TOP SECRET
UNITED STATES
SECRET SERVICE
CRIME REPORT

OFFENSE:
Kidnapping

VICTIM:
Jonathan Starr,
President-elect of the United States.

SUSPECTS:
Middle East terrorists. The Soviets.
Political enemies. Or anybody.

America has fallen into dark times. With the President-elect missing and the Constitution utterly unclear about the process for succession, political forces on all sides collide in a struggle with devastating consequences for the nation. . . .

OATH OF OFFICE

Steven J. Kirsch

FAWCETT CREST • NEW YORK

A Fawcett Crest Book
Published by Ballantine Books
Copyright © 1988 by Steven Kirsch

Library of Congress Catalog Card Number: 88-91118

ISBN 0-449-21654-3

Manufactured in the United States of America

First Edition: October 1988

To my grandparents,
Samuel and Rose Fridkin

Acknowledgments

I would like to thank Diane Hirte for her editorial assistance; Sue Gerlach for her loyalty in typing and retyping the manuscript; Henry Morrison for his confidence in me and the story; my parents, Harold and Mildred Kirsch, for their undying encouragement and support; and the three most important people in my life, Amy, Abby, and Brian Kirsch, my children, for their patience and understanding while I was writing this book.

If, at the time fixed for the beginning of the term of the President, the President elect shall have died, the Vice President elect shall become President. If a President shall not have been chosen before the time fixed for the beginning of his term, or if the President elect shall have failed to qualify, then the Vice President elect shall act as President until a President shall have qualified; and the Congress may by law provide for the case wherein neither a President elect nor a Vice President elect shall have qualified, declaring who shall then act as President, or the manner in which one who is to act shall be selected, and such person shall act accordingly until a President or Vice President shall have qualified.

—United States Constitution, Amendment 20, Section 3

If, by reason of death, resignation, removal from office, inability, or failure to qualify, there is neither a President nor Vice President to discharge the powers and duties of the office of President, then the Speaker of the House of Representatives shall, upon his resignation as Speaker and as a Representative in Congress, act as President.

—3 United States Code, Section 19(a)(1)

PROLOGUE

SIX MONTHS BEFORE THE ELECTION

A COOL NIGHT WIND BLEW SOFTLY AS THE TWO MEN STOOD outside the Oval Office, in the Rose Garden, each pondering his next move.

"J.W.," President Arthur Sutherland said, "win or lose this election, our deal must be made."

J.W. McBee, chairman of the Senate Foreign Relations Committee and senior senator from Texas, turned to face his old Senate comrade, touching him gently on the left arm.

"Arthur," he began slowly, "Ah've been workin' on this deal for five months. . . . We'll git it through befo' the election."

"I know," the president responded, "it's best for our country . . . and Israel."

"Hell," McBee grunted, "the damn thing will be great for the entire world. You'll go down in history as the president who brought everlastin' peace to the Middle East."

The president nodded, his brow creased in deep, painful thought. "But it's risky," he said softly.

"Shit, Ah know that," McBee drawled, "but we'll git it wrapped up tight . . . no holes."

"Will the Arabs go for the concessions we proposed last month?" The president asked.

"Ah think so. The A-rabs want this as bad as we do."

"And the king?"

McBee smiled. "Ah think our king wants this *more* than we do."

"Remember, J.W., no one," the president leaned toward

1

McBee and whispered, "no one, except the secretary of state, not my aides, not Congress—no one must have an inkling of what we're proposing until the Arabs and the king agree. When we're close, I'll discuss the plan with the Israelis and determine how much we disclose to the nation. Parts of it must never be discussed publicly—never."

"Ah understand, Mr. President. Or we wouldn't be talkin' out here beyond the range of your microphones," McBee responded, gesturing toward the Oval Office.

A sly grin took shape at the corners of Sutherland's mouth. "I promised the American people I would never turn off those microphones. I intend to keep that promise. Besides," he said solemnly, "we both know executive agreements can be difficult."

"And even more difficult if your political opponent, or the Israelis, get wind of this befo' you go public," McBee added.

"Speaking of my opponent," the president asked, "what are his chances? You've got a good feel for these things, J.W."

The tall, lanky Southerner became fully alert, his gaze sharp and penetrating, as he pointed to the sky.

"Arthur," he asked, "are you familiar with astronomy?"

"No, I'm not."

The Texas senator smiled. "Your good friend, the Speaker," he began sarcastically, "and I are amateur astronomers. 'Bout a week ago, we agreed on a theory concernin' the loyal opposition."

The president sighed softly and shrugged his shoulders as he thought about the power-hungry Speaker of the House.

"Spare me his opinions," the president snapped, "and just give me yours."

"I would equate Jonathan Starr with a nova star," McBee said, nodding his head toward the sky. "You see," he continued, "a nova is a variable star that suddenly increases in brightness to several times its normal size and then shrinks to its original appearance."

The president detected a subtle condescension in his friend's smile.

"So," McBee summarized patiently, "Jonathan Starr's victories in the primaries and his probable nomination constitute his bright light. He'll return to his original status, a United States senator, in 'bout six months, after he loses the election,'' McBee concluded triumphantly.

"But," the president shot back, "my astronomer friend, if it takes Starr years to return to his former brightness, it may mean he will win the election and won't return to his original appearance until he leaves office."

"Arthur," the senator replied, patting the president's back gently, "you need a drink."

The president took one step toward the Oval Office but stopped suddenly and turned toward McBee.

"J.W.," he said softly, "you've got to conclude this deal soon, like you said. If I lose the election, agreement with the Arabs and the king may be impossible." The president pronounced the words without anger. Nothing in his manner or tone displayed his interior storm.

"Arthur," McBee replied sincerely, "the deal is critical, but if it doesn't work, it's not the end of the world."

The president sadly shook his head. "It may be, my friend," he replied intently. "It may be the end of the world as we know it. Our failure could lead to World War III."

Chapter 1

The Passenger

7:00 A.M.
Wednesday, November 3

THE TWO MEN RODE IN SILENCE. THEY HAD LEFT SAN FRAN-cisco over three hours before. The front-seat passenger rubbed his scratchy beard nervously. His protruding belly stretched the last hole of his new forty-four-inch belt. He leaned forward impatiently to change radio stations again, feeling the strain in his midsection and cursing himself for not buying the next size belt.

The early-morning disc jockeys had been replaced. Their substitutes lacked the resonant sounds so pleasing to their regular audience. Today, the dull, nameless voices sounded like accountants, spewing out figures and statistics, analyzing, state by state, the presidential election returns.

The driver kept his bleary, sunken eyes on the road. He drove precisely 50 mph. There would be no speeding ticket today; one encounter with the police was enough.

The driver, dressed in brown double-knit pants, smiled as the returns were reported. Though he had never voted in an election, he listened intently.

As they approached the outskirts of Los Angeles, the sun began to rise. Its rays penetrated the smoggy haze of the Southern California sky. The driver took his eyes off the road just long enough to check the time. Cars began entering the freeway with more frequency as a nearby factory changed to its early morning shift. The driver became more tense. Increased traffic amplified the potential for danger. He would . . . he must foresee the unforeseeable.

An obnoxious-sounding horn momentarily startled the driver, until he observed a near collision in his rearview mirror. He felt the sweat and heat his hands were producing on the steering wheel. His heart slowly returned to its normal beat. Damn horns, he thought to himself.

The horn had startled someone else. His head felt like a runaway merry-go-round. He strained to open his eyes.

DARKNESS.

He immediately experienced movement. A steady, boring, smooth movement. When he attempted to change positions, he realized his hands were tied behind his back.

He felt something gentle, like a pillow, smooth and soft, under his right cheek. He was able to move his head forward several inches before the dizziness became unbearable. He kept

hearing the same noise. He concentrated and became very still
. . . trying to make some sense out of the strange situation.

Cars.

The outside sounds were cars passing him. He was a prisoner
in someone's trunk.

He opened his eyes again. The trunk was dark, but he forced
himself to think. Where had he been last night? He panicked
when his memory failed him. He tried to lift his head from the
pillow again. The dizziness was gone.

There was a dryness in his mouth. His tongue felt a foreign
object. It was soft, yet firmly implanted so he couldn't put it
out. Cotton. By moving his jaw back and forth he discovered
that the cotton was secured by heavy masking tape over his
mouth. He could feel the tape over both cheeks. He began to
monitor his breathing rate, realizing for the first time his nostrils
were his only source of air.

Nob Hill. Last night he had been at Nob Hill. As he probed
his memory, tracing last night's events, a luxurious hotel room
flashed across the wide screen of his mind. The room had several television sets situated next to each other, adjacent to an
elegant and spacious, powder blue couch located near the center
of the room.

Faded images were becoming clear. His wife. A large group
of men who had spent the evening with them watching television. Then his mind went blank again.

He slowly moved his head from side to side and tried desperately to reconstruct the past few hours. He raised his head
again from the small pillow. He struggled to recall, permitting
the free association of his memory, digging, straining, forcing
his mind to function as a finely tuned instrument. Sweat broke
out on his forehead, his pulse quickened.

He was remembering.

Men with guns. Secretly and safely secured in shoulder hol-
sters. Phones strategically placed throughout the fashionable
room. Electronic equipment that constituted an independent
communications center. Last night's images were returning to
him. All those people had been watching the presidential election returns. The networks had announced the winner early in

the morning. He remembered the drinks. The stories. The congratulations and back patting.

His eyes were stinging—he was sweating profusely. He tried to shrug his shoulder toward his face, but couldn't. His shoulder struck a hard, woodlike object above him. In frustration, he dropped his head back onto the pillow.

He lay quietly for a few moments. Thinking. The celebration. The phones. The guns. The Secret Service. Panic overcame him as he finally realized two things.

He was the president-elect of the United States.

He had been kidnapped.

CHAPTER 2

ELECTION NIGHT

Tuesday, November 2

JONATHAN STARR AND SEVERAL AIDES SAT BEFORE AN ARRAY OF carefully arranged television sets in a three-bedroom suite at the Fairmont Hotel, anxiously awaiting network confirmation of what they already knew to be true.

For several hours Starr and his associates watched the returns with a mixture of elation and expectancy. Finally, and mercifully, at 11:00 P.M. San Francisco time, Jonathan Starr, along with the rest of the nation, watched while the anchors of each network projected him as the next president of the United States.

For a man who had been elected to the United States Senate from California just eight years before, winning the presidency seemed nothing short of a miracle. But the evening's real surprise was that Americans for the first time had elected a Jewish president.

"To the President of the United States," Paulson Orear toasted, as he proudly raised his empty martini glass to the Starrs. In unison, everyone raised their glasses to salute the nation's new leader.

Starr left his wife's side and approached his campaign manager.

"Well, Paulie, you managed the upset of the century!"

The short, stocky genius, who had orchestrated the Starr campaign, broke into a broad grin and embraced his candidate.

Paulson Orear had traveled the presidential campaign route before during the 1970s. He then left politics to start his own advertising agency in Southern California. He met Jonathan Starr when he was named chairman of the Governor's Drug Commission. Starr and Orear struck an immediate friendship. Though the campaign manager was more conservative than his maverick friend, together they won two Senate races in a politically unpredictable state.

The election-night party continued. It was now almost 1:00 A.M., and the celebrants in Starr's suite of rooms showed no signs of fatigue.

"Listen, listen," Orear shouted, as he tried to get everyone's attention. "Our new president-elect and his first lady elect need a few hours alone. What do you say we move the party down the hall?"

The gathering cheered as Starr motioned for silence. He was six feet tall with a wholesome, healthy look: strong, handsome features, a tanned, smooth-skinned face, broad shoulders, and black hair, streaked with gray.

"Words escape me now," Starr began. "I appreciate . . . really, I should say Judy and I appreciate, everything . . ." He couldn't continue. The tortuous months of campaigning, coupled with the emotion of winning, were too much. Judy walked over to her husband, took his right hand, and lovingly raised it toward her mouth, kissing it gently.

"Johnny thanks you all," she said emotionally, as she squeezed his hand.

"Listen," Orear interrupted, "let's move the party to my room. I'll run over to campaign headquarters, make a quick appearance, and tell them Johnny will make a statement." And then, glancing at Starr for approval—"What time, Johnny, 10:00 A.M.?"

Starr nodded. "Thank them for me. They know why I won't say anything tonight."

Starr had informed his staff, win or lose, he would make no public statement until the morning following the election. A fiasco four years ago had left a bad taste in his mouth, and he vowed that nothing like it would happen again.

The previous election had gone down to the wire. Four years ago Arthur Sutherland and his Democratic challenger fought a grueling and bitter campaign. At 5:00 A.M., when Sutherland was finally projected the winner, he held an impromptu press conference. Under the influence of alcohol and euphoria, he made unkind comments about his opponent. Shortly after his speech, the press quoted some off-color jokes by President-elect Sutherland that were to have been "off the record."

Starr intended to avoid even the possibility of such a spectacle. The practical result of the new media election law passed by Congress meant that election tallies were not released until the polls closed in all states, except Hawaii and Alaska. Starr felt it appropriate and "presidential" that any victory or concession speech wait until the next day. Cooler heads would prevail, and the public could then watch their new president while sipping morning coffee. The president-elect would choose his words carefully, and extend an olive branch to the loser.

Starr supporters everywhere were celebrating their candidate's victory, but at no place was the frivolity equal to that at the Hyatt Regency, Starr campaign headquarters. The twenty-story structure at the foot of Market Street was about to burst with enthusiasm for San Francisco's favorite son. The interior glass elevators, rising through the multi-tiered lobby, carried a steady stream of celebrants with drinks in hand.

Starr's friends and neighbors had already found their places in the main ballroom and were reminiscing about their experiences with the senator. They shared in the victory, feeling privileged to celebrate in the hotel that they believed housed their candidate. None of them knew Jonathan Starr wasn't at the Hyatt Regency this night . . . thanks to Andy Reynolds.

Andrew Reynolds, the head of Starr's Secret Service detail,

had decided to take extra security precautions. Guarding a presidential candidate any election year is an enormous task, but protecting a *Jewish* candidate complicated Reynolds's assignment. Starr's Middle East policy made him a target of several radical Arab terrorist groups. Additionally, his Judaism brought neo-Nazi groups from the underground. Several unconfirmed threats, foreign and domestic, convinced Reynolds to play his own "campaign dirty trick." The public thought Starr would spend the evening in his suite of rooms on the top floor at the Hyatt, where his campaign headquarters dominated the hotel.

However, up the hill, just a short cable-car ride away at the Fairmont, with the assistance of the hotel manager, another security check had been quietly undertaken. Orear had made arrangements with Michael Irving, a wealthy businessman and close friend of Starr's, to rent the elegant and spacious three-bedroom suite at the end of the third floor. Irving was ostensibly renting the room for a wealthy and important business associate who would be spending the week in the Bay Area.

The living room was enormous, complete with grand piano, fireplace with marble mantel, and enough furniture for the East Wing of the White House. Around the corner from the living room was a game room, equipped with a pool table and ample tables for card playing. Moorish chandeliers dangled from the ceiling, and stained glass windows would usher in the California dawn with the colors of the rainbow.

The Secret Service had checked the route Starr would take to and from the Fairmont and the Hyatt. Elevators and stairways were scrutinized. The names of all hotel employees were placed into the Secret Service computers. The technical services branch of Reynolds's crew inspected the suite for bombs. It was just routine. No one expected to find anything. After all, no one knew Jonathan Starr would be the guest of Michael Irving this election night.

Early in the evening of election day, Starr's three Senate aides had arrived at different times wearing various disguises. Each received a specific time and place to enter the Fairmont. They had left campaign headquarters by the back stairs of the Hyatt, and the Secret Service had arranged their own "cab service" to transport the Starr entourage in secrecy.

Even Judy Starr was forced into the charade. At 7:00 P.M. she had entered the "employees only" entrance, wearing a maid's uniform and a brown wig. She took the freight elevator to the third floor, where she unlocked the linen closet, grabbed two towels and a bar of soap, and made her way to the end of the corridor, where she inconspicuously entered the last suite of rooms.

"Andy, everything is running like clockwork," reported Roger Jefferson, a cocky, curly-haired assistant to the agent-in-charge, as the two men met in the back stairwell.

Reynolds ignored Jefferson's good news. "Where's Jo?" he asked crisply.

"Behind the front desk," Jefferson answered, sensing his boss's sour mood.

Reynolds quickly moved down two floors of stairs. Though the election was over, his job had just begun; he was now responsible for the well-being of the next president. For a black man from Brooklyn, who had risen to lieutenant colonel in the Marines and later distinguished himself in the Secret Service, Reynolds should have felt more elation than he was feeling this night. His preoccupation with security measures prevented him from enjoying the historic moment.

Reynolds walked hurriedly through the lobby, covering the pink-and-black carpet with giant steps. He ignored the agent who was stationed outside the Squire Restaurant, adjacent to the main lobby.

He entered the office behind the hotel's front desk and noticed Jo Decker talking to the hotel manager.

"Josephine, may I have a word with you?"

The short, powerfully built, thirty-year-old woman quickly turned toward Reynolds.

"Excuse me," she said softly, gently touching the manager's arm, "I'll catch you later." She walked over to her boss, eyeing him intently.

"What's wrong?" she wondered out loud.

"Nothing," Reynolds replied, taken somewhat off guard. "Why?"

"When you call me Josephine, you're normally angry."

Reynolds forced a grin. "I'm just uptight. Give me a report."

"Everything is fine. Starr's guests moved in and out without fanfare. None of them tipped off the press or other hotel guests. All agents have checked into rooms near the Starr suite to serve as a buffer . . ."

"For the noise and celebrating," Reynolds interrupted. "I was up there. I don't think any guests will be disturbed. Let's go over positions one more time."

"Again?" Decker feigned surprise.

"Humor me," Reynolds smiled, "just one more time."

"We have one agent outside the suite, posing as a maintenance man, working on a pipe in the hallway ceiling. Another agent will periodically appear to repair the service elevator. No one should be suspicious if he walks into the hall late at night."

"And if the press sees us, you or me, what do we tell them?"

"You and I are checking security because the candidate is moving here tomorrow."

"Good. How many agents in the rooms?"

"Six. We also have a painter in the back stairwell. Andy . . . everything's covered."

"Your dad would be proud."

Decker visibly flinched. "Don't get sentimental on me," she responded tersely.

"How come you won't talk about him?" Reynolds inquired.

"He's dead," she replied coldly, showing no emotion.

"You were made my assistant after four short years of service. You were an outstanding Green Beret, and yet you can't cope with the death of your father?"

"Death?" she snapped. "You mean murder."

"Jo . . . Jo," Reynolds said softly, putting his arm around her. "He was my best friend . . . don't forget that."

"I know, Andy." She had regained her composure. "Let's talk about the good colonel some other night."

A loud bang startled Reynolds. Two carpenters were removing a large mural from the top of scaffolding, in order to begin remodeling the back office.

Reynolds smiled as he watched the men work. "I'm really jumpy tonight," he said, as he shook his head.

Decker took his arm as they walked toward the lobby. "Look around," she said, waving her arm, "there's not a soul here who suspects anything. Starr is at headquarters. Everyone *knows* that, right? There's nothing to worry about. We have enough agents to protect him, but not enough to cause suspicion.''

"What are you trying to tell me?"

"Go see Starr. Then go to bed. I have the night shift. Everything's cool." She smiled reassuringly and pushed Reynolds away. The agent nodded and moved toward the stairs. He would take her advice.

Paulson Orear gulped down another drink and carefully put on his disguise. His arms were as thick as totem poles but he slowly and methodically struggled to wiggle into his sport coat. The Senate aides had already departed.

"Leave it to Paulie to wear a Nixon mask on my election night," Starr chided.

"Our election night," corrected Orear. "I'll go down the back stairs, and then walk two blocks toward the Hyatt before I take a cab. No one will know where I came from."

"Don't let them follow you back here," Judy cautioned.

"Look, if I have it my way, I'll just stay out all night, celebrating. After all, it's not every day a guy wins the presidency."

"Paulie, don't stay out all night. I'll need your help in the morning."

"Okay, okay," Orear gave in waving his arms, "I'll be back." As he slowly opened the door he turned to Starr, "I'll check on you before I go to sleep. I'll be back in a few hours."

"Paulie," Starr said, as he grabbed a drink, "thank you." He walked to Orear and the men embraced, patting each other softly on the back.

"I'll just have a few drinks at the Hyatt. With our campaign people. Reynolds will be pleased . . . it will make everyone think you're there," Orear said, trying to rationalize a few more drinks. Anything and everything for the sake of security.

The Starrs were finally alone. It was 1:30 A.M.

"Judy."

"Back here, Johnny."

Starr walked into the master bedroom. It was lavishly decorated with powder blue carpeting and matching draperies. The king-size bed looked comfortable and appealing, but Starr didn't feel tired. He didn't want the night to end. Not yet. There was time for one more bourbon.

Judy was in the bathroom brushing her teeth. While Starr supporters all over the country celebrated, the future first lady prepared for bed. She wore a blue negligee that accented her gorgeous California tan. She saw him coming in the mirror. He leaned over and kissed her gently, his right hand squeezing her buttocks.

"Mr. President," she said in mock respect, "how dare you!" She turned to her husband and saw his gentle blue eyes, now swollen and bloodshot. She leaned forward and touched his arms, gently pulling him closer. They stood in silence, enjoying the comfort of each other's body.

"I'm going to sleep. I'm just too tired to stay up." Judy walked into the bedroom and crawled over to the right side of the bed. She turned toward Jonathan, raising her eyebrows Groucho Marx style, and said, "Wake me up when you come to bed."

"You can bet on it," he responded, as he winked at his wife. Starr looked into the mirror. He was tired. The strain of the presidential campaign was enormous.

He quietly removed his shirt and tossed it toward the corner of the bedroom. He looked at Judy. She was already asleep. How Jonathan envied her ability to go to sleep quickly. He couldn't begin to calculate how many hours of his life he had wasted trying to fall asleep. He walked out of the room, quietly closing the bedroom door behind him. He was alone. An exhausted candidate and three television sets.

He planned to watch the updated returns for a while and then turn in. He would get up early in the morning to finish his statement to the press. He wasn't too worried about the wording of the speech; his staff would use just the right words, the proper dignity.

Starr dropped into a chair, taking another look at the elaborate bar. He decided he was too tired for a nightcap. Just a few more minutes of TV, that's all he wanted.

He didn't hear Reynolds opening his suite door with the pass key.

"Jonathan, are you still up?" Reynolds asked, as he quietly

shut the door. He was the only Secret Service agent who addressed Starr by his first name.

"Seriously, it's late. I won't go to sleep until I know you're tucked in."

The athletic-looking Reynolds walked toward Starr, flashing a grin as he extended his right hand.

"I haven't had a chance to tell you this, but you've accomplished what very few men have ever done. Congratulations. You'll make one helluva president."

Jonathan took Andy's right hand between both of his extended hands.

"I couldn't have done it without you. I trust you with my life," Starr said sincerely.

Starr had met Reynolds, one of the few black students in the class at Hastings Law School, when they were both first-year students. Jonathan was drawn to his quick wit and dry sense of humor. After two years of private practice, Reynolds understood the law couldn't satisfy his desire for instant action. A man who had fought in the Vietnam jungles for several years wasn't going to have his thirst for challenge and excitement quenched by drafting corporate documents or defending drunk drivers. At least not the free-spirited Andy Reynolds.

After a two-year stint in the Treasury Department, Reynolds was assigned to protect President Carter. Some years later he became involved in high-security, high-risk, special-investigative work for the Treasury. Starr had kept his friendship with Reynolds over the years, and specifically requested that the Treasury Department assign Reynolds to spearhead his Secret Service staff.

"Get some sleep," Reynolds suggested as he walked toward the front door. Starr slowly followed his good friend, feeling the last ounce of energy drain from his body. He would bask in the glory of the returns for a few minutes, and then join his sleeping wife.

"Andy, I'm impressed. Your decoy tonight appears to have fooled the press."

"Yeah, even Katherine Wilson. You're up shit creek, my man," Reynolds replied, gently poking Starr in the shoulder with his finger.

Katherine Wilson.

She was the best political newspaperwoman in the country, the pride of *The Washington Post*. She had been promised an exclusive interview this very night from the Democratic candidate for president.

"She'll understand, Andy," Starr replied, halfheartedly.

"Sure," Reynolds grunted, knowing his boss would talk his way out of another problem. He always did.

Especially with Katherine Wilson.

Kate Wilson's slim, sexy body and fine brown hair were the subjects of many of Jonathan's high school dreams. They wrote each other in college, but eventually went their separate ways. When Jonathan entered politics, his high school sweetheart treated him to a rousing column in the *Post* Sunday edition. She described her classmate in one word.

Integrity.

Kate's writing style varied, depending on her subject matter. At times her reporting was mundane and unimaginative, as if she wrote the first words that came to mind. Other times, her articles were moving and dynamic, showcasing her creative skills and innate writing ability. This happened when she covered politics.

As the years went by, Jonathan and Kate kept in touch. She encouraged his political involvement, and when he finally arrived in Washington, she volunteered to help the Starrs find a home. Their friendship was rekindled, and a unique closeness developed between Kate and Judy Starr.

"She'll forgive me," Starr said softly, breaking his momentary reverie. He smiled and nodded assurance to Reynolds as the agent quietly shut the door.

Starr scanned the suite. The television sets began spewing election statistics. He'd watch for a few more minutes. The goose bumps just wouldn't go away.

CHAPTER 3

THE KIDNAPPING

4:00 A.M.
Wednesday, November 3

THE TALL MAN IN THE BROWN DOUBLE-KNIT PANTS HAD BEEN pacing the laundry room of the Fairmont Hotel for one hour. He was waiting for the phone call that would change his life.

Len Allen had been employed by the hotel for three months. During that time, Allen and his associates had worked out the details of the abduction down to the second.

He stared at his watch. 3:00 A.M. Allen cleared his throat and nervously twisted his neck, hearing the familiar, obnoxious, cracking sound. He scanned the laundry room again. Other than the huge machines and mountains of dirty linen, he was alone.

The loud ring of a nearby phone disrupted his pacing.

"Speak," he commanded into the phone, anticipating what would be said.

The caller slowly enunciated each word of the message. "All systems go. Riley and Olson will be there in ten minutes. At precisely 3:23 A.M., the scaffolding behind the front desk will collapse on two workers. The Secret Service will be asked to assist in the emergency. Agents will leave their posts. Use your passkey . . . third-floor executive suite."

The silence at the other end of the phone signaled the end of the message. He quickly dialed the night supervisor.

"Boss?" Allen asked calmly.

"Yes," came the dull response from the lazy night maintenance supervisor.

16

"As usual, we're backlogged in the laundry. I took the liberty to call Riley and Olson to help."

"Three nights in a row now, isn't it, Len?" The supervisor responded, trying to calculate the effect on his budget.

"Must be done, boss, or we won't have clean sheets for morning." Allen glanced at his watch. 3:16 A.M.

"Do it," the boss responded, then quickly added, "I'll be going on my meal break. I'll check back in a couple of hours."

Allen chuckled to himself as he placed the phone back into its cradle.

Due to the enormous interest in the November election generated by the California senator's candidacy, the Fairmont was filled to capacity, creating havoc with an already overcrowded laundry. During these hectic days, Secret Service agents responsible for securing the hotel observed that three laundry room employees worked all hours of the day in order to supply the hotel guests with clean linens.

Allen's angular face looked both purposeful and anxious as his fellow kidnappers entered the room. Their early-morning arrival caused no undue concern to the Secret Service agent stationed nearby.

"Let's get moving," Allen commanded, as the three men quickly changed into their white coveralls. Allen, who had previously loaded two large washing machines, pushed a button to start the forty-minute cycles.

Starr's room was located near the back exit and stairwell on the third floor. At approximately 3:30 A.M., Allen rolled a large laundry cart into the service elevator and pushed the button to the third floor. At the same time Jim Olson and Paul Michael Riley strangled an unsuspecting Secret Service agent, who had been stationed near the second-floor landing at the back stairwell. The stunned agent was posing as a painter, and never had a chance to warn the others of danger. The two men covered the agent with his large painting canvas, tucked him neatly into a corner, and raced to the third floor to meet Allen.

"Hey, can you help me?" Allen asked, as the elevator door opened onto the third floor. The repairman, hard at work on some leaking pipes, smiled as he descended his ladder. He would be happy to assist one of the laundry boys.

"If you can hold the door, I'll try to get this damn cart over the opening," Allen said, as he glanced quickly down the corridor.

No one.

Agent Ray Stewart placed his pipe wrench on top of his toolbox. The box contained a walkie-talkie and a .38 magnum.

As Stewart approached the elevator, he started to open the door so Allen could push the laundry cart out. When he put his hand on the elevator door, Stewart was knocked in the head from behind. Allen, with the assistance of his two associates, quickly injected fluid from a hypodermic needle into the right arm of the helpless agent. The three men quietly dragged Stewart's body from the elevator entrance to the stairwell of the third floor, where they kept the body hidden for a few minutes before entering Jonathan Starr's suite. During these frantic seconds they hoped that no one would appear in the hallway. They were armed and prepared to use force to take Starr with them. They were professionals. Kidnappers. Murderers. They would not fail. They had one other order. Jonathan Starr was to be taken alive. If he was killed, all three men understood their lives were over. They knew their employer all too well.

The president-elect never knew what happened. As he was sitting on the couch, with his back to the front door, he heard a key turning in the lock. He was going to turn around, but NBC flashed the White House on the screen for a live report.

He felt arms all over him. One covered his mouth, the others his arms and legs. He was pushed violently to the floor, and he started to scream, but it was futile. The hollow needle of the syringe slid into his right arm. The stab of pain shocked his senses. His body heaved as he struggled for freedom. He slowly became dizzy, slipping into a comalike, dark sleep.

Within these long, seemingly endless seconds, Starr felt empty, lifeless. He had been injected with a fluid similar to that used by the three abductors on Ray Stewart minutes before. Allen administered an additional injection into Starr's left arm to slow his breathing rate.

To the onlooker, Jonathan Starr would appear dead. Riley

stood by the cracked open door. He hoped he wouldn't hear running footsteps or other signs of trouble. His gun was drawn, held tightly in his left hand, just in case. He wiped the sweat off his brow, tugged at his crotch, and turned toward his partners.

"Johnny, come to bed. It's late."

Allen motioned for Riley to get near the bedroom door. It opened.

"Johnny, I said . . ."

Riley hit the woman in the doorway over the head immediately, catching her as she fell back into his arms.

"What should I do?" asked Riley.

"Hold her while we move Starr. Keep an eye on the fuckin' door," Allen commanded.

Olson and Allen dragged Starr over to the door. Olson placed his hand under Starr's shoulders and Allen grabbed his legs. They put Starr in a huge laundry bag, literally folding him in half, bending his body in a yoga position. The bag was tied and placed in the bottom of the cart.

Moving in perfect precision, the kidnappers went to the back stairwell and grabbed the drugged Secret Service agent, dragging him back into Starr's room and tossing him into the bed.

"Let's get the lady," Allen ordered, glancing at his watch. He wanted to be off the third floor within three minutes.

Olson started for the door, but then suddenly stopped. "Len, take a look at him."

Allen immediately noticed Stewart had a physique similar to Starr's. He quickly pulled the covers over the lifeless agent.

"That way," Allen began, "if a sympathetic aide sees him sleeping so soundly, he may let him sleep longer. By not killing him, the bastard continues to breathe . . . and it *might* buy us more time. And it's the last place anyone will look for this agent."

"What if someone misses him?" Olson asked.

"Then they miss him," Allen responded briskly. "They won't look for him here."

The two men left the bedroom to assist Riley. They found him sitting on the floor, with the future first lady resting in front of him. Both his hands were firmly attached to Judy Starr's breasts as her head slumped against his right shoulder.

"What a piece of ass," Riley muttered as Allen and Olson injected Judy's right arm. The two men carried her to the bed, placing her on the right side of Stewart.

Riley followed them into the bedroom, not wanting to miss an opportunity to see Judy Starr's body.

"How do you know she sleeps on the right side?" Riley asked, unable to take his eyes off Judy's firm, tanned thighs as the negligee bunched around her waist.

"I sniffed the sheets . . . asshole," snarled Allen. "Can't you smell the perfume? She was lying in here five minutes ago."

The three men secured the laundry basket and walked down the third-floor hallway, dropping the top sheets of the basket into the linen closets as they normally did every workday, simultaneously picking up piles of dirty linen.

Though Allen had been up and down the halls of the third floor numerous times, he never realized until now how well lit they were. The lights seemed as hot and bright as those that had shone on Allen in police stations. Len Allen had seen the inside of many police stations and jail cells working for his employer. He had beaten hundreds of poor souls, dismembering many, killing most. It was his job. And he loved it. As Allen and his two comrades approached the service elevator, their footsteps on the elegant, well-vacuumed carpets seemed to make an inordinate amount of noise.

Within minutes of the kidnapping, the abductors made their way to the floor below. As Allen shut the linen door, he noticed two well-dressed men approach him. He glanced toward his cohorts, making an automatic reflex move to his shoulder holster. He observed the bulge under the suit coat of the taller man. The shorter man, a blond, with shoulders that would shame a professional wrestler, was dressed in a conservative blue suit. He looked like a banker.

Secret Service.

Allen's professional eye noticed the walkie-talkie clipped to the short agent's belt, causing his well-tailored trousers to sag to the left. A thin wire disappeared under his suit jacket only to emerge at his collar, finally ending at a seemingly innocent plastic plug in his left ear. Under his left shoulder was a gun.

Allen stared at the men. "Damn laundry room, we just can't

keep up,'' Allen said, his voice friendly, his eyes not. Olson and Riley calmly continued to drop dirty linen in the basket, occasionally glancing toward the middle of the large cart, praying they would see no movement. So far, the injected drug was effective.

"Cigarette?'' asked the taller agent, as he started to strike a match.

"No thanks,'' Allen replied calmly, hoping to avoid a shootout.

The agent casually flipped his match in the laundry basket. Allen reacted immediately, lunging for the cart.

"Hey . . . it's out,'' the agent said quickly. "I know linen could catch fire.''

"Sorry,'' Allen replied, gripping the side of the cart with his right hand, suddenly terrified that he might lose control. "What gets you guys up this early?'' Allen asked carefully, trying to act friendly.

"Early-morning flight to Denver . . . we're attorneys,'' the shorter agent offered. Allen noticed neither carried any luggage.

"You'll miss the '49ers this Sunday, won't you?''

"Yeah,'' the blond agent answered, "but we'll catch the Broncos. . . . They play the Vikings; it'll be a better game.''

"We better get back to work . . . have a good trip,'' Allen said, as he slowly walked away from the agents, motioning his assistants to follow. Olson turned around, relieved that the agents had left.

"I thought the Vikings play the '49ers?''

"Shut up. Let's get the fuck out of here,'' Allen said, as he wiped his sweating palms on the top sheets and walked toward the service elevator, pushing the cart as fast as he could.

Finally, the journey through the hotel's corridors had ended. Allen quickly changed into his brown double-knits, while Riley and Olson emptied the remaining laundry from their cart.

Allen had made a point of doing his own laundry at the Fairmont during the past few weeks. When he dragged the overstuffed laundry bag to the trunk, anyone watching from the hotel would see nothing he hadn't seen before—Len Allen trying to save a few bucks on his laundry bill.

It was a crisp wintry morning. The air felt cool and soothing as Allen gently shut the trunk. He would stop the car again before Starr's drug dosage wore off. Then he would properly secure his prize. Riley walked around the car and entered through the front passenger door, his eyes scanning the empty streets.

No one.

Olson, who had left the laundry room through a separate exit, hustled to his car and drove off in the opposite direction.

Riley nervously rubbed his oversized stomach and smiled at Allen.

"We did it," he observed proudly, "it went just like . . ."

"Shut up," Allen grunted, as he placed the keys in the ignition.

"We haven't done anything yet. Not until we make L.A."

The two men traveled west to Van Ness Avenue, where they turned south heading toward the highway to Los Angeles.

"As soon as we get out of town, I'll tie up Starr," Allen said, as he noticed a flashing red light behind him.

"Fuck!" Allen exclaimed. He slammed the steering wheel with his palm. Riley quickly turned around and saw the cause of Allen's sudden outburst.

"They know. How the hell do they know?" Riley wondered, as he removed his gun.

"Put that away. They don't know . . . they can't. It must be something else.

"You weren't speeding, were ya, Len?"

"Of course not, asshole. Just shut up," Allen snarled, as he pulled the car off the road. "You stay in the car . . . and let me do the talking . . . all the talking."

San Francisco Patrolman Brian Nyberg entered the license plate number and a brief description of the vehicle in his patrolman's notebook, and made his way to the car in front of him, his every move being scrutinized by the attentive eye of Len Allen through the rearview mirror.

"He's taking his sweet time," Riley observed.

"He didn't call for a backup, either," Allen added, touching the gun in his shoulder harness. Allen rolled down his window, feeling the crisp wind from the ocean.

"May I see your identification, please?" The officer was being very polite. Allen handed him his license, carefully looking over another potential victim. The officer's left hand pushed his brown hair from his forehead, the wind playing havoc with his recent haircut.

"Your left taillight is out."

Allen acted surprised. "I'm sorry, officer. I just had the car serviced."

Nyberg shined his flashlight into the car. "What are you guys doing out so late?"

"We work downtown," Allen responded, "we're headed home from work."

"You guys work together?"

"Right," Allen quickly replied, placing his right hand on his belt buckle.

"Anything in the trunk?" The officer's question stunned Riley. He jumped three inches off his seat. Did this cop know? Maybe he was stalling for time. Allen was thinking the same thing.

"It's clean laundry. My laundry. I clean it at work."

"Why don't we take a look?" the officer suggested, "sometimes you can knock a wire loose."

Allen quickly glanced at Riley and pulled himself out of the car. "Sure, officer."

As the two men moved toward the trunk, Riley took out his gun and slid behind the steering wheel. At the same time, Allen saw approaching headlights. He had to make an instant judgment. Was the cop for real, or just stalling? He raised his hand to his shoulder harness, but instinct told him to wait.

The approaching car passed, leaving Allen and Patrolman Nyberg alone, next to the trunk.

"Open it," Nyberg said impatiently, shining his flashlight on the trunk.

Allen inserted the key and opened the trunk. He looked at the officer. "Just a big laundry bag." He tried to force a smile, but Nyberg wasn't looking. His light was aimed in the trunk.

"Fairmont, I see," the officer said, as he reached toward the bag, gently poking it with his right hand.

"What?" Allen said in a surprised tone.

"You must work at the Fairmont."

Allen said nothing, but followed the shining light. The Fairmont insignia was on the bag.

"My friend and I work there together." Allen stared at the bag, praying there would be no movement.

The officer leaned forward for a closer look. He moved the flashlight across the left front of the trunk.

"Loose wire," he observed, "you must have knocked it when you threw the bag in. I'll hold the light . . . see if you can fix it."

Allen reached into the trunk and within seconds had reconnected the wire. Even with the cool wind at his face, Allen felt perspiration all over his body.

"Thanks, officer, that should do it." He looked at the patrolman, whose gaze had become fixed on the laundry bag.

"That's a helluva big bag," he offered, looking intently at Allen.

"It's just sheets, pillowcases, and blankets," Allen responded, hoping his voice wouldn't betray his true emotions. "Here," Allen continued, "if you really want to see it, I'll open the bag."

Riley, who had been straining to hear the conversation from the front seat, gritted his teeth when he heard Allen's offer. He cocked his gun, fully expecting to use it.

"That won't be necessary," Nyberg replied, walking to the front of the car. He motioned toward Riley.

"Hey, flip on the headlights."

"They work," a relieved Allen shouted from the back of the car, quickly slamming the trunk and walking closer to the officer.

"Is this where I beg forgiveness?" Allen asked, smiling at the officer.

"Well," Nyberg began, "your record is clean. I suppose no harm done." Allen moved into the front seat as the patrolman pushed the driver's door shut.

"Well," the officer continued, "it's not every day our senator becomes president," he said with a grin.

The officer looked into the car and addressed both men.

"You guys did vote for Starr, didn't ya?"

"Absolutely!" they replied in unison. Allen wanted to add "and the bastard's in the trunk," but decided against it.

The young patrolman took two steps from the car. "I'm getting married in two days, and my favorite senator is now the president." Nyberg laughed and waved his right arm. "Ya caught me in a good mood. No ticket. Get going."

"Thanks, officer," Allen replied, as he rolled up his window and quickly drove away.

Patrolman Nyberg walked to his car and took his pen out. He scribbled Len Allen's name next to the car's description and license plate in his notebook.

Allen had driven ten miles on Highway 101 when he saw a roadside pay phone. He pulled over and placed his call.

"Why are you calling?" came the unemotional response.

"Fifteen minutes ago, patrol car 18 stopped me for a taillight violation. No ticket was issued."

"Keep the car . . . and continue as planned."

"I just thought . . ."

"You said no ticket," the voice rudely interrupted. "We can handle any problem like that on our end. Your car has special breathing holes in the trunk, armor-plated sides, bulletproof glass, and an arsenal under the backseat that would intimidate any National Guard unit. We won't have you ditch that car unless the problem can't be handled."

"Understood," Allen replied, but the other voice had already hung up.

CHAPTER 4

THE SCENE OF THE CRIME

6:00 A.M.
Wednesday, November 3

AT 5:45 A.M. PAULSON OREAR STAGGERED ON THE BACK STAIRS of the Fairmont Hotel. He gripped the handrails, struggling to pull himself up each step. He could hardly see where he was walking, due to the Nixon mask blocking his vision, and a combination of fatigue from lack of sleep and several recently consumed drinks.

As he paused to catch his breath on the second-floor landing, he noticed that the painter had left quite a mess; a large canvas had been carelessly thrown into the corner. As Orear painfully continued his now physically exhausting journey, he began to wonder where the painter was. He would be sure to report this to Reynolds if he reached the third floor before passing out.

He silently cheered to himself as his legs reached their destination. He felt terrible. His eyes were swollen and bloodshot. He knew Agent Stewart would never let him forget this night. Well, he thought to himself, it had been worth it. The drinks . . . the stories . . . the promising future. He was ready to take whatever abuse the sarcastic agent might dish out. He slowly opened the stairway door. He watched his hand grip the handle, but he felt nothing. He knew instantly something was wrong. Where was Ray Stewart? His first reaction was to pound on Starr's door, but he held back. Maybe Reynolds knew what was going on. He quickly ran past two rooms and firmly knocked on Reynolds's door.

"What the fuck do you want, Paulie?" Reynolds was annoyed. He hadn't been sleeping long.

"Where is Stewart?"

Reynolds looked intently at Orear, wiping his eyes and trying to get his bearings. Orear was capable of deviousness, but Andy could tell he was serious. Without answering, Reynolds shot out of the room and, while running to Starr's suite, took the passkey from his robe. Orear quickly followed. Something was wrong.

"The TV's still on."

"Sshh," Reynolds motioned for Orear's silence. He went for his shoulder harness.

"Shit, Paulie, I hope I don't have to use this," Reynolds cussed in a barely audible whisper. Both men tiptoed toward the bedroom.

"Whew, that was close," sighed Orear upon seeing the two figures in bed. "Come on, Andy, let's go."

Something wasn't right. Reynolds suddenly felt sick. He could feel the tension in the air. All the razor-sharp thinking in the universe wouldn't help him now. He tensed, his heart pounding furiously, ready to explode, as he walked over to the male figure lying so still. The agent's entire body began to shake. He felt panic sweeping over him, as he looked toward Orear.

"It's not him." He struggled to say each word. His breathing stopped, his legs froze. He was barely able to move.

"Oh my God!" Orear ran to Judy.

"Andy, she's bleeding." Reynolds quickly examined the blonde. He felt her pulse. Orear's words had startled him back to reality.

"She's okay. Must have been knocked out. Don't touch a fuckin' thing."

Reynolds ran to the bathroom. He didn't know what to look for. He just ran. His heart was pounding so fast he could hardly breathe.

"Go get Jo," Reynolds commanded.

Orear ran outside the bedroom, through the main room into the hallway.

"Help!" he screamed. Several agents arrived within seconds. Reynolds took control as the other agents stared helplessly.

"Jason, Mark, David, go downstairs, check the parking lot, check with the bellhops, anybody working all night."

Before the three left, Reynolds cautioned, "Keep this quiet." But as they ran away he mumbled, "If you can."

Reynolds darted to his room and pulled his trousers on. He went over to the nightstand and reached for his walkie-talkie.

"Get me . . ."

"I'm here, Andy." Reynolds was startled to hear her voice. He just stared at her, still trying to understand. He sat on the edge of the bed.

"What happened?" he asked, staring in disbelief at his aide.

Josephine Decker was fighting back the tears. She walked toward Reynolds and leaned against the desk behind her.

"The scaffolding behind the front desk fell on two carpenters."

"So what?" he interrupted.

"So," she continued, "I was nearby and saw they needed help. They were being crushed. At 3:30 A.M. there's not much help around. I called a few agents from their stations." Decker couldn't look at Reynolds. She stared at the floor and waited for her boss's temper to erupt.

"Excuse me, sir," said the agent, as he cautiously entered the room.

"What is it, David?" Reynolds asked, still trying to digest Decker's story.

"Agent Bob Martin is dead."

"Oh my God!" Decker exclaimed as she turned from the two men.

"Was he the painter?"

"Yes, sir," the agent replied, unable to hold back his tears.

"Check with everyone else and report back in fifteen minutes."

"Yes, sir."

Reynolds followed the agent to the door and slammed it shut. He turned toward Decker. She could see the anger in his eyes.

"You know what you have done? You've violated every rule. You *never* take men away from their assigned posts without checking with me. . . . Never."

"I thought you would do the same thing. I never . . ."

"You *thought*!" Reynolds screamed. "It didn't require moving that many agents. One or two with hotel personnel could have moved that scaffolding. I know . . . I saw it."

Decker moved closer to Reynolds and whispered, "I never dreamed this could happen. I only needed those men for fifteen minutes."

"Fifteen minutes," Reynolds repeated slowly, shaking his head in frustration. He went to the bathroom and splattered his face with cold water. Decker watched in silence as he slowly dried himself off.

"Get me a full update within twenty minutes. I have a few phone calls to make."

Decker said nothing and walked toward the door. She grabbed Reynolds's arm.

"Andy . . . what will we do?"

"We've got to find him. One more thing . . . get me on the next available plane to D.C."

CHAPTER 5

THE WHITE HOUSE

Wednesday Morning
November 3

ARTHUR SUTHERLAND KNEW HIS PRESIDENCY WAS OVER. Although he had made valiant attempts, his foreign and domestic policies had failed. The president, approaching his sixty-fifth birthday, was not a man who accepted defeat gracefully. He would have rather spent election night at home, in Indianapolis, but due to the growing tensions in the Middle East, he felt it imperative that he stay in Washington.

Sutherland was a big man, muscular with broad shoulders, well built and in good physical condition for his age. His rapidly graying hair matched his thick eyebrows and neatly trimmed sideburns. He had aged gracefully over the past four years, and, like his predecessor, loved to spend time outdoors in robust physical activity.

Well, he thought to himself, stretching his arms far above his head as he sat behind his desk in the Oval Office, if J.W. McBee closed their deal within the next several weeks, maybe he could redeem a major portion of his presidency. Lame duck or not, his foreign-policy coup could work. History would treat his administration far better than the voting public had today.

The president reached across his desk and selected a pipe to fit his mood. He chose a lightweight black briar with an oversized bowl. Sutherland lit his pipe and sucked, watching the smoke waft toward the ceiling.

The president was interrupted by his campaign manager, Ray Bailey. Bailey had gone over all of the votes, looking at the plurality, past presidential history, and popular vote. He compared it on a scale with the electoral vote, and now felt he could accurately project the election results to President Sutherland. The president looked at each state's tally and did not need the three networks to tell him he had lost the election. He accepted what had been known all evening. He no longer would be the president.

"Well, Ray," the president sighed, "at least it was fairly close."

"I'm sorry, Mr. President."

"Hey, hey," Sutherland waved his hands, "it sure as hell isn't your fault. I saw it coming."

"Do you think the Jewish issue mattered?" wondered the campaign manager.

"I think it helped Starr. Look, not only is he Jewish, but his wife's not. A mixed marriage. The country could give a shit anymore."

"I'll give Starr credit, though," the president continued, "he kept both the Jews and Arabs happy. For the country's sake, I hope that continues."

Bailey listed a litany of statistics for Sutherland's review. The professional and business voters, as they had done four years ago, went with President Sutherland, though Starr held his own and picked up a tremendous number of votes from the white-collar workers. Voters over fifty years of age seemed to vote almost equally between Sutherland and Starr, but those voters between thirty and forty-nine supported Senator Starr. Though the Protestant vote stayed with President Sutherland, the Catholic vote was split. The Jewish vote strongly favored Senator Starr. Starr also received votes from a greater number of Independents, and was able to garner a high percentage of Democrats, many of whom came back to the party after leaving it four years earlier.

The president stayed up all night. He talked with campaign aides and staff members. Reminiscing. Making jokes about the campaign. The atmosphere wasn't as bad as expected. Perhaps most of the president's staff had been prepared for the defeat.

It was almost 9:30 A.M. when Arthur Sutherland completed the draft of his concession speech to the nation. He had not requested assistance from any of his speech writers. He wanted to make this speech his own; one in which he could speak sincerely to the American people. Just as he was going upstairs to shave, the president was told that Federal Bureau of Investigation Director Donald Hagstrom was in the White House and had to talk to him about an urgent matter.

Sutherland sat in his chair with his mouth open, horrified, as he listened to the FBI director relate some of the information from San Francisco.

Hagstrom's four-year tenure with President Sutherland had been routine. No major crisis, no scandal, no sticky domestic issue causing the public or Congress to stir . . . until now. The FBI director sank slowly into a chair in front of the president's desk. He was a medium-sized man, narrow at the hips with strong arms and wrists, strong enough to drive a golf ball three hundred yards. He pulled out a handkerchief and wiped his broad forehead.

"So," the director continued nervously, "everything is sketchy. Reynolds is on his way back. He'll be here by 1:30. His report is being transmitted, and you'll have it within the hour."

"Jesus," the president mumbled, staring in disbelief, petrified by the news.

"We don't know why, how, or who," Hagstrom continued. "Reynolds can't understand how they found the room or snuck through security. There's no ransom note, no phone calls, no fingerprints. We're tracking down three laundry room employees who were observed by agents. They, evidently, killed one of our agents, and we're running this information through the computers."

"Was Judy Starr injured?"

"She's still in shock, but she'll be all right."

"Mr. Director, how the hell can the FBI not know when something like this is planned? How could the Secret Service let something like this happen?" the president demanded, his disbelief turning to fury. Hagstrom paused before answering, took a deep breath, and then looked the president square in the eye.

"Mr. President, we have no idea how they did this. The Treasury Department and the FBI are taking full responsibility."

Sutherland bellowed as he shot up out of his chair. "Mr. Director, I am not asking who is going to take responsibility, I am trying to understand how and why this happened!"

Sutherland struggled to regain his composure, sat back in his chair, and looked out the window, trying to think what to do next. The backyard of the White House looked so serene, a peaceful contrast to this new crisis, the most difficult he had faced during his presidency. And it had come on a day when his presidency was all but over. He turned his chair back and apologized to Director Hagstrom.

"Sorry for the outburst, Donald, but I'm shocked that something like this could happen in our country, and to make it worse, happen under these circumstances." Sutherland looked at the FBI director intently. Here was a man who had been on the force for over thirty years and he, too, was dumbfounded.

Minute by minute Washington became a web of activity. Word got out to Special Counsel Whyte that the president wanted to see him immediately. All cabinet members, along with top Pentagon officials and the vice president were summoned to the White House.

Within an hour, official Washington had gathered in the White House basement crisis center. The Republican leaders, Speaker of the House Charles T. Durkin of Illinois and Senate Majority Leader Jay Johl of New York, were among the first to arrive. After Director Hagstrom briefed the group, the president took immediate control.

"We don't know if there is a conspiracy. It could be an international plot. The Russians, Cubans, or some radical group from the Middle East could have done this. We just don't know yet."

The president walked around the room, tieless, in shirtsleeves. There were dark circles under his eyes, his gray hair was rumpled, and an irritating black stubble of beard covered his chin.

"We have alerted allies and enemies that our internal problems are of no concern to them. That we have the situation under control. We have placed our military forces on red alert." Noticing a reaction from a few cabinet members, the president quickly added, "Solely as a precaution.

"The Secret Service contingency around the president and other key members of government has been tripled. We've done the same for Starr's family. I will address the nation when we know more. I want everyone to be available. Let's meet again at four o'clock. I'm meeting with Andy Reynolds soon, and I hope to God he has something we can go on."

Reynolds was nervous. His hands were sweating. He had never spoken personally to the president. For the past six hours the only clue he or the FBI could uncover involved three laundry room employees who had been working the early morning following the election . . . about the same time Starr was kidnapped and one Secret Service agent murdered.

The president greeted Reynolds and ushered him to the chair directly in front of his cluttered desk. Sutherland collapsed into his chair and reached for several papers in front of him. He said nothing as he scanned a report Reynolds recognized as coming from the bureau.

Reynolds gazed around this historic office. To his right was a huge four-screen television console with family photos and memorabilia tastefully placed directly above.

The curving west wall was inset with light blue bookshelves, lined with sets of books chosen by color and the design of their bindings rather than for the contents of their words. Everything appeared so neat . . . so peaceful.

Between the northernmost window and the curved door leading to the president's secretary's room were impressively large bowls filled with beautifully colored flowers. On the perfectly painted walls on either side of the windows hung oil paintings of scenic Indiana farmland.

The north end of the room was dominated by a large fireplace of classic design. An oil portrait of George Washington hung over it in a frame appearing as old as the original.

Behind the president's desk were floor-to-ceiling rounded windows covered by light blue drapes. Beyond the tinted glass was the magnificent Washington Monument.

Reynolds looked out the French doors behind the president's desk into the elegant Rose Garden. So quiet and tranquil; a reminder of better times.

To his left, five tall flags of the armed services with their bright battle streamers, topped with large gold eagles, were proudly displayed for all Oval Office visitors and guests.

The president flipped the FBI report back on his desk, his arm causing a little American flag to fall over. His desk was replete with symbols for all occasions. The miniature Republican elephant was conspicuously displayed on one end of the desk and was counterbalanced by a huge, elegant, marble pen set with a large mounted clock at its center on the other side of the desk.

"Andy, I want you to take personal charge of the investigation. Work with Hagstrom." The president knew of Reynolds's relationship with Starr.

"Are you planning to head back to Frisco?" the president wondered.

"Yes, sir," Reynolds replied, and then quickly added, "we've checked all phone calls made from the Starr suite."

"Go on," the president said.

"No calls were made to the room. Three calls were placed by Starr according to the switchboard operator."

"How do you know for sure Starr placed the calls?"

"She identified his voice for us," Reynolds replied quickly, trying to convince the president there was no need for optimism.

"Sir," he continued, "the calls were to his parents, Johnny Carson, and the vice president elect."

"Shit," the president snapped, his hopes of finding an early clue eliminated. "No suspects there."

"Hardly," Reynolds agreed.

"Why Carson?"

"Jonathan was accepting Carson's offer to appear on the show next week. It was a pledge he made one week before the election. Win or lose. This is all confirmed by Carson himself."

"Andy, I'm trusting you with an awesome undertaking. Director Hagstrom thinks you can handle this and so do I. No one is holding you responsible."

The president's words hit Reynolds like a bolt of lightning. Responsible.

Of course, he was responsible. Starr was taken from under his nose. The president was giving him a chance to save his reputation and career.

"Andy," the president said, his voice subdued, "I'm about to let you in on a top-security item." The president left his chair and walked around the desk, leaning over the still sitting Reynolds. The president held out his left hand.

"Take a look at this ring." Reynolds awkwardly held the president's hand and observed what appeared to be a wedding ring.

"Starr has one identical to mine. It has a high-frequency transmitter inside the gold band."

Reynolds sat back in his chair as the president handed him a manila folder.

"The history of the ring's development is in here. For eight years the president, vice president, and the opposing party's candidate for president have worn these rings. If their plane would crash, the transmitter would help authorities locate them. Or . . ." the president stopped.

"Or if they're kidnapped," Reynolds finished the sentence for him.

The president sat down behind his desk and eyed Reynolds.

"It's an enormous task. Especially since much of the work is up to you . . . alone. You must locate Starr by using the special monitors. Obviously, we can't have you doing this with an army."

"I can't attract attention."

"Right. But once you locate him, you are to immediately contact me, and I'll decide what action must be taken."

Reynolds thumbed through the report in silence. When he looked up at the president, Sutherland was staring at him.

"You're thinking what I am, aren't you?"

"What's that, Mr. President?"

"Is he alive?"

Reynolds nodded his head, but said nothing.

"I've thought about that all day. He *must* be alive. Otherwise, whoever did this could have made it easier by just killing him."

"I'll locate him, sir," Reynolds said, his voice firm. He stood up, carefully holding the manila folder.

"I think we've already located him," the president replied. He noticed Reynolds's surprise. The president tried to explain. "When we heard of the kidnapping, we immediately began tracing the ring from Washington. The monitor readings are weak but we think he's in the L.A. area. I'm flying you to L.A. International. An FBI equipment expert will brief you on the tracing mechanism on the flight. Your car and special gear will be waiting for you. You will be bringing the only tracing device we have. You're in charge . . . take whatever manpower you need . . . just check in with me before you make a final move."

Reynolds grabbed the president's hand.

"I know what you're thinking, Andy," the president began, "but you are *not* responsible. No more than the agents in Dallas, or the Ford and Reagan attempts. If I thought otherwise, I sure as hell wouldn't place you in charge of the most important investigation of my career."

Reynolds had taken all of the precautions. The building had been so thoroughly checked, he found it hard to believe that the kidnapping had taken place. Even with President Sutherland's gracious and compassionate remarks, Andrew Reynolds felt responsible. As head agent assigned to a presidential candidate, it was Reynolds's duty to make all decisions concerning security. Where had he gone wrong? Somewhere, somehow, a mistake had been made.

After meeting with the FBI technical equipment expert, Andrew Reynolds sat alone while the Air Force jet streaked to L.A. He studied the combined report prepared by the FBI and Secret Service.

The Russians, as always, were suspect, but there were no motives. Why get rid of Starr? He wasn't president yet. The Cubans, Libyans, and Iranians all had motives, but it was doubtful Starr would be a target. Their arguments were with the Sutherland administration.

Several Arab terrorist groups were on the suspect list. Starr's Judaism concerned them a great deal. But he apparently was trying to eliminate the appearance of a pro-Israeli posture and had brutally criticized Israel's recent Lebanon invasion.

Then the Israelis themselves had to be considered suspect. The CIA had documentation that suggested an underground faction of the Mossad, the Israeli secret police or "the Institute," wanted Starr dead. They believed he would be no friend to Israel. Inferences, piled upon innuendos, piled upon rumors. No concrete evidence linked any foreign power to the kidnapping.

Reynolds closed the report and flipped it on the empty seat next to him. He shut his eyes in anger and frustration.

At 9:00 P.M., Wednesday, November 3, Arthur Sutherland addressed the nation. He hoped to ease the country's fear about the kidnapping and to alert the world that the United States would not tolerate any foreign interference during this crisis. He had no answers on why there was no ransom note, nor could he respond to legal questions regarding succession to the presidency—the ultimate question that troubled the nation, the country's allies, and the entire world. The president, as leader of the free world, was the most important and influential person in the universe. This one person, this one office, literally could control the destiny of all mankind.

The abduction in San Francisco was now the focus of worldwide attention. Even more newsworthy than a presidential assassination, since succession laws covered such an eventuality. But here, the world faced an unprecedented event. America's problem was now a problem for the citizens of the world.

The Washington Post summarized the country's dilemma most succinctly. Their morning headline echoed the troubled feelings of a worried nation. "WHO WILL BE PRESIDENT ON JANUARY 20?"

CHAPTER 6

CAIRO

Wednesday, November 3

THE EGYPTIAN GENERAL SAT NEXT TO HIS PHONE, QUIETLY tapping the glass coffee table to his right. He stared out the window of his second-story apartment, then glanced at his watch. Again. The lady was late. Why can't she even make a phone call on time, he mumbled to himself.

The general rubbed his mustache with his left hand, gently twisting the neatly trimmed hair. He was growing impatient, now glaring at the telephone.

It rang; the loud noise didn't even startle the experienced army leader.

"Yes," he said quickly.

"My general," she began, "I call as instructed."

He glanced at his watch but said nothing sarcastic. "Has the Englishman filled you in?"

"Yes," she responded quickly, "but I want to know, from you, is everything under control?"

"Indeed, Madame," he replied confidently, "our man is in place and we're on top of the situation."

"I don't like our plans being tied into American politics."

"Nor do I," the general sighed, "but we all knew the risks."

"This can't lead to the signing of the peace plan. It just can't happen," she said forcefully.

"It *won't* happen!" the general shouted, leaning forward in his chair. "There will be *no* peace plan. We have matters under control." The general paused, not wanting to lecture his colleague. "Do you want to know any specifics?"

"No," she responded quickly, "your assurances are enough."

"Fine. We'll talk in three days, unless you call before."

"Agreed."

"Good-bye, Madame," the general said, placing the phone into the cradle. He stood up and walked to the bathroom. The military leader stared at himself in the mirror. His mouth tightened, eyes squinted as he pounded the sink before him in defiance, "There will be no peace plan . . . *never.*"

CHAPTER 7

THE RESCUE ATTEMPT

Early Morning
Thursday, November 4

REYNOLDS GRIPPED THE STEERING WHEEL FIRMLY WITH HIS left hand while with his right hand he forcefully shifted into park. He leaned forward and carefully made a few calculations on the TV screen, located between his right knee and the front-seat passenger, Jo Decker.

The cold rays of the moon raced down from the night sky and bounced off the hills near the little farmhouse located twenty miles outside of Los Angeles.

"The screen still shows about two more miles," Reynolds observed, glancing quickly to his right. Decker took out her walkie-talkie and returned her boss's stare.

"Base to scout," she said in even tones, tapping her fingertips gently on the sensitive instrument. Several seconds later a calm voice replied.

"Status quo remains. Turn headlights off three quarters of a mile from present location; right past northerly sixty-degree turn. I left a beer can in the middle of the road. You're on your own from there. Over and out."

"Check," Decker replied, turning to Reynolds. "What next?"

"Look!" Reynolds exclaimed, pointing to the electrical dot in the middle of the screen. "Jonathan has quit moving."

Decker leaned closer for a better look. The lines, the numbers, degrees, and angles confused her, but she also noticed the stationary circle in the middle of the scope.

"My god, that machine is sensitive," she offered, wondering when Reynolds would move.

"It is, when you're this close. That's why we had to stay in the car, to make sure they didn't make a run for it." Reynolds looked through the front window and slowly maneuvered the car to their destination.

"How did you know we were this close?" she asked.

"Gut feeling," he replied, not moving his swollen eyes from the roadway. After he reached Jonathan, he planned to take a three-week vacation, anywhere.

"The farm fields indicated to me that no other farms or access roads are in the area. Plus the beeper was getting closer, and Jonathan's movements mimicked someone walking around in a house. I knew we were close and didn't want headlights to spoil our surprise party."

His mood changed quickly as he reached forward to kill the headlights, noticing the Budweiser can in the middle of the road. He leaned back in the seat, stretching his legs and arms. "Get me the phone."

"Go ahead, Andy," President Sutherland responded to his early-morning caller.

"We have six men in place. There was no way to alert the National Guard. This place is too open. I've got L.A.'s best FBI people."

"Will six be enough?"

"It certainly looks that way. There's very little movement inside . . . and only a beat up VW in front. Not the best escape vehicle."

"What do you recommend?" the president asked, staring at the carpet next to his desk.

"I'll go in and try to get Starr. That's the easiest. In all probability I'll flush them out, and a man stationed outside the front door will grab him."

Reynolds held his breath and listened intently. Nothing. How long could it take? What were the man's options?

"Do it," came the firm reply, with the president quickly adding, "but a word of caution. If, after you have personally surveyed the farmhouse, you feel your plan won't work . . . immediately abort. That's an order."

"Yes, sir," Reynolds replied quickly and respectfully. He was about to hang up when the president spoke again.

"What have the agents been told?"

"The truth . . . there is no other way. They must know the stakes."

"Call me when you have Starr," the president replied, terminating the conversation.

Reynolds and Decker crouched near the road, using the black of night and the nearby tall grass as their shield.

"It looks like someone is moving in the living room," Decker whispered, as Reynolds peered through his binoculars.

"Shadow of some kind. The lighting in there is dim."

"Everyone is in place," Decker said, finishing her contact with the other agents over the walkie-talkie.

"I'm going around the back." Reynolds glanced at his watch. "Give me eight minutes, then work your way near the VW."

"Andy," she grabbed his arm tightly before he could move. "Be careful . . . it could be a trap."

"The thought has crossed my mind." He forced a smile and started into the high grass, zigzagging toward the nearby trees.

The mission brought back Vietnam memories. Reynolds shook his head, feeling a thousand pounds of pressure on the back of his neck. The wind, grass, and trees—being out in the open . . . Vietnam again. He couldn't shake it. He stared at the binoculars hanging from his neck. He shook his head again, not wanting to relive that tragic night so long ago.

Colonels Thomas Decker and Andrew Reynolds had personally been responsible for the deaths of hundreds of Vietcong. In the jungle these two leaders headed platoons whose mission was to destroy roads and bridges and to cut supply lines behind enemy lines. They had performed their task to perfection . . . until Colonel Thomas Decker was captured.

Like the daughter who would follow him, Tom Decker excelled as a Green Beret. Those who watched him master parachute training and the special forces "Q" courses knew he would be a leader. Decker was at the top of his class in unconventional warfare: sabotage, subversion, guerrilla tactics, and demolition. At times, his detachment equipped, trained, and led forces of fifteen hundred men into the hot jungles of Vietnam.

His reputation grew faster than Reynolds's. He raided enemy headquarters, captured generals, destroyed supply lines, and soon became a marked man.

When Reynolds was informed of his friend's capture, he immediately took steps to save him. But there was only one way to save Tom Decker. Andrew Reynolds would have to go alone.

The daring rescue mission was further complicated by a political dilemma. Tom Decker had been captured during a cease-fire. Several of his best friends had recently been butchered by the Vietcong. Decker decided to retaliate when the enemy least suspected his reprisals. Andy had argued long and hard with his good friend the night before he left on his "revenge mission." But to no avail. He knew Decker would violate the cease-fire. Andy saw it in his friend's eyes, which glittered with a ghoulish anticipation and malice.

After traveling all day, Reynolds located the camp and saw Decker, asleep in a small see-through hut right in the middle of the camp. The small bamboo cell was guarded tightly. Enemy soldiers were strategically located with rifles all around the colonel.

Reynolds planned the escape, knowing a diversion and quick exit was the only way out. He set five claymore mines alongside a nearby roadbed. He carefully placed the detonator far away, near the escape path he and Decker would travel. He prayed the enemy would chase him along the roadway.

All the necessary traps had been set throughout the jungle. Reynolds carefully memorized their escape route. It would be difficult because his rescue effort had to be done at night . . . when it was pitch black, except for the moon, whose great light was diminished by the forest engulfing the enemy camp.

Reynolds crawled toward the camp, not daring to go any closer. The high grass bent with the breeze. The earth under him was hard, sun-baked, unlike most of the mud he'd encountered getting there.

The Vietcong had the camp lit up like New Year's Eve in Times Square . . . lights were everywhere. He saw what was occurring, but didn't want to believe it. Decker was being tortured—it would be a slow, agonizing death. Reynolds understood enough Vietnamese to know what was being said. He squeezed his eyes shut as he listened in silent horror.

"Colonel Decker," the enemy commander shouted, "for killing so many of our people, you too will be killed." Then taking a long steel-bladed knife, the officer slashed off one of Decker's fingers. The colonel grimaced in pain but didn't scream. The soldiers in camp cheered, enjoying the gruesome display of torture.

Reynolds grabbed his binoculars and saw three fingers were missing from the colonel's left hand. Decker was sweating profusely, standing straight in his uniform, tied to a post behind him. Blood was oozing from the left side of his mouth where the colonel had bitten a small hole into his lip.

Tears began rolling down Reynolds's face as he viewed the unit's security. Men with rifles, their backs to Decker, were peering into the jungle. Certainly any diversion would cause them to kill Decker immediately.

There was no way out. Reynolds watched in agony as three

more fingers were removed from the blood-filled hands of his beloved friend.

"Now, colonel," the officer hollered, "you are a brave man. No screaming. You must be respected. But we demand our satisfaction. My men have had their brothers slaughtered by your butchers. They demand justice." The men around the commanding officer cheered again as the repulsive scene turned into a sporting event. The commander rubbed his muscled right arm, made permanently brown by the hot Vietnam sun.

"Take down his pants." The order was greeted by an enthusiastic outburst from the soldiers. A nearby officer followed orders and rolled down Decker's pants. The colonel closed his eyes but said nothing, more blood flowing from the side of his mouth.

Reynolds felt his knees go from under him. He couldn't let his friend, his brave friend, suffer any longer. Reynolds understood he would have time for only one or two shots. He quickly moved his way toward the nearby roadway. He wanted the enemy to assume that this was his escape route. That's the angle he had to shoot from. It was a more difficult shot, being 150 feet farther from his target . . . his best friend.

Reynolds took a deep breath and aimed. He saw the commander raise his right hand with the butcher knife.

"May God forgive me," Reynolds uttered, as he squeezed the trigger. The bullet entered the center of Decker's forehead, killing him instantly.

The commander stopped his swing and turned toward the fallen Decker, seeing the hole in his head. He quickly turned around, his twisted face showing the agony he was feeling.

"The shot came . . ." A second shot hit the commander right between the eyes. He fell to the hard ground below. Reynolds dropped his rifle and began running into the forest. His heart was beating so hard, it felt as though it would blast through his chest.

He went right to the detonator and listened. As he squatted under the brush, he wiped the tears from his eyes. He heard voices in the distance. The assholes were on the roadway.

The explosion caused screams that pierced the night air. Screams they never heard from Colonel Thomas Decker. That was a small consolation to Reynolds, as he frantically stepped through his escape route . . . alone . . . to safety.

Reynolds stared at the binoculars around his neck. "Shit," he mumbled to himself, checking his watch. Five minutes had elapsed. It was another "do or die" rescue effort. He couldn't fail.

Reynolds made his way to the back door. He peered in the glass window on top—there was no one. It was pitch black inside. He leaned forward and picked the lock. Fortunately, it wasn't a dead bolt—every second was important.

There were no agents stationed behind the house, but Reynolds's actions didn't go unnoticed.

A man perched high in a nearby tree watched through infrared binoculars. The branches and limbs hid him completely. He took a piece of gum from his pocket, carefully gripping his rifle with the telescopic lense.

Reynolds slowly entered the house. A rush of stale air escaped from the kitchen where something had been decaying, for weeks. Andy's batlike sonar told him the house was empty . . . but how could that be? As he moved toward the living room, he heard voices. He could see light, then shadows, just around the corner. He wiped the sweat from his palm on his pant leg and held his gun high over his right shoulder, inching forward.

"Starr's been a model prisoner." The first voice came in a monotone.

"Yeah," agreed the second man, "but consider what his options are." Then there was silence. Reynolds inched closer to the voices. He waited. His eyes quickly adjusted to the dim light ahead.

"When will we move him again?"

"Whenever the boss tells us."

Reynolds noticed this time that the voices appeared to be coming from somewhere in the middle of the room. Why would they be sitting so close together? There was silence again. Something was wrong. An uneasy feeling overcame Reynolds as he felt beads of sweat trickling down his armpits. He wouldn't wait any longer.

"Freeze," he whispered as he burst into the room, his gun aimed toward the voices.

Nothing.

The room was empty. Reynolds saw the tape recorder on the small table in front of the fireplace. He scanned the room. A small fan circulated. Light was being supplied by a burning candle over the unlit fireplace, and two small lamps positioned nearby. That was the silhouette he had seen from outside. He noticed a miniature train-set track that circled the living room on shelves surrounding the walls. The tracks went upstairs through shelving over the bannister.

The living room was filled with antiques and World War II memorabilia. He wiped the sweat from his brow and took a deep breath as he scanned the room for clues. An uneasy, nauseating feeling almost overcame him. He stood silently hoping to hear something upstairs.

"Choo-choo." The train startled him as it began its journey up the stairs. Was it a trap? He decided not to use the walkie-talkie. Not yet.

He rushed up the stairs, taking two steps at a time, until he reached the top. He was breathing hard, his heart pounding as he approached a dimly lit room. Hearing nothing, he leaped into the room.

"Freeze!" he screamed, instantly feeling foolish. Reynolds found himself standing in an empty room.

He dashed into the bathroom, the only other second-floor room. He pulled the walkie-talkie to his mouth.

"Nothing. No one here. I'm coming out."

He heard the train stop in the next room. He put his gun in his shoulder harness and dejectedly entered the room. The train had a small caboose that raised Reynolds's curiosity. As he got closer, he reached down for a small package in the little red car. He quickly opened the small box and stared at the contents in disbelief.

Jonathan Starr's wedding ring.

They knew. Somehow they must have electronically searched Starr, and when they found the ring, they had enough time to set this elaborate charade. It must have bought them hours of a head start, Reynolds thought to himself as he walked out the back door.

Then he caught something . . . someone out of the corner of his eye. He beamed his powerful flashlight toward a large nearby oak tree. There was a man.

"Halt!" Reynolds shouted, grabbing his gun, running toward the man who had descended from a nearby tree. Reynolds caught a quick glimpse of his face as a beam of light swung across the darkness. As he fired his gun into the dark abyss behind the farmhouse, he heard another shot.

"Shit!" Reynolds yelled, as he fell to the ground, "I've been hit."

As soon as they heard the gunfire, the two agents who had been walking alongside the farmhouse sprinted toward Reynolds.

"Get the bastard!" Reynolds barked, holding his right leg tightly, just below the knee. Without breaking stride the agents disappeared into the woods.

"My God, Andy!" Decker hollered, as she ran to his side. She watched silently as Reynolds tried to pull himself upright.

"Let me," she said as she grabbed his left arm firmly. She tore his pant leg off and closely examined the wound under the steady rays of her flashlight.

"God, you're so lucky. It's a flesh wound."

"I'm not *lucky*," he snickered, leaning back on both arms, holding himself steady by his muscular wrists.

"What do you mean?" she asked.

"Look at the wound," he shouted, shifting his weight so his left hand could point to the leg. "He wanted a flesh wound . . . instead of blowing my leg off. He's that good a shot . . . but why?"

"How can you know that?"

Reynolds leaned back on both arms and stared at Decker. "I've seen that face before . . . it's different . . . perhaps foreign. Dark features, very well built."

"So what?"

"His eyes. I could see it in the eyes. For some reason he didn't want to kill me . . . even hurt me . . . just slow me down."

"He did that," she replied, taking another look at the wound. The two didn't speak for several minutes. Decker finally broke the silence.

"What was he doing here?"

"How the hell do I know?" he snapped. "Help me up."

He leaned on Decker's right shoulder as they slowly walked back toward the car.

Where had he seen that man? Was it the wavy dark hair . . . maybe the eyes . . . or the buggy eyeballs. He pushed his memory . . . photos . . . files . . . Vietnam . . . or maybe a foreign agent.

Sweat broke out on Reynolds's forehead as he reached the car. He felt his pulse quickening. He heard footsteps.

"He's gone, Andy."

Reynolds turned and looked at the two FBI agents.

"He disappeared into thin air," the tall agent said in a low voice, waiting to be chewed out. Reynolds forced a smile.

"At least *you* didn't get shot."

"It could have happened to any of us," Decker said reassuringly.

"Not you," Reynolds responded, hopping into the car and collapsing into the front seat. He eyed Decker. "You wouldn't get hurt. Green Berets are tough."

"The colonel was a Green Beret . . . and he got killed," she replied coldly.

Reynolds didn't respond to her but addressed the agents.

"Give us a few minutes alone," he said softly. Then he turned toward Decker.

"Let's not talk about the colonel tonight, Jo."

She nodded her head and helped Reynolds elevate his right leg onto the front seat.

"Why did he spare me . . . what does he want?" Reynolds mumbled, as he straightened himself in the seat. He observed Decker for a few seconds and motioned for her to come closer.

"Get me the phone."

She knew the tone too well. Her boss didn't relish giving bad news to an anxious president.

Chapter 8

Journalism to the Rescue

Tuesday, November 9

Guy Hirte paced the length of his spacious fourth-floor office, located in the *Washington Post* building. He had just spent two hours discussing the legal ramifications of the Starr kidnapping. During the past six days, most newspapers had extensively covered the government investigation into Starr's abduction, with little mention of the constitutional crisis facing the nation.

Hirte had researched every applicable case and statute concerning the dilemma facing the nation. The law was not clear as to who would become president on January 20. The paper's hierarchy had decided to run a daily feature on this issue, which would overlap a series of articles on Jonathan Starr as an individual, not a politician. Hirte's task was to convince the *Post*'s ace reporter, Katherine Wilson, to write the sensitive stories about Starr.

Wilson's journalistic intuition told her the meeting with Hirte would be important. She had spent five frustrating days in San Francisco, attempting to learn what the government's investigators had not. Who kidnapped Starr . . . and why?

Wilson grabbed her notes from last week's interviews, and gulped down a lukewarm cup of coffee while she scampered toward the elevator. She cursed herself as she noticed a small stain of French dressing left over from a hurried lunch just hours ago. She stopped by the water cooler but failed to remove the red smudge. She tugged and pulled on her brown jacket, trying to cover the obvious spot on the sleeve of her new white blouse.

"Katie, good to see you. Come on in." The attorney greeted her with a sincere smile and firm handshake. The two had dated several years ago. Kate stopped accepting dates when Hirte apparently wanted more than temporary companionship.

She sat down in the chair directly in front of the attorney's desk. He had several neat piles of paper on the right side of the large brown cedar desk, but the left side had only one law book. Wilson noticed the remaining two chairs and couch were completely covered with other law books. Only two certificates were displayed on the otherwise bare walls—the attorney's diploma from Hamline University School of Law and a certificate from the Order of the Coif.

"Katie, we have a special project, a *very* special project for you to work on." The attorney was shrewd and businesslike, and as usual, avoided any small talk.

"It's about Jonathan's kidnapping," Wilson unhesitatingly replied, making more of a statement than asking a question.

"It is. We know of your close relationship to the senator . . ."

"President-elect," she interrupted quickly, wondering what the attorney was about to propose.

"Yes," he agreed, looking the reporter squarely in the eyes. "The project is twofold. First, based on my research, you will find we face a legal crisis. We want the reader to understand the position this country is in."

"I have several questions about that, but tell me about the second fold?" she said, flashing an annoyed look at the attorney because she sensed she would have no choice on this assignment.

"We all believe this will be the greatest project this paper has ever undertaken."

"Greater than Watergate, or the Iranian crisis?" Wilson countered.

"It has that potential." Hirte hesitated slightly. He was coming to the difficult part. "If the stories are based on exclusive interviews with Judy Starr."

"How cruel," Kate snapped. The paper's lawyer held his hand up, attempting to stop any tirade from the reporter.

"We can . . . you can do it tastefully. The country will want to know as much about Starr as possible. He won the election, we know about him politically. Now, what about the man— through the eyes of his wife.''

"She'll never agree to it.''

"She will if you sell it, if you believe in it. By giving us an exclusive, she can keep the bloodhounds away.''

"You mean our competitors,'' she said icily, not relishing the thought of approaching Judy for the interviews, but strangely, from strictly a journalistic viewpoint, grudgingly admiring the paper's proposal.

"What about the legal issue?'' she asked, still debating in her own mind the propriety of taking advantage of a terrible situation.

The attorney adjusted his glasses, opened the law book in front of him, and turned to the first bookmark among many. Kate noticed that his fingernails were perfectly manicured.

"Under the Twentieth Amendment, if Starr dies, Edwards, the vice president elect becomes president.'' The attorney stopped, glanced toward Wilson, then continued.

"If he doesn't die, the vice president elect *could* be president or acting president, but it depends on what the electoral college does. A special election may be necessary. Even the Speaker could act as president.''

Kate was beginning to understand the dilemma. She uncrossed her legs and moved forward in the uncomfortable little chair as the attorney continued, after clearing his throat.

"Obviously there's no precedent to draw from. The amendment gives many options, but politics and the electoral college will ultimately decide.''

"What's the president's decision?''

"Who knows,'' Hirte replied. "He's got to go through the same books I did.''

Kate sat in silence. After a grueling week in San Francisco, this was no way to be greeted. But the proposal was a reporter's dream. The country would get a double dose of news: the constitutional dilemma and the memories of Judy Starr.

"I'll think about it and call you tonight. Bye, Guy,'' she said, as she quickly left the attorney's office, not allowing the speechless lawyer a chance to respond.

CHAPTER 9

BRING ON THE LAWYERS

Thursday, November 11

DURING THE NINE DAYS FOLLOWING THE STARR ABDUCTION, President Sutherland did his best to reassure the country and its allies that he had the situation under control. He signed several bills from Congress and kept all appointments with foreign diplomats.

But it was not business as usual. Ironically, all of his energy was being spent trying to rescue the man who had just defeated him for the presidency.

Starr had been missing for over a week, and there had still been no ransom note, no one claiming responsibility for the kidnapping, no hint of what the motive might have been for this shocking, incredible act.

The Situation Room in the basement of the White House West Executive Wing had been converted into a central command post. Ordinarily this room, which adjoined the smaller area where the National Security Council met, held little furniture other than a long table and chairs, a direct telephone line to the Pentagon War Room, and a "hot line" to Moscow. Today the room was a hub of activity.

The Joint Chiefs of Staff had persuaded the president to place the armed services on a red alert. Though there was no evidence of foreign involvement in the kidnapping, Sutherland concluded this precautionary first step was necessary. The Pentagon delegated an army general to report any new activities around the world that might relate to the San Francisco tragedy.

FBI Director Donald Hagstrom and his staff controlled the other part of the makeshift command post.

A large map of California and San Francisco covered one wall as multicolored ribbons marked off unsuccessful leads. Enlarged highway maps highlighted roads, bridges, hills, towns, and rivers in the general vicinity of the Bay Area. All airports were marked by thin blue tape.

Hagstrom manned the teleprinters that had been utilized from a nearby communications room. Adjacent to the machines stood several television sets and radios. A marine sergeant at a typewriter table kept a minute-by-minute log of developments. The chairman of the Joint Chiefs of Staff stayed in contact with the army general from the Pentagon. Hagstrom handled the nest of phones that linked the command post to the Justice Department, the FBI, and the outside world. The tired FBI director was also in constant communication with agents from California. Though almost totally exhausted, the director knew the work in the basement command post didn't come close to that in the Oval Office.

In the afternoon President Sutherland met with Attorney General Paul Gilbertson and Thomas Whyte, the president's special counsel, to develop preliminary legal opinions in order to answer the question of what effect this kidnapping would have on Jonathan Starr's swearing-in ceremonies.

After two hours of discussion the president ordered Attorney Whyte to summon the two constitutional law experts from the law firm of Christenson & Griswold, retained by the administration to render legal opinions concerning an incident which had never before occurred in the history of the United States.

Ken Christenson stood six feet four inches, with long, thick, brownish gray sideburns. The middle-age spread was visible around this fifty-five-year-old's stomach. He was the person who did most of the legal research for the firm. (Don Griswold, the shorter of the two, was sixty-three years old, with white hair, and did most of the talking.)

The four men sat in velvet-cushioned chairs perfectly spaced in front of the president. Several stacks of unsigned letters covered the famous desk in front of them as the president took a pen from his top drawer, slowly rotating his neck to loosen the stiffness that had been bothering him since election night.

Griswold understood this was one of the rare times an attorney could act on his own judgment and instinct, make decisions without interminable discussion and compromise, and get something accomplished right away, when time for a solution was ripe. With this in mind, he began the day's discussion.

"Mr. President, one of the amendments that certainly is applicable to this crisis is the Twentieth Amendment, adopted as law on January 23, 1933. It specifies that the terms of the president and vice president shall end at noon on the twentieth day of January. Section 3 of that amendment is extremely important." Griswold leaned forward and placed a photocopy of the amendment before the president. "Please read along with me, sir."

> If, at the time fixed for the beginning of the term of the President, the President elect shall have died, the Vice President elect shall become President. If a President shall not have been chosen before the time fixed for the beginning of his term, or if the President elect shall have failed to qualify, then the Vice President elect shall act as President until a President shall have qualified; and the Congress may by law provide for the case wherein neither a President elect nor a Vice President elect shall have qualified, declaring who shall then act as President, or the manner in which one who is to act shall be selected, and such person shall act accordingly until a President or Vice President shall have qualified.

The president stared at the paper for several minutes. He sighed, leaned back in his chair, and intently eyed the attorneys.

"I have read your memorandums. All of them. I even read the research from Westlaw. I have also discussed this entire situation with the vice president elect. He called me. He respectfully informed me *his* attorneys have concluded *he* will be the next president, assuming Starr isn't rescued and the Republicans don't play politics."

"Mr. President," Griswold began, "the president-elect, Jonathan Starr, has not died, so under Section 3 the vice president elect cannot automatically become president. In addition, Mr. President, this section indicates that if a president has not been chosen before the time fixed for the beginning of his term, or if he fails to qualify, then the vice president elect could *act* as president until Jonathan Starr . . . or someone else . . . would qualify.''

Sutherland was confused: he uncrossed his legs and looked around the room for his pipe. "Well, tell me this, Don, what do you mean by 'qualify'? And," the president sighed, "let me also add this to my question. I am assuming Starr *won't* be back by the time the electoral college votes. If he's back, there's no crisis. Of course he'll be qualified. But I'm forced to face reality. One rescue effort has failed. Whoever took him may end up calling the shots.''

The attorney pulled another legal pad from his briefcase, balancing the papers on his lap as he responded.

"Mr. President, we don't have an exact definition for 'qualify,' but during this discussion, let's equate it with the electoral college voting for or 'qualifying' Starr and Edwards, or anyone else for that matter, under the Twelfth Amendment."

Sutherland leaned against the chair, calmly explaining his dilemma. "If the electoral college doesn't qualify either Starr or Edwards, for whatever reasons, I'm faced with a political issue as well as a constitutional issue; and if I throw this election into a Republican Congress, you can rest assured that a Democrat is not going to come out president."

For the first time Attorney General Paul Gilbertson spoke. Historically a liberal, the Harvard scholar was a surprise choice for Sutherland's Cabinet. A former judge with an outstanding reputation for intelligence and integrity, Gilbertson was easily approved for the position by Congress. "General," as he was known, was in his fifties, always immaculately dressed, and exhibited the crew cut and bow tie that had been his trademark for years.

"President Sutherland, there are some other areas of the law that may apply, which we should discuss. Title 3 of our United States laws under Section 19 covers vacancies in office of both the president and vice president. The language is so important that I have taken the liberty to have it typed on a separate piece of paper." Walking over to the president, he showed him a copy of the law. Sutherland brought both hands to the sides of his head, massaging his aching temples gently with his fingers as he read in silence.

If, by reason of death, resignation, removal from office, inability, or failure to qualify, there is neither a President nor Vice President to discharge the powers and duties of the office of President, then the Speaker of the House of Representatives shall, upon his resignation as Speaker and as a Representative in Congress, act as President.

"Here is the problem this raises, Mr. President. Jonathan Starr has not died, he has not resigned, he has not been removed from office. We really can't say he has an inability, or at least not yet, and if the electoral college qualifies him for the presidency, he hasn't failed to qualify. Still, there may be neither a president nor vice president to discharge the powers and duties of the office of president by January 20. Your term of office by law expires on this date, and neither you nor the vice president could serve. If the electoral college has not voted in Jonathan Starr or Martin Edwards, then those people can't serve. So under this section, it would be Speaker Durkin who *acts* as president."

Sutherland looked at Thomas Whyte for help. The president was becoming frustrated—his right ear was getting sore from the constant tugging.

Whyte thought the president wanted to hear from him. "President Sutherland, the recommendation you make to congressional leaders and to the electoral college really will decide the next president of the United States."

The president nodded, his forehead deeply carved with worry lines. During his four-year term he had aged very little. Now he was making up for lost time.

"You all have referred to the electoral college and their decision. I read your memorandum, but it wasn't clear. By tomorrow, I want a shorter memo detailing the specific procedures the Constitution provides for in the event the electoral college doesn't qualify anyone and the election gets thrown into Congress."

Christenson raised his hand almost as if asking for permission to speak. The tall, quiet attorney had listened attentively, trying to pick and choose the most logical solution to the legal dilemma.

"But we must keep in mind, Mr. President, that you are the president until noon, January 20, and if no one comes in on January 20, if neither Starr nor Edwards—nor anyone else— qualifies, then the Speaker of the House in my opinion has got to be the acting president of the United States. And he could conceivably serve four years."

"That's right," interrupted Griswold. "For once I agree with my law partner," he said with a grin. "Let's face it. If the electoral college doesn't vote anyone in for president, the House will only have about four weeks to choose a president. It won't happen that fast. Too much politics. At least on the twentieth the country would have a president. Call him acting, temporary, interim . . . whatever. The Speaker is our man."

"Goddamn it!" the president bellowed. "I don't want to keep hearing that." Sutherland quickly checked his outburst, raising both hands apologetically. "Sorry for my sudden burst of . . . eh . . . energy," he said, now completely in control. "But let's shape this discussion toward a resolution away from the Speaker. You know how I feel about the power-hungry bastard. The country won't survive if he's in."

"There may be no choice, Mr. President," Christenson replied softly. "Besides, if the Speaker campaigns during the next month for the electoral college vote, he could probably take a major chunk of votes away from both you and Starr, almost assuring a deadlock. Then, as acting president, he could go for broke when he has the votes or stall the Congress; either way . . . he'd be here," the attorney said, pausing for effect. Then looking at the president he added, "And sitting in your chair."

The president frowned, but his eyes reluctantly accepted the attorney's logic. "Paul, any way we can force the electors to vote for Starr?" the president asked.

"Of course not," the attorney general responded and added quickly, "even without the kidnapping, they wouldn't have to vote for Starr. Remember, the country really only elected members of the electoral college, not the president. They are free to vote for anyone."

Sutherland tapped his fingers softly on the desk, staring at the stack of legal memorandums in front of him. No one said anything; they waited for their leader to speak.

· "Listen," the president began slowly, "let's focus on the first issue. We must do all we can *politically* to convince the electoral college to qualify Starr and Edwards. That's my job. It won't involve you guys. This presumes Starr won't be back by the time they vote. I'll talk to the majority leader and others to get this ball rolling."

The president paused, and glanced at the document on top of his desk. He looked at the lawyers seated quietly before him.

"I want all of you to put together a plan of attack on what I can do, and should do, *legally*, if Starr is *not* qualified by the college. I also want to know what the law is if he *is* qualified but doesn't show up on January 20 to take the oath of office. I have to deal with one issue at a time, but be prepared for anything. Especially keeping one step ahead of that bastard Durkin."

CHAPTER 10

THE SPEAKER OF THE HOUSE

Friday, November 12

IT WAS AFTER MIDNIGHT, BUT THE AMBITIOUS, POWERFUL Speaker of the House of Representatives sat in the law library of his attorney, reviewing statutes, Supreme Court decisions, and legislative history.

"Well, Paul," he asked the attorney, his gravel-like voice ricocheting around the room, "after one week of legal research, am I closer to becoming president?"

Paul Douglas, senior partner from the law firm of McKeen and Douglas, eyed the Speaker with admiration, straightening his glasses as he sat down next to his client.

"Mr. Speaker, if certain contingencies can be worked out, and with some luck, I believe you will be the next president of this country," the attorney responded without hesitation.

Charles T. Durkin, a seventeen-term congressman from Springfield, Illinois, mulled over the words. Smiling, he gently touched the lawyer on the arm. "Paul, I've been waiting a week to hear that. Give me the specifics. I want to plan the attack tonight."

Douglas crossed his legs and delicately hitched up the crease of his trousers. Taking a deep breath, he began his legal analysis.

"The Twentieth Amendment states if the president-elect isn't dead and qualifies, he'll serve as president. If Starr is rescued before December 13, when the electoral college votes, they will no doubt qualify him . . . as if he never had been kidnapped. But here's the tricky part." Douglas leaned over the desk, his long arm reaching the red volume of the *United States Code Annotated*. He quickly found the relevant page.

"Now, listen carefully to these two sections. They are under Title 3, Section 19, which I explained briefly to you yesterday."

"Refresh my memory."

"Okay," the attorney replied, nodding his head. "To paraphrase, if by reason of death, resignation, inability, or failure to qualify, there is neither a president nor vice president . . . the Speaker acts as president."

"All right . . . I remember that."

"Good. Now Section (c)(1) reiterates that if the *president-elect and the vice president elect* fail to qualify, the Speaker *acts* as president . . ."

"Until someone qualifies," the Speaker finished the sentence for him. "I knew that."

The attorney ignored the sarcasm in Durkin's voice and continued. "Section (c)(2) says that, if the Speaker's powers are founded in whole or in part on the *inability* of the *president* or *vice president*, he acts until the removal of the *disability* of one of these individuals." The attorney carefully enunciated each key word as he intently eyed the Speaker.

The man who meant so much to Illinois politics rose from his chair, his tie undone. The untidy roll of fat he never managed to control, despite all of his sporadic efforts at dieting, spilled over the top of his belt and trousers.

"Paul . . . what does this mean . . . in English?" the Speaker snapped, his tone evidencing a lack of patience.

"The first section refers to *president-elect*. The second refers to *president*. If one made the argument that the latter would also apply to *president-elect*, which is only natural to presume, one could then make the argument that Starr must have *no disabilities*, if he is to serve as president."

"And if he has this disability . . . he can't serve until the disability is gone," the Speaker bellowed, his fiery eyes wide open and focused on his lawyer.

"Starr could be brainwashed or tortured . . . all kinds of mental or physical problems could arise. Permanent, irreversible disability. This gives me much more ammunition than just *failure to qualify*." The Speaker sighed in relief. "If I can get to be acting president, it gives me more time to collect my IOUs . . . and get this matter out of the hands of the electoral college . . . and into my own backyard."

The attorney concurred excitedly. "Right. Congress would qualify *you* . . . if neither Starr nor Edwards gets the nod."

The attorney handed the Speaker a copy of the Twelfth Amendment. "For you to become a full-time president, two situations can occur. First, you *must* be in the top three electoral votes to qualify for president. You . . ."

"Shit, Paul," the speaker interjected, "that's perfect. I was going to run my own campaign anyway, to prevent Starr from being qualified. If Starr isn't returned by the thirteenth, I'll give the electoral college plenty of reasons not to qualify him. The election was close enough that I'll pick up the necessary votes to prevent either Starr or Sutherland from getting 270. I'll run them a good third. I'll pick states where I'm strong and have congressmen who will help me. What's the second scenario?"

"If Congress can't decide on any of you, and stays hopelessly deadlocked, not qualifying a president or vice president . . . you *could* act as president for years."

"I'll do better than that. The House will *qualify* me within weeks of January 6. I won't be *acting* president long."

"Now, Mr. Speaker," the lawyer said, hesitating thoughtfully, "we do have some problems."

"Let's hear them."

"First, if Edwards gets qualified for vice president, that causes you problems under Section 19. This law was passed in 1948 in response to the Twentieth Amendment. It strongly implies that, if Edwards gets qualified, he will be acting president, or full president. Section (c)(1) indicates that if you take power due to a failure of both Starr and Edwards to qualify, you act as president only until either one of them qualifies."

"So if Edwards qualifies as vice president . . . and no one is yet qualified as president, he could sneak in the back door."

"Right."

"But," the Speaker countered, "I plan on getting qualified right away. Can Edwards be qualified for president directly?"

Douglas shrugged his shoulders. "I'm not sure. The electoral college could qualify Edwards as president if they want the Democrats in the White House and they feel Starr won't be back. If this happens, the game's over for us. Or," he continued, "Edwards could be among the top three vote-getters from the college for president, if they substitute him for Starr, and be eligible under the Twelfth Amendment to be qualified by the House. If this scenario occurs, you'll win, if you are also in the top three."

"If Starr is returned before the thirteenth, any suggestions on how I persuade the electoral college not to qualify him?"

"That's going to be very difficult. We must center on his disability . . . maybe physical, certainly mental. Convince the electoral college he's unfit. If we have time—a week, let's say—we might be able to influence the appropriate doctor."

The Speaker raised his brown eyebrows at this suggestion. "And how do we accomplish this, counselor?"

"Eric Von Hoff has been Starr's personal physician for years. We just have to dig up dirt on him."

"Well. Go on."

"I'm not that quick," the lawyer chuckled, "but I have someone discreet working on it."

"I'm not too sure that will work," the Speaker said, his voice displaying the uncertainty he felt. "How else do I convince the electors?"

"First," explained the attorney, "assuming Starr *isn't* rescued, you could personally visit electors before they meet or vote. Use your charm. Convince them that Starr won't come back and that Edwards is just a political hack."

Durkin nodded his head. "That could lead to electors voting for their own personal choice, and if no one gets 270 votes, I'm going to be *acting* president. As long as we keep Edwards from being qualified as well."

"Until you," Douglas added, "from your own backyard, collect those political IOUs to qualify you as *the president*."

Paul Douglas reached for his briefcase, pulling out several typed pages that were stapled together. He handed them to the Speaker.

"What's in this?"

"I have taken the liberty," he began, "to put down on paper, in legal form, the script that will probably be followed. It presumes Starr won't be returned safely. You can show this to the president at the appropriate time."

The congressman started to thumb through the pages, stopped, and gave a growling, scornful laugh. "You are one clever cookie. But what's in all of this for you? After all, some of your suggestions may be illegal, or at least unethical."

The attorney smiled. "Fair question," he responded. "I'm from a small Iowa town, went to Drake Law School, and married the farmer's daughter. The big time has only recently come my way. I want to grab the whole thing. I see this as my opportunity to be the next attorney general."

"My, my," Durkin responded, smiling as he looked at his lawyer, "I do admire ambition."

CHAPTER 11

RECOLLECTIONS OF A HOSTAGE

Saturday, November 13

NOVEMBER IN WASHINGTON, AND ANOTHER RAINY DAY. FOR the past two weeks the weather had fit the mood of the country: dreary and lackluster. Yesterday it was a light snow, today rain; tomorrow was to bring more rain. But would tomorrow bring Jonathan Starr home?

A dejected Andrew Reynolds made his way to M Street, walking the streets without noticing the other pedestrians quickly moving from building to building, avoiding the rain as best they could with an assortment of umbrellas and rain jackets.

He avoided several puddles as he ran through the intersection of 18th and M Street, oblivious to his surroundings. He entered the old Baker Building, pushing the revolving door by instinct, his thoughts still fixed on that special San Francisco hotel room. He slowly made his way to the elevator, wiped the rain from his face and collar, pushed the button, and waited, drumming the fingers of his right hand unconsciously against his thigh.

He noticed the small sign to the left of the elevator. "Out of order." Some observant agent, he thought to himself, as he dragged his body up three flights of stairs to the office of Orear and Fridkin, political campaign consultants.

"Paulie, it's been a long time. It's good to see you," Reynolds began.

"Sit down, Andy, we've got a lot to talk about," responded Orear, as he motioned to an empty chair. He stared at the agent before speaking again. Reynolds's eyes were dull and red-lined with fatigue.

"Almost two weeks have gone by, and we don't have one goddamn clue as to what happened to Jonathan. I hear the president has been meeting every day with people, with FBI agents, with Secret Service agents, and yet he knows nothing. Do you have anything to report, Andy?"

Reynolds sat with a dejected look on his face as he glanced around the office.

Orear's room was total chaos. Little pink phone messages were spread all over his already cluttered desk. His walls were full of pictures from politicians, all of whom had written their own personal notes.

Files and papers were piled on top of three old chairs in the room. Reynolds was lucky to be sitting in an empty fourth one. It was obvious Orear's large fees didn't go toward overhead. His only published book on politics, *How to Win Elections and Still Influence People*, was prominently displayed in triplicate on the corner of his bookshelf.

Reynolds thought to himself, How do I tell this man I know nothing—that the whole fucking election was for nothing. After waiting a few moments, Reynolds responded.

"I'm going to tell you something top secret." Reynolds began, gently rubbing his right elbow with his left hand, looking at Orear. "The day following the election we failed in a rescue attempt outside of L.A." Orear began to interrupt, but Reynolds stopped him.

"I'm not at liberty to tell you how we knew Jonathan was there. But he was. Perhaps as little as two hours before we got there."

"No one knows?" wondered Orear.

Reynolds shook his head. "It must stay that way. The president doesn't want any more of our failures to be known."

Orear leaned back in his chair and stared at the ceiling. He knew the conversation was difficult for the agent. Orear leaned forward and in a hushed voice spoke to Reynolds.

"You must have some leads by now."

"The president has appointed me to spearhead the investigation. I'll be going back to Frisco tomorrow. We've checked the hotel and all witnesses. The only lead appears to be three laundry room employees. They evidently kidnapped Jonathan and got him out of the hotel.''

"How?"

"In a laundry cart. They even engaged in casual conversation with two of my agents that very morning.''

"Shit,'' Orear blurted out, unable to control his frustration. Reynolds understood, all too well.

"Their signatures don't match any computer records. Their references and prior addresses don't check out. There are no fingerprints or records for any of these men. It's as though they don't exist.''

Reynolds looked at Orear. He knew the campaign manager could sense his guilt feelings. It was as though Reynolds was shouldering the entire responsibility for the kidnapping. The agent couldn't function, couldn't think. He wasn't even capable of reading "out of order'' signs. Reynolds knew he had to snap out of his depression . . . and soon. For his sake, and for Jonathan Starr's.

"Paulie, there's one thing I will do, one thing I'm going to dedicate every second of my life to, and that's to get Jonathan back alive. By God, I'll do it. I'll get him back.

"I'm going to San Francisco tomorrow morning to follow up leads. I've got my own hunch but I haven't told the president about it. Someone had to have the contacts to get into the Fairmont Hotel. Someone had to know that Starr was going to be there. How they found that out I don't know. We didn't even know until three weeks before the election that we were going to stay at the Fairmont. He didn't talk to anybody. The president didn't even know where Starr was that night. It doesn't make sense. And someone had to have a motive. "I don't know, I just don't know.''

Reynolds stood up, and the two men shook hands. They had been through a presidential campaign together, and respected each other immensely. As the Secret Service agent walked dejectedly out of the door, Orear could hear him mumbling, "I don't know . . . I just don't know.''

There was another man in the United States who didn't know how this abduction had been planned. He didn't know who was behind it or why he had been kidnapped, but Jonathan Starr was afraid . . . afraid of losing his life.

The time passed slowly. He was a man elected to the highest office in the country and the most powerful position in the world, but was confined to a room, the basement of an abandoned warehouse. As he sat on his bed, thinking, trying to sort out the facts in a logical manner, as he had done for ten days, he tried to piece together what had happened on that election night.

The security plan appeared to be foolproof. The Fairmont was a perfect secondary location because everyone was told he would be at campaign headquarters. There was no reason for anyone to suspect otherwise. But someone did.

Starr got up and started slowly walking around the room in his familiar walk—the walk he had been taking day after day. The room was rectangular with a hard, gray cement floor. The walls were white with no windows. The ceiling was unfinished, and looking up he could see wooden support beams under the first floor. He had not been confronted by his abductors nor had he received any information from the outside world—only two meals a day. Two meals to keep his sanity. He was already to the point where he was playing games with his food. Chewing each piece of food twenty-five times, seeing how many pieces he could break a sandwich into—kid games—anything to break the monotony. Fortunately, he still had his watch, so he knew every morning at 10:00 the door would open and a tray would be left there. Every morning it was one egg and a piece of toast with a glass of water. Initially, Starr didn't feel like eating, but after the first few days he realized he needed his strength. At 4:30 P.M. every day the door would be opened and the tray removed, replaced by a second tray. For almost two weeks Jonathan Starr had been eating hamburgers and hot dogs with a healthy spread of mayonnaise on the buns—always mayonnaise.

Occasionally, during his captivity, Starr would think of freedom and what it means to be free. He thought of the Supreme Court debates and cases on First Amendment rights—freedom of speech—and wondered how something like this could happen. Today, like yesterday and tomorrow, Jonathan Starr would think about the freedom that he so often took for granted. He promised himself, when he got out, if he got out, freedom would no longer be an abstraction to him.

To live in a rectangular basement, not much larger than 25′ × 20′, and sleep in a corner, in an old bed, for days upon days, and weeks upon weeks, painfully reminded Starr how sweet and precious freedom really is. What did these people want? Did they want to break his spirit? Did they want to brainwash him? Or worse yet, did they want to torture or kill him?

At night he shivered convulsively and brought his knees up close to his chest, curling into a tight ball. His captors had provided no blankets.

He thought of his wife and three daughters. How were they holding up? Would he make it? Would they? Tears came to his eyes as he thought of them. During the long arduous days of captivity, Jonathan's thoughts also went back to his start in politics—the appointment to chairman of the Governor's Drug Commission. The group, which eventually became known as the "Starr Commission," heard testimony for nine months from various political leaders, social workers, medical doctors, and educators, to determine what effect illegal, and in some cases legal, drugs were having on the youth of California. When the commission reported its findings, Starr was praised both by liberals and conservatives for proposing legislation that all Californians could live with.

Under normal circumstances, spearheading a citizens' group on drugs in California wouldn't bring a chairman statewide publicity. This commission, however, took a giant leap that similar commissions in other states were afraid to take. The commission suggested that the dealers and pushers of serious drugs, as defined by state law, be subject to the same penalties as those committing first-degree murder. The death penalty.

Starr and his commission demonstrated common sense throughout their deliberations. They realized marijuana had become a recreational drug tried by some fifty million Americans, with over sixteen million using the weed regularly. Their studies showed ten percent of high school seniors claimed to be daily users.

Once the commission submitted their findings and specific proposals for new legislation, the California legislature acted with uncharacteristic dispatch. The commission's proposed bill was passed verbatim. Jonathan Starr had achieved statewide recognition.

Ten months later the Democrats were talking about running a strong senatorial candidate against powerful Republican incumbent, Gary Bielenberg.

Bielenberg, a two-term senator, was considered unbeatable because he was a moderate—appealing to many of the Independents and the more conservative branch of the Democratic party in California. The Democrats were divided on who to run against Bielenberg, finally agreeing upon a compromise candidate in Robert Willard, secretary of state from Los Angeles. Unfortunately, Willard was in an automobile accident that paralyzed him from the waist down, leaving him unable to undertake the grueling, physical aspects of the campaign. The accident left the Democratic party with a serious problem. Who could they find to run on short notice against such a powerful senator?

Later that year the California Democratic party approached Jonathan Starr to see if he would run for the Senate. After several discussions with his family, Starr entered his first political campaign. Months later he easily defeated his two opponents in the Democratic primary.

With the assistance of Paulson Orear, his newfound political friend, and effective campaign fund-raising, Starr pulled an upset in California politics. He defeated a powerful incumbent.

His meteor-like rise had occurred within one year . . . from Drug Commission to United States Senate.

CHAPTER 12

"SENATE SELECT COMMITTEE TO INVESTIGATE ORGANIZED CRIME"

TOMMY DUNCAN LEANED BACK IN HIS SWIVEL CHAIR AND looked out the window. The sun shone brightly on the modern sculpture proudly displayed in front of the International Union's headquarters. The labor leader's eyebrows furrowed as he glanced toward his desk. Jonathan Starr's Senate Select Committee had just served him with several specific subpoenas. Duncan's attorneys had already reviewed them—there were no legal loopholes—and he would have to turn over his records.

Tommy Duncan, however, was no man to fool with. Even at age sixty-six, his broad shoulders and powerful arms gave him an imposing physique. He was graying at the temples, and signs of baldness were setting in, slowly winning the war against his remaining hair.

In the forties, after a brief career in banking, Duncan served as a bookkeeper for the New York Textile Union. During that time he gained the confidence of several New York Mafia families. By the early 1950s he was in the employ of both the Gambino and Genovese families.

With the Mafia's help, Duncan took over the local New York Textile Union, which eventually led to his position as secretary-treasurer for George Meany and the AFL-CIO. As secretary-treasurer, Duncan was an important member of the union, giving financial advice and keeping its books.

Years later, in an effort to consolidate and unite the labor movement, Duncan took the bold step of forming the International Union. With the AFL-CIO as his base, Duncan convinced the Operating Engineers, United Textile Workers, the Meatcutters, the Carpenters, Hotel and Restaurant Workers, the Sheet Metal Workers, and various other existing unions to join the powerful IU.

His newly formed union was the most powerful labor organization in America. By controlling IU pension funds, and the authority to make investments, Duncan's political clout in Washington exceeded that of most elected officials.

Republican Arthur Sutherland's election brought unforeseeable problems to Duncan and the IU. Shortly after his swearing-in, President Sutherland was pressured by big business and powerful politicians to investigate allegations of corruption against the IU.

A committee was formed with only one lawyer member, Senator Jonathan Starr. The Senate committee's function had been made clear by President Sutherland. First, was organized crime influencing and infiltrating the International Union? Second, if organized crime was involved in the International Union, was there a need for special legislation to correct the situation, and prevent its recurrence?

The committee realized that it needed the assistance of the FBI to obtain and research the numerous documents that had been accumulating as a result of the investigation. The FBI diligently obtained documents concerning Duncan's business transactions and interviewed numerous witnesses.

Starr worked closely with many accountants during the investigation. Several documents indicated that, in addition to embezzlement and transferring union funds, Duncan had ordered the murders of those in the labor movement who were opposed to the merger. Miscellaneous payments to alleged hit men were uncovered in ledgers, many dated only days before the deaths of various union officials. Through painstaking investigation, the FBI was able to reconstruct ingeniously planned fake financial transactions. They uncovered extortion and collusive agreements between the union and various organizations that were in violation of federal law. Starr and his staff spent tedious hours talking to people who were associates of those killed, and to many who were losing their pensions because of Duncan's financial practices.

Soon it became apparent that the committee had enough information to indict and undoubtedly convict Tommy Duncan. Starr was concerned that Duncan would take the Fifth Amendment, and with his silence, all the committee's work might be futile. He convinced the committee's chairman to approve using the press to box Duncan into a corner and force him to testify.

When Starr held his press conference shortly before the hearings, every major newspaper in the country had their headline. He challenged Tommy Duncan not to take the Fifth Amendment. The very next day Duncan responded just as Starr had hoped. He was quoted in *The New York Times* and the *Los Angeles Times* as stating he would not take the Fifth Amendment, because he had nothing to hide. Further, Duncan added that his decision was against the advice of his lawyers. Duncan quoted J. P. Morgan to one of his lawyers, bellowing, "I don't want a lawyer to tell me what I cannot do; I hire him to tell me how to do what I want to do."

Jonathan Starr's strategy had worked. He had publicly dared Duncan to come forward and answer the challenge. The stage was set. The scene was the United States Senate. The plot was murder, embezzlement, and organized crime. The actors were the Senate Select Committee and, as leading man, Jonathan Starr. Tommy Duncan's role had been cast years before—the villain. The play would have the largest audience possible . . . the American public.

CHAPTER 13

THE HEARINGS

JONATHAN AND JUDY STARR BEGAN THE SECOND MILE OF THEIR twice weekly jogging session. The senator was sweating profusely, neatly dressed in the navy blue running outfit that Judy had given him last month. The holiday snow had almost melted, but the two runners couldn't avoid some of the slush swept onto the neighborhood sidewalks from shoveled driveways.

Curious neighbors watched the senator and his wife, wondering what they could be thinking about on the eve of Tommy Duncan's televised Senate testimony. The unusually warm Washington winter temperature tired Starr as he ran at a grueling pace.

Judy knew the mood. Jonathan's thoughts were on tomorrow. His jogging tonight was just a physical ritual. No conversations about the kids, the neighbors, or Judy's League of Women Voters meeting.

No conversations at all.

During the past several weeks Starr had been preparing for the hearings as if it were the biggest trial of his life. Every witness was thoroughly prepared, every document carefully checked.

The first week of the hearings had gone as expected—groundwork and preliminary matters leading to the labor leader's own testimony. The media was building the Starr-Duncan confrontation as the biggest news story since Watergate.

This same night across town, Tommy Duncan was discussing his defense with his lawyers. The head of Duncan's legal team, Alan Ryan, was again trying to persuade his client on the merits of pleading the Fifth Amendment before responding to Starr's questions the next morning. Duncan stared at Ryan, pointing a warning finger toward the frustrated attorney. His voice was loud, crystal clear, and had the ring of supreme authority.

"Al, we have rehearsed for months what Starr can ask me. He isn't the brightest guy in the world. He has been investigating me for months trying to find out what we already know. There is no way he has found out about everything. I know all of the questions. I'm prepared to answer them. All my life I have been under investigation and all my life I have been able to fight it. And this is no different. This Jew boy isn't going to get the best of me in front of the American people. He may think he can use this as a stepping stone to the presidency, but he's fucking crazy. There is nothing to worry about."

Confidently, Tommy Duncan leaned back into the armchair and gazed at Ryan, who nodded quietly.

The Senate hearing room overflowed. Top network commentators were present, and reporters from the leading newspapers in the country were in attendance. The tension mounted as technicians hurriedly set up cameras and adjusted lights. The room was already very hot by 9:00 A.M. when Tommy Duncan walked in with Alan Ryan and numerous members of his law firm. Mobs of reporters and photographers jostled for position, as Duncan, smiling confidently and waving, moved forward to take his chair. The senators had not yet entered the room. Duncan was joking with members of the press. There he was—Tommy Duncan— the king of labor. He looked like a businessman . . . neat, trim, grandfatherly, a real family man. Duncan felt great. He was looking forward to making a fool out of the headline-grabbing Starr. He felt comfortable. He smoothed out his three-piece suit, straightened his flashy red tie, and waited.

The gallery was packed with union members, news media personnel, and the few members of the public who were able to squeeze in.

At 9:05 A.M. the senators slowly entered the Senate hearing room. Jonathan Starr took a sip of water, swishing it around his mouth. The wetness didn't help.

The hearing would be television theater at its best. Chairman Hoffman, the conservative senior senator from Minnesota, had to climb over cables and through a maze of electronic equipment to find his chair. The hearing room was dominated by the lighting towers and camera platforms.

Duncan pulled his chair toward the small rectangular table before him. He looked up at the raised platform. He observed long tables with the requisite number of chairs, microphones carefully in their place in front of each one, and the flag of the United States proudly displayed center stage against the back wall. Several desks with stenotype machines were crowded below the platform on the main level to record the hearings.

Though he was frightened, Starr looked calm, as if he was ready to leave for a relaxing night on the town. He began to organize his papers as Senator Hoffman gave Duncan an opportunity to make a brief opening statement.

Duncan leaned toward his attorney, whispering, as his eyes gazed upon the full gallery behind him. He winked at Kate Wilson, who was seated in the press section off to the left of Duncan. She politely smiled at the gregarious labor leader. Duncan placed both hands on the table before him and began reading from a prepared text.

"This committee, under Chairman Hoffman, has attempted to be fair to our great union. We have cooperated because we have nothing to hide. There are those . . ."

Duncan paused and lowered his hands, placing the text on the table. He then glared toward Starr.

"There are those who are on a witch-hunt, confusing union issues with slanderous innuendos of murder and organized crime. I *will not* tolerate these grievous claims against the greatest union in the history of this country." Duncan slammed his fist on the table as he shouted the last sentence, his face turning red.

During the next two hours Starr methodically went into Duncan's relationships with various union officials. Duncan's early-morning freshness and confidence were starting to wilt. It was apparent Duncan did not want to take the Fifth Amendment. What he was doing, based upon the advice of his attorneys, was claiming a bad memory. Starr relentlessly pursued every area he could, at times playing recorded phone conversations, when Duncan denied ever having known the person he was talking to.

STARR: Mr. Duncan, do you deny spending two hundred thousand dollars of International Union money to build a summer house?

DUNCAN: Well, Senator, to the best of my recollection, and I must rely on my memory, I just can't remember.

Duncan had to fight the urge to grin. Starr couldn't touch him.

STARR: To the best of your recollection, you have to rely on your memory, but you can't remember—is that your answer, Mr. Duncan, or are you telling me a joke?

DUNCAN: Sorry, Mr. Starr, I guess I just don't have as good a memory as you.

Duncan was not easily upset.

STARR: The issue, Mr. Duncan, is not what kind of memory you have. The issue here is what is or what isn't the truth. And that is what I would like to talk about, the truth.

For Starr, it was like cross-examining a witness at trial. He wouldn't always get the answers he wanted immediately, but he would relentlessly pursue the line of questions until he was satisfied with the response. It was also apparent that attorney Alan Ryan was concerned. His client was too evasive, trying to be cute for the cameras. Duncan was starting to lose credibility. Ryan thought to himself that it had been a big mistake for his client not to take the Fifth Amendment.

That night the top floor of the International Union was a hub of activity. Duncan and his attorney ate sandwiches as they reviewed the day's transcript.

"We were hurt," Ryan admitted, keeping his head down as he reviewed Starr's questions.

"Bullshit, Al. Ya goddamn high-price lawyers panic whenever the opponent scores a point. Roll with the punches. Starr shot his wad today . . . that's all there is." Duncan's confidence was joined with zeal. It was in his voice.

"Look, Al," Duncan said, his voice descending to a hollow sound, "Starr can't win. The press leaks about people coming forward is bullshit. People know that if they come forward, there will be . . . reprisals."

"I suggest you take the Fifth Amendment, if they will let you. It will be embarrassing, but you'll stay out of jail," the short, black-haired attorney said quietly, feeling no need to amplify.

Duncan smiled and shook his head, walking to the corner of

his spacious office to turn on the television set. He looked at his watch and then glanced toward his attorney. Another gutless wonder, he thought to himself, as he poured a drink and sat before the set, watching himself on the ''NBC Nightly News.''

''Jonathan Starr has insulted the noble traditions of this Congress and this country, and he will continue to abuse his authority because Senator Hoffman lets him ramble on and on. He is a rich, spoiled senator, trying to become president. I just want to say to you and to the public that America does not belong to the rich and exclusive club of Jonathan Starr and his friends. It belongs to all of us. The common man.''

Duncan grinned and pulled himself out of the chair, walking toward his attorney.

''Al, I'm not going to roll over and play dead. The union is too important. Why don't we meet at 7:00 A.M.''

The two men silently shook hands. As the attorney shut the impressive mahogany double doors, Duncan sat behind his desk. He didn't have to playact anymore . . . he was worried.

There was a light sprinkle of snow over the nation's capitol, much of it melting by mid-morning. Many of Washington's visitors had a chance to observe the capital city's beauty in between Senate sessions. However, those following the Senate hearings paid little attention to the weather or the winter appearance of the cherry blossoms. Round two was about to begin.

At the start of the session Tommy Duncan fixed his stare on Senator Starr. It was a penetrating expression of intense hatred. He looked like a man obsessed with winning. He would not take his eyes off Starr, like a heavyweight boxer eyeing his opponent between rounds. It was as if he wished his eyes could shoot a laser beam through the head of Jonathan Starr.

Starr knew Duncan was trying to intimidate him, and to some extent, it was working. The testimony Starr heard on Tuesday convinced him he was right in his pursuit of Duncan. Duncan had stifled democratic procedures within the union, ordering murders of union rebels and any dissenters who dared to speak out against him. He had misused over nineteen million dollars of union funds, had taken money and other favors from employers to promote his own personal welfare and ambition, and was using Eastern gangsters and organized crime to consolidate his control over all of the unions, through the International Union. He was not running a labor movement or organization, he was running an institution within the country that answered to no one, and abided by no laws.

Starr peered at Duncan. The labor leader appeared confident. Perhaps too confident for what was in store for him. Starr took a deep breath. It was time to attack.

STARR: Mr. Duncan, isn't it true that in your past you have been associated with the Gambino family in New York?

DUNCAN: Never heard of them.

STARR: I see that you are starting with your good memory again, Mr. Duncan.

DUNCAN: Well, Senator, I have just learned from you to tell the truth. Isn't that what you wanted me to do?

Duncan was still calm. He wasn't going to let Starr rattle him.

STARR: Isn't it true, Mr. Duncan, that you are also associated with the Genovese family of New York?

DUNCAN: No.

STARR: Isn't it true, Mr. Duncan, that you're just a front man for the New York Mafia families and that they are running the International Union?

DUNCAN: Complete fiction.

STARR: Mr. Duncan, Jerry Pedlar will be testifying before this committee, and he will swear under oath that he witnessed you ordering numerous murders of Chicago labor officials. Do you deny that?

DUNCAN: Yes.

STARR: We will also hear the testimony of Tony Shern. He will testify that you ordered the hit of Big Joe Marsh of Detroit, because Marsh was going to make public some of the pension dealings you manipulated through a New York insurance agent who was a member of the Bonnano family. Do you deny that, Mr. Duncan?

DUNCAN: Yes.

STARR: Mr. Duncan, I am going to read to you what the perjury law is for Senate hearings, and I want you to listen very carefully.

It was apparent Jonathan Starr had played his trump card. He had given specific names of witnesses who would be called later to testify that Tommy Duncan had ordered murders of various union members. Duncan was visibly concerned. He was taking longer to answer questions and using more time to consult with his lawyer. He had underestimated his adversary. Starr had been able to find individuals who were coming forward to link Duncan with organized crime. The union boss never thought this could happen. This was one of the reasons he decided not to take the Fifth Amendment.

The sweat on Duncan's brow started to flow freely. The blood from his head was rushing toward the top and he was feeling faint. He felt the walls of the Senate hearing room closing in on him and he finally realized why Jonathan Starr had been so cocky during this investigation. Tommy Duncan was in trouble. The senator spent the rest of the day confronting Duncan with allegations of embezzlement documented by Duncan's own records. The union dictator slowly and carefully looked over the records. He was stalling. He couldn't deny their authenticity. They were in his name, had been notarized and certified by the International Union's accountants.

"The committee will take a thirty-minute recess," Chairman Hoffman stated as he pounded the gavel in front of him.

Hoffman quickly made his way to Senator Starr and placed his right arm on Jonathan's shoulder. "You're scoring points!"

Starr shrugged. "We've got a long way to go," he said. "But progress is being made," he added with a smile. "I'm going to the john."

"Our john is out of order," Hoffman replied.

Starr turned toward him and grinned. "I'll go to the public restroom . . . and I won't even bring any reading material."

Starr entered the closest stall to the urinals and dropped his pants. He noticed his upper thighs were wet, perspiration almost covering his entire body. The hot lights from the television cameras and the confrontation with Duncan had been a grueling experience. He wished this part of the hearings was over, but he was very pleased with his performance.

He stared at the closed door in front of him, reading the latest in Capitol Hill graffiti; "Be a page—Fuck a congressman" brought a chuckle from Starr as he reached for the toilet paper. Out of the corner of his eye he saw a pair of men's black shoes start to enter the next stall. Evidently, the man changed his mind, because the shoes quietly disappeared.

As Starr turned around to flush the toilet, the room went pitch black. He sat in silence and listened. He could hear what sounded like dripping water coming from the corner to his right. He felt the sweat pouring from his forehead as he wiped his brow.

He quietly stood and pulled up his trousers. His hand reached forward carefully and slowly opened the door to his stall. The constant dripping rang in his ears . . . but there was another noise. . . . Someone was breathing.

Starr almost panicked, instantly feeling short of breath. He closed his eyes, thinking he would hear better. It only frightened him more. He knew it wasn't a power outage or practical joke . . . someone was there.

The senator started to feel his way toward the front door, constantly stretching his right hand and arm in front of him in case he would run into something . . . or someone. His left hand just slid along the marble wall, not wanting to lose contact with the only way out of the room.

The dripping sound was getting louder. He strained even more to hear the breathing.

Nothing.

He sighed out loud, hoping his imagination had played a trick on him. Even so, he remained motionless . . . just in case someone was there.

"Damn," he said, as he stumbled into a wastebasket. His cover was blown. If anyone was in the room, they now knew exactly where their prey was located.

He continued to grope the wall with both hands. The switch. He had made it. The lights went on and Starr stared right into the eyes of one of the biggest men he had ever seen. The man was hoodlum personified, right from central casting: dark black suit, black shoes, white shirt, and muscles everywhere.

The man said nothing, but knocked on the bathroom's entrance door behind him. Starr sensed something over his right shoulder and quickly turned toward the mirrors.

"Sorry we had to meet this way, Senator. You barely got a chance to flush the toilet."

Starr shook his head slowly. It all made sense.

"Tommy, if I have to look at you all day in there," he said, motioning his hand toward the hearing room, "why can't I shit in peace?"

Tommy Duncan moved closer to Starr and peered into his face. He didn't see the fear he had expected.

"No one takes my union from me," Duncan snarled, pointing a menacing finger at Starr. The senator stepped back.

"Why the goon?" Starr asked, pointing to the apelike man standing near the front door. "Can't you handle me one-on-one, Tommy?"

Duncan ignored the sarcastic comment, wiping sweat from his upper lip. "I'll run the union from behind bars, if necessary. . . . No Jew bastard will take it from me."

Starr was surprised at how calm he felt. He had never quite encountered such a situation, but his coolness boosted his confidence. He knew Duncan wouldn't resort to violence. Not on Capitol Hill . . . in a men's room.

"I'm not *taking* the union from you. The Mafia did that. I'm *giving* it back to the membership."

"Bullshit!" Duncan bellowed, "you're running for president."

"You won't run the union from prison, either," Starr continued, ignoring the last response, "because the membership won't let you. And neither will the mob."

"I'm more powerful than you think."

"You're six months from life imprisonment."

"You'll never pull it off," Duncan countered, again wiping the moisture from his upper lip.

"I'm doing it now, Tommy." Starr walked toward Duncan. The two stared at each other. The guard at the door started popping his knuckles, expecting to break up a fight any minute. Starr broke the deadlock.

"Listen to the testimony. Talk to your lawyer. It's over, Tommy. It's already over."

"Fuck off, Starr," Duncan said, as he passed by Jonathan and walked to the door. He stopped abruptly and charged toward Starr, stopping just inches from him. "If I lose the union or go to jail . . . you'll pay the price." The veins in his neck were grotesquely stretching his skin and his face had turned red.

Starr slowly shook his head, whispering back to the furious Duncan, "You have already lost."

Jonathan watched while Duncan charged out of the bathroom. The senator looked at his hands. He was shaking, almost uncontrollably. He looked at himself in a nearby mirror, splashing water on his troubled face. He glanced at his watch and tucked his shirt into his pants. He quickly combed his hair and exited the bathroom. He was going back to work . . . more determined than ever.

STARR: Mr. Duncan, are you aware that over thirty-five union officials earned in excess of $100,000 last year? And that four of them earned over $200,000, and that your union salary, Mr. Duncan, is $400,000? Are you aware of that?

DUNCAN: Yes.

STARR: Isn't it true, Mr. Duncan, that at least forty relatives of these top officials are on the payroll, and at least nine of them earn more than $100,000 per year?

DUNCAN: That is not true.

Duncan's hands were now under the table sweating, pressed together so tightly that there was hardly any blood left.

STARR: Mr. Duncan, we have sworn statements from court employees. Birth certificates and records from your union show some of your top officials do have these relatives on the payroll. With that information, are you still denying my question?

DUNCAN: Yes.

STARR: Are you aware, Mr. Duncan, that Dave Beck was
          convicted in the late fifties, but President Ford par-
          doned him in 1975? Are you familiar with that?

DUNCAN: I wasn't sure.

STARR: Are you aware that Jimmy Hoffa was pardoned by
          President Nixon for some of the crimes he commit-
          ted as a union official?

DUNCAN: Yes.

STARR: Let me tell you this, Mr. Duncan, if you are indicted
          and convicted, I certainly hope that no president *ever*
          pardons *you*!

At that point Attorney Ryan bolted forward. He was furious.
His face was flushed as he directed his fury at senators Starr and
Hoffman. "This is a witch-hunt. Senator Starr's statement is
totally improper and violates this committee's code of conduct."

"Sit down!" Starr shouted back at Ryan. "We've heard
enough evasions from your client to last a lifetime. If you don't
like my questions, counselor, you can take whatever action you
deem appropriate. But," Starr chided, "that does not include
grandstand speeches."

The New York Times and *Los Angeles Times* had big head-
lines. The *San Francisco Chronicle* stated "OUR FAVORITE
'STARR' HITS THE JUGULAR—DUNCAN FINALLY MEETS HIS
MATCH."

Eighteen months after Starr's encounter with Duncan, the
labor leader had been indicted, tried, convicted, and sentenced
to San Quentin for life. All of his appeals had been rejected.

It was clear that the Senate hearings had produced a new
American hero. Starr had been aggressive and dynamic during
the proceedings. One junior senator complained to Chairman
Hoffman that Starr got all the publicity. Hoffman laughed and
responded with his typical wit, "I treat Jonathan Starr the same
way I would any other future president of the United States."

After the committee had finished their hearings and while
Tommy Duncan was on trial, Jonathan Starr received a message
that he would cherish for the rest of his life. It was a handwritten
note from President Sutherland, praising the senator for the

work he had done on behalf of the American public, and for all the good that work would do for the labor leaders, the labor members, and their families. Sutherland praised Starr's leadership abilities and integrity. It would be ironic that, during the later heated presidential campaign, Sutherland would claim just the opposite.

CHAPTER 14

THE VIRTUES OF EXPERIENCE

DURING THE TWELVE MONTHS FOLLOWING THE SENATE HEARINGS, Starr found himself on the road constantly. His landslide Senate reelection, coming on the heels of his televised confrontation with the dethroned Duncan, skyrocketed the junior senator from California into national prominence. Starr's handsome face had graced the covers of *Newsweek*, *Time*, and *People*, all in the same month. Articles about the Starr family were as common as the daily sports scores.

As winter was about to die, the gregarious and always plotting Paulson Orear paid a visit to his friend's Senate office.

"Greetings, Paulie," Starr said, not getting up from his chair behind an impressive oak desk. Papers were neatly stacked in large piles on the credenza behind Starr, adjacent to the flags of California and the United States. Nearby bookshelves contained trinkets and photographs from the senator's family.

"I'll be with you in a second, just finishing some dictation." Starr motioned for Orear to sit down in the chair directly to the left of his desk, reserved for intimate conversations. Orear took off his sport coat, and hung it on the back of the door. He quietly pushed the door shut, and sauntered to the chair next to the senator, trying not to eavesdrop on Starr's letter to an irate constituent.

"This guy from San Diego thinks I can solve their housing problem," Starr said with a grin, sliding his chair toward Orear. "Well, Paulie, what brings you to my neck of the woods? My secretary said you needed some private time."

"The presidential election," Orear replied quickly, grabbing notes from his briefcase.

"That again?" Starr asked, as he moved even closer to his campaign manager, sliding several folders to the other side of the desk.

"Jonathan, we've taken surveys throughout the country and your name recognition is very good. We also find the fact that you're Jewish wouldn't stop people from voting for you. The country is in very bad shape under Sutherland, and if the Democrats don't get together to run someone who can beat him, and I don't think Senator Jennings can beat him, we're going to have another four years of Sutherland and, by God, the country can't take another four years."

Starr sat quietly for a moment, reflecting. He had been giving some thought to running for president.

"You know, Paulie, sometimes I want to run, sometimes I just want to open up the window and scream that I'm a candidate and then get to it. But deep down inside I think—I've been a U.S. senator for seven years. Does that give me the qualifications to lead this country?"

"But Jonathan, you've been a senator just a few years less than Sutherland was, and yet he easily got his party's nomination, and he beat a guy who had been in the White House as vice president. I think you are eminently qualified, and by the time you run, you will have been in the Senate for eight years." Orear began pacing the room. His squinting blue eyes stared at Starr.

"Let's look at your record. Grand jury reform, cameras in the federal court system, with acceptable guidelines. Your revision of the tax code was super, not to mention your watchdog bill to independently monitor defense spending. Besides, you're also one of the leading opponents of nuclear weapons. You've got whatever it takes, whatever it is, that certain magic that will allow you to lead people."

Starr shook his head and smiled, but he could see his campaign manager was getting worked up.

Orear wasn't about to give up. He could see the uncertainty in the senator's eyes. If only he could come up with the right words. The proper argument to convince Starr that the nation would accept him.

"I want you to give some thought to hiring a professional pollster. My firm has done a lot of work on this and I think the votes are there. I think you should get in the race and you should get in early, if you want to get the nomination. It looks like Jennings is running, Governor Gregory is running, and that female senator from Massachusetts . . ."

"Cindy Morris," Starr interrupted, "is only a first-term senator, who has authored very little legislation. And she hasn't been active on any Senate committees. Governor Gregory is not qualified. I hear that Senator Edwards is getting into the race and he may be qualified, but I don't think he has a chance to win. I personally think Senator Jennings would be good for the country and I could support him. He's qualified—fair—honest. The only problem is, I'm not so sure he could be elected. I think what I may do is meet with him to get his thoughts. If no one has enough delegates by the time of the convention, then maybe I would consider a draft. But I want to keep my options open . . . at least for now. I can't commit to getting into the race."

"A draft won't work, Jonathan," Orear responded, barely concealing his disappointment. "If you run, get in early or the primaries will kill you."

Starr didn't respond as he leaned back in his chair, folding his hands behind his head, staring at the ceiling.

"I knew you were going to discuss this," Starr began, eyeing Orear intently. "Judy and I were up all night talking about it. I even called my father this morning. Because I have some doubts about running, we all agreed I shouldn't run."

"What doubts?" Orear wondered.

"I think Jennings is more qualified. If I help him, my conscience is clear. We get Sutherland out. His regime is killing this country."

"Is that your only doubt?"

"What do you mean?"

"Is it because you're Jewish?"

Starr shook his head. "No. That's really not a factor."

Orear watched him closely. Jonathan appeared to be uncomfortable. "You think you can't win, don't you? That's your real doubt."

Orear got out of the chair and walked over to Starr.

"Jonathan, at the presidential level, everyone has doubts about winning. That's natural, the stakes are so high, your personal life becomes so public, but you can win."

Starr stood up and put his arm around the stocky man's shoulder. "I really do appreciate your viewpoints. You're very convincing. But until something, or unless something, drastic happens, I'm going to support Jennings."

"If that's your decision . . . I guess I can help him, too."

"Good," Starr replied with a smile, "I've already told him that."

Orear pushed Starr away. "You son of a bitch. You . . ." Then he stopped. Starr was just grinning, a wide smile covering his whole face. Orear shook his head in amazement and forced a smile.

"Maybe the vice presidency," Orear said, the excitement in his voice returning.

"Out!" Starr commanded, as he ushered Orear to the door. "I've got work to do, Paulie, I'm just a senator."

Orear walked out the door and turned back to Jonathan, "For now, anyway."

After the first few state caucuses, it was apparent that Jennings did not have enough support to win the nomination. Though he had a slim lead over Edwards, Governor Gregory was doing better than most people had anticipated. In early February Jennings called Starr, requesting the California senator meet him in Zebulon, North Carolina, prior to a debate between Gregory, Jennings, Morris, and Edwards.

Jonathan traveled alone to the scenic state of Bill Jennings. The good-looking California senator never felt better. He was comfortable in the Senate, respected by his peers, and his personal life couldn't be happier.

What did Bill Jennings want?

Jennings's senior aide ran to Starr as he got off the plane. It was pouring rain as the two dashed under an umbrella toward the waiting limousine.

"Nice weather you bring from California," kidded Jennings.

"I left sunshine and happiness for this shit," Starr replied sarcastically as he shook hands with his colleague. Starr sensed something was wrong. There were no press . . . no photographers. He looked at Jennings. The senator from North Carolina didn't look well. His soft brown eyes appeared tired and his receding hairline made him look every bit of his sixty-seven years.

"I'm running out of money and ambition for the White House."

Starr did not respond. He looked out the window, watching other passengers fight the rain. The downpour had formed several large puddles, forcing passengers to walk carefully over the runway area. Several children were having a great time splashing each other, as an irate father swore to himself he would get even in the privacy of their hotel room.

"Jonathan," Jennings whispered, barely controlling his voice, "I'm also running out of time."

Starr quickly turned back toward his colleague. Tears rolled down the fat pink cheeks of the North Carolina senator.

"Cancer," he said matter-of-factly. "I may have three more years, with cobalt. I found out five days ago. No one knows except Jimmy," motioning to his aide in the front seat, "and of course, my wife."

"Bill, I'm so sorry," Starr said, fighting his own emotions. The two sat quietly for some time . . . each thinking what to say next.

"I don't want Edwards, Gregory, or Morris to win. They can't beat the president." Moving closer to his younger colleague, Jennings whispered in a hushed voice so his aide couldn't hear him, "Sutherland's no good for the country. If he wins, there will be war in the Middle East. His peace plan stinks."

Starr started to interrupt, but Jennings grabbed his arm.

"Sshh . . . I know. Believe me, I know." Motioning toward the outdoors, Jennings got hold of himself, addressing Jonathan in a clear, strong voice.

"They need you. All those people. The country, Jonathan. The country needs you."

"Bill, I've been thinking about it. Orear's polls look good, but you're more qualified."

"Senator," Jennings replied emphatically, "you don't listen. I'm a dead man."

"Bill, give me a minute. Let me collect my thoughts. You have caught me by surprise."

Jonathan leaned back and shut his eyes. Orear could put together a campaign staff within a week. His family would support him. Now that Jonathan's candidate was out of the race, his self-doubts about not being the most qualified person were eliminated. *He* was the best candidate. The other contenders in his party could never overcome the incumbent.

But he could.

"I'll do it," Starr finally responded, taking Jennings's right hand in his own. "I'll do it for you, and people like you. God bless you."

Jennings smiled but said nothing. Tears were streaming down his face.

"Let me make a few phone calls before this becomes public," Starr said, looking back at Jennings. The two were still holding hands. Starr didn't know what to say. Jennings reached over and patted him softly on the cheek.

"Don't worry, Jonathan. We were all born to die."

Senator Jennings called a press conference the next day at the Raleigh-Durham Airport in North Carolina and announced to the nation what he termed the "Treaty of North Carolina."

"My fellow Americans, I have called this press conference to make an announcement. Though I have received more delegates in the caucus and primary voting to date than Senator Edwards, Governor Gregory, and Senator Morris, I have decided that it would not be in the best interest of the Democratic party or the United States for me to continue my candidacy for the presidency. Though I feel I am qualified to serve as this country's chief executive, I feel there is someone in our party who is more qualified.

"I believe there is someone who can mend wounds and appeal to both moderates and liberals in our party, and more important, appeal to the nation. And that is why this morning I am withdrawing my name from all future primaries, and I am asking all of those committed to me through past party elections to give their support to the candidate that I now support, Senator Jonathan Starr of California."

CHAPTER 15

THE LAWYERS RETURN

Sunday, November 14

THE PRESIDENT ARRIVED AT THE OVAL OFFICE AT 6:30 A.M. Sleep had been impossible. He was hoping for a prompt legal solution to the ever-gnawing constitutional crisis. The stock market was dropping. Even the Treasury secretary had called late last night, expressing his concern that foreign markets were devaluing the dollar.

The *Washington Post* lead story wasn't helping, either. Every day, America was reading about Jonathan Starr and his family, through the slick writing of Kate Wilson.

The president's secretary buzzed the intercom. The lawyers were present. Sutherland nodded glumly. He was slouched in his chair, legs extended with his feet resting on the rim of a metal wastebasket.

Whyte and Gilbertson had spent all night in the White House library. The men quietly entered the room, each shaking the president's hand. Sutherland felt like the bereaved receiving the condolences of friends. He noticed the attorneys were wearing the same suits as last night. Christenson had evidently borrowed someone's electric shaver and Whyte was wearing a different shirt. The president felt guilty. He had rested two hours and showered. Not much, but with fresh clothes, far ahead of his comrades.

Griswold sipped his morning coffee. At his age, all-nighters were dangerous to his health. Normally, the senior partner of one of Washington's most prestigious law firms would delegate legal research assignments to one of his associates, or in some cases, to a junior partner. But when the president of the United States called, one did his own research, even if it took all night. He faced the president.

"Mr. President, last night we researched some other laws that have some relevancy in this matter. Chapter 84, Section 1751, deals with presidential assassinations and kidnappings. Part of that law indicates that whoever kidnaps anyone designated under the section, which includes the president-elect, shall be punished for life or by death. The attorney general of the United States is authorized to offer a reward of up to $100,000 for information and services concerning any violation of this section. It would be our recommendation that the attorney general take that action immediately, so at least we can get the public helping federal authorities."

"I think that's an excellent idea. Paul, will you issue said order immediately?"

"Yes, Mr. President," Gilbertson responded, "I have my office working on the publication of this information right now. It would be my recommendation that we issue a presidential order to the army, navy, and air force to assist the FBI and the California state, federal, and local agencies in any way possible. I have taken the liberty, Mr. President, to have my office prepare something along those lines, if that's all right with you?"

The president nodded his assent. "Are there any other actions that can be taken in the interim, before we decide this? Thomas, can you come up with anything?"

The president felt good. Finally the group was able to arrive at a consensus on some issues that would lead to immediate action on the part of the government. The president poured coffee while Whyte responded to his inquiry.

"Mr. President, the electors of president and vice president of each state meet and give their votes on the first Monday after the second Wednesday of December, so you understand that we are really dealing with December 13. We have one month to make a decision on this issue. I think we need to give guidance to the electoral college on what they should do."

Sutherland interrupted Whyte, with a quizzical look. "What do you mean, Thomas? You mean we have to tell them what to do?"

"No, Mr. President. What I mean is this. If you tell them you think Jonathan Starr is dead, or that he is never going to be returned, then I think the electoral college probably will not qualify Starr, and then could qualify Martin Edwards as vice president elect who, under the Twentieth Amendment, could be sworn in on January 20 as vice president and immediately take over as acting president. On the other hand, if you want to say that we're going to get Jonathan Starr back, then I think it's reasonable to presume they will vote for Starr on December 13. Then we can hope that he is around on the twentieth to be sworn in and serve as president. If he's not, once being qualified, then the law is unclear whether it's the Speaker or Edwards. And if it's Edwards, is he acting president until Starr returns, or president for the full term . . . who, under the Twenty-Fifth Amendment, can choose his own vice president?

"I think we need to give some guidance on what to do. This may turn into the worst political bloodbath we have ever seen. Everyone starts playing the political game and the country has no president on the twentieth. I think, if that happens, we're going to have the Speaker of the House as acting president, who will put pressure on the House to qualify himself."

"Yes, Thomas, you are right. By the way," the president snapped, "did you guys listen to Dan Rather last night?"

Before anyone could respond, the president answered his own question.

"That SOB accused me of stalling," Sutherland said angrily, flashing an annoyed look toward his audience. "He claimed we should have an answer for the country by now. He even had the audacity to accuse me of playing politics, and trying to twist the law to the advantage of the GOP.''

"We know that's a bunch of crap," the attorney general said reassuringly. The president wasn't satisfied.

"But the country doesn't know. Starr, Edwards, a compromise candidate, the Speaker of the House, and even myself, for God's sake, were mentioned as possibilities for the electoral college vote or those the House could consider after January 6. The country wants guidance, needs encouragement, and I give them nothing.''

"We're doing the best we can," Whyte pointed out, but the president continued as if he didn't even hear his special counsel.

"Rather claims his sources point to the Arabs as the kidnappers. Goddamn irresponsible journalism. The Middle East is tense enough. We don't need to accuse the Arabs of kidnapping a Jew . . . let alone a newly elected president.''

"Do we have anything more on the kidnapping?" Griswold inquired.

"Nothing. Not a fuckin' thing. Reynolds and the FBI are baffled. We don't even know if it's domestic or foreign. We don't even have a damn ransom note.''

Then the president turned to face the group, his mood became solemn, almost mournful. "We don't even know if Starr is alive." The men were silent. What could they say.

"I've got two tough decisions to make," the president continued. "One, I have to make a legal recommendation to the electoral college, which they don't have to follow. I also must make a *political* decision as to what's best for the country.''

The president poured another cup of coffee. He tilted the cup back and forth while he pondered his next move.

His lawyers had spoken, shifting the burden to his shoulders. Whyte would remember later that, at this juncture, a vise slowly began closing on his good friend. Sutherland would recall the moment as one of instant loneliness.

The president rose and rubbed his palms together. He was ready for action. But as he looked about the room for a show of confidence, he could see doubt in the eyes of his trusted aides. They were thinking their president was untried in crisis.

They had discussed their options for three hours and were all learning to walk with the crisis. Sutherland sensed a spirit of camaraderie. He had often wondered how he would behave in a time of national emergency when he alone could set in motion a chain of events that could alter history.

He was close to a decision. Once that decision was made, each new choice dwindled in magnitude. Right or wrong, he was confident in his judgment. He now flowed with the events. He tasted the rich wine of power in a time of national crisis.

He stood up to his detractors. Countless voices lashed out at him. Radio stations blared. Pollsters conducted surveys, and the loyal opposition unfurled spangled platitudes. Reporters hammered typewriters and television talk shows spilled with advice.

High school civics classes discussed the law, taxi drivers rendered their free opinions to helpless passengers, and businessmen kept a wary eye on the stock market. This single event—with the potential to politically explode the nation into tiny fragments—had almost the opposite effect. The tragedy was a unifying force. So far.

CHAPTER 16

GOVERNMENT BY CONSENSUS

Monday, November 15

CHIEF JUSTICE OLIVER ROBERTS HAD SERVED ON THE EIGHTH Circuit Federal Court of Appeals for twenty years, prior to his Supreme Court appointment. The chief, never known for his legal scholarship, was considered a strict constructionist by constitutional law experts. His conservative law-and-order opinions and public criticism of lenient judges made him a favorite target of liberal activists.

The chief took off his robe, placing it gently on a nearby hanger. He glanced at his watch. In five minutes the president would be in his office. He straightened the piles of papers on his desk. As he reached for the phone, he was startled by the president's unannounced entry.

"Mr. President, please come in."

"Good to see you, Oliver," the president said, as he shook hands. "Thank you for seeing me. I know this meeting puts you in an awkward position, but I can't help it."

Without saying anything, the chief walked across the room and shut the door.

"I'll do what I can, Mr. President. Off the record."

"Okay, Oliver, off the record."

The chief was visibly relieved. The short, stocky, bald-headed justice slowly took a seat in a chair next to the president.

"Oliver, is there any way out of this dilemma?" the president asked.

"The Supreme Court can't give an advisory opinion. There is no 'case or controversy' before us. Eventually, whenever a decision is made, those who object may have standing to appeal your decision or course of conduct, as well as any decision by Congress to the Supreme Court. Then we'll have jurisdiction."

"This is most unusual," the president began. "As you know, there is no precedent. I wanted your thoughts about what we discussed over the phone."

The chief scooted about in his chair. He didn't like the hot seat. He was a judge, not a politician. He felt perspiration forming on his forehead.

"The Twentieth Amendment is vague. It may not cover this situation. Especially when read with the Twelfth Amendment and Title 3, Section 19. Plus, there are so many possibilities. Will Starr qualify or not? Edwards or not? Both of them, neither of them, one of them, and each scenario triggers different and inconsistent laws. However," the chief continued, looking the president straight in the eyes, "this is a political issue to be decided by Congress. If the electoral college doesn't give a candidate the majority votes on January 6, the law says the House picks the president. It all depends on—and starts with—the electoral college."

"Yes," the president interjected, "but what if no one is chosen by the twentieth of January . . . who will govern?"

"Either the Speaker or Martin Edwards, probably Edwards, assuming he qualifies as vice president elect. But there are too many elements involved to give a definite opinion."

"Thank you, Oliver. It looks like it's boiling down to those two. Another quick question. Give me a rundown on what would happen if this thing gets thrown into Congress."

The chief responded to the president, with his notes on his lap, fully expecting the question.

"The Twelfth Amendment outlines the procedure for electing the president if the election would go to the House of Representatives. And keep in mind, Mr. President, that the presidency has only been decided by the House twice: 1800 and 1824. The procedure outlined in the Twelfth Amendment is that members of the electoral college meet in mid-December in each state to cast secret ballots for president and vice president. Then the electoral vote is opened at a joint session of Congress on January 6. If no candidate would receive the majority of electoral votes, the presidential election would go to the House. The president must win a majority of the electoral college votes . . . 270. However, if no candidate whom the college voted for has a majority, then a maximum of the top three candidates become the eligible individuals from which the House would qualify a president."

"Only three?" asked the president.

"Right," the chief responded quickly. "However, this assumes that neither the Twentieth Amendment nor Section 19 has changed this very old amendment. Those two laws imply there is no limit of three, but until I find law to the contrary, I'll stick by this approach.

"So, if the electors start to split their votes, it's likely no one would get a majority. It's also very, very probable that the top two vote-getters would be you and Starr, with perhaps the Speaker being third. At least he's the next most powerful politician. And one to whom many favors are owed."

"Shit," the president muttered, "that's what I'm trying to avoid. Tell me," the president asked, pausing a moment to reflect, "how would the House procedurally act after this?"

"The votes are taken by states. All of the congressmen from each state have one vote. Each state delegation would caucus. The winning candidate needs twenty-six states. States reaching a tie vote in their caucuses would vote *present*."

"Christ!" the president exclaimed, "can you imagine how this could strangle our government? All Congress would do during this period would be to try to choose a president. Tell me, Oliver, how would the vice president be chosen?"

"There are two differences from what I just described. First, only the top two vote-getters would be eligible for vice president, once again, probably Edwards and Vice President Stevens. Second, the Senate, the newly elected Senate, would vote individually, not by states, to elect or qualify the new vice president. Fifty-one votes would be needed."

"Unbelievable," the president sighed, forcing a smile.

The chief justice tapped the president's knee softly. "Arthur, you're taking all the right steps . . . making the correct moves. It will work out."

The president felt reassured. The chief, though noncommittal, supported the president's preliminary conclusion. The nation didn't need Congress fighting over this issue. Especially in light of a secret cable, received by the president from the Middle East early this very morning. The delicate Middle East peace was hanging by a thread. The election and kidnapping of the Jewish candidate bothered the president. Was it a coincidence, or was there a Middle East connection to San Francisco? There was no proof . . . yet. Could this be the reason the Arabs were stalling J.W. McBee?

The president said his good-byes to the chief and walked quickly with the Secret Service to the waiting presidential limousine.

Though he had only a few minutes, the president grabbed his favorite pipe for a quick toke or two. It was probably a psychological crutch, he thought to himself. During times of decision he would catch himself toying with it, fondling it, and always packing and repacking the bowl; scraping the burned-out contents into a nearby ashtray with methodical precision. Today, he held the pipe so tightly between his teeth, the force caused the muscles of his jaw to stand out.

Part of his apprehension was the crisis. The other part was his disgust at the necessity of personally calling on the Speaker of the House. His irascible reputation was deserving, and certainly apparent during this presidential visit. The abrasive Durkin was dictatorial, petulant, and unpleasant. But his skill as a politician was irreproachable.

"Mr. President, so good to see ya." The Speaker proudly ushered the president to his private office. Before the president could exchange amenities, the Speaker pled his case.

"Under the Twentieth Amendment, if neither the president-elect nor vice president elect qualifies, then Congress has already decided, by enacting Section 19, that I am to serve. With Starr's future so uncertain, I think your administration should suggest to the electoral college who to vote for." The president raised his hand trying to slow down the speeding Durkin.

"Wait a minute," cautioned the president. "Edwards may qualify as vice president elect, or even president-elect."

"Not if you handle the electoral college," Durkin replied quickly, interrupting the president.

"That stinks."

"Don't be stubborn, Mr. President. Call it politics or statesmanship. The country didn't elect Edwards."

"Yes they did," corrected the president. "They elected Starr and Edwards, the ticket."

"We've got a Republican House. If no one qualifies for president, someone must be chosen by the House. Why not you?"

The president was startled. The Speaker noticed, thinking Sutherland might be vulnerable.

"You got more votes than anyone but Starr. You could serve. The electoral college would go with you, if they think Starr won't be back and if they don't care for Edwards. Or," Durkin hesitated a moment, "the Speaker could be interim president, giving Congress more time to choose someone."

"And who might that be?" the president asked sarcastically. Durkin got out of his chair and walked toward his desk. He held up a stack of papers.

"Mr. President, these are political IOUs. I'm calling them in. From both Democrats and Republicans. I have enough support to be chosen for president if the electoral college doesn't qualify one.''

The president's expression changed. Facial muscles twitched involuntarily. He closed his eyes briefly and bit his lips together. The Speaker decided to go for the kill.

''Look, Mr. President,'' he began, his tone respectful and condescending, ''the country has enough problems. The Middle East is tense. We don't need a constitutional bloodbath. If you join me now, support me for president, things will be best for the country. But if you don't,'' the Speaker's tone was threatening, as he stared squarely into Sutherland's eyes, ''I will campaign all over this country, to the electoral college, and you know the general election was close enough that I don't need to siphon too many votes from Starr to get this election to the House. If I do that . . . and I will,'' he said firmly, motioning to his large stack of political IOUs, ''the House, *my* House, will choose me as president.''

Durkin walked toward the president, stopping several feet away, his voice harsh and ruffled. ''Unless you get Starr back, whether you accept this or not, you are looking at the next president of the United States!''

''Durkin, you disgust me,'' the president said, as he started toward the door. ''We can't play politics now. For once, think of the country.''

''I am, Arthur, I am.''

This lack of respect by the arrogant, plotting Speaker was all Sutherland could stomach. He would get nowhere with Durkin. The president knew he would receive a different reception from the Senate majority leader.

The senior senator from New York had been one of the President's staunchest supporters, carrying forward a strong friendship developed from their Senate days together. The majority leader was the most wily and skillful of those who toiled in the labyrinths of Congress.

''Arthur, Arthur, please come in,'' Senator Johl said, his friendly smile a marked contrast to the president's last host. Being an old-time friend of the president's earned the majority leader the privilege of addressing Sutherland by his first name.

"It's been one helluva day," the president said, as he walked over to the senator's central bookcase.

"Now if I remember, it's right, here." The president pushed a small button partially hidden by a book. He was pleased with himself as the bookcase opened into a full bar, complete with running water.

"It's just like sex, Mr. President, some things a man will never forget," the senator joked as he started to pour his old friend a drink.

"Still drink those god-awful martinis?"

"Some things a man will never forget." Sutherland was looking around the bar for something else. "Can't have a martini without an olive."

Johl broke out into a broad grin as he pushed another button. Sutherland watched as a small refrigerator came into view.

"I had this put in three years ago," the senator said proudly, admiring his newest piece of office equipment. "But I know you aren't paying a social visit."

"No," the president responded, shaking his head, "this is business. Serious business."

"Let's sit down." The senator finished mixing his drink and motioned for the president to sit on the couch. The senator's office, like the majority leader himself, was immaculate. Though in his late fifties, Johl was in good health and looked ten years younger. He didn't exercise as much as he did years ago and lately was feeling the extra weight. He looked down at the slight bulge of his stomach.

"Jay," the president began, "I just saw our mutual friend," the last word spoken with extreme sarcasm, "and he wants to be president." The majority leader said nothing. He took a sip from his drink and carefully set the glass on a nearby table. He had wide, penetrating eyes, and spoke slowly and precisely as he looked toward the president.

"I am prepared to show my confidence in your judgment. Whatever . . . whatever you decide, I know will be in the best interest of this country. I do privately, and publicly, support you."

"Jay, I can't tell you what that means," the president responded gratefully. Jay Johl was an extraordinary man, of unparalleled integrity, with a complete commitment to his fellow man.

Sutherland related his entire conversation with the Speaker to Senator Johl, who sat in stunned silence. The majority leader was aghast.

"Durkin must be stopped," Johl responded firmly. The majority leader rose and walked toward his desk. Suddenly he raised his right hand and banged the top of his desk. The noise startled Sutherland. The veins in the majority leader's neck stretched his skin grotesquely, as he stared at the president.

"This could ruin the country. What Durkin wants to do lacks constitutional precedent, and it sucks! In 1800 and 1824 there was no winner in the general election; Congress had to decide the issue. Here, Starr has won . . . and goddamn it, he should have a chance to serve. You should have a chance to get him back."

The majority leader's fists tightened until the knuckles almost burst through the taut, stretched skin. He gulped his drink and paced before his desk.

Sutherland had never seen his friend this angry. He watched Johl's every move. The majority leader had a frightening gleam in his eyes. A sardonic smile formed on his lips as he approached the president.

"I'm okay," he said softly, patting Sutherland on the shoulder. "I've also got a plan."

"Go ahead," Sutherland replied, anxious to hear any news that would neutralize the Speaker.

"I'll go on the stump for Starr and Edwards. The ranking Republican senator in the country will campaign for the winning Democratic ticket. It's unheard of, but so is this entire dilemma."

"Beat Durkin at his own game," the president said, warming to the proposal.

"Exactly. The Speaker can't win if Starr and Edwards get qualified. We must keep the election out of the House. There the Speaker can win."

"You could do the dirty political work and . . ."

"And keep you above it all," Johl continued, "so you can

be president, and do what you have to do to get Starr back alive."

"Isn't it amazing," the president said, nodding his head. "If I had told you three weeks ago you would go on the stump for Starr . . . why hell . . . you'd have had me committed."

Johl laughed, taking a sip of his drink, feeling the excitement circulate through his body.

"The laws are unclear. We can't change that. But I will convince the electoral college that Durkin's actions stink. I'll line up politicians on both sides. Arthur, we will win this election!"

CHAPTER 17

THE INVESTIGATION

Tuesday, November 16

"BRIAN, WILL YOU GET BACK IN BED?" COOED THE SEXY NEW-lywed, sitting up to comb her hair, the sheets falling from her naked breasts.

"I've got to reach Studer," he replied impatiently, tapping his fingers on the table next to the phone. He nervously looked at his watch.

"Greg must be in by now."

"Honey," his wife said, carefully combing her long red hair, "I'm sure there is a reasonable explanation."

"I hope so too," he nodded, "then I won't worry anymore."

San Francisco Police Captain Greg Studer leaned back in his chair and sipped a hot cup of coffee. His feet rested comfortably on a desk overrun by paper. The captain was reading the sports page. The one time in the morning he wouldn't be disturbed.

"Goddamn '49ers," he mumbled to himself, as he smoothed his black hair with his left hand, "they traded Harvey to the Cardinals for a fucking draft choice."

"Captain Studer, line three," shouted the voice in the intercom. The captain turned the page, swallowing more of his coffee.

"Take it," he replied.

"Long-distance from Patrolman Nyberg," came the response.

Studer smiled and reached for the phone, stretching his fingers from his still reclining position.

"What's up, Brian," Studer began, "besides your dick?"

Nyberg shook his head before answering. His boss was as crude as ever.

"Come on, Brian," he continued, "Diane probably won't let you stay out of bed for more than three minutes." Studer took another sip of coffee.

"We were married the day after the election. I heard the news, but not the details. We haven't watched television or read a paper in two weeks. We're in a cabin. Just a bed and a phone."

"How can you fuck for two weeks straight?" Studer quipped.

"I just read a newspaper article that gave some details of the kidnapping."

"Yeah," Studer responded, still reading the paper. "It's out of our hands. The Feds are all over town."

"Well . . . ." Nyberg hesitated, taking a deep breath, "I think it's back in our hands."

Studer stopped reading. "So," the captain said quizzically.

"So," Nyberg replied carefully, "I think I saw the kidnappers. I stopped them that morning."

Studer leaned forward, spilling the coffee all over the sports page and his lap. "Goddamn it," he snarled, grabbing Kleenex to wipe his soiled pants.

Nyberg gave the details of the early-morning taillight incident in chronological order.

"Are you sure that bag was big enough to carry Starr?" Studer interrupted, jotting down as many notes as he could.

"Yes, I'm sure. Two men from the Fairmont, the laundry room . . . it's too coincidental."

"But you didn't give them a ticket."

"True. But I entered the name and license plate in my log-book."

"Shit, yes!" Studer exclaimed, unable to control his excitement. "Where is that goddamn book?"

"Locker 438, 18–20–34. It will be on the upper right shelf, next to my shaving stuff." Studer didn't even reply. He ran straight to the locker room.

Nyberg laid down the phone and walked to his bride. She was sitting up in bed, looking understandingly at her husband. He kissed her softly, his right hand slowly caressing her uncovered breasts. "I'll be back here in a second to give these my complete attention," he said as he rubbed her firm nipples. He went back to the phone and waited.

"I'm here, Greg."

"The pages aren't numbered."

"I know, go to the date."

"November 3 is missing."

"What?" Nyberg screamed.

Studer's mood turned solemn. He noticed tiny pieces of white paper inside the spiral notebook.

"Someone has ripped out the pages since October 29."

Nyberg collapsed into a nearby chair, dumbfounded.

"Honeymoon or not, give me your phone number," Studer commanded, "I'll get back to you."

Andrew Reynolds took another bite of his club sandwich. The Squire Restaurant in the Fairmont was almost empty.

"Mr. Krochock, I can't tell you how much I appreciate your setting up the meeting this morning."

Arthur Krochock smiled and nodded his acceptance of the compliment. He had been hotel manager for sixteen years, and was cooperating fully to minimize the bad publicity now associated with one of San Francisco's finest hotels.

"My pleasure, Mr. Reynolds. But I'm still shocked at what you've found."

"Remember, Art," Reynolds said softly, "whatever we discuss must be kept in complete confidence."

"Understood."

Reynolds drank his iced tea. "We know almost every hotel laundry room in this city had changes in laundry room personnel approximately three to six months before the election."

"So?" Krochock wondered.

"That's how they did it. They were ready for any hotel we would stay at."

"How did they know it was my hotel?"

Reynolds shrugged his shoulder. "That, my friend, is the question of the hour."

"But the personnel changes seemed so . . ."

"So natural . . . so normal," Reynolds continued. "That's why it worked. Whoever masterminded this knew the plan quite well."

"How did they know he would stay in a hotel? After all, he was from San Francisco."

"Is," Reynolds corrected.

"Sorry," replied the embarrassed manager.

"They knew Secret Service protocol. We use hotels for all kinds of reasons." Reynolds stopped for a moment, reflecting upon his words.

"Anything wrong?" Krochock wondered.

"No," Reynolds replied, finishing his club. "Thanks also for the free room and board. It makes the investigation easier for me . . . to have headquarters here."

"The scene of the crime," Krochock quietly stated.

"I still can't figure out why those injured carpenters didn't check into a hospital."

The hotel manager looked puzzled. "I went over that with your assistant."

"Who?"

"The girl . . . Decker."

Reynolds looked surprised.

"Didn't she tell you?"

The agent nodded his head and smiled. "I'm sure she did, but I have a lot to remember. Refresh my memory."

"On election night I told her the carpenters would leave at midnight. They were working overtime, but not all night."

"Go on, Art."

"Well, Mr. Reynolds, it's simple. The men who were work-ing at 3 A.M. were *not* my men."

Reynolds took the napkin from his lap and folded it neatly, placing it on the table. "Who were they?"

Krochock shook his head. "I have no idea. That's what's so strange."

"Who have you told this to?"

"Only Decker . . . and now you."

Reynolds leaned closer to the bearded hotel manager. "Let's keep this quiet."

Andrew Reynolds wasn't the only person investigating the kidnapping.

Kate Wilson stood across from the Transamerica Building and made her phone call.

"Mr. Morgan, please."

"Mr. Morgan will be out of the office all day. May I take a message?"

"I'll try later."

Kate hung up the phone and walked along Montgomery Street. She had been following Tommy Duncan's San Francisco attorney for one week. Even though the law firm receptionist had insisted Kevin Morgan was absent all week, she saw the attorney enter the building every day. She had stopped to buy a diet soda from a street vendor when she saw the curly-haired attorney leaving the building. He appeared to be heading toward the Embarcadero Center as he briskly walked along Clay Street.

She put on her sunglasses and crossed the street, careful not to be seen. She placed a scarf over her head, fighting the winds that whirled through the tall downtown buildings.

The attorney switched the big briefcase from his right to his left hand. He quickly turned around, causing his tie to fly in his face. It appeared he was looking for someone. He hurriedly walked into an alley off the Clay and Battery Street intersection.

Wilson surveyed the crowd around her. The streets were crammed with tourists and businessmen. She peered down the alley, but saw no trace of the attorney. From what she observed, the alley was narrow but not long. Several wires were strung across overhead, appearing to connect the nearby buildings in some fashion. She walked by an overfilled trash barrel, smelling the alcohol that permeated from within. She noticed most of the windows above her were shattered; her shoes were stepping on the glass below. As she trudged slowly up the slight incline toward the center of the alley, she wondered why Morgan would take this route.

"Out for a morning stroll, Miss Wilson?"

She quickly turned around, caught off guard by the person behind her.

Morgan moved toward her and stopped. She watched his intent blue eyes, staring at her, waiting for a response.

"I can't wait to hear what you're doing in this alley," he said sarcastically, noticing her surprise.

"I'll be honest with you," she said cautiously, trying to regain her composure.

"That's good for starters. Why have you been following me?"

"How did you know?"

"That's not important. I asked you a question."

She moved several steps away and felt the cold wall behind her blouse. "You're Tommy Duncan's lawyer."

"So."

"You've been to San Quentin twenty times during the past four months."

He smiled. "He's my client. They won't let him come to my office."

She looked him over intently. Her years of training served her well in detecting liars. With this man, however, she wasn't sure.

"What did you discuss with your *client*?"

"You know better than that. Attorney-client privilege."

"The appeal period has expired."

"Wrong, lady. We still have avenues to explore."

"You represent the International Union, don't you?"

"You already know that answer." The attorney looked down the alley. It was the first time he had his eyes away from her.

"You also represent the hotels along with the union, don't you?"

He suddenly became irate and charged toward the reporter,

waving a threatening finger in her face. The veins in his neck stood out in anger.

"I know what you're trying to do," he snapped. "You can't get away with this—neither my client, nor myself, had anything to do with Starr. If you follow me anymore, I'll sue you and your shitty paper for harassment."

Kate didn't have to respond. She finally saw what she had suspected all along.

Fear.

Reynolds had just stepped out of the shower when the phone rang.

"Andy, it's Jo."

"Anything to report in L.A. ?"

"Nothing," she said, her voice flat and unemotional. "We've been watching the farmhouse for two weeks, but no activity."

"Have the police uncovered anything?"

"No. Do you want me to stay here?"

Reynolds thought for a moment before answering. His eyes stared out the hotel window.

"I think he still may be in L.A. Stay there for a few more days."

"Have you made progress?"

"Not really," he responded.

"Andy . . . what is it?" He noticed an uncertainty, a lack of confidence in her voice.

"Everything is fine, Jo. I may have one lead. But it's such a hunch I won't lose credibility with anyone, until I check it out."

"You're strange, Andy. All these years together. We're supposed to share."

"You're right," he conceded. "The bullet in L.A. may give us clues."

She sounded relieved. "Good. You mean Roger did some work?"

"Right," he replied, "and as soon as I learn more I'll call you."

Reynolds placed the phone in its cradle and pondered what he had just said.

He dialed Washington.

"Hello."

"Roger, it's Andy."

"I was just going to call you."

"Is it good news? I need some."

Other than Jo Decker, Roger Jefferson was Reynolds's most trusted confidant. The young, ambitious agent had risen within the service in record time and greatly admired the man he worked for.

"The bullet dug out of the ground at the L.A. farmhouse was not made in America."

"What?" Reynolds exclaimed, drying his hair with the towel.

"It's a teflon-coated bullet."

"A cop killer?"

"No. This type has unusual patterns. I've checked with several large companies to confirm my findings. This bullet has been outlawed."

"What do ballistics show?"

"Had this been shot from a .357 magnum revolver, it would penetrate two inches of cold-rolled steel. The teflon lubricates the bullet along. You could have been standing in front of the farmhouse and this guy could kill you from the back."

"It would go through the walls?"

"All of them . . . I'm glad he missed."

"He missed on purpose," Reynolds said coldly, throwing the towel in the bathroom as he observed his strong nude body in the mirror.

"Do me a favor."

"Anything, Andy."

"If anyone asks when you told me this, tell them it was yesterday."

"Okay," Jefferson replied, trying to control his curiosity. Andy could sense his mood.

"Roger, there's a reason for this."

"I know. You don't have to give me reasons."

"Thanks. Then do me another favor."

"Shoot."

"Send me the personnel files of all agents who were stationed with Starr in San Francisco."

"All the files?"

"Yes."

"Of everyone except you and Jo, I suppose?"

"I said everyone," Reynolds replied flatly. "And keep the request confidential."

"How can I do that?"

"Steal them."

CHAPTER 18

THE ALLIANCE

Wednesday, November 17

THERE WAS A LIGHT KNOCK AT THE DOOR. REYNOLDS GRABBED his watch. 12:30 A.M. "Who the hell . . ." he muttered, as he grabbed the wet towel from the bathroom floor.

"Andy, is this a bad time?"

He peered into the beautiful eyes of Kate Wilson, who in turn was staring at the agent's almost naked torso.

"No . . . no," he responded, as he opened the door wide enough for her to enter.

"How did you find me?"

"First," she replied, nodding at his towel, "shouldn't you get decent?"

He smiled and motioned her to a chair as he grabbed his bathrobe, quickly changing behind the bathroom door.

"Nice outfit," she commented, as Reynolds tied the strings to his bright red robe.

"Can I get you something?"

"I've taken care of that."

Wilson walked to the door and quietly rolled in a cart with wine and cheese. He shrugged his shoulders.

"You aren't shy, are you?"

"Now Andy, I didn't embarrass you, did I?"

He grinned and poured them each a glass of wine, reading the label as he carefully returned the bottle to the tray.

"Straight from Napa Valley."

"Only the best," she kidded.

He sat down on the bed. Kate's navy blue skirt had ridden high on her leg. Reynolds noticed how firm her breasts looked under a tight white blouse.

"My contacts in Washington told me you were here. That made sense to me."

"How did you find me?"

"I looked at the guest register. I figured 'Jonathan Reynolds' had to be you."

"I'm not that original."

"Your being here is really no big secret."

Reynolds agreed. "I suppose not."

He smiled at her and sipped the wine. Kate's long brown hair looked beautiful in the light from a nearby table lamp.

"He's alive, isn't he, Andy?" Kate said, breaking the awkward silence.

"You love him like I do, don't you?" he asked.

"Yes," she smiled softly at Andy, then quickly added, "that's why I'm here."

"That was going to be my next question," he responded.

She got up and poured herself another glass of wine. She kicked her shoes against the nearby wall. She sat across from Andy, placing her left leg under her body, once again showing off her upper thighs.

"First, I have a request."

"Go on," Andy nodded, reaching for more cheese.

"This conversation must be off the record."

Reynolds chuckled. "That's got to be a first for you. I can see the headlines, 'Pulitzer Prize Winner Denies She Was Agent's Source.' "

"Do we have a deal?"

"Only if it goes both ways."

"Deal," she said quickly, adjusting her leg on the bed and swallowing her wine, wiping her lip softly with her right hand.

"I think Duncan did the kidnapping." She watched Reynolds closely for a reaction. There was none.

"Why?"

She related the story of her encounter with Duncan's attorney and his representation of the union. She was very excited.

"And he didn't deny or explain all those visits to the prison. And another thing . . ."

"Hold on," Reynolds interrupted. "What gives you the authority to get involved in a federal investigation?"

She was surprised by his tone. Surely, they were on the same side. "I'm a reporter, I'm doing my job," she replied matter-of-factly.

"Are you covering the news or making it?"

"That's unfair, Andy."

"By interfering . . . *you are* the news," he snapped.

"When the values of good journalism and humanitarianism collide, I opt for the latter."

"You're doing both. Get your exclusive story and be the hero, too."

"Are you jealous, Andy?"

"Of course not."

"Years ago, in Atlanta, a man lit a match and almost burned to death. The reporters present filmed it, making no effort to stop . . . just to report the news."

"So," Reynolds replied icily.

"So," she continued, "that's the rule. My paper says, if I cover a news event, I must not participate for whatever reason."

"Kate," Reynolds responded, trying to control himself, "you're proving *my* side."

"That's just it, Andy, normally you would have every reason to be pissed . . . but the next president has been kidnapped. This must be an exception to the rule."

Reynolds didn't respond, but conceded that Kate was persuasive. He sipped his wine and watched her in silence. She returned his stare.

"Look, Andy," she continued, moving her right leg under her buttocks, and leaning over the bed, supporting herself with her right hand, "if I was covering a crash I would observe the burnt victims being pulled from the car . . . not render assistance. I would watch little kids being dragged from the river and report on their sobbing parents. That's my job.''

''That's journalism,'' he said softly.

''It's a summons to tell the truth as best . . .''

''As best you determine it,'' he interrupted.

She ignored the sarcasm and continued to plead her case.

''In this situation, I'm an American citizen first . . . reporter second.''

''You're being paid to report the news.''

''I've met my commitments. My articles on the legal issues involving the kidnapping and Judy Starr are being carried in almost every paper.''

''Why won't you write what you've told me?''

Wilson stopped in mid-sentence and eyed Reynolds carefully. Her voice had dropped.

''Because this isn't only my story. I had to talk with you. When someone's life is at stake, Jonathan's, I become a participant . . . not an observer.'' She tried to fight the tears, gritting her teeth in frustration. Reynolds moved to her and placed his powerful hand around her shoulder.

''You're right,'' he said softly. He poured two more glasses of wine.

''No more disagreements,'' he toasted. She smiled tolerantly.

''Getting Jonathan back is so important. We have a society desperately looking for quick cures. We . . .''

''Kate,'' he said gently, ''no more politics or journalism.''

She smiled. ''I'll drink to that,'' she said, raising her wineglass. There was a brazen sexiness in the way Kate held her lips. The agent leaned over and kissed her softly on the lips.

''Maybe we can be a partnership. I assume I am the only person who knows about your investigation?''

''Yes,'' she replied, ''but a true partnership must share. Agreed?''

''What does that mean?''

''It means telling me about a little farmhouse in L.A.''

Reynolds flinched, totally surprised the enterprising reporter knew about the failed mission.

But he told her everything.

"What I conclude from all of this. Well, the same as you . . . Duncan."

"He has the motive," she replied.

"Revenge," he continued. "He also could place laundry employees in hotels . . . and pull off the kidnapping. Our agents actually saw these men in the hallway . . . with Starr in the bottom of a laundry bag."

"We know why . . . how . . . but now the hard part . . ."

"Right," interjected Reynolds, "where is he?"

"How did they know about the Fairmont . . . Jonathan even stiffed me out of an interview. I was cooling my heels at the Hyatt."

"I know," Reynolds said quietly. He leaned over and kissed her again. "Tomorrow, partner, you and I will figure out how they knew about the Fairmont."

She looked into his eyes and moved closer to him, pushing her body against his chest. Her eyes were warm and inviting as he leaned against her, kissing her forcefully, feeling her mouth open to greet his exploring tongue.

She moved quietly, pressing her soft pink cheek against his. He felt her breath against his face and her ripe firm breasts against his chest.

His penis hardened and shoved demandingly through the bathrobe. She dropped her hand and squeezed it.

Her warm tongue agilely continued darting between his trembling lips; then she suddenly pulled away.

"Is this right?" she whispered, still staring into his eyes. He stood next to her, pushing her brown hair from her eyes. He smiled and kissed her softly on the lips. "It's right."

She nodded her assent and quietly made her way to the bathroom. Reynolds stripped off his robe, jumped into bed, and waited.

As the door closed behind her, Reynolds blinked, staring at her gorgeous figure. She was completely naked. His eyes made love to her, first fixed upon the pink pouting nipples of her satiny breasts. He next made his way to the brown silky curls which nearly hid her fig-shaped vaginal lips.

She crawled in next to him. Her lips parted and her tongue entered his waiting mouth, her hand fondling the velvety head of his aching cock. His strong muscular body leaned over her, gently cupping her breasts. Kate closed her eyes and arched her knees, spreading her firm legs wide, granting total access to her soft, yielding flesh.

They moaned, feeling the cohesion of their bare skin. His strong fingers made their way to her quivering breasts, stroking their sides as he positioned himself on top of her.

She reached down and guided his penis into her, biting her lips as he entered.

"I'm so wet . . . I'm so turned on," she gasped, meeting each of his powerful thrusts.

"I wish I could do this all night," he groaned, kissing her firmly on the lips. She gripped his shoulders, raising herself to feel the penetration of each thrust.

He held her tightly, saying nothing. He was still inside her, cherishing every moment of their experience. Using his left hand as leverage, he shifted his body weight and gently wiped the sweat from her brow with his right hand, noticing that her hazel eyes looked violet.

He whispered softly into her ear. "I'm glad this was off the record."

CHAPTER 19

ROSE GARDEN REVELATIONS

Thursday, November 18

THE FRESHLY FALLEN SNOW BLANKETED THE WHITE HOUSE gardens that led toward the Ellipse, where the White House Christmas tree would soon be flashing its brilliance.

"Mr. President," Senator McBee said, wiping the snow from

his shoulder, "Ah know you said every conversation in the Oval Office would be recorded for historical purposes, that you'd never be ashamed to record anything said there, but please, either make an exception, turn off the recorder . . . or let's meet somewhere else."

The president laughed, rubbing his hands together to stay warm. "It's beautiful out here, J.W. Just look at the Washington Monument . . . isn't it glorious?"

"Arthur, please, it's only goin' to git colder. Remember," he drawled, "Ah'm from Texas, and to me, this is cold weather."

"Alright," Sutherland reluctantly conceded, "for you, I'll turn the microphones off. This is our last Rose Garden rendezvous."

"Thanks," McBee muttered in appreciation. "By the way, any news on Jonathan Starr?"

"Nothing," he replied sadly. "Hagstrom is checking a list of six hundred people considered to be potential assassins or kidnappers. There are also about thirty thousand names in the Secret Service computer being checked. It takes time."

"A commodity Ah wish we had more of."

"Listen," the president said seriously, "as usual, I need a favor."

"Name it."

"Spy on the Speaker for me. I know you're friends, but I also know where your loyalties are. Not to me, but to the office of president, and this country."

The Texas senator nodded his head in agreement. "Ah've heard his plan. Ah think it stinks. Ah'm fixin' to go see Jay Johl tomorrow. Ah will do what Ah ken. Mah loyalties are with you!"

"Thanks, J.W.," the president responded, appreciatively. "I've only got a few minutes, I'm meeting the vice president in the warm Oval Office," Sutherland said smiling, pointing behind them to the closed French doors.

"At your request, Ah've delegated more responsibility to the secretary of state. Ah can't keep meeting with A-rabs in Texas and Washington all the time. They are makin' concessions . . . but the Starr kidnappin' has slowed things down. They don't like not knowin' who's goin' to be president. They may not sign until this entire matter is resolved. They also think too much has gone public."

"Some of that was beyond my control," the president retorted.

The Texas senator buttoned his overcoat, shivering, and frowned at the president.

"I said this was the last outside meeting. Go on."

"National Security Decision Directive 218 is finished. Twenty agencies have drafted specific proposals for enforcing an anti-terrorism policy. Of course, none of the agencies knows the exact problem we may be dealin' with."

"Can our proposal work?"

"Yes," McBee replied, but then quickly added, "There need to be some modifications . . . but they're minor."

"What about the companies?"

"Ah think all problems have bin ironed out. Westinghouse, Sperry, Rockwell, and that California company have agreed totally with your proposal."

"Excellent," the president said enthusiastically.

"What effect does the kidnappin' of Starr have on this?" McBee asked.

"I don't know. If I get this thing worked out, and the Arabs agree to our terms, under these circumstances, this will be an executive agreement under the new law and not a treaty, so I avoid any fight with Congress. The problem with this executive agreement is if Starr or Edwards or the Speaker—once one of them becomes president—decides not to honor it."

"To undo what you've done?"

"Right."

"Well, Reagan went along with Carter's Iranian settlement even though he didn't like it."

"Right. That's what I'm counting on. This government must stand behind her agreements, regardless of which president makes them."

"Ah agree," McBee responded. "But, you can understand the hesitancy of the A-rabs if they know the deal may hinge on a Jewish president to carry out your wishes. Besides, they may want to wait. If Starr is rescued and will be president, knowing what he feels about the peace plan, they may say screw it. Starr will never honor it. It may be too late for the plan if Starr comes back. Everyone knows his position."

"Yes," the president agreed, "but it's not my agreement, it's an agreement of this government."

"You know, Arthur," J.W. said softly, "at some point you might have to deal with the Speaker."

"You mean the agreement for his presidency?"

"Maybe," J.W. replied cautiously, "maybe."

The president blew into his hands. He looked at McBee but didn't say anything.

"Ah thought about our conversation last night," McBee said. "Ah don't think any less of you cause you're havin' second thoughts."

The president stared silently at McBee. His troubled eyes gave away the conflicting emotions he was feeling. The president, like his former Senate colleagues, found something irresistible about McBee's Southern accent. His languid, drawling syllables just seemed to make emotions sound bigger.

"The Speaker really disgusts me," the president began slowly, "but if he can prevent Starr from getting 270 electoral votes why shouldn't I take advantage of his strategy. If he succeeds, why shouldn't I pressure the House to qualify me?"

"Ah know where you're comin' from," McBee said softly.

"I know you do, J.W.," the president responded appreciatively. "But will the country? This deal with King Hussein and the Arabs could really bring peace. Israel and the Arabs need a third party they can trust. My presidency has supplied that trust. A Jewish president, or the Speaker, might not."

"What's you plan?" McBee asked softly.

The furrow between Sutherland's eyebrows, a definite sign of stress, made him look distant and alien. "I know what a president feels," he continued, "to get his name in history. I was with Reagan when the nuclear talks with the Soviets took place. He did so much, but there was more left undone. So much unfinished work. I felt his pain. Any man holding this office wants to do something, to accomplish some feat that will last for decades. Our deal with Egypt, and our agreement to stand back and let Hussein take over like he wants to, is the break this nation has been looking for for close to forty years. I just can't let it slip by.''

"Hussein won't be able to act before January 20," McBee offered matter-of-factly, "even if things worked out tomorrow.''

"I know,'' Sutherland agreed. "But the deal with Egypt could be in place, as well as their agreement to support Hussein's plan. It's the only way to save Israel.''

"Too bad,'' McBee mulled out loud, "this country doesn't know your true feelings toward Israel.''

"I know,'' the president nodded in agreement. "I should have stated my position years ago, before anyone could accuse me of politics. In 1942 and '43 this country knew Jews were being slaughtered in Europe. FDR and Secretary of State Sumner Wells knew too. Headlines in American papers graphically reported on the mass murders in Poland. Even a 1943 Gallup poll indicated almost one half of those polled believed two million Jews had been murdered since the war began. But we didn't do anything about it.''

McBee noticed the president's eyes were moist. Sutherland stared toward the Ellipse, watching the traffic on Constitution Avenue. The president returned the Texas senator's stare.

"We,'' the president said softly, "this nation, owes the Jews. We owe Israel. They can't survive this way forever. There are too many people, too many resources against them. I only wish I could have convinced Starr. His victory may doom the entire thing. Since both Israel and Egypt know his views, his return may kill the plan. Unless I can do some quick talking when he returns.''

"What will ya do?'' McBee asked.

The president sighed. "I'm going to watch the Speaker's plan. If it looks like it may succeed, I'll have to decide to step in myself or stop it.''

"What about Johl's counterattack?''

"I'm going to let him do as he sees fit. I've got a week, at least, before I jump off this fence.''

"Ah'm with you, Arthur,'' McBee said solemnly, placing his arm around the president's shoulder. "Ah'm with you no matter what.''

CHAPTER 20

THE PRISONER

Thursday, November 18

"SOMEBODY ANSWER ME!" SCREAMED JONATHAN STARR. IT HAD been over two weeks since his kidnapping, and he had not seen or heard from his captors since the night they fled from the farmhouse outside of Los Angeles. The loneliness had become unbearable.

"Will somebody talk to me? I know you're out there; I can hear your voices. I just want to talk . . . I just want to talk."

The hellhole Starr had been staying in smelled like a sewer. He had not showered for weeks, and the one roll of toilet paper provided him was long gone. Fortunately, the toilet was still working, and Starr was able to wash his hands with fresh water after each flushing. Without toilet paper Starr's anus was infected . . . swollen . . . painful.

He had become very weak. He still got two meals a day, but without companionship, was slowly losing his grip. He had his desire to survive—to live—but the uncertainty was overwhelming.

He was totally frustrated. He had become the first Jewish president-elect of the United States—now, not only was his future presidency at issue, but his very survival was paramount. He could only assume, and hope, the deadly silence would be broken soon.

He considered himself a strong man, able to withstand any physical or mental torture. It was the solitary confinement, the loneliness, that was becoming his biggest enemy.

Spending hours staring at the wall, meditating, he would begin to break into a cold sweat. FIGHT IT—GOT TO FIGHT IT. GOT TO STAY STRONG—DON'T GIVE UP.

In the end, in the battle between his body and mind, the mind would win. He would not succumb to his kidnappers. Somehow, someway, he would get out of this predicament. YES, I'LL WAIT THEM OUT, I'LL JUST WAIT THEM OUT.

He walked to the corner of the room and collapsed onto his cot-like bed. The narrow mattress was hard under his aching body. He slowly rubbed his sore legs, trying to stay active, to do something . . . to keep his sanity.

The green army fatigues he had been given reeked. He slowly unbuttoned the matching green shirt, tossing it to the floor in disgust.

His right hand reached for the chain around his neck, the mezuzah he had proudly worn since his parents presented it to him on the day of his Bar Mitzvah. He gently kissed the gold Star of David that was affixed to the rectangular religious ornament hanging from the chain. Inside the mezuzah was the most sacred prayer of his religion. Someday soon, he thought to himself, he would take the tiny container apart, his way of getting closer to God.

He continued to fondle the mezuzah as he prayed for the strength to get him through this crisis. He willed himself to wait it out. He had no other choice.

Len Allen and Vicky Roe were playing cards. They had been playing cards for weeks, helping pass the time. Allen had received explicit orders that they should have no communication with the senator. No conversation, no radio, television, or newspapers. He was to remain in solitary confinement, served only two meals a day.

"Man, that son of a bitch sure can yell," snickered Allen. He looked at his hand. He was one card away from gin.

"Len, I think we ought to talk to the poor guy. I mean, my God, he's been kept there for weeks, and no one has even said 'boo' to him."

"Shut up, you cunt!" hollered Allen as he stood up from the card table. "Don't you even think about communicating with that asshole. Until we get the word, nobody does nothing. You understand?'' Allen suddenly grabbed the young, beautiful blonde from her chair, picked her up, and threw her against the wall in one motion.

"All right . . . back off, Len . . . back off." Roe legitimately feared the power, strength, and unpredictability of this madman, as she rubbed her sore right shoulder.

"There's no reason for you to get upset, Len. I was only talking out loud. If you don't want me to talk to him, I won't. My God, can't a girl talk out loud?"

"Get back over here and finish the game!" he grunted. Like a trained dog moving on command, Vicky hustled back to the card table. No need to get herself injured again, she thought as the two continued playing cards. She, like Len Allen, would have to wait for further instructions.

CHAPTER 21

THE PEACE PLAN

Friday, November 19

ARTHUR SUTHERLAND SAT BEHIND THE MASSIVE OAK PRESIDEN-tial desk framed from the timbers of an old British ship, and given to President Hayes by Queen Victoria. He turned excitedly to the last page of the report, carefully reviewing the conclusion, typed in bold print and capital letters.

The president reached under his desk, turning off the power to the Oval Office microphones and recording system. It was easy, he thought to himself, to erase history in advance. How ironic—that simple flipping of a switch could have saved Richard Nixon's presidency.

"We're getting close, J.W.," the president said, smiling at the Texas senator.

"Yes, sir," McBee responded quickly, pointing to the French doors behind Sutherland. "Ah'm just glad to be inside."

"J.W.," the president grinned, shaking his head, "you're one unusual fella."

"Ah know. Just a good ole boy. But Ah'll say this. It's sure good to see you laughin'. "

"I feel good. Johl called this morning. His campaign with the electoral college is going fine. People seem willing to place their vote where it should be," the president paused for a moment.

"Go on," McBee urged.

"Let's just say Senator Johl has a few surprises up his sleeve for our friend, the Speaker."

"Speakin' of Johl and Durkin, have ya decided what to do 'bout the electoral college and Durkin's campaign?"

"I have, J.W.," the president replied confidently, "I certainly have." The president was steely nerved, regardless of the chaos breaking loose all over the country.

"I had an argument with Johl just last night," the president elaborated. "He thought I was power-hungry. I told him I respected his opinion immensely, even when he's wrong. I think I convinced him that the bottom line is I should be president for the next term if Starr can't serve."

"What did he say?" McBee inquired.

"He said, if he told the electoral college members to vote for Starr, but then in the same breath told them, if not Starr, vote for me, it would sound like he was really campaigning for me."

"He is Senate majority leader. Ah could see how people might think that."

"Yes," the president conceded thoughtfully. "I told him I could too, but in the long run my serving the next four years is better for this country than the Speaker."

"And?"

"And," the president continued, "he agreed. He said he knew I was trying to rescue Starr. He didn't think I was totally innocent in stealing the election from Starr, since I won't publicly deny my interest in serving four more years, if the fight is between the Speaker and myself.''

''Johl supportin' ya?''

''He is, with some reservations. But you know, J.W., if I don't get Starr back,'' the president paused, a trace of concerned doubt in his voice, ''I will be accused of playing the dirtiest kind of politics. Keeping the winner away so I can take advantage of another term.''

Sutherland stopped and stared intently at McBee. He gave a long, exasperated sigh and shook his worried head slowly. ''*You* do believe me, J.W., that I want Starr back, even if it meant the Middle East peace might fail?''

''Ah certainly do, Mr. President,'' McBee quickly replied, firmly and convincingly.

Sutherland carefully opened his top right desk drawer, pulling out two cigars.

''Where's the pipe?'' McBee asked.

''Don't feel like a pipe now. My mood compels me to tackle this swisher sweet.''

McBee shrugged his shoulders. ''Arthur . . . when are you goin' to start smokin' a man's ceegar?''

The Texas senator chuckled to himself, reaching inside his left suit pocket. ''Here,'' he offered, ''Ah've got a punch panetela.''

The president leaned over his desk and tossed McBee a small cigar, still wrapped in cellophane. ''Today, J.W., you'll smoke *my* cigar.''

''Arthur, Ah'm not much for readin', but Ah know that English fella . . . John Galsworthy . . . once wrote, 'By the cigars they smoke . . . ye shall know the texture of men's souls.' Hearin' that, Ah wondah if we should smoke these?'' McBee asked, twisting the cigar around in his right hand between the fingers.

''Smoke!'' the president barked, puffing on his cigar. ''Since you've displayed your literary skills, I find it necessary to quote Rudyard Kipling, who once said, 'A woman is only a woman, but a good cigar is a smoke.' J.W., *this* is a good smoke.''

Sutherland smiled as he closely watched his friend. With every crisis, there comes a time when a president must rely on one or two men from his trusted circle of advisers, close intimates with whom he feels completely at ease. FDR turned to Harry Hopkins after Pearl Harbor. JFK listened to brother Bobby during the Cuban missile crisis. Now Arthur Sutherland had been turning to Thomas Whyte and J.W. McBee.

"J.W.," the president said seriously, placing his cigar in a nearby ashtray, "you've done well. If things continue, there's a chance we'll get this through in January. The kidnapping complicates matters, knowing Starr's not around and his views on the plan. But I would be pushing it as a lame duck even if he were sitting next to me." The president paused and sighed, "I'm just not sure the Arabs will sign until we know who our next president will be. Are you ironing out the final problems?"

"Ah think so. The A-rab coalition will allow American companies to build nuclear power plants in Egypt and Saudi Arabia."

"This will pump billions of dollars into our nuclear industry, but of course, that's only a small side benefit."

McBee nodded, taking another reluctant puff on his cigar. The taste was too sweet for his liking. "The A-rabs will agree to follow every provision of the Atomic Energy Act of 1954, and the Nuclear Nonproliferation Act of 1978."

"They damn well better follow them. They have agreed not to recycle the nuclear fuel. Our 'executive agreement' simply allows the construction of these reactors. If there is ever any recycling of used radioactive fuel, against our guidelines . . . that could build nuclear weapons, we must have the right to shut down the reactors, or if necessary, dismantle them."

"That's a god-awful tough condition for the A-rabs to meet. But they did agree. That's how badly they need, and want, nuclear energy."

"Damn right they need it. To get their own people into the twentieth century. And," the president said proudly, "we can now insure Israel's safety as well."

"Israel will protest, claimin' they can't live next door to A-rabs with atomic weapons. One bomb on Tel Aviv, and goodbye Israel."

"That's the point," the president replied calmly. "There will be no bombs. The reactors will take ten years to build. By then, if this thing works, Israel will be peacefully coexisting with her neighbors."

"But this only works because of your initiative with Hussein. The reactors are only step one in the big picture you've set up," McBee said, stretching his legs as he tapped ashes from the cigar into a nearby ashtray. "Even the king is havin' second thoughts," McBee added quickly. "Starr's victory, and his peace plan position, which he made crystal clear durin' the debates, have the king concerned that this country, under Starr, won't honor *your* last-minute executive agreement. The fact *you* may still be president for another term, if Starr isn't rescued, allows everyone to continue our negotiations. But we're all in limbo."

The president nodded in appreciation, taking a long puff from his cigar, watching the smoke rise to the ceiling.

"Think of it, J.W. We monitor the power plants. Not only do they follow our federal laws—they let us inside *their* plants, knowing full well if they *ever* try to use the plants for weapons— well, they know the consequences."

"That's a key to this entire deal," McBee added.

"Right," the president quickly agreed. "The International Atomic Energy Agency established by the U.N. in 1957 to promote the peaceful use of atomic energy would never, alone, be enough of a safeguard for the Israelis. Even though the IAEA monitors nuclear plants and fuel processes to prevent their being used to make nuclear weapons, Israel needs more assurances. This agreement gives them every safeguard imaginable."

"And," McBee quickly noted, "that report we talked about a few days ago . . . concernin' terrorists, clearly sets forth an acceptable plan to protect the reactors."

"What we must do," the president said patiently, "is convince the Israelis that any fear they have is unfounded or protected against. Just like Reagan did years ago when he supplied the Saudis with the Stinger antiaircraft missiles."

"Mr. President," McBee said sincerely, "we're gittin' close. But I still need to get some loose ends tied. And it's goin' to get worse. Even if the A-rabs will sign before Starr is back, or after he gits back, the Israeli position will be tough to change. They know Starr's attitude. Why should they sign when the Jewish president-elect is negative. They may want to wait to see if Starr comes back. If he does, why would they sign? Why not wait and deal with Starr?'' McBee stopped and suddenly grinned at the president. ''This is a gosh-awful hard deal to put together.''

''J.W., you did this faster than—what's your saying—faster than corn through a goose?''

McBee broke into a belly laugh, slapping his hand on his knee. ''Damn good, Arthur . . . but it's faster than a turkey on a June bug . . . but Ah like yours better.''

He put out his cigar and eyed Sutherland intently. He was amazed at how well the president had withstood the enormous pressures of the kidnapping and the growing tensions in the Middle East.

''Mr. President,'' McBee drawled, his voice quiet and reflective, ''we need to make final revisions in our agreement so this deal is an executive agreement comin' under that new federal law that expanded your Emergency Powers Act authority, so no one will claim this could be a treaty.''

''Go ahead and do it,'' the president replied immediately. ''This agreement is the type that comes under the new law. If I have to get congressional approval, as a lame duck . . . we've got problems. In early January, the House and Senate undergo some significant changes. The GOP barely kept a majority, and with this kidnapping—I know I couldn't sneak it by if it was ever construed as a treaty. Make those changes.''

The president studied the ''Eyes Only'' report before him. This was his Middle East plan. He carefully reviewed, once again, each proposal.

1. THE UNITED STATES WILL ARRANGE, THROUGH DESIGNATED PRIVATE CORPORATIONS, THE CONSTRUCTION OF NUCLEAR POWER PLANTS IN EGYPT AND SAUDI ARABIA, BY EXECUTIVE AGREEMENT, CONSTRUCTION TO BE COMPLETED WITHIN 10 YEARS. SEPARATE DOCUMENT 11-804, COVERS SECURITY ARRANGEMENTS AND AGREEMENTS.
2. SYRIAN PRESIDENT HAFIZ ASSAD WILL BE ASSASSINATED BY KING HUSSEIN'S ARMY UPON HIS RETURN TO HAMA (EST. 6 MONTHS). MOD-

ERATE SYRIAN ARMY LEADERS SUPPORT HUS-
SEIN COUP. THE THREE SYRIAN VICE
PRESIDENTS WILL BE ELIMINATED AT THE SAME
TIME, INCLUDING ASSAD'S BROTHER, RIFAAT.

3. HUSSEIN WILL TAKE OVER ALL OF LEBANON,
EXCEPT THE 20-MILE SOUTHERN BORDER,
WHICH WILL BE UNDER ISRAELI CONTROL. HUS-
SEIN WILL CONTROL THESE THREE COUNTRIES
UNDER A NEW REPUBLIC, RECOGNIZING AND
PLEDGING ISRAEL'S RIGHT TO PEACEFUL EXIS-
TENCE. HUSSEIN WILL CONTROL MAJOR MEDI-
TERRANEAN PORTS AND ACCESS TO THE RED
SEA.

4. NO UNITED STATES TROOPS OR PERSONNEL, CI-
VILIAN OR MILITARY, WILL BE INVOLVED.
BASED ON EXECUTIVE AGREEMENT, EGYPT,
SAUDI ARABIA, AND ISRAEL WILL ACQUIESCE
TO HUSSEIN LEADERSHIP.

5. ISRAEL WILL ANNEX THE WEST BANK TO FORM
A SEPARATE PALESTINIAN NATION. SECURE
BORDERS ON ALL SIDES GUARANTEED BY EGYPT
AND HUSSEIN.

6. SYRIAN SOVIET SUBMARINE BASES WILL BE DIS-
MANTLED. 7,000 SOVIET ADVISERS IN SUBURB
OF DAMASCUS WILL BE EXILED. NO MILITARY
CONFRONTATION WITH SOVIETS.

7. BY EXECUTIVE AGREEMENT, UNITED STATES
WILL RENEGOTIATE INTEREST RATES ON EGYPT
AND SAUDIA ARABIA LOANS FOR PURCHASE OF
MILITARY EQUIPMENT. ECONOMIC AID TO BOTH
COUNTRIES WILL BE INCREASED. JOINT DEVEL-
OPMENT PROJECTS DECREASED.

8. UNITED STATES GOVERNMENT WILL URGE THE
INTERNATIONAL MONETARY FUND TO RE-
SCHEDULE DEBT OF ISRAEL, EGYPT, SAUDI ARA-
BIA, AND JORDAN.

9. HUSSEIN HAS ACCORD WITH ARAFAT AND PLO.
WILL BE GOVERNED BY 15-MEMBER EXECUTIVE
COMMITTEE. FATAH, ARAB LIBERATION FRONT,

    AND DEMOCRATIC ALLIANCE TO BE CON-
TROLLED BY PLO AFTER HUSSEIN COUP.
NATIONAL SALVATION FRONT, PALESTINE
LIBERATION FRONT, AND HABASH GROUP TO BE
NEUTRALIZED AFTER HUSSEIN COUP.

10.   ALL PARTICIPANTS TO PEACE PLAN AGREE TO
FIGHT TERRORISTS. INTERNATIONAL ANTI-
TERRORIST COMMITTEE TO BE FORMED. TAR-
GETED GROUPS INCLUDE WEST GERMANY'S
RED ARMY FACTION, FRANCE'S DIRECT ACTION
GROUP, BELGIUM'S FIGHTING COMMUNIST
CELLS, ITALY'S RED BRIGADES.

11.   COLONEL MUAMMAR QADDAFI CLOSE TO AC-
QUIRING NUCLEAR CAPABILITIES FROM BEL-
GIAN CONCERNS. HUSSEIN WILL ELIMINATE
QADDAFI AND HIS AIDES IN TRIPOLI WHEN AS-
SAD IS NEUTRALIZED IN HAMA. THE LIBYA NU-
CLEAR FUSION FACILITY WILL ALSO BE
DESTROYED. PLAN WILL MINIMIZE CHANCE
OF INJURING SOVIET TECHNICIANS ON THE
SCENE.

12.   ISRAEL WILL AGREE TO AN OPEN JERUSALEM.

The president's eyes were unsettling, cold as a crypt. He eyed
McBee intently. Without speaking, Sutherland drew a fresh cigar from his humidor, leaned back in his chair, and bit off the
wrapper.

McBee glanced outside. The sky was gray and baleful, hiding
a bright moon. The Washington night was cool, but not the usual
cold for this time of year.

"For over three quarters of a decade," the president began,
his jowls sagging noticeably, "people have envisioned a free
Israel. This country gives Israel billions of dollars of foreign
aid, weapons, and support worldwide. Yet we've just been buying them time."

"Until now," McBee offered in an admiring tone.

"With the Mediterranean on one side, Lebanon, the new
Jordan on the other, a friendly Saudi Arabia below, an equally

friendly Egypt to the southeast, and a controlled Palestinian State, Israel may finally have her chance.''

"Mr. President," McBee said seriously, "Israel's been fightin' Arab refugees and their neighbors forever. We must hope you and the next president can convince the prime minister of the urgency of this plan.''

"J.W.," the president whispered excitedly, "this plan even ends a three-thousand-year-old fight over Jerusalem. Sure,'' the president conceded, "there will be some bloodshed. But nothing compared to the past forty years.''

"Or the next forty,'' McBee added, "if this plan doesn't work.''

Sutherland took a puff from his cigar and slowly shook his head. "What a time to elect a Jewish president.''

Chapter 22

The Speaker's Campaign

Friday, November 19

IRV GRAYSON SHUT HIS OFFICE DOOR AND SCANNED THE ROOM once again. He hadn't been able to sleep the night before—ever since his congressman had called. The Speaker of the House of Representatives was making a personal call to Grayson's Shoe Store in downtown Quincy, a store he had operated successfully for over twenty years in the quaint and peaceful river town.

Grayson straightened his tie and carefully rearranged his desk. Every paper was neatly stacked on the right side of the desk. He hurriedly reached down and grabbed a paper clip from the carpet. He wanted his small office to be immaculate for his visitor. The soft knock on his door startled him for just a moment.

"Honey, the Speaker is here."

Grayson scampered excitedly across the room, his wife opening the door just as he got there.

"Irv, it's a pleasure to meet you," the Speaker bellowed, extending his right hand to Grayson. "Meet my attorney, Paul Douglas."

"A pleasure . . . a real honor to have you in my store," Grayson said sincerely, smiling at his wife as he ushered the two men into his office. He shut the door and walked toward his desk. Both the Speaker and Douglas had taken their seats in nearby armchairs.

"Always love comin' to Quincy," the Speaker began, "so much history in this little town. Paul here," he said touching his attorney on the arm, "is from Iowa, so he knows all about Quincy . . . and your great basketball tradition," he added with a grin.

Grayson nodded, but said nothing. He looked quizzically toward Douglas.

"Paul is here," the Speaker offered, catching Grayson's eye, "to answer any legal questions you may have."

"How long you been in business, Irv?" the Speaker asked, his tone still very cordial.

"Over twenty-two years," Grayson beamed proudly, "this very store, right on Maine Street."

"Mighty fine," the Speaker replied, "mighty fine." Durkin cleared his throat and sized up the man before him.

"You do know why I'm here?" the Speaker asked seriously.

"Yes."

"Since you're one of the twenty-six Democratic electors from Illinois, I wanted to take this opportunity to chat with you about Jonathan Starr."

Grayson pulled his chair closer to the desk, leaning forward, near the Speaker.

"I should tell you," he said, hesitating momentarily, "that Senator Johl called several days ago."

"And what did he want?" the Speaker asked sarcastically.

"He said give the system a chance. That Starr would be returned, and that our Founding Fathers would never have wanted what . . ."

"Go on," the Speaker said, waving his arm.

"That the Founding Fathers would be turning over in their graves because of what you're doing."

"Hogwash!" the Speaker snapped angrily. "This dilemma was never anticipated. I don't think you, as an elector, should waste your vote on a corpse."

"But what if he's not dead?"

"What if he is?" Douglas asked, speaking for the first time. "If he's dead, you couldn't give this government to Edwards, who just balanced the ticket. He's not qualified to be president. But," he said gesturing to his left, "you *know* the Speaker is. *He* should get the vote from his own home state."

"But Senator Johl . . ."

"Screw Johl!" the Speaker shouted. "Look, Irv," he said icily, his voice returning to normal, "Johl is really campaigning for Sutherland. He calls folks like you, using Starr as a facade. He wants electors to switch as much as I do, only he wants the votes for Sutherland. Well, Sutherland lost. And," he tartly added, "Starr is probably dead. That leaves me."

Grayson nervously played with his tie. It was patently obvious the Speaker was intimidating him.

"Look," the Speaker said calmly, "I don't want an answer today, but I want a call within the next few days. Okay?"

Grayson nodded, forcing a smile. "That's fair. I want you to know I respect you a great deal, and I will give your proposal serious thought."

"Good," the Speaker quickly replied, standing up to shake hands with Grayson. "You know you can vote for whomever you want, you're not bound to Starr."

"Yes," Grayson said softly, "I'm certainly aware of that. Over the past few weeks I've learned a lot about my responsibilities."

"Fine," the Speaker said, as he exited the office. He turned to face Grayson one more time. "Let me hear from you."

"You will."

The Speaker and his attorney left the store quickly, not stopping to talk to several surprised customers.

Grayson's wife ran to the office and hurriedly shut the door behind her. Her husband was on the phone.

"That's right, Senator Johl, he did exactly as you said he would. What? Well, as I told you last night, when Arthur Sutherland called me this past week, and explained the situation to me, I knew then what was the right thing to do."

Grayson leaned back in the chair and confidently winked at his wife, enjoying his newborn notoriety. "Tell the president he can count on me."

"How much longer to the airport?" the Speaker asked impatiently from the backseat.

"Baldwin Field is five miles away," the cabdriver replied.

The Speaker moved closer to Douglas. "So what you're saying," he whispered, "is Article 2 of the Constitution requires Starr to be there on the twentieth of January?"

"Right," Douglas replied softly. "Section One, Clause Seven, says the president, *before* he takes office, *shall* take the oath of office. *Shall* means mandatory."

"Good. Now tell me about Dr. Von Hoff?"

The attorney squirmed as he shook his head sideways.

"What does that mean?" the Speaker demanded.

"We've come up with nothing. Maybe I've been reading too many books. I thought he would be a Nazi war criminal or something."

The Speaker remained silent, looking at the miles of farmland surrounding them. He leaned back against the seat cushion, lost for a moment in private thought. Douglas didn't dare interrupt. Slowly, a smile, a newfound confident smile, formed around the Speaker's lips.

"Paul," he said quietly and calmly, "if Starr is returned, wouldn't the government require him to go to the best psychiatrists around?"

"Of course," the attorney responded curiously, watching the cab turn left into the airport entrance.

"And what hospital would Starr go to?"

"It would be Walter Reed. No doubt about it."

The Speaker smiled again. "Don't do anything more about doctors. I'll handle it myself."

Douglas nodded his assent. "What about Grayson?" he asked.

"I think we'll lose him. Johl's campaign is effective. We've got a big fight on our hands, but Starr only won the election by ninety-two electoral votes. If I can get most of Illinois, I'll be halfway there. We must concentrate our efforts in states where Starr won but where the GOP has its strongest roots. Then, I can pick away, vote by vote, and cause enough erosion to deny Starr 270 votes. Even if I fall short, and Starr wins, he must be sworn in on the twentieth. If he's not around, even assuming Edwards is vice president, he could only act as president, since the Twentieth Amendment won't apply. Presumably Starr won't be dead and he won't have failed to qualify. Then Congress will have to decide how to choose the new president. A Republican Congress with no precedent to draw on won't bend over to give it to Edwards. I'll see to that. As to our friend from Quincy," the Speaker concluded, "Grayson's obviously a Jew—his nose gave him away. He'll stick with the Jew Starr."

Douglas was surprised by the Speaker's last statement.

"Mr. Speaker," he asked nervously, "your fight for the presidency—well—it's not based on anti-Semitism?"

"Of course not, Paul," the Speaker responded quickly, affectionately patting the attorney on his leg. "I was just making an observation, one I believe to be entirely accurate. Now let's get going to Chicago. I must be in Jacksonville tomorrow."

CHAPTER 23
THE ARGUMENT

Saturday, November 20

REYNOLDS FIDGETED UNCOMFORTABLY IN THE CHAIR NEXT TO his bed, his feet propped over the neatly folded bedspread.

He looked outside his room, through the window to his right. Dusk lingered, the orange sun inflaming the San Francisco skyline. Downtown traffic barely existed.

He glanced at his watch and peered over his left shoulder, toward the woman sitting at the desk. She was poring through documents that were neatly piled behind her on the bed.

Reynolds stared at the stack of folders he had arranged on the small circular table in front of him. His attention returned to the folder on his lap. He scanned the document quickly and tossed it on the bed.

"I'm done," he exclaimed, "how about you?"

The intent young woman sitting at the desk replied without taking her eyes off the documents in front of her. "This is the last one."

He stood and gathered up the manila folders that were scattered throughout his hotel room, carefully placing them in a king-size brown briefcase.

Jo Decker shook her head in frustration as she handed Reynolds the last folder.

"No leads at all," she said, stretching her arms high above her shoulders, rotating her head in a circle, stretching and loosening her tired neck muscles.

"Nothing for me either," he replied, locking the briefcase and placing it in the corner of his closet.

"Did you really think one of our agents could be involved?" she asked softly, still rotating her head in a circle, rubbing her neck.

"Not really. But I wanted to check everything. I'll report this to the president. At least we eliminated another possibility."

"You're thorough," she said, then quickly added, "but not completely thorough."

He looked surprised. "What did I miss?"

"Our personnel files aren't here."

He laughed. "If you and I aren't above suspicion, we might as well give up."

Decker didn't return his laugh. Her mood became solemn.

"Do you think that will satisfy your president?"

"Why the sarcasm?"

She walked toward the window and looked outside, not noticing the gorgeous sunset. "Sutherland's playing politics with this situation."

"How?"

"He should name Edwards, or the Speaker. He's just dragging this out for the publicity."

"Where did you get your law degree?" he responded, returning her sarcasm. "The president must follow the law. He can't name anyone."

"Bullshit, Andy," she snapped, "he can do whatever he wants."

Reynolds sensed something about her tone. It wasn't just anger at the president. He stared at her, but her eyes wouldn't meet his.

"Jo," he said, "what's eating you?"

"You really want to know?"

He nodded his head, moving backward to sit on the chair at the desk.

"It's the hypocrisy of our entire government."

"That's a broad statement, Jo, want to get specific?"

"For instance," she began, pacing the room before him, like an attorney delivering a closing argument to a jury. "You and my father fought your asses off in Vietnam. My father lost his, and what did our distinguished government do?''

Reynolds shook his head. "I don't follow."

"In 1982 they dedicated a memorial to the dead servicemen. It took years for our government to do this. When it was dedicated, Reagan couldn't make it."

"So what?" he responded quietly, still confused by her attitude.

"So what!" she exclaimed. "Don't you think that's important? They had a ceremony at the National Cathedral, where the list of 57,000 was read by candlelight . . . *we* were there . . . but no president."

"Jo . . . I don't . . ."

She cut him off. "For fourteen years citizens fought the war of politicians. . . . When it's over, the country and those same politicians ignore us.

"Probably 500,000 wounded Americans . . . over four million who served . . . and what do they get . . . not gratitude . . . just exposure to Agent Orange."

"What does this have to do with Sutherland?" Reynolds wondered out loud, shocked by the uncharacteristic outburst of his closest aide.

"It's the government. Not just Sutherland . . . but the Congress and the stinking bureaucracy."

"How long have you felt like this?"

She ignored the question, but finally her eyes met his. She stared at him intently.

"There are 2,500 Americans still unaccounted for in Southeast Asia. There are still 300 missing from the Korean War. Shouldn't this government care?"

He shrugged his shoulders in exasperation. "Why now, Jo? Why these bitter feelings now?"

"I'm just expressing them now."

"No government is perfect. But we try . . . we all try."

"You of all people, Andy. A Vietnam veteran is one thing. But how can you stand what the government does to blacks?"

Reynolds stood up in anger. "For Christ's sake, Jo, how many social issues do we discuss today?"

"Too bad you weren't in Chicago for the mayor's election in

1982,'' she replied coldly, the veins in her neck strained with hatred. ''You could have seen how these good Americans treated a black candidate. And what they did to Jesse Jackson when he tried to get involved in the system is just as bad.''

''It's not all the government's fault. Society has problems . . . why today, Jo . . . why the concern today?''

''We have 2,000 agents and we can't even protect our own president-elect.''

''Is that it? Are you blaming me for Starr's kidnapping? Is that the bug you have today?'' he shouted at her, his anger causing him to shake.

''I don't blame you . . . Andy,'' she replied flatly. ''I blame a society where a violent crime occurs every twenty-four seconds. Where 12,000 handgun murders occur annually because the gun lobbyists control Congress. Where eight presidents were victims of assassination attempts, and four were killed.''

Reynolds harshly interrupted her. ''And where this Jewish president doesn't make it to office.''

They both stared at each other in silence. He looked at his watch. ''Your plane leaves in an hour. Should I take you to the airport?''

''Do you really want me back in Washington?''

''I do. There is work needed on our network between California and the Capitol. We've been through this once. I just . . .''

''I'll take a cab,'' she replied, grabbing her purse from the desk near the front door. She patted his arm as she left, making an effort toward reconciliation. ''Take care of yourself, Andy.''

''I'll call you tomorrow,'' he mumbled softly, shutting the door behind her.

CHAPTER 24

THE TRANCE

Midnight, November 20

THE SOFT KNOCK ON THE DOOR STARTLED THE AGENT, WAKING him from his stupor. He pulled himself up out of the chair next to his bed and glanced at his wristwatch. He had been daydreaming for thirty-five minutes. He tucked his shirttail into his pants and fumbled with the door chain before getting it open.

"Andy, what's wrong?" the brunette said sympathetically, as she entered the room. Kate kissed him gently on the lips, holding his chin with her soft hand.

"I must have dozed off," he whispered, as he entered the bathroom to splash water into his weary eyes.

"What time will they be here?" she asked from the other room.

"The doctor will be here in twenty minutes. I'm glad you're early." He wiped his face and entered the room smiling.

"Now that's better," she said, reaching up to kiss him again.

"This room has been the hub of activity lately," he said as he dialed room service.

"You mean last night?" she kidded, sitting on the bed behind him.

He smiled and spoke into the receiver. "Five Cokes and five coffees, room 318."

"I don't like Coke," she said as he hung up the phone.

"Tough," he replied laughing, opening the bottom drawer of his dresser.

As he turned to her, his mood changed. "Remember our discussion about Jo Decker last night?"

Wilson nodded her head. "How did your meeting go?"

"Terrible," he replied, handing her a manila folder. "Take a look at this," he said, pointing to the last page.

The reporter scanned Decker's personnel file. Reynolds reviewed the page, leaning over her left shoulder. Wilson looked up at him, confusion in her eyes.

"This seems to be discussing your relationship to her father, Colonel Decker."

"Right, keep reading."

She pointed toward the bottom of the single-spaced, typed page. "What does this mean?"

"It says the 'Eyes Only' file on her father is missing."

"So?"

Reynolds sat down next to her, moving closer to smell her perfume. "It means someone took the classified version of her father's death."

"Do you think she has seen it?"

"I do now, after today."

"What does the report say?"

"I killed her father," he said flatly without emotion.

"Oh, Andy," she muttered, putting her arm around him.

"There's more," he said quietly, his voice caught in his throat. "I could never tell Jo I killed Tom. I was ordered not to. Anyway, she would never understand or accept it. There's always a way out to Jo. She was told the official story. Tom disobeyed orders and attacked during a cease-fire. That's why his death didn't bring the 'honor' she wanted. She never fully understood why he did it."

Kate hugged Andy tightly. "Get it off your chest, Andy," she whispered, her voice velvety soft.

He gazed dumbly back at her, his mouth partially open, his hands trembling. "I filled out a top secret report. There was a big stink with the brass. I told them the Vietcong had violated this political cease-fire, and Tom was avenging the brutal murder of several of his men. Since the enemy wasn't abiding by the cease-fire, Tom wouldn't either." Reynolds shuddered, his breathing escaping in a rush. His mouth was dry. He looked at Kate. Tears were rolling down his face.

"The brass decided it would hurt the war effort if it was known a colonel intentionally violated the cease-fire. The president, at the time, was assuring the world that the United States would abide by the politically arranged cease-fire. This incident, if made public, would make the president look like a liar."

"A cover-up you could do nothing about," she muttered with understanding and compassion, still holding him tight.

"I was under orders to keep this secret. My report was sealed, and Tom's relatives were never to know. He was really a hero, but to the world he died in disgrace. This has haunted me all these years. And now, Jo must know. Which explains her recent behavior."

"What does it all mean, Andy?"

"I'm not sure," he responded, but pointing to the document in front of her, he added, "The entry is dated March. If she took it, she has known for eight months."

"Why would she take it, after all these years. Why now?"

"I'm not sure she took it. Maybe someone else did and gave it to her."

"Why?"

"I don't know, but she was a different person today. She really has been acting strangely for some time. I'm not sure what I think."

"Did you tell her about the doctor?"

"No," he said patiently. "I don't know why, but I didn't feel I could completely trust her, or her judgment."

Reynolds placed the folder back into the bottom drawer and watched Kate move toward the window to close the curtains. Her firm hips swayed seductively under her tight slacks. She turned around and caught him staring. They both smiled.

"Do you think this doctor can really hypnotize Nyberg and get the license plate number?"

"If anyone can, he can. Remember the Chowchilla kidnapping case in California. I think it was 1976. The driver of the bus remembered all but one digit of the involved vehicle's license plate number. Dr. Michaels was the person who hypnotized the subject."

"Would it be admissible in court?" she wondered.

"If we keep in mind he's a witness, not a victim or a defendant, I think over twenty states allow it. Anyway, I'm not concerned about arresting anyone yet, just getting Jonathan back."

"This will be one hell of a story, when it's over," she said sincerely, flashing a hopeful glance at Andy.

There was a loud knock at the door. Reynolds greeted the visitor.

"Thank you for coming, Doctor. As I indicated this morning, Kate Wilson will be observing."

"It's an honor, Miss Wilson," Dr. Michaels replied in a hoarse voice, as he firmly shook Kate's hand. She noticed a small scar below the doctor's Adam's apple. Other than his hoarse voice, the scar was the only remaining piece of evidence from a near-fatal automobile accident when he was attending medical school.

The distinguished-looking, middle-aged doctor took a chair from the nearby desk, pulling his suit pants up at the thighs before sitting.

"When will the subject be here?"

"Thirty minutes," Reynolds responded, sitting next to Wilson on the adjacent bed.

The doctor cleared his throat before explaining the evening's procedure. "As you both know, hypnosis is a temporary condition of altered attention in a subject that may be induced by another in which a variety of phenomena may appear spontaneously or in response to verbal or other stimuli."

Reynolds laughed at the explanation. "Sorry, Doctor, but remember to talk English to us laypeople."

Michaels smiled and cleared his throat again. "If Nyberg is in a highly suggestible state, and is willing, I can alter his consciousness and memory, thus increasing his susceptibility to suggestion."

"He'll be in a sleeplike state," Wilson offered.

"Exactly," Michaels replied, smiling at the reporter. "But keep in mind, hypnotic subjects have been able to pass lie detector tests while attesting to the truth of statements they made while under, which researchers knew were utterly false."

"Will you use truth serum?" inquired Reynolds, offering the doctor a Coke that had just been delivered by room service.

"Thank you," he replied, sipping from the eight-ounce bottle. "Sodium amobarbital won't be necessary. Nyberg has no motive to manufacture or invent false statements."

Reynolds handed Kate a cup of coffee. "I assume you don't want a Coke."

She smiled, carefully placing the cup and saucer on the round table next to her. "Go on, Dr. Michaels. This is fascinating."

"Hypnosis is not a mechanical device that attempts to serve a truth determinative function. Rather, it restores memory of an event that has been forgotten or psychologically suppressed. It's immaterial how the memory is quickened. Whether it's a song, face, or even newspaper," he added, smiling toward Kate, "it's sufficient if, by some mental operation, I can stimulate Nyberg's mind."

"What is the major difference," Reynolds began, "in being asleep or awake?"

The doctor cleared his throat again, placing his Coke on the carpet next to him. "In normal waking state, there are units of mind power and streams of suggestion. In hypnosis there is no mind power available to take notice of other things. The stream of suggestion represents one hundred percent concentration.

"Nyberg won't be asleep or lose awareness. He'll be more alert because of increased physical relaxation. He will be in complete control, able to come out of it at will."

"Dr. Michaels," Reynolds said seriously, his mood somber, "what if you draw a complete blank, what can be done?"

"As we discussed over the phone," the doctor replied, "there are drugs named amino pyridines . . . which have been remarkable with animals . . . but not proven safe with humans. Medical ethics would prevent me from using them today."

"Even with a direct order from the president of the United States?"

"Well," the doctor replied gently, "if that happens, I just . . . well I just don't know."

"Maybe I could administer the drug?" Reynolds offered, eyeing the doctor intently.

"No way," the doctor replied quickly, shaking his head. "The synthesized 3-4 diamino pyridine, which is more potent than 4 amino pyridine just hasn't been tested enough. But large doses of either one can cause convulsions . . . and other damage we don't even know about yet. They work on rats . . . but . . . ."

"They're here," Reynolds interrupted, hearing the knock on the door.

"Captain Studer, Patrolman Nyberg, thanks for coming." Reynolds extended his hand to the two policemen.

At Reynolds's request both men were dressed in street clothes. Nyberg was visibly nervous, his hand trying to keep his light brown hair off his forehead.

Dr. Michaels placed his arm gently around the patrolman.

"Brian, why don't you go wash up? It will help you relax," he said, motioning to the bathroom.

"As Mr. Reynolds knows," the doctor began, "I would prefer it if no one were present during this session." Looking toward the bathroom door, the doctor lowered his voice and whispered when he turned back to the others.

"Understanding the importance of this session, I have agreed you all may observe, but you must stay here, behind the subject. I don't want him to be in a position to see anyone but me. There can be no inadvertent communication. Understood?"

They all nodded their agreement. Michaels opened a case containing the tape recorder he had carried in with him. As he placed it upon the desk close to where Nyberg would sit, Wilson motioned for Reynolds to step outside the room.

"What is it?" Andy asked, gently pulling the door behind him.

"I had a scary thought. What if Nyberg is part of the kidnapping conspiracy? Suppose he has been programmed to give us a license number to start off a wild-goose chase?"

Reynolds leaned hard against the hallway wall, his left foot rubbing the carpet back and forth. He stared ahead, saying nothing, thinking.

"No problem," he responded, grinning at Wilson. "Let's look at it objectively. First, if they wanted to do that, why tear the pages from his book? Why not give us a phony number then? Second, how could anyone plan on, or guess, we would use hypnosis? I only thought of it two days ago."

Wilson laughed. "That's why you're the agent and I'm the observer."

He reached for her, pulling her hand toward the door, murmuring, "You're much more than that."

Reynolds thought about Kate—great looks, intelligence in abundance—but other women he had known over the years possessed these qualities. Perhaps it was her drive, her will, her talent, her restless, volatile energy that attracted him.

Inside, Dr. Michaels had positioned Nyberg in his chair facing the bathroom, his back to the others. Michaels methodically went through the facts concerning the day in question, taking notes as rapidly as Nyberg spewed out his story.

"Brian, I'm going to start. I won't add any new elements to your recollection. You must use recall, your memory won't work solely on suggestion. Don't change any events, just remember them."

Studer, Reynolds, and Wilson watched as Michaels started the tape recorder and tested Nyberg's hypnotic susceptibility. Finally, the subject entered a deep hypnotic state.

"Remember the events of early Wednesday morning, November 3, as they actually occurred, but as though it was on a television screen. We'll go forward or back in time, or even use stop action. It's just like watching a football game."

Captain Studer began to pace in front of the window, using extreme caution not to make any noise. Though the policeman had been a precinct captain for twenty years, he had never been involved in a major investigation. He could feel the perspiration on his forehead as he listened intently, praying Nyberg would remember.

"You are going to feel as if your body and mind have been completely rejuvenated, and you will be able to remember very clearly everything that happened. Now that memory is very clear in your mind, this does not disturb you."

The room was almost silent. The only noise was the soft-spoken voice of Patrolman Nyberg, who carefully recalled the entire event, except the license number.

Dr. Michaels sipped his Coke and tried another approach.

"Brian, describe again what happened when you saw the big laundry bag."

"Just that, a big bag. I saw a loose wire that the guy fixed."

Nyberg stopped talking. It appeared his breathing was becoming irregular. Studer took one step toward his officer, but Michaels held up his hand to stop him.

"Go on, Brian. Don't fight it. What do you see?"

"The entire left side of the trunk was solid steel. Not like a normal car. So was the other side. I noticed the driver's side of the car. It was thick, like it had been reinforced by steel. It was like an armored car, but it looked so ordinary at the time.

"There was also something funny about the paint. It was spotty, like it had been painted over several times. I thought my flashlight was bad at the time, but something was peculiar about that blue paint."

Michaels moved closer to Nyberg, eyeing his subject closely.

"What about the license number?"

"I see it. It's . . ."

Everyone in the room held their breath. Reynolds prayed this was the break that would blow the case open. Studer moved forward, gripping Reynolds's shoulder. Michaels never took his eyes off Nyberg.

"Go ahead," he began softly, his voice sounding emotionless, "tell us the license number."

"C . . . P . . . J . . ."

"Go ahead, Brian, give the rest."

Brian was sweating profusely, searching his memory.

"I didn't see the rest."

Reynolds grimaced as Kate put her head in her hands. They had been so close. So close.

"Reynolds," Studer whispered so softly Andy could hardly hear him. Studer put his hands over Andy's ear, cupping them as he hurriedly relayed the message.

"He wrote the numbers in the book . . . the book with the missing pages."

Reynolds quickly grabbed a piece of paper from the nearby table and scribbled a note for Dr. Michaels. The frustrated doctor saw the commotion in the back of the room and motioned for Reynolds to place the note on the bed next to Nyberg. Michaels leaned over, stretching his arm across the bed.

"Brian . . . the book . . . the notebook you write reports in . . . what license number did you write down?"

Nyberg sat expressionless. Then he said "CPJ807 . . . the blue Impala."

"All right!" Studer shouted as he grabbed Reynolds. Dr. Michaels quickly took Nyberg out of his trance. Nyberg appeared dumbfounded by the backslapping he was receiving.

"You're a good cop, son," Studer said shaking the patrolman's hand.

Reynolds escorted Dr. Michaels from the room, grabbing his right hand firmly. He shut the door and pulled a folder from his desk.

"Captain Studer, you will call the LAPD tonight to inform them this car was involved in a local bank robbery. I will have the FBI coordinate the investigation with you. You are now the local officer in charge from this end on the city level. My contact in the San Francisco FBI will take care of all the paperwork."

"You move fast," Studer replied.

Reynolds quickly wrote two lines on the report and pushed it into Studer's waiting hand.

"I've described the car. Even if they have changed the plates, we have enough to identify this car. If we can find it."

"The bank robbery sounds like the perfect cover. I suppose it's in my jurisdiction."

Reynolds smiled and nodded. "Of course. Our friends in L.A., on the city, state and federal level, won't suspect anything else. We'll mark it urgent. We'll tell them the robbers are suspected in a related Texas kidnapping."

"I suppose the . . ."

"The paperwork will be taken care of," Reynolds replied quickly, cutting off the captain in mid-sentence.

"I know you and Patrolman Nyberg will keep things quiet."

"We will," Studer said, hugging the dazed Nyberg.

Reynolds walked into the hall with both officers. "I can't tell you what this means."

"We know," answered Studer. "Just get him back alive."

The men bear-hugged in the hallway, patting each other's backs. "Good luck," Studer mumbled, as he walked down the hall with his right arm around Nyberg's shoulder.

Reynolds entered the room, looking for Kate.

"Bingo!" he shouted, raising his clenched fist in the air.

He knocked on the bathroom door. "We're going to L.A. tomorrow. I want to be there when they find the car. I'll call Jo in the morning." Then thinking out loud he added, "but I won't tell her why we're meeting in L.A."

Kate opened the door slowly and entered the room. She had a towel draped around her body, but it didn't cover her ample cleavage. Her firm, tanned thighs looked inviting.

She dashed to the bed, pulling the covers up as she dropped her towel. Reynolds undressed and turned off the lights as he joined her under the covers.

He kissed her passionately, his hands reaching between her legs. His index finger entered her, as he felt her wetness.

She leaned close and whispered in his ear. "Bingo."

CHAPTER 25

TORTURE

Sunday, November 21

HE OPENED HIS EYES SLOWLY, AWARE OF THE SICKENING STENCH of his own body. He felt the sweat on his shirt and trousers, the result of an unseasonably warm autumn evening in Los Angeles.

Starr sat up, pushing himself forward with his hands. He dropped his head on his upper chest, still not fully awake. He unbuttoned his shirt and closed his eyes again as he tossed the soaked fabric to the side. How much longer could he go on? How much stamina did he really have?

The daily reverie always ended with thoughts of his family. His three daughters, so energetic, so eager to learn. Their ambitions and plans needed the thoughtful guidance of two parents. Their futures, alone, gave him the resolve to survive.

Then there was Judy. He recalled the times he rolled over in bed and quietly watched her in the early morning. How she would move, stretching, her face bathed in the glorious sunlight that streamed through their bedroom window. As he remembered her gentle, peaceful sleep, he tried to imagine what she must be going through during his absence.

He also remembered her body. Her wonderful body. Muscular thighs, firm legs, always cleanly shaved. So smooth. So soft. How he loved to run his hands up and down those legs. Judy loved the long and sensual rubdowns he gave her, which would almost always lead to passionate lovemaking.

Lovemaking. It had been almost three weeks for Jonathan. Other than the three pregnancies, and the six-week, post-birth waiting period, this was the longest Jonathan had gone without sex. He missed it. He was horny and frustrated. With all the other worries and turmoil he suffered through each day, he ached enormously for Judy.

Jonathan found it difficult to sleep. On more than one occasion he had nightmares about losing his children. Sometimes his dreams were pure fantasy, allowing him to see the son he never had. The boy who would carry the Starr name and family tradition. Sometimes he cursed when he woke up in the night . . . the nightmare being reality . . . not a dream.

During the first few days of his captivity, Starr had little contact with his kidnappers. Len Allen, the obvious leader of the group, had not said more than six words to him. Allen was a big man, with strong, wide shoulders, a thick neck, and skin as tough as mule hide. He was boorish, pompous, and petty. His heavy features and thick eyebrows, along with his personality and build, made him a perfect candidate for head bouncer at any big city bar.

Paul Michael Riley, member two of the kidnapping team, was short, with a squat body, like a Little League catcher losing the battle of the bulge.

The third man controlling Starr's destiny, Jim Olson, was a physical anomaly. His head was large, but not out of proportion to his neck and shoulders. However, his arms and legs were thin, his hands and feet small, almost dainty. He had short, thin fingers with pink tips and neatly manicured fingernails. His skin was ruddy, making him look younger than his years.

There was a fourth person involved with the captivity team: Vicky Roe. She was a living centerfold from the pages of *Playboy* or *Penthouse*. She had beautiful blond hair, which she wore in a ponytail. She had the perfect 36–24–36 build. The first time Jonathan saw her, she was wearing a tight white sweater and pink shorts. Her legs and thighs were very well built, finely muscled, and deeply tanned. Though he could tell she was wearing a bra, he could still see her erect nipples through the sweater. At least Jonathan had not lost his hunger for sex. Vicky Roe was able to trigger sensual dreams . . . and more thoughts of Judy.

Something very peculiar was happening this November morning. As Starr pulled himself out of bed, all four of his wardens made their way into the basement dungeon.

Allen perused the basement jail house with great pride. He walked over to the toilet near the middle of the room and spit forcefully into the water. Riley and Olson could barely contain themselves, knowing full well what was in store for the senator.

Allen glanced at Roe in silence. He understood his employer wanted to determine how much information Starr really possessed about the activities of organized crime, the information he never used at the Senate hearings. Vicky's job was to befriend the unsuspecting captive so he might divulge that desired information when he was in a less resistant mood.

Allen eyeballed his pathetic-looking prisoner and motioned Starr to his bed.

"Mr. Senator," Allen began in mock respect, "we are hereby authorized to advise you that within the next few days Tommy Duncan will make it known to the president of the United States that he was the person who arranged your kidnapping."

Starr was expressionless as he listened to Allen explain how the kidnapping had been carried out. He was not surprised. The only person Starr had been able to think of who had the motive, and obviously the means and opportunity, was Tommy Duncan.

Allen smiled to himself as he explained to Senator Starr what would be taking place in the future.

"We were told yesterday by Mr. Duncan to start making life

miserable for you. Whether you're ever going to be returned alive is seriously in doubt. Whether you'll return with all parts of your body is also seriously in doubt," Allen said icily, staring directly at Starr.

Allen walked over to Starr and brutally pushed him back against the wall.

"You're going to go through excruciating pain," Allen began, unable to conceal the pleasure he derived by this encounter. "We'll break your toes, then crack your ankles. We'll work up your fuckin' body and break and crush your legs and knees."

Starr said nothing. He closed his eyes, took a deep breath, and silently prayed to himself. Allen continued to preview his tale of torture.

"We'll spring your arms right from their sockets. Your wrists will be twisted until they break. You'll be punished just enough to stay alive. You will then experience the ultimate humiliation. The removal of your *cock*!" Allen shouted the last word and Starr flinched, sliding into the corner of his bed, placing his back against the wall. Starr's lips began to tremble, his eyes watered, but he said nothing. He couldn't. He was physically and emotionally drained. Starr looked around the room. He could feel Allen's stare, feel the sting in his eyes, but no one spoke.

Allen looked down at his pathetic prisoner and shook his head in disdain. "And to think the country elected such a spineless asshole," he snarled, reaching into his pocket and pulling out a large syringe.

Starr sat motionless, his hands folded before him as though in prayer, until he saw the needle. As he lunged forward toward Allen, the large man unexpectedly and with great ease and force kicked the stunned prisoner in his Adam's apple. Starr grabbed his throat and coughed violently, gasping desperately for air.

Allen grabbed Starr's head, holding him in a hammerlock as he maneuvered the needle into Starr's right arm.

A terrified scream ricocheted from one wall to another around the windowless room. Jonathan Starr knew all about the effects drugs could cause the body, and considering the source, he feared the worse.

Allen angrily pushed the exhausted Starr against the wall. His body slumped on the bed as he curled into a ball.

But Allen wasn't finished.

"Hey!" he shouted, "I've got something to tell you. Listen up." Allen pushed Starr in the shoulder, feeling little resistance or strength left in the prisoner.

Suddenly Jonathan experienced gut-clutching agony.

"What have you given me?" He struggled with each word as his eyes found Allen. Starr tried to focus, to regain his equilibrium as he struggled to push himself up into a sitting position.

"With all your experience from the Drug Commission, I expect you to be able to answer your own question in a few days," Allen responded sarcastically.

The powerfully built man leaned down toward Starr. "Which daughter should we kill first?"

Starr's body jerked erect in the bed. He stared at Allen in shocked horror, his mouth opened, but the words wouldn't . . . couldn't come out.

He squeezed his head tightly. Allen's statement and the obvious effect of the drug made Starr dizzy and incoherent. He strained and struggled to reply, visibly grimacing as he scowled in disgust. "I swear . . . I'll kill *you*!" he screamed the last word, "if you ever go near my kids."

"That's a laugh," Allen snapped, "*you'll* never go near your kids."

The kidnapper walked to the door and turned to Starr. "Duncan will negotiate his release. You can bet your life on it . . . and," he added bitterly, "you are."

Allen forcefully slammed the door.

Silence.

Jonathan lay in his bed exhausted, even after three hours of sleep. He had been through the most dehumanizing and degrading experience of his entire life. Being made to feel dirty— treated like the lowest scum. He noticed that the lights in the room were turned on. He twisted to his left and saw Vicky Roe. She was wearing a white T-shirt and a red bikini bottom. As she walked closer to him, he noticed she had tears in her eyes.

"Mr. Starr," she said emotionally, almost sobbing, "they

made me do it. I'm a prisoner here as much as you are. I had nothing to do with the kidnapping. I am being forced to help these men. If I don't, they will turn me over to the police. I have a criminal record and have been living in Los Angeles under an assumed name, and Duncan and these guys know it. I'm very sorry if I hurt you.''

She walked closer to Jonathan and sat on the side of his bed. He eyed her suspiciously. His instincts told him she was being honest with him. He put his right arm around her and brought her face toward his shoulder. She looked up at him, and slowly moved over to kiss him. It was a gentle kiss . . . then a red-hot kiss. As their mouths opened, Jonathan began to feel passion. Within seconds Vicky's right hand was rubbing his crotch. His left hand slowly moved to her shirt, and within moments he had raised the T-shirt above her breasts. As they continued their erotic kiss, Starr began fondling her breasts, feeling the firmness, the erect nipples. He slowly moved his hand down her stomach, inserting his finger under the red bikini.

Her fingers softly traced over his legs, up and down, but he remained almost totally motionless, as if his body, his very soul, were detached from his brain.

When her gentle and sensuous lips engulfed his penis he wanted to say no. To protest in some fashion that he really didn't want it this way. He thought of Judy. That he wanted to kiss her again . . . to touch her again or hold her against his body. But he surrendered—peacefully, still the prisoner. Only this time a prisoner to her irresistible sensual powers, a willing captive to her own act of submission.

He collapsed, totally drained, completely limp. She moved toward him, and without saying a word, kissed him on the cheek. She smiled softly, rose from the bed, and walked out of the room, locking the door behind her.

Allen got up and turned the monitor off, quickly returning to the table to discard.

"She's a good actress," said Allen, "and Starr must know by now she's a good whore," he added with a grin, and a touch of jealousy.

"Do I get a blow job as part of the deal?" asked Riley, becoming aroused just thinking of the beautiful blonde, tugging his crotch with his left hand.

Allen shook his head. "Not now . . . but maybe later."

"I think she likes him," Olson said, picking up a card.

"It will make her job easier, more convincing to Starr," Allen responded. "Gin."

"Fuck you, Len," Olson snickered, dropping his cards on the table. "Does Vicky know the room is bugged?"

"No," Allen replied quickly, "and it stays that way. We only turn on the monitor when she's in there. That's why I got it hidden."

"What will we do with our *Actress* once she delivers the information . . . or fails?" wondered Riley.

Allen grinned: "The same we always do. We'll kill her."

CHAPTER 26

UP, UP, AND AWAY

Monday, November 22

REYNOLDS HELD THE TELEPHONE TIGHTLY IN HIS RIGHT HAND as his left hand firmly gripped the steering wheel. He glanced at the speedometer—35 mph. He would be there in twenty minutes.

Finally, mercifully, he was twenty minutes from Jonathan Starr.

"That's right, Mr. President," Reynolds responded, peering into the rearview mirror for a quick look at Kate Wilson, who sat silently in the back seat.

"The LAPD was told this was the car involved in the San Francisco bank robbery. Within twenty-four hours a patrolman located the car in a parking lot on Spring Street, the warehouse district.''

"Did it have the same license plate number?" wondered the president.

"It did, and by using Nyberg's hypnosis description, we're sure we have the same car.''

"Do you know the exact warehouse?''

Reynolds hesitated and glanced at Decker, who stared ahead through the windshield. Her face was expressionless, her mood solemn.

"No, Mr. President,'' Reynolds conceded, "Jonathan's in one of three warehouses. They form three quarters of a rectangle, like a courtyard without the fourth building. The car was parked in a common parking lot.''

"Was?'' the president remarked, "what does 'was' mean?''

"The car isn't there anymore,'' Reynolds responded flatly.

Sutherland leaned back in his chair and stared at the ceiling. He looked over at Thomas Whyte, who had been listening on the Oval Office squawk box. Whyte shrugged his shoulders.

"What choice do we have?'' the president muttered, as Whyte reluctantly nodded his head in approval.

"Beg your pardon,'' Reynolds said, noticing his speed was up to forty.

"Sorry, Andy, I was talking to Thomas Whyte. Do you think he's there?''

"I do.'' Hearing no response from Sutherland, Reynolds offered his rationale. "I think we got lucky. . . . The patrolman must have spotted the car at a time the kidnappers were returning. They must have hidden the car later.''

"Or else it's a trap,'' offered the president.

"I doubt it. Anyway . . . we really have nothing to lose. Everyone is in place.''

"Give me the rundown.''

"The entire area is surrounded . . . a two-block radius. There's no way out for them. The men are waiting for my arrival.''

The president sighed and took a long drag off his pipe.

"Do it, Andy.'' The president's voice had a dreadful finality. "And call me when you get our man.''

As Reynolds cradled the phone, Jo Decker spoke. "I can't understand how you can be so hypocritical," she exclaimed, turning an ugly glance toward Wilson. "Her presence endangers the mission and violates specific Service rules."

"I'm making the rules now . . . and the exceptions," Reynolds responded crisply, trying to control his anger. He stared at Decker. "Kate and I have an understanding. This mission won't be front-page news *unless* we get Jonathan back."

"*Then* she gets her exclusive," Decker added sarcastically.

"Damn right she does!" Andy shouted, gripping the wheel with both hands. "Kate has been a great help. I *owe* her this."

Decker wasn't satisfied with the explanation, but she moved on to another subject.

"Why am I going with you in the same car?"

"I want you with me."

"Normally," she emphasized the word emphatically, "standard operating procedures would have us approach the target from both sides. I'm second in command . . . why don't I hit the back of the warehouse?"

Reynolds was silent and so was Kate Wilson. She stared at the dark carpet under her feet. Decker raised her eyebrows, and her voice.

"I *am* second in command?" It was a question, not a statement.

"You are. Look," he began, trying to explain his strategy, "under these circumstances we need to work together. We know each other's moves, and we don't know which warehouse. It will work out."

Reynolds knew he had to sound convincing, but he was disappointed in his performance. Decker was absolutely correct about SOP—that's why Roger Jefferson would be entering the back of the middle warehouse when Andy walked through the front.

Decker rolled down her window for a breath of fresh air. Even at 10 P.M. on a November evening, L.A. was warm. She eyed Reynolds carefully. He could feel her eyes staring.

"You took a few big swipes in the Senate yesterday."

Reynolds forced a grin. "Yeah, they said Sutherland was to

blame because he entrusted the investigation to me, instead of the sacred FBI.''

Decker nodded her head, but said nothing. Senate criticism didn't make this mission easier. It really didn't matter; the stakes couldn't get any higher.

Reynolds stopped the car at the roadblock. The street intersecting Spring was dark; not even the streetlights were working. At least they didn't have to worry about a traffic jam or innocent bystanders being involved, not at this hour, or this location.

"Kate. Stay here."

She held up her hand and smiled, "I understand. We've been through this at least . . . ten times."

"Good." He shut the car door and turned toward the cop who addressed him by name.

"As I live and breathe, Andy Reynolds." Andy shook hands with Dick Roodman, the bureau chief from L.A. The big redheaded officer grinned as he continued to grasp Reynolds's hand between his own.

"Andy, I knew when I heard you would be here we weren't dealing with bank robbers, but I suspect the kidnapping part is right."

Reynolds forced a smile and looked admiringly at his colleague. "Same as always. You're right. Is everything set?"

"We've got this area completely surrounded. By the way, who's the broad?" Roodman inquired, pointing to Wilson, who was sitting straight up in the back seat of Reynolds's car, listening intently to each word.

"Let's just say she's an assistant."

Roodman frowned but nodded his assent. Reynolds motioned for Decker.

"Dick, this is my second in command."

"Pleased to meet you . . . Miss . . . .''

"Jo Decker," she responded, firmly shaking his hand.

Reynolds joined them as he set down the walkie-talkie.

"They tell me there's been no movement anywhere, no lights, no nothing."

"Right," agreed Roodman. He took Reynolds aside and placed his arm around the agent's shoulder.

"I don't think the bastards are in there," he whispered.

Reynolds leaned toward the redhead and whispered louder, "I do."

Roodman, Reynolds, and Decker walked a block and a half in silence, looking for any movement, any sign of life.

They finally arrived at the parking lot. The building to their left was eight stories, with almost every glass window broken. The years had been unkind to this deserted structure, its bricks chipped and discolored. As they crept closer, not using their flashlights, they heard the crunching sound of broken glass.

"Shit," Roodman uttered, "it's all over."

"Tiptoe," Reynolds commanded as they moved toward the middle building.

The six-story, red brick warehouse appeared about ready to collapse. Because it was in such shambles, and its facade looked so vulnerable, Reynolds decided they would start here. It was a hunch, but the kidnappers had a history of unpredictability. He noticed, however, the building to his right had windows that were completely boarded from top to bottom. Reynolds took two small steps toward Roodman, realizing they weren't stepping on glass any longer.

"Dick," Reynolds whispered, "you go into that building." He motioned to his right. "Jo will stay out here and let us know if she hears or sees anything. If someone gets in trouble, fire two quick shots. We don't need dead heroes."

Reynolds moved forward in almost total darkness to the front door. It was unlocked. He took one step inside and then heard a loud crash.

"What the . . ." He stopped in mid-sentence. Jo Decker, his number one aide, Green Beret extraordinaire, had just fallen over a trash can.

Roodman, who had crawled into the other warehouse after removing two loose boards, looked over at Decker in disgust, mumbling to himself, "Goddamn women."

Len Allen dropped the cards he was holding on the table and motioned for silence. He stared toward a nearby window he had covered with plywood, but said nothing. He barked out his next command to Riley.

"See what that noise is." Riley quietly peered through a

small opening between the boards, straining to see into the darkness. The bright moon above was his only light.

"The trash can's down, but I don't see anyone."

"Fuck," Allen snarled, jumping from the table. "The wind didn't do it. They've found us." He turned toward Olson who still sat stiffly at the table.

"Go to the roof and get ready; take Vicky. Paul Michael and I will get Starr. And remember," Allen added in a firm voice, "shoot to kill."

Olson and the girl ran quickly to the back stairs. Riley and Allen drew their guns and silently descended the nearby stairs to the basement.

Reynolds walked carefully in the darkness, feeling the wall to his right as he moved past a hallway. He was still cursing about Decker's stupidity. He was dumbfounded. There was no way she should make such a mistake. Not after all her years of training and experience. Sweat was pouring from his face as he finally came to the realization he had been fearing for days.

She had not made a mistake.

He stood motionless and listened, his eyes staring into almost total darkness. He glanced around quickly, his pupils transmitting a barrage of information to his brain. His keenly trained mind ingested all the details in these brief, precious seconds.

Some moonlight from a nearby window forced itself into the building. He tried to make out what was in front of him. It appeared to be stairs. Hearing nothing, he decided to use his flashlight.

A spiral staircase. Now he faced a dilemma. Did he stay on the main floor, or climb the stairs?

He observed the staircase carefully, straining his eyes, looking up as far as he could. He didn't dare shine his light in that direction.

He gripped the handrail firmly, still not sure whether he should go further. His heart beat so fast he could almost sense a pain in his chest.

Then he heard something. From the other end of the warehouse. It wasn't voices . . . maybe a rat . . . maybe.

The faint sound was heard again. Reynolds took three steps

away from the staircase, shuffling his feet, sliding slowly over the wooden floor so he couldn't be heard. There it was again. This time he knew.

Another staircase. It had to be; footsteps. He had found them. He excitedly fumbled for his walkie-talkie.

"Don't move," came the command from the darkness, as the man from the corner moved toward Reynolds. "Or you're a dead man," he intoned in his mellifluous baritone.

Reynolds gripped the walkie-talkie in his left hand. "May I turn around?" the agent requested, trying to decide in the split second he might have whether he could call for help.

"Drop it . . . now," the other man barked.

The walkie-talkie dropped from Reynolds's fingers as he opened his left hand, the clinking noise echoing near the staircase. Reynolds slowly turned around and eyed his captor.

"Who the fuck *are* you?" the agent asked in astonishment.

"My name is not important," the man replied, keeping his gun pointed at Reynolds.

The agent looked over his shoulder, at the staircase. "I'm going to sit down."

"Fine."

"Why do you keep following me?" Reynolds inquired, staring into the gun held in the other man's steady hand.

"On the contrary," came the calm reply, "you really keep following me. I guess it's our quest to find our mutual friend."

"Why do you want Starr?"

"That's not important."

"It is to me," Reynolds replied, raising his voice.

The man quietly moved to his prey. "It would serve you well to remember who has the gun."

Reynolds remained quiet for a few seconds. If he could stall the man, just for a few more minutes, the FBI would be there.

"Why didn't you kill me at the farmhouse?"

"I have no reason to kill you. Anyway, killing a man of your stature would only complicate matters."

"For whom?"

The man smiled. "It's not important . . ."

"Wait a minute," interrupted Reynolds, "if you want Starr, why didn't you take him. He's here."

"That statement will be true for another . . . two minutes."

Reynolds answered him with silence, his eyes full of both loathing and resignation. The man knew those eyes, he had seen the combination of hatred and the recognition of mortality.

"Two minutes, I don't . . ."

Reynolds was startled by the loud noise above. He could sense a vibration. The sound was getting louder, a shrilling, sickening noise.

"My God!" Reynolds exclaimed, staring at the man, "you knew."

The man nodded his head and stepped backward, away from Reynolds.

"I will find them later. I won't stop them now. I suspect you will foolishly try."

Reynolds lurched off the step and stared at the man with the gun. "Shoot me, pal, because I'm going up to the roof."

The man eyed Reynolds with admiration. "I won't stop you now. You don't have enough time." Reynolds cupped his hands and shouted toward the front door. "Jo . . . call the LAPD— get a helicopter over here!" He screamed the last few words, his eyes wide, straining as he focused on the top of the stairwell.

The man watched in silence as Reynolds leaped up the spiral staircase, two steps at a time. He yelled into the walkie-talkie, trying to catch his breath. "Get to the roof. They've got a copter."

Reynolds saw Starr being shoved into the helicopter. He was alive. At least he was alive! Reynolds drew his gun. He aimed— he couldn't fire. The helicopter was off the roof.

He acted on instinct—running as fast as he could, his athletic ability the only asset that could get him there on time. He saw a man leaning out of the copter. And he saw his gun.

Reynolds was almost at the end of the roof. The copter was hovering above at the end of the building. He had made up his mind. In one second he would grab the copter or he would fall to his death.

Reynolds leaped in the air as the helicopter soared upward, far above the building. He was gripping the bottom rail with both hands, his body swinging back and forth. It was like being on monkey bars . . . only as he glanced below he saw he was one hundred feet above ground.

He desperately pulled himself up, trying to look into the copter. Now that he was here, what would he do, what could he do?

"Goddamn instinct," he muttered to himself as he saw the gun pointed toward him. He swung his body under the copter and avoided the bullet he heard go over his head.

The noise from the helicopter was deafening. He thought he heard shouting from above. He was hanging on with both hands, but his arms were tiring fast, too fast. He had to make one last attempt to get inside.

He started swinging his body, feeling his momentum sway the copter back and forth.

"Kill the black bastard!" screamed Olson over the noise of the helicopter as he desperately tried to keep it balanced.

"I'm trying, asshole," Allen snarled as he leaned out the copter, frantically searching below for his prey. His left hand was gripping the inside of his seat as he stretched himself, waiting for another opportunity to shoot.

Reynolds started to swing himself again, feeling the strain in his arms. If he didn't make it this time, there wouldn't be a next time. As his body moved back and forth, he glanced at the large guns mounted at the base of each side of the copter. Whoever had Starr had come prepared. The artillery made the Vietnam copters he knew so well look like kiddie cars.

He pulled his left leg onto the bottom bar of the copter. He lunged forward into the cab, knocking the gun from Allen's hand.

Starr lurched forward, trying to keep Allen away. Reynolds glanced at Jonathan. He was screaming something at the top of his lungs. Reynolds strained to hear but the noise was too much.

Starr moved forward again, briefly grasping Reynolds's hand. Riley struggled with Starr in the back of the copter, finally knocking him unconscious with the butt of his gun.

Reynolds desperately tried to grab something, anything, from inside the copter. He balanced his body with his left knee as he lunged for the pilot.

Allen punched him in the face, momentarily stunning the

exhausted agent. Riley took his gun and aimed, trying to move around Allen, whose large frame was screening his target. Reynolds saw the gun out of the corner of his eye and quickly moved back, trying to reach the outside bar, but it was too late.

He felt the bullet strike his left arm. He struggled toward the opening . . . grasping the railing below him. The pain in his left arm was making him dizzy. He glanced below.

A building, a tall, twelve-story structure, was about fifty feet below. The agent could feel Allen beating on his shoulders and understood that it would be only seconds before he was shot again.

He stared at the roof below, taking one quick glance at Riley's gun. He let go, just as the bullet passed his left ear, barely ticking him as he fell.

CHAPTER 27

SKY DEATH

Midnight, November 22

BOB MACK HOVERED ABOVE, AS IRATE PILOTS ARGUED THE MERits of their case to each other. Fortunately, there were no apparent injuries. The officer grabbed the microphone to his right.

"Copter 18 to base. Come in base."

"We acknowledge, report."

"Two-car accident at intersection of Mark and Jason Streets. No apparent injuries. Send squad car. The two young fellas look like they want to go a few rounds."

Mack chuckled, put the microphone down, and turned north toward the outskirts of the warehouse district. Other than the accident, it was an unusually peaceful night for the LAPD lieutenant.

He reached for the lunch box his wife had packed, pulling out a few carrots from a cellophane bag.

"Copter 18 . . . come in."

"This is copter 18."

"Bob . . . you're not going to believe this," said the panic-stricken voice from base. "I know you're sitting down . . . well, here goes, seconds ago we received an emergency call from Roger Jefferson of the Secret Service."

"What?" Mack whispered excitedly.

"You are to head to Spring Street in your district, near the old Murnane Warehouse. There is a helicopter. You must follow it."

"Only follow?"

"Right."

"What if it's armed . . . or . . ."

"Just follow them," came the cold reply.

Mack was two minutes away from the target area. He tried to slow down his breathing, fearful he would start to hyperventilate. He nervously checked his control panel.

"Base . . . this is copter 18."

"Bob . . . this is Commander King."

"Larry . . ." Mack interjected, "what exactly do you want from me?"

"Just follow them. We have six more copters that should be there within ten minutes."

Mack took a deep breath, he would be at Spring Street within ninety seconds. "Why can't I defend myself?"

There was no response.

"Larry, we've been friends too long. Who's in that copter?"

"Jonathan Starr," the commander replied. "All copters have the same orders. You'll be there first. We can't lose them. Acknowledge."

Mack stared at the radio in disbelief. "I acknowledge," he weakly responded, his mind flashing back to his wife and daughter. He glared ahead, leveling the copter. He wasn't moving forward any longer. His lights beamed straight ahead.

"I've got the target helicopter in front of me . . . wait . . .

there's a man . . . my God . . . there's a man hanging outside the copter . . . Jesus . . . what should I do?''

"Nothing," came the reply through the radio. "Just observe and report.''

"Larry . . . that man will fall . . . somebody is hitting . . . or pushing him. He's . . . oh my God!'' Mack screamed into the mike, "he fell out.''

The horror-stricken lieutenant maneuvered the copter toward the target, shining his searchlight for the body. He clutched the throttle, panic running through his body.

"Larry!'' he cried into the mike, "that man may be okay. By some miracle he fell on the roof of a nearby building.''

Mack turned off his light and hovered where Reynolds had fallen. He could sense the target helicopter would determine his fate.

Len Allen surveyed the entire area. No other helicopters were in sight. He glared toward Mack.

"Let's see how these guns work.'' He moved to the controls.

"What are you going to do?'' inquired Olson, clutching the steering mechanism firmly with his trembling hands. They were shouting at each other, as the ferocious blades produced near-deafening noise.

"I'm going to blow the bastard to hell,'' Allen shouted confidently as he aimed the weaponry toward Mack. "He knows who we are. He's been ordered not to shoot. If we don't blast him, others will follow. This is our only chance to get out.''

Allen aimed the guns toward his target. "Move twenty degrees to the left,'' he ordered the pilot, as the long steel tubes of death focused on their ultimate mark.

"Good-bye, asshole,'' Allen muttered as he pushed the button, a little red button that could destroy so much.

Mack saw the blast of fire from the enemy copter. Surprisingly there was no pain, only remorse mixed increasingly with mellower tranquility. He saw his seven-year-old daughter, her curly black hair flying in the wind as she kept running in slow motion toward his outstretched arms.

The helicopter exploded with devastating vehemence, causing a red flash to burst upon the skyline. Broken rotors flailed all around, and suffocating smoke engulfed the dead pilot as he crashed into the ground.

"Go to the waterfront," Allen directed without any emotion, "I'll show you where we land."

"God . . . no!" Kate Wilson screamed in horror as she watched the explosion above. Agents were running all around her, trying to impose some order on the tragic event.

Richard Roodman grabbed her arm firmly. He thought the reporter was in shock.

"Where is Decker?" he shouted directly into Kate's ear.

She collapsed against the FBI agent as he wrapped his arm around her.

"You're not used to this, are you?" he asked in a gentle tone.

She nodded her head, trying to fight back the tears, as she clutched his shoulders. Finally, Wilson moved out of Roodman's hold.

"I haven't seen Decker at all."

He grabbed her arm. "We've located Andy. He's going to be all right."

She smiled, no longer trying to control her emotions. Big tears rolled from her eyes as she ran with Roodman toward a nearby building.

Kate was out of breath when they reached the roof. An agent was dressing Reynolds's shoulder wound. He had been propped up against a nearby planter so he could sit upright. Wilson saw the pain in his eyes, and it wasn't physical pain.

Roodman leaned down and patted Andy's knee. "Thought you might want some company."

Reynolds looked at Kate. "Thanks, Dick," he responded, motioning for Kate to move closer. His head was spinning like a top.

"You see that bed of flowers over there?" Reynolds asked, motioning with his head. "I landed right in the middle. The flowers and the thick soil cushioned my fall. It saved my life."

"My God," she uttered, surveying the area, "another ten feet . . . you . . ."

"Another ten feet," he conceded, "in either direction, you and I wouldn't be talking."

"Where do you hurt?"

He tried to laugh but the pain was too intense. "Where don't I hurt would be easier to answer."

She leaned on her knees, scooting closer to him. She held out her hands and gently placed them behind his neck, pulling him close to her, kissing his forehead.

"Thank God, Andy . . . I . . . when I saw you fall . . ."

"There . . . there," Andy whispered, comforting his sobbing girlfriend, "I'm going to be fine. My shoulder is only bruised, the other one doesn't have much more than a flesh wound. My legs and butt are killing me, and my back is numb. But I'll make it."

She wiped his forehead with her handkerchief, then looked over her left shoulder. "The ambulance attendants are here. I'll go with you."

He stared at her, but said nothing. She noticed a change of mood . . . from despair to reflection.

"Penny for your thoughts?" she asked softly.

He began speaking, grimacing in pain as he moved his shoulders. "I'm in this whole mess because Jonathan talked me into heading his Secret Service detail. I can remember how excited he was during the primaries . . . I remember . . ."

"Andy!" Kate shouted, shaking his head violently when his eyes closed. She felt a strong hand on her shoulder and looked up.

"It's okay," Roodman said reassuringly as he helped Kate to her feet. "He's just passed out."

Kate stood silently as they carried Reynolds away on a stretcher. Like Andy, her thoughts went back to the primaries, the convention, and the great debate.

Those had been happy times, challenging times, as Starr took his campaign to the people.

CHAPTER 28
THE RELIGION ISSUE

Six Months Before the Election

STARR STOOD SILENTLY BY THE ROYAL BLUE DRAPES, OBSERVING the cluster of taxis haphazardly switching lanes as only New York cabbies do. His view from the eighteenth floor of the Waldorf-Astoria focused on Park Avenue at 50th Street.

"It's about time," Orear mentioned as he looked at his wristwatch. "Nervous?"

Starr turned to face him. "Not really. But it does hit the Jewish issue head-on."

"Look," Orear began, "the media and politicians are finally talking about it. Don't worry; it's to our advantage. Nobody but one crazy senator and his evangelist friend ever says anything anti-Semitic in public."

"Yeah," retorted Starr unconvincingly, as he straightened his tie in front of the mirror. "But a group of rabbis might cause trouble," Starr said, as Orear helped him with his navy blue suit jacket.

"Leave the worrying to me. It's late April and you've won ten out of the past eleven primaries. You're getting 6 P.M. news while Sutherland has to pay for his airtime."

"He's unopposed."

"Sure," Orear replied, "that's his problem. This primary is where the action is. Within ten days, though, this one will be over, too!"

The quiet knock at the door signaled the candidate—time to leave for another meeting.

The entourage quickly made its way to the Empire Room, walking over a huge medallion, the "wheel of life," embedded on the foyer floor by Louis Rigal many years ago.

As Starr entered the room he was warmly received by the group of rabbis who were gathered there to meet him. Jonathan noticed the large room's three huge chandeliers, each with over one hundred individual candles, complete with elegant dangling crystals.

Jonathan briskly moved to his left, pacing over the green carpeting, sprinkled with gold and blue leaves symmetrically designed.

Starr extended his hand to Rabbi Sidney Rothman, a short, distinguished-looking man who had arranged the meeting. Starr stood behind a table centered in front of the room next to two rabbis. Jonathan scanned the vast audience before him, recognizing representatives from the National B'nai B'rith, United Jewish Appeal, the American Israel Public Affairs Committee, the Union of American Hebrew Congregations, and the Board of the American Jewish Congress. Rabbi Rothman himself was co-chair of the Committee of Concerned American Jews.

The religious leaders had an opportunity to share and express their concerns with the candidate. The questions and answers were candid and serious. But after thirty minutes Jonathan was becoming uneasy. Many of the questions presumed he would automatically favor Israel—on any issue.

Then lightning struck.

The words were spoken by the short, articulate Rabbi Rothman—words that were a flame, which might ignite the fire.

"Senator, we are somewhat concerned that President Sutherland does not support the independent state of Israel like he should and that our foreign alliances with the Arab nations, because of oil, are becoming increasingly dangerous to the security of Israel. And we know that you, a Jewish president, will see to it that Israel remains strong and independent." Then the rabbi unfortunately added, "And we've even forgiven the fact that you married, forgive me Senator Starr, a goy."

Jonathan could not believe his ears. The blood rushed slowly to the top of his head as he felt his anger mounting. He listened to his heart. Thumping hard but steadily. The adrenaline pumped through his veins and his nerve ends pulsated—making his entire body throb with anticipation. He understood the rabbis were sensing his growing hostility.

The room was silent. Starr was trembling; trying to compose himself, he thought of his family. As a little boy, he and his younger sisters always fought their parents about going to Friday night services. Other kids attended high school football games, why couldn't they? His parents never wavered. Religion came first. So he went, he learned, he understood his heritage. He listened to stories about his ancestors, and became proud.

He became a man one August day many, many years ago. He recalled looking out over the congregation and observing his mother's new yellow hat. And seeing the pride swell in his parents' eyes.

The hours he spent training himself to read Hebrew. Right to left: symbols, heritage, history. And yet these educated men, the leaders of his religion still could not bend their ways.

Then there was Israel. He had spent his honeymoon there. He and Judy loved the small, scenic country where there was so much love, yet so much hate. He remembered tears uncontrollably running down his cheek when they visited the Wailing Wall in Jerusalem, the only remnant of the Jewish temple of biblical times.

Trying to control his anger Starr began, barely concealing his emotion, his gaze fixed on the audience as he spoke in a monotone.

"Rabbi Rothman, there is separation of church and state in this country. If I'm elected president, I'm the president of all the people of the United States. And that includes Jews and non-Jews. That includes whites and blacks. It includes everyone. I am not going to favor Israel just because I'm a Jew. I've got to do what is right for the country. And let's face it—Israel has had some policies that aren't right for this country. The strong majority of Americans favor a strong and independent Israel, but over the last few years there has been quite a change in public opinion. Israel can do wrong now, when in the past they could do no wrong. They invade foreign territories, kill innocent people, and are close to starting a war as we speak here today. The Arabs, however, are becoming more cooperative with us, and

I'm not just talking about oil. I'm talking about human rights and politics. I will not be dictated to by a group of religious leaders into doing something that is against what I think is best for this country.''

Starr stopped to look at the entire audience. Nothing. An uncomfortable silence. Many of the men had their heads down, staring at the carpet below their feet.

''And as to the comment about my wife, let me tell you that I married my wife because I love her. The fact that she wasn't Jewish did not matter to me. And if you really think that you are going to keep the young Jews in this country believing in their religion when you fail to compromise, when you fail to change when society changes, then I think you're living in a fantasy world.'' Starr was livid. He was sweating profusely and quickly wiped his forehead with his right hand, not taking time to pull out his handkerchief.

The rabbis were stunned. Appalled. Never before had this esteemed group of religious leaders been talked to by anyone, let alone a political leader soliciting their votes, in the chastising tone that Starr had just used to address them. He had lectured them. He had embarrassed them like the schoolmaster taking a child's hand on the table and pounding it with a ruler. But Jonathan Starr had not finished.

''I'm going to do what I think is right for the country, and if it happens to be against Israel, so be it. I will not compromise my position as president of the United States. And I think you're doing a tremendous disservice to our religion by criticizing my marriage and possible political transactions with the state of Israel. Don't misinterpret anything I have said today. I still love my religion. And I certainly want your support, but it will have to be under my conditions, with no strings attached. I still think that under those conditions I'm much better for the Jewish people than Arthur Sutherland. But it's *not* because I'm a Jew. It's because of the policies and beliefs that I have . . . it's not because I'm a Jew.'' He literally whispered the last few words.

Starr was shaking after he had finished his speech. He had come to New York intending to meet with these leaders and to walk away from the meeting with their full support. As he stormed out of the meeting the news media swarmed around him.

"No comment!" Starr barked, as he pushed his way through the crowd of reporters.

"Give us a brief statement," insisted a nearby journalist trying to hold a camera and microphone with one hand. Starr said nothing, but jerked the microphone from the startled reporter.

"No comment," he shouted, making no attempt to hide his anger. The others backed away. Starr could sense their disbelief.

Jonathan's feet stomped over the heavy blue carpet that graced the historic lobby of the Waldorf. Those having drinks in Peacock Alley, immediately adjacent to the lobby and the famous Statue of Liberty clock, were stunned by Starr's adamant refusal to speak with the press.

As Starr headed for the Lexington Avenue exit, one bar patron was overheard saying to his drinking chum, "What's he so pissed off about? He was meeting with his fellow Jews."

It had been a lively, entertaining dinner. The Starr family, and their guest, the ever-present Paulson Orear, had thoroughly enjoyed Judy's home cooking. The unusual family get-together, in the middle of the grueling campaign, was a temporary cure for Jonathan's acute case of homesickness.

The cross fire of talk—on the campaign, the latest movies, the girls' upcoming recital—had been ceaseless, dominated by the head of the household.

"Amy," Jonathan said smiling, "pass that dessert over here."

The petite, brown-haired, pug-nosed twelve-year-old nodded her head and handed her dad a large cold dish.

"Paulie," Jonathan said, admiring the food in front of him, "this is a dessert recipe Judy stole from her sister." Jonathan dished out a scoop for Orear.

"Chocolate ice cream over Oreo cookies, covered by semisweet dark chocolate. A dermatologist's delight . . . we all love it, don't we girls?"

"Right," the three girls exclaimed enthusiastically in unison.

"Unbelievable," Orear mumbled, his mouth full of the delicious cold chocolate.

"It's our welcome home to Dad," Judy offered. "Abby," she said, "tell Dad what Marnie asked you."

Abby, even though nine years old, was still the baby of the family in the eyes of her dad. Today, her light blond hair was in pigtails. Her energetic and rambunctious personality always kept her parents on their guard. Her short, squat legs peaked out from under her blue dress as she strained forward in her seat.

"Daddy," she began excitedly, "Marnie wants me to spend the weekend with her."

"The whole weekend?" Starr asked, feigning surprise. "What does Mom think?"

"She says it's okay with her if it's okay with you."

The little girl paused for a moment, tilting her head on her shoulder, her eyebrows furrowed. "Please, Daddy, I've been good all week."

Jonathan grinned and nodded his head, "I suppose."

"Yeah!" she shouted with glee, scooting out of her chair.

"Where are you going?" Judy inquired.

The girl looked back toward her dad, "Can't I call Marnie to tell her?"

Jonathan spoke to Judy. "Let her go, hon. She's excited."

Judy shrugged her shoulders and touched Paulie gently on the arm. "See who's the soft touch around here, and who must be the bad guy?"

"Mom's right," Andrea interjected, "Dad's just a soft touch."

The oldest Starr daughter was approaching her fifteenth birthday. She looked very much like her mother: short, well built, with a deep tan and long blond hair. Her blue eyes sparkled as she rose out of her chair, walking toward Jonathan to give him a hug. "Welcome home, Dad."

"Thanks, baby," he replied, patting her softly on the back.

"Paulie, there's no place like home," Starr said sincerely, still hugging Andrea.

Amy ran over to her dad, sliding on his left knee. "Will you come to Abby's and my recital?"

"Wouldn't miss it for the world, sweets," he replied, leaning over to kiss her on the cheek.

"The man has hardly ever yelled at those girls . . . and I can't remember him ever giving them a swift hand on the butt," Judy said to Paulie, as the campaign manager helped himself to another bowl of dessert.

"Now, Judy," Jonathan said in defense of himself, "When it's necessary . . . I've disciplined them."

"Sure," she laughed, "for a second. Then you leave it up to me. Why Paulie," she said, turning her head toward Orear, "he yells at you and me all the time, but at his daughters . . ."

"All right, you've made your point," Starr replied, resigning to the fact he wasn't a modern-day Attila the Hun. "But the girls *are* pretty good."

"Judy, super meal . . . and dessert," Orear said as he walked around the table to kiss the hostess gently on the cheek.

"Hey girls, let's go out to the back for a whiffle ball game," Jonathan suggested, as the girls darted from the table, arguing about who would get Dad as a teammate. Jonathan winked as he walked by Orear, "You do the dishes."

"Come on, Paulie, I'll help," Judy offered. The two cleared the table and began loading the dishwasher in the kitchen, looking out the back window, watching Jonathan and the girls play.

"It's too bad we waited so many years to have kids," Judy said with a touch of remorse in her voice.

"Why, everything seems great."

"Oh it is," she quickly responded, "don't get me wrong . . . it's just that . . ."

"You didn't have a son," Orear said the words for her.

"How did you know?"

"Jonathan and I talk about many things . . . not just politics."

The two stood washing dishes, saying nothing. Occasionally they would look out the window when they heard Jonathan arguing about a called strike.

"Can he win?" wondered Judy out loud, looking at Paulie.

"He can and he will, Judy. He's going to be a great president."

She smiled, but didn't respond.

Within the hour father and daughters came back to explain the game to Paulie. After Jonathan showered, he and his campaign manager went to the study. It was time for business.

"Did you know Gregory had the audacity to challenge us to a debate in Michigan?" Orear began.

"Challenge *us*," Starr emphasized the last word, "I thought it was only me."

"Easy, Jonathan," Orear said with a smile, "just because you won the whiffle game . . . by cheating, according to Amy, doesn't mean you should have a big head. Seriously, what's your response to the good governor?"

"My dad once told me never to get into a pissing contest with a skunk. There's no way I would debate that skunk."

The two men talked for hours. The Starr den was so comfortable, neither one wanted to turn in for the night. Jonathan was sitting behind his big oak desk, feet propped up as if he didn't have a worry in the world. Orear was lying on his backside, covering the nearby couch, puffing on an after-dinner cigar. Judy allowed smoking only in this room, and Paulie was taking full advantage of the privilege. Law books filled the built-in bookcases surrounding the room, giving the appearance of a small law library.

Orear attempted to flip his ashes into a nearby tray, but missed.

"Better clean that up," Jonathan cautioned, "or you'll be on Judy's shit list."

Orear paused before speaking. "I would like to comment on your speech last week in New York."

Starr grinned. "I wondered when you would bring it up. At least they endorsed me."

"Say what you want," Orear replied, "but try to give me some warning in advance."

"I wonder what the prime minister said?"

"Who knows," Orear replied.

"He probably ordered a hit," then catching himself quickly Jonathan added, "that's not so funny, is it?"

"No it's not. Many of those PLO leaders are claiming top civilians are being brutally murdered, one by one, on direct orders from the Israeli Prime Minister. Anyway, you won't be the first American president who occasionally talked harshly to Israel."

"Our government did condemn them during the 1956 war."

"And," Orear countered, "don't forget that Carter had harsh words for them too."

"So did Reagan. Especially in 1981, when they destroyed that Iraq nuclear reactor."

"They claimed self-defense."

"I know," chuckled Starr, "that's what they claimed. Even Sutherland has had words with them. Being Jewish is going to complicate matters."

"I know," Orear agreed, "damned if you do and damned if you don't."

"Anything I do will be subject to criticism by the Arabs or the Israelis."

"Well," cautioned Orear, "don't say anything too bad about Israel until you win."

"Why?"

"Money, my boy," Orear said pointing to his wallet, "Money."

Jonathan nodded his assent and walked over to help Orear from the couch. "I'll be glad when this election is over," he said, a trace of fatigue showing in his voice.

"Why?" Orear responded, "the presidency will be much harder."

Jonathan quietly opened the bedroom door, surprised to see Judy reading in bed.

"Whatcha reading?"

"One of your disgusting magazines," she kidded, pulling out the centerfold. "What does she have that I don't?"

"Nothing," he said softly, sitting next to her in bed. He leaned over and took off his shoes and socks. "Paulie thinks the nomination is in the bag."

"It appears that way," Judy said. "You're not going to be too many delegates short."

"We're sending Michael Irving, Ron Harens, and Jay Crane to L.A. to make the last-minute arrangements."

"It'll be difficult to top the San Francisco extravaganza four years ago."

He reflected for a moment. "That was great fun. Being on the sidelines . . . feeling no pressure."

"Those days are over, Mr. President."

He stood over her and slowly removed his pants. Then his underwear.

"What on earth are you doing?" she asked in mock surprise.

"I'm going to rape you."

She reached out and touched his leg, running her finger up his thigh. He moaned softly and looked at her as she wrapped her hand around his penis. His knees knelt on the bed beside her and he leaned forward to kiss her.

He pushed her lips apart with his tongue and thrust it farther back into her mouth. He abruptly pulled it out, running it softly around the circle of her lips, until she moaned with pleasure.

"I love you, Johnny," she whispered, shutting her eyes tightly.

He began kissing her neck and moved his mouth down to her breasts, pressing his lips around one of her nipples, sucking it tightly between his lips.

"I love you too, dear," he muttered, crawling on top of her, and not caring at all about Los Angeles.

At least for the moment.

CHAPTER 29

THE CONVENTION

LOS ANGELES CAN BE TROPICALLY WARM AND HUMID IN THE summertime, especially when the Democrats meet for a convention. Senator Starr arrived in the City of Angels less than forty delegates short of the nomination—confident the uncommitted votes would put him over on the first ballot.

The festivities began Monday, July 12, with Convention Chairman Senator William Jennings giving the opening address.

Former President Jimmy Carter would give the keynote address on Tuesday, followed by the adoption of the platform. The roll call for the presidential nominations and the expected anticlimactic balloting for the presidential nominee would take place on Wednesday. Many observers felt Thursday would be the most interesting day of the convention. Reporters from all over the country were speculating on whom Starr would choose for his running mate. The balloting for the vice presidential nominees would take place on Thursday night, followed by the acceptance speeches scheduled for prime time. Chairman Jennings, making no attempt to hide his support for Starr, assured the networks the convention would run on schedule.

"Good meeting," Orear said, as he and Starr entered the campaign manager's room. Jonathan took off his suit coat and tossed it on the couch.

"Want a drink?"

"Sure," Orear replied from the bathroom. "Your staff . . . our staff did a magnificent job on the VP candidates' backgrounds," he shouted, as he washed his hands after urinating.

Orear took his drink from Jonathan, and the two men relaxed on opposite ends of the large green couch.

The pugnacious campaign manager's room was just like his office—paper cluttered every available space—walls, chairs, beds, and even dresser drawers. Large charts, each containing the name of every delegate, hung securely next to his bed. Little stars, of every color, were strategically placed next to the delegate names—and only Orear knew their significance.

Orear was jubilant. The campaign, so far, had run like clockwork. He sipped his drink, loosening his tie as he faced Jonathan.

"Your friend Michael Irving did one hell of a job on the platform. Even the abortion issue worked out fine."

Starr nodded in agreement. "Look. We've got the other votes. Now who gets the consolation prize?"

Orear placed his drink on the small end table next to him. "The staff is split between Jennings and Edwards."

Starr took a sip from his drink, stretching his legs as he addressed Orear. "Jennings is popular, but he's old. Edwards is popular enough and is close to me on most issues. He's much younger than Bill, and certainly qualified.''

"You've made up your mind, haven't you?'' Paulie said in a loud voice, punctuating his stentorian delivery with highly dramatic pauses. Orear grabbed a cigarette from the table, taking a long drag while he eyed Starr intently.

"You know something I don't know about Bill Jennings. Do we have secrets from each other?'' he asked facetiously.

"No secrets, Paulie,'' Starr responded awkwardly, carefully choosing his next words, "but let's equate it with the attorney-client privilege. I just can't talk about it.''

Orear understood. Beads of sweat began to appear on his furrowed brow. Some ashes fell on his shirt as he took another puff from his cigarette.

"I would suggest you talk to Edwards. And if he is agreeable, make your peace, personally, with the other candidates. We must be unified when we leave here Thursday.''

Starr watched his chargé d'affaires closely, shaking his head slowly, whistling softly. A low swelling whistle, the sound made by a man genuinely astonished.

"You just roll with the punches, don't you, Paulie? Nothing gets in your way.''

"Look,'' Orear replied smiling, "I know when your mind is made up. I trust your instincts, too. Besides,'' he added with a sly grin, "I was for Edwards.''

Standing at the window of his room at the Century Plaza Hotel, Starr looked out over the bright lights of Los Angeles. His wife and three daughters, along with top campaign aides, had decided to stay at the Century Plaza to watch the presidential balloting on TV. In Starr's luxurious suite, intermixed with Coke cans and pretzels, were three TV sets, each tuned to the three networks covering the convention. Starr, who continually upset the Secret Service by standing at the window, was admiring the beauty of Los Angeles at night. However, this particular night would be even more beautiful for him, since the state of Texas had just given Jonathan Starr enough delegates to be the presidential nominee of his party. He was now the first Jewish candidate for the presidency of the United States. Starr looked around the room with great appreciation and humility for those who had made this day possible.

"This is a great day for the Starr family," Jonathan exclaimed, as he took Judy's hands and linked them with his. The girls joined in and the family formed a circle. Jonathan began singing Jewish songs, trying to reach the deep resonant tone of a cantor as the family danced the horah.

"I'm glad I kept the press out," Orear quipped, as he, the Secret Service, and Starr's campaign staff began clapping their hands to Jonathan's singing.

Paulson walked over to the small bar at the end of the room. Reynolds was watching television and devouring an entire bag of pretzels himself. He grinned at Orear but said nothing.

"What are you smiling about?"

"You, Paulie," Andy replied shaking his head. "This means as much to you as it does to Jonathan."

"No," Orear said quietly, then breaking into a wide smile he chuckled, "but almost as much."

The campaign manager poured himself a drink, carelessly dropping an ice cube on the carpet. He looked down and kicked the cube against the curtain, raising his hands as the official signifying a field goal, while spilling part of his drink on his shirtsleeve. He turned around to see if Reynolds saw his foolishness, but the agent's attention was once again focused on the screen.

Orear slid a chair near Reynolds and watched the demonstration.

His demonstration.

He had been on the phone all night—bantering—pleading—praising the campaign workers, yet always wanting more.

He hoped the bandwagon psychology would carry them through November 2. His wish for three nights of free national television exposure had been granted.

From the ornate suite on the top floor of the Century Plaza, Paulson Orear sat in a large, overstuffed chair enjoying the fruits of his labor. For the past several hours he had been using an elaborate phone communications system to keep in contact with the convention "floorwalkers" representing the campaign. He had persuaded enough Edwards defectors during the days before the vote to swing the first ballot coup. Delegates and alternates had received a personal letter from Jonathan Starr, complete with a handwritten postscript. Orear felt it could convince the fence sitters to jump for the Starr ticket.

He even arranged for hosts to greet the delegates as they exited their planes. Followed by the buses that safely transported the Democrats to their hotel. On the buses, pens for the men, flowers for the ladies, and booze for everyone was the norm of the day. Paulson Orear didn't miss a trick.

"Look!" Amy screamed with excitement, pointing to the TV, "Michael's on the screen."

"Sshh, sshh," Starr turned to quiet everyone down as Irving was being interviewed. The noise of the convention could be heard in the background as the Starr demonstration had been going strong for over twenty minutes, balloons and all.

"All right, Michael, your man is the nominee," began the network commentator, "who is the running mate?"

"We did it, Jonathan, we did it," Irving shouted, the puffy red cheeks of his Irish face stretched to their fullest as he grinned from ear to ear.

"The senator will announce his choice tomorrow. No one on the staff will comment until then," Irving said, finally answering the question. Before the newsman had a chance to ask another question Irving had left, shaking hands with members of the California delegation.

"He follows orders well, doesn't he?" Starr said, chuckling to himself as he mingled with his friends.

"Congratulations, good buddy," Andrew Reynolds said sincerely, as he patted Jonathan on the back. "Not bad for a frustrated lawyer."

"Thanks, my man," Starr replied as he bear-hugged the big Secret Service agent.

Jonathan noticed the television screen again. Chairman Jennings had recognized Senator Morris. The convention was quieting down, and Starr motioned for his group to do the same. He happened to catch the gleam in Orear's eye as he looked at his campaign manager, who shrugged his shoulders and held up both hands as if to say, "I don't know what's going on." Jonathan knew differently. He was about to observe another Paulson Orear production.

"Mr. Chairman . . . Mr. Chairman!" Morris shouted, trying to quiet the convention delegates, "I would like to address this great convention."

"Would the distinguished senator from Massachusetts care to come to the podium?" Chairman Jennings asked, his excitement evident from the tone of his voice.

"She would," came the reply, as the cameras caught Morris making her way toward the speaker's stand. She was a beautiful woman, Jonathan thought to himself: well built, athletic looking, as if she were a jogger. But on this night Jonathan noticed a sensual quality about her he had never observed before. The way her thighs moved when she walked and the gentle, slightly noticeable bouncing of her breasts, the kind of action that normally didn't go unnoticed to Jonathan's well-trained eyes. He knew something was prearranged. Jennings wasn't about to give the podium to someone, on prime time television, without knowing the script in advance. This time when Starr glanced at Orear, the clever little campaign manager winked back.

Morris was greeted with enthusiastic applause as she began to address her captive audience. She graciously motioned for them to quiet down before speaking.

"Mr. Chairman," she began, as she looked out over the vast audience of delegates and visitors in the convention center. "I have just talked with Senator Edwards and Governor Gregory. They, along with me, wish to move that this convention nominate by acclamation Jonathan Starr, who *will*," she said firmly, looking the cameras straight in the eye "be the next president of the United States."

The roar was deafening. Chairman Jennings embraced Senator Morris as they both gave the victory sign to the screaming delegates. It had been a media extravaganza, orchestrated by Paulson Orear, to show the nation, the party, and the president that this year, unlike elections of the past, the Democrats were, in fact, united.

"Nice job, Paulie," Starr said, shaking his head in admiration, "maybe you should be president."

"Just doing my job, Jonathan," Orear said politely, comfortable with the pats on the back he was receiving.

Thursday night finally arrived. The evening progressed with perfection. Edwards, after easily winning the second spot on the ticket, delivered an eloquent and powerful speech praising Starr's leadership ability and chastising the president's.

Senator Cindy Morris, who had been chosen to introduce the California nominee, followed Edwards to the podium with grace and confidence.

Starr stood backstage with Paulson Orear, listening to Morris pound the Republican administrations over the last decade. He realized that within moments he would be in front of millions of people . . . trying to convince them he was the person best able to lead the country in the next four years. Starr slowly felt an enormous surge of electricity and power enter his body. People throughout the country who had never seen or heard Jonathan Starr would get their first look at this "new hero" of the Democratic party.

Senator Starr heard the end of Morris's speech and his own introduction; he slowly but authoritatively walked on the platform, to the standing ovation from those in the Los Angeles Convention Center. Never before had Starr seen so many screaming people, raising their blue-and-white "Starr and Edwards" banners throughout the auditorium. Balloons came down from the ceiling as campaign aides mingled with their walkie-talkies throughout the floor, trying to encourage those around them to scream their lungs out and shake their noisemakers so the American public could see that the Democrats were very pleased with their nominee. After what seemed like an eternity, Jonathan Starr had the opportunity to address his beloved Democrats and the American people. Dressed neatly in his favorite navy blue suit, Starr faced the delegates and the nation. His time had come.

"Chairman Jennings, delegates to this convention, my fellow Americans:

"I have made many speeches in my political life, yet never have I found it more difficult to find the words that would be adequate to express what I feel here tonight.

"I would like to quote the words of the great Harry Truman, who once said, 'It isn't important who is ahead at one time or another in either an election or a horse race. It's the horse that comes in first at the finish that counts.' This horse will finish first."

The roar of the crowd was genuine enthusiasm. It was more than "my party, right or wrong." These delegates believed in Jonathan Starr. That was the clear impression millions of viewers were getting as they watched the speech in their living rooms.

Starr smiled and took a deep breath. The applause gave him an opportunity to catch his wind. He wiped his sweaty palm on his thigh behind the podium, undetected by the cameras.

"America has become a nation that can't keep peace at home, so it can't be trusted to keep the peace abroad. America has become a country where a president who isn't treated with respect at home will not be treated with respect abroad. America has become a country that can't manage its own economy, and consequently it can't advise others how to manage theirs. If we are to restore prestige and respect for America abroad, the place to begin is at home. The place to begin is to get Arthur Sutherland out of the White House and the Starr-Edwards ticket elected.

"I pledge to you that the attorney general of the United States will open a new front against those dealing in narcotics. Let this message come through loud and clear—time is running out on the merchants of crime and corruption in this society. And the wave of crime is not going to be the wave of the future under the Starr-Edwards administration."

Starr paused to sip a glass of water as the convention erupted again. Though Jonathan was tired from the week's activities, he gained strength and encouragement from the crowd's response. He looked over the mass of humanity in front of him. It was a breathtaking sight. Gathering his second wind, he pledged himself to lift their spirits higher. As he approached the end of his speech the conventioneers were buoyed by his sense of mission.

"I see a day when our nation is at peace and the world is at peace. And all of those who live and all of those who aspire and all of those who crave liberty will look to America as a living example of hopes realized and dreams achieved.

"The time when one man or a few leaders could save America is gone. What this country needs now is nothing less than the total commitment and the total involvement of the American people if we are to succeed. Thank you."

The response to Jonathan Starr's speech was spectacular. The reaction of the audience was spontaneous. Delegates in the aisles were screaming and shouting. People throughout the country who did not know Jonathan Starr, were now duly impressed; but they were not alone. The White House had been watching the Democratic convention. And Arthur Sutherland knew, with total certainty, the battle for his political life was about to begin.

CHAPTER 30

THE PRESIDENTIAL CAMPAIGN—PART I

THE TWO BLACK LIMOUSINES PULLED IN FRONT OF ERNIE'S AT 847 Montgomery Street, in San Francisco. The Secret Service had spent the morning checking the restaurant's food service and security layout. Several agents were inside already assigned their tables in strategic locations throughout the restaurant. By waiting until 2:00 P.M., Andrew Reynolds hoped to avoid the spectators and media who always surrounded the candidate.

For the first time in his life Starr was wearing a bulletproof vest, snuggly fit under his hand-tailored, thousand-dollar, brown Mariani suit. Orders from Reynolds, on orders from the head of the Secret Service. No chances this year.

The agent who had been in the kitchen all morning discussed his findings with Reynolds. The White House food services coordinator had trained several agents in the art of testing food for poison.

Ernie's decor recalled the city's opulent days before the fire of 1906, and many of its furnishings came from the elaborate mansions that once covered the top of famous Nob Hill. The walls were covered with red brocade; the carpets were thick, red, and plush. The elaborate mahogany and stained-glass bar was a relic rescued from a saloon in the old, raucous Barbary Coast.

Agents Reynolds and Jefferson escorted the two diners into the dimly lit, almost empty restaurant. They were seated in a secluded corner for privacy . . . and security.

After they placed their orders, the two men were alone.

"It's not the Four Seasons Clift Hotel or Stanford Court," Orear began, "but this is nice."

"It should be, I'm buying."

"You really love this city, don't you?"

"Paulie, it's the greatest city in the world."

A smiling waitress nervously placed cocktails on the table, honored she had been chosen to serve candidate Starr. Starr sipped his bourbon and seven, and Orear gulped his dry martini. Orear could sense Starr was preoccupied; he had been in a state of semi-awareness since the meeting with President Sutherland.

"Jonathan, what's bothering you?"

"You're perceptive."

"In my business, it's a prerequisite."

The waitress returned and served them their lunches. Then she stood motionless, staring at Starr. She didn't leave until the candidate smiled at her.

Starr took another sip from his drink and leaned his elbows on the table, getting closer to his friend.

"I've seen cables from the CIA, at least hinting the ten-year peace between Israel and Egypt may be coming to an end because of the Israeli invasion of Lebanon."

"So," Orear replied, chewing on his lunch as he reached for a drink of water—his small hand gripping the glass carefully.

"If I'm elected president, will the Egyptians trust me to keep the peace?"

"Why not? Why wouldn't they?"

"My religion."

"Look, Jonathan," Orear placed his fork on the table, pausing to finish his bite, "you were Jewish when the campaign started. You're Jewish now. You know the Middle East is dangerous territory, why worry about it?"

"Because I realize I may win this election. The problem won't go away. I want to defend Israel . . . not because of my religion, but because I believe in their independence." Starr gulped down a French fry as he waited for a response.

"Look," Orear responded, a rueful little smile breaking out, "don't get hung up on the Israel angle. Your instincts will get you through. They always do."

"There's more, Paulie." Starr's voice dropped to a low and troubled tone.

"Go on," Orear urged.

"Sutherland is working on a secret peace plan. It involves moderates like Hussein, Egypt, and the Saudis. I'm not sure how much he's told Israel. It could put me in a tough spot. Sutherland could bring the religion issue to a head, right before the election, and box me in a corner. I've got to be on my toes regarding this plan."

"He's playing hardball—trying to keep you quiet on Israel will make religion more of an issue. He'll claim you can't handle the situation . . ."

"But if there *is* a war . . ."

"If there is one—you'll handle it as you would any crisis . . . as president," Orear said flatly, wiping his chin with the napkin.

"Look, Jonathan, the moderate Arabs dealing with this country *will* trust you when they get to know you. They know our system. You wouldn't get elected in the first place if the citizenry thought different."

"It also makes criticism of Israel difficult," Starr said reflectively. "God knows there is enough fault on all of them."

"Criticize when necessary, but be careful," Orear added.

"I know," smiled Starr, "money."

"Anyway, you can criticize the Arab oil money to even things out," Orear added reassuringly. "Besides, our polls show people do *not* feel you will let your Judaism interfere with decisions. You don't have to do anything to prove yourself. You already have."

"I wish it was that easy," Starr replied, placing the napkin on his lap and cutting into his lunch. "There's a war taking place in boardrooms across this country . . . against Israel."

"Oil money again?" asked Orear.

"The Arabs have over four hundred billion to invest from their profits, and it's in this country. It's not just the Arabs either. Foreign investments worry me."

"How so?" responded Orear, content to let Starr dominate the conversation so he could continue attacking his lunch.

"Howard Johnson, Baskin-Robbins, Alka-Seltzer . . . almost an American Who's Who, are owned by foreign investors. They own American farms and dominate some of our banks."

"What's the solution?"

"No solution yet. It's just a problem. But the petrodollars blackmail some companies into being against Israel . . . even to the extent of not hiring Jews."

Orear looked around the room and noticed they were no longer the center of attention. Most customers had gone back to enjoying their meal. Paulson took a sip of water before responding.

"Percy talked about this years ago, in Congress, this is nothing new."

"Thirty of our largest banks have petrodollars. It's grown worse over the past decade. Some of these banks won't hire Jews, just to appease their Arab investors."

"There's discrimination everywhere . . . just ask Andy Reynolds."

"I know," Jonathan replied, slowly chewing a piece of the tasty prime rib before him. "But we must do something. Nixon worked out a deal in '74 where the government agreed never to publicly list a detailed breakdown of Arab holdings in this country."

"You can change it. But it's a two-way street."

"Why?"

"A public list detailing Israelis' holdings would be fair game."

"No problem," Starr quickly responded, wiping his mouth with the napkin.

"Maybe . . . maybe not," Orear wondered out loud.

"Look," Starr began, "whatever their interest is, it won't

come close to the Arabs. The Saudis receive 150 billion a year in oil revenues. They invest in treasury bills, American corporations, and banks. Hell, even the PLO invests over here. I just think . . .''

"The public should know," Orear finished the sentence for him. The campaign manager placed his knife and fork on the table and stared intently at his friend.

"Methinks you want the public to know too much."

"Maybe . . . maybe not," Starr chuckled, cutting another piece of his lunch.

"Jonathan," Orear said patiently, "enough work—let's get back to this super meal."

It had been a good lunch, with privacy. There were not thousands of people standing in front of him, cheering his name, waving "Starr and Edwards" signs—there were no political reporters shoving microphones in his face, no media asking questions, no band playing "happy days are here again," and his face was no longer projected on the screen of the three networks for millions of people to view. Here he was one man, eating lunch with a friend.

It wouldn't be this way for long.

The campaign moved forward. City to city, county to county, state to state. The six o'clock news displayed the candidate's handsome face every night, talking with local leaders, discussing issues with townspeople, and giving his opinion on any topic raised. He was trying to build momentum for the nationally televised debate scheduled for October 18 in St. Paul, Minnesota.

The California senator's political reputation was spreading around the country like a blazing, uncontrolled fire, in great part aided by his uncanny ability to deal with the media. He quickly became the master of the thirty-second response that fit in perfectly with the national evening news.

During the first month of the campaign Starr had encountered some anti-Semitism. As he mingled through crowds he heard comments coming from unseen faces. As the campaign approached its last month, the "religion issue" began to surface with more regularity.

Orear knew literature from anti-Jewish groups or crackpots was being circulated on the campaign trail by those who would never vote for Starr—to people who probably would not vote for Starr. These pamphlets were surfacing in states with large numbers of Protestant and Catholic voters, who were trying to evaluate Starr as a man, as a potential president. Though they might not want a Jew in the White House, they feared religious intolerance even more. In addition, the anti-Jewish campaign would only consolidate the already strong Jewish support Starr had in some very close electoral college states. It was in these states that Paulson Orear managed to point out the existence of the terrible scandal sheets. He understood what it took to win presidential elections. He planned on winning this one.

"It's great to be back home!" the president shouted, his voice giving away some of the weariness he felt, as he sat down behind his desk in the Oval Office for the first time in ten days.

"Nice to have you home," replied Vice President Stevens, who, along with the chief of staff, campaign manager Ray Bailey, and Press Secretary Brandt were gathered to discuss the president's campaign schedule for the next week.

The president signed a few letters and quickly glanced through his phone messages. As usual, when he was away from the office, the paperwork deluged his desk.

"Shit," the president mumbled, noticing the latest poll results Bailey had placed before him. He scanned the numbers, and grabbing his pipe, joined the others on the two couches adjacent to his desk. The president was tired, and somewhat irritated.

"Why am I eight points behind Starr?" demanded the president as he tried to light his pipe.

"Mr. President," Bailey began, "I believe the religion issue is hurting us. We talked yesterday about the effect of the speech he gave in Rhode Island. He seems to be making an issue out of it, and it puts us in an awkward position."

The president nodded. He knew that, as a Jew, Starr had a right, perhaps even a responsibility, to answer any attacks that were made against him because of his religion. However, Starr was using the religion issue to his advantage. The Rhode Island speech brought the issue to a head. Starr argued convincingly that he should not be denied the presidency on the sole basis of his religion. The speech was being used in some Starr campaign literature, and in television advertising markets where electoral votes were highest. *The New York Times*, *St. Paul Pioneer Press & Dispatch*, *Cleveland Plain Dealer*, and *St. Louis Post-Dispatch* all had headlines during the past eight days discussing the religion issue.

"Mr. President," Campaign Manager Bailey said reassuringly, "for four years Jewish leaders in this country have praised you. Only Starr's Judaism has changed that. It's nothing you've . . ."

"Yes, I understand, to a point," the president interrupted, gently puffing on his favorite pipe. "But Starr has it both ways. Republican Jews are being urged to vote for Starr because he's Jewish. Protestants are told to vote for him to prove they aren't anti-Semitic. Who does that leave?"

"Indiana," Bailey replied, getting a small chuckle from the president, who appreciated his sense of humor. Vice President Stevens did not.

"What about the debate? Are you going to discuss it?"

"I'd rather not," the president said, pondering the issue that might cost him the election. "Things are close. I don't want to blow this. If I'm asked a question, I will just say it has nothing to do with the questions facing the people and shouldn't be a factor for any American."

"That's a cop-out," blurted Jim Brandt, the president's long-time press secretary and the only one in the room who could ever get away with that comment.

"No," the president replied gently. "It's the God's truth."

"You know," the chief of staff began, handing Brandt and Bailey their coffee, "we can use some circumstances to our advantage."

"For instance," Bailey asked, sipping his coffee, but listening intently to the sometimes devious chief of staff.

"War."

"War!" shouted Bailey in anger, almost spilling his coffee, "it's been said I'd do anything to win an election but never this . . . I . . ."

"Easy, Ray," the president said calmly, sitting in his rocking chair, moving back and forth gently, smoking his pipe. He looked like he was ready for a bedtime story, not a discussion about war. "Let him continue. He sometimes has a knack for coming up with . . . shall I say . . . unusual ideas."

"Thank you," the aggressive adviser replied. "Eisenhower had his Korea and Lebanon. Kennedy had Cuba. Ford had Mayagüez and Carter had Iran."

"What's the point?" Bailey interrupted icily, still suspicious of the chief of staff.

"We've had Russians in Cuba. Now we have problems on the Sino-Soviet border and a war stirring in the Middle East. We could move troops somewhere, perhaps a peace force in Lebanon. The public would rally around the president during the crisis, and it would be enough for us to squeak by in November," the chief of staff concluded triumphantly. Bailey was about to speak, but the president cut him off.

"I would never do that," Sutherland said firmly, his tone controlled, but the pipe puffing and rocking had stopped. "Ford lost fifty-four men in the Mayagüez incident and Carter lost eight Americans . . . and the election. The Middle East situation is already at a crisis level. I won't play politics on this issue of war or peace. Even if it means losing."

"Starr will," Brandt pointed out matter-of-factly.

"Starr is not president," Sutherland responded loudly, his voice showing the anger he felt on this issue, "and he won't be, if we do our jobs."

"I agree with the president," Vice President Stevens said, his voice exhibiting uncharacteristic firmness. "The Israelis and Egyptians are yelling at each other. Almost everything accomplished in the late seventies has eroded. The Arabs are fighting among themselves, and the PLO aggravate everything. Take that, plus the Soviets placing troops near the Chinese border. Well, we've got enough problems."

The president nodded his head, frowning. "We're watching the situation. Secretary of State Long is working night and day for a peaceful solution. We aren't going to alarm the nation, not yet anyway. But Starr is liable to burst the bubble. Besides, anything I do in the Middle East, running against a Jew, will be considered suspect. To put it bluntly . . . my tits are in a ringer.''

"Yes," the vice president agreed, "all of our tits are in the ringer.''

"You know," the president continued, "I can't do a damn thing about the sharp slowdown of Jewish immigration from the Soviet Union." The president began puffing again, his voice calm. "If I speak out on the issue, the press will accuse me of going after the Jewish vote. So I stay quiet. And those poor bastards have to stay in Russia.''

"Starr has to be quiet on it too," Stevens added, his mood solemn as well.

"Starr has more problems than he knows about," the president said, changing the subject. "When the country goes to high school football and basketball games, he's suppose to go to services. And what's he going to do when he sits down with Arab or PLO leaders, talk to them or have them searched. I . . .''

"It's going to be an incredible problem," interrupted the vice president. "Anything he does or says will be treated as suspect by all parties in the Middle East. How will the Egyptians trust a Jewish president?''

"They won't," Sutherland replied simply. "They barely trust a non-Jew as president. Starr's election will upset the delicate rapport we have established over there." Then shaking his head, he added, "The people don't understand . . . do they?''

"Neither does Starr," the vice president concluded.

"You know," the president said somberly, wagging a cautionary hand, "religion and politics is a fact of life. Those who condemn school prayers are accused of religious intolerance. Our money is emblazoned with 'In God We Trust.' Both houses of Congress start their sessions with prayers and have chaplains; and the IRS allows a tax deduction for charitable contributions.''

Bailey was confused. "If the religion issue comes up, what's your response?''

"It is not an issue.''

"That's not good enough," Bailey said shaking his head.

"That's my response. Period. And if I'm asked about the Middle East, I'll be consistent with my record. Starr will have more trouble on that question. He can't afford to give the impression he's so pro-Israel that his religion would influence his decisions. We'll see how he handles the peace plan.''

The meeting lasted all day. The upcoming debate was the key to the election. The winner would be the next president of the United States.

The president sipped from his iced tea, observing a White House gardener trim some bushes in the Rose Garden. Sutherland had been talking for thirty minutes.

"Mr. President," J.W. McBee responded, pulling his yellow lawn chair closer to Sutherland, "Ah agree that you must win this election. The A-rabs are havin' hard enough time agreein' on your terms. Havin' a Jew headin' the country may be too much for them to swallow.''

"We don't have much time, J.W.''

"Ah know. The Egyptians aren't the problem. The Saudis will come round, but because of Israel's invasion of Lebanon, well, that's holdin' up things. Hussein wants most of Lebanon. Soon, contact with Israel will be necessary. Hussein will only give them twenty miles. The king isn't quite ready to eliminate Assad. The PLO problem is comin', though. It won't be too long befo' we're ready.''

"I've told you Starr's position on nuclear arms and Israel. If he wins, I'm afraid he'd terminate the executive agreement. That's not how a government should be run, but it's a cold fact. And without that agreement, Egypt and the Saudis will be a problem.''

"Arthur," McBee said seriously, "Ah'd piss on a spark plug to git this agreement wrapped up. But you'd better git ready for this upcomin' debate. Leave the Middle East to me.''

"You'd better hurry," the president cautioned, "with Israel's actions and those Arab troop buildups, there might not be a Middle East for long.''

CHAPTER 31

THE GREAT DEBATE
THE PRESIDENTIAL CAMPAIGN—PART II

THE ONLY DEBATE IN THIS PRESIDENTIAL ELECTION WOULD BE a grueling four-hour marathon session sponsored by the League of Women Voters. During the hectic days prior to the debate, both weary candidates used every precious spare minute of time preparing their opening statements, going through mock questions from their staff and rehearsing the cross-questioning procedure.

Taking a few breaks from their debate preparations, Starr and Orear visited St. Paul's downtown indoor park under glass, Town Square. They observed exhibits at the downtown science museum and had lunch with several business leaders at the stately red-brick building housing the St. Paul Athletic Club. The afternoon was spent with Minnesota's governor at the state capitol, sporting the largest unsupported marble dome in the world. The busy day culminated in Minneapolis at the Orion Room located on the top of the fifty-seven-story IDS Tower, the highest structure between Chicago and California, where the Starr entourage dined in seclusion. Before ordering dessert, Jonathan made his way to a nearby phone.

"Judy," he said, "it's me. How's that flu bug?"

"Fine, Johnny, it should be gone by tomorrow. The kids waited up, why couldn't you call earlier?"

"I've been in meetings. I miss you."

"I miss you, too," she said, her voice disclosing the nasal sound that had bedridden her for two days.

"Paulie has promised me a day off after this debate."

Her spirits were immediately lifted. "Great," she responded enthusiastically, then added softly, "I love you."

"Wish me luck."

"You don't need it. I know you'll do fine. Sleep well, my love, and send my best to Paulie."

"I'm wearing my gray suit tomorrow."

"Good. I was tiring of the blue one."

"I'm sick of hotel rooms, aren't you, Paulie?" Starr said, as he tossed his suit coat on the nearby bed.

"Yes, but the end's in sight. Another couple of weeks and you'll earn yourself a nice, big White House," Orear remarked with a wink.

Jonathan chuckled as he poured himself a drink. "Want one?"

"Is it one of your kiddy cocktails?"

"Nothing wrong with seven and seven," Starr replied, as he mixed his campaign manager a drink.

"When you become president, I'll teach you how to drink," Orear said half-seriously, taking his drink from Jonathan. He walked to the closet and pulled out his briefcase, grabbing a stack of documents with his chubby hand.

"Jonathan, let's go over these surveys."

"Paulie . . . I'm too tired. Can't it wait?" Starr replied, exhausted from the day's work.

"Give me fifteen minutes," insisted Orear, not wanting to call it quits.

"Shoot," Starr said in mock defeat, shaking his head at Paulie's stubbornness.

"Well, first . . ." Orear stopped abruptly, motioning for Starr to listen. Jonathan smiled, but Orear was alarmed. "What the fuck is that?" Orear whispered, cautiously inching his way toward the hotel room door.

"Is Andy out there?" Orear asked, still whispering. Starr nodded. Then in one violent motion Orear pulled the door open, surprising a stunned Reynolds, who was sitting on a chair in the deserted hallway. As Reynolds faced Orear, they both heard Starr laughing hysterically.

"What's going on?" Reynolds asked. Orear was standing next to him, speechless.

"He heard your animal noise," explained Starr, still unable to control his laughter. "Paulie, when Andy was in law school he made all kinds of animal noises."

"Tell him my nickname," Reynolds said, as the three men moved back into the room.

"Since one sound was like a cricket, we called him the 'chocolate cricket.' I knew it was him all the time," Starr explained to his irritated campaign manager.

"Cute, Jonathan," Orear replied, unable to see the humor in the situation. He pushed Reynolds out the door—"You stay there, chocolate cricket, I'm trying to win an election," he said, as he slammed the door.

"OK, Paulie," Starr assured him, sitting on the bed, "I'm all yours." Orear regained his composure, and his heartbeat returned to normal.

"Our private survey shows Sutherland is regarded as super cool and aloof by many Americans. You are regarded as more friendly and outgoing."

"What about our trustworthiness?"

"You both are considered trustworthy and competent," Orear responded, as he thumbed through the stack of papers in his hands. "You can win the debates on humor, friendship, and old-fashioned decency."

"Act myself?" Starr smiled.

"Yeah, make animal noises with your friend," chided Orear. "At least you're not yelling that you only want to talk about issues and solutions. That alone won't win the debate or the election."

"I know," Starr said, agreeing wholeheartedly with Orear. "Sutherland will be the third incumbent in the last four elections to lose. I'll charm them with my decency."

"That's the spirit. But," Orear added, his brow turned upward, "remember these people see Sutherland every day in one way or the other. In fact, for four years his words were conveyed to the public, his picture on TV or in the newspapers or magazines. He is the president. He lives in the big house. Every day he's there, he carves out reasons to stay longer."

"Thanks for the encouragement."

"Listen," Orear said sincerely, "you're more confident,

hardworking, and dedicated. You can lead. Emphasize those traits and those traits will make you the next president of the United States.''

Senator Starr was ushered briskly through the hotel lobby into his waiting limousine. The debate was less than two hours away. Dusk lingered. The orange sun partially inflamed the St. Paul skyline. The temperature was dropping and gray clouds filled the darkening sky; even in October, snow was in the Minnesota air.

Starr slid across the backseat, leaning over to kiss the attractive lady on his left. Orear slammed the front passenger door and motioned for the Secret Service agent to start the caravan.

"You look great, Kate," Starr said as he squeezed her small right hand. Orear turned around from the front seat.

"Katherine, friend or no friend, this is a shitty time for an interview, especially since we're only three blocks away."

"Look, Paulie," Starr interceded, "it was the only time I had, unless Kate wanted to watch me take a shower."

The reporter liked the idea. "I would have, but what would Judy have said?" she replied, her radiant smile disarming Orear.

"Kate, I know this is under less than optimal conditions, but time is a problem. Shoot."

"How important is this debate?"

"Very important, but I question whether it will really change the outcome of the election, unless," he added nervously, "one of us screws up."

She was attempting her shorthand when the limousine swerved to the right to pass a car. The pencil in her hand made a line across the entire top page of her notebook.

"Less than optimal conditions," she mumbled just loud enough for Jonathan to hear. He turned toward her and took an admiring view of his first love. Her red skirt had risen to mid-thigh.

"I notice you don't have your favorite blue suit on. I thought you were superstitious?"

"You didn't fly out here to ask me about my wardrobe, but yes," he said smiling, "the blue is my good-luck suit . . . I think this one fits me better, though. I've put on twelve pounds since July.''

"Good chicken on the banquet circuit, I suppose,'' she quipped. "Do you expect religion to dominate the debate?''

"It shouldn't be an issue.''

"You haven't answered my question.''

Starr shook his head, admiration in his eyes. "You're tougher than tonight's panel,'' then lowering his voice, "can we go off the record?''

She shook her head no, but said nothing.

"For the record,'' he began, seriously, his tone flat and unfriendly, "it won't be discussed at any length because neither of us can use it to our own advantage.''

Wilson spent the remainder of the trip trying to pinpoint Starr on other important issues. She sensed her friend wasn't really concentrating on her questions.

"Look, Jonathan, this isn't working too well; bad timing on both our parts. I've got enough for my story. Why don't you think about tonight.''

He nodded his appreciation and took her right hand into his. She could feel the trembling, but somehow it comforted her.

Starr's limousine pulled into the lower level of the Civic Center. He was there two hours before the debate for a makeup session. He needed it. Earlier in the day he'd cut himself shaving, and hoped the gel being applied to the right side of his chin would do the trick.

"It's almost a packed house out there, Jonathan,'' observed Orear, keeping one eye on the network makeup man, the other on the closed-circuit TV that showed the overflow crowd gathering outside the Civic Center.

"No hockey game tonight,'' Starr muttered, careful not to upset the strange substance being applied to his shaving wound.

"Maybe not, but the Stanley Cup, World Series, or Super Bowl never had this drama.''

"You can always put things in proper perspective, can't you, Paulie,'' Starr cracked as he rose from the chair. "Give me a mirror.'' Starr looked over his face closely, rubbing his chin and neck. "Not bad, I might just make it.''

The following one hundred minutes were the slowest of Starr's life. Every time he glanced at the clock, or impatiently stared at his watch, time seemed suspended.

Technicians from KSTP, the Twin Cities' ABC affiliate, were hurriedly making last-minute camera adjustments. Their equipment was being pooled with the other major networks for the simultaneous broadcast.

Starr stared into the mirror, admiring the perfect knot he had just tied . . . his red tie with tiny flags complimenting his freshly pressed suit. "Paulie, didn't you . . ."

"No time for chitchat," Orear broke in. "They just told the crowd the ground rules . . . let's go."

Starr and Orear walked through the tunnel and met Bailey and Sutherland close to the center's entrance. All four men shook hands, but no one uttered a word. Starr wore a heavy three-piece gray suit that was already causing him to perspire. The president, dapper as usual, wore a trim navy suit and a conservative tie, and appeared ready to do battle. The two candidates were greeted with a standing ovation from thirteen thousand cheering Minnesotans. Starr gazed at the people in the auditorium. He nodded to the three panelists as he took his place behind the podium. The special lights being used were unusually bright, and hot.

The three panelists sat on the left side of the stage, with Starr standing behind a lectern, approximately thirty feet to the right of President Sutherland. Both lecterns faced the panelists at a diagonal; yet both men were facing the audience as well.

Before the debate, Ray Bailey whispered into Sutherland's ear.

"You know, Mr. President, if you hadn't decided to form the Senate Select Committee against Tommy Duncan, there probably never would have been a Jonathan Starr."

"You're not the first person who has told me that," Sutherland replied, forcing a smile.

Starr began, speaking effectively. He hit the president's economic policies and the unemployment rate, and discussed the administration's lack of effort in eliminating discrimination. He condemned the administration for not instituting any strategic arms limitation talks during the last four years. For the first time publicly, Starr proposed a United Nations committee that would be formed and implemented immediately. He suggested fair and enforceable agreements that would immediately halt the production of all nuclear military weapons, and would also prohibit the superpowers from transferring them to other countries.

Starr had forced the president to take the defensive. In Sutherland's opening ten-minute speech, he defended his administration. Sutherland attacked Starr's proposals that would place an additional cost on federal government programs. The Republican president emphasized the importance of individual initiative and corporate enterprise.

Crime in the United States had been a serious issue for both candidates. Once again Starr attacked the president's policies, forcing the incumbent to defend the past four years. When President Sutherland had finished, he and Senator Starr got into a heated question-and-answer period themselves. The excitement was apparent from the audience reaction; people were squirming in their seats, eyeing the candidates intently, and the nation was witnessing a real old-fashioned debate.

Starr was starting to sweat under the hot lights, and was amazed at how cool and comfortable President Sutherland appeared. Here he was, a big, well-built man, in his sixties, every hair in its place, his shirt neatly pressed, the tie just right.

Sutherland flashed a smile when Starr concluded his answer concerning the president's energy program. He stared intently into the nearest camera.

"It's easy when you run for president to talk about things that you'll do if you win, but I won four years ago, and when I make a pledge to the American public to do something four years from now, I have a track record to show that I'll do it. Senator Starr has no track record."

As the debate continued, both candidates realized they didn't have an opportunity to answer all of the questions in depth. And because the members of the panel continued to jump from one subject to another, there was really no effort at continuity.

The experienced and versatile female panelist, known for her penchant for controversy, was ready to add more fuel to an already hot fire. During the first hour the religion issue had not been raised. It was her turn to ask the president a question.

"Mr. President, we all know that you are running for the first time against a Jewish candidate. The campaign has approximately two weeks left—yet the religion issue has not been raised by your camp. We all know that the voters are concerned, or at least aware of this issue. What are your thoughts on the religion issue?"

"In my mind there is no question that Senator Starr is loyal to his country. I firmly believe that if he were elected president of the United States, he would follow the Constitution, and would be able to separate church from state. This issue has not been made by Senator Starr or myself; it's something that has been played up by the press. I'm not asked a question on the campaign trail about religion, and I doubt Senator Starr is. I believe both of us don't consider religion a real campaign issue, but neither one of us has been successful about taking it out of the campaign. It has no place in this, or any other, political campaign in this country."

All eyes turned toward Jonathan Starr. "Well, I can probably say for the first time in the campaign that I wholeheartedly agree with President Sutherland. I don't wish to make any additional comments on the religion issue, nor do I wish to ask President Sutherland a question on that subject."

During the next ninety minutes a relative calm settled under the high ceiling of the Civic Center. Both candidates were exercising extreme caution in the delicate responses they were espousing. Now Starr made an instant judgment; his political instincts, which had never failed him, called out to him to be the aggressive challenger—and the perfect opportunity arose.

"Senator Starr, do you believe the country has a dependence on Arab oil, and if so, what would you suggest to rectify it?"

All right, Starr thought to himself, the time had come. The Civic Center was completely silent.

"We are still dependent on Arab oil. In the last four years, as in many other instances, President Sutherland has done nothing to stop our dependence.

"During hearings in the Senate Foreign Relations Committee, some economic experts felt that, if there was another war in the Middle East, the United States would be jeopardized in helping Israel, because the Arab league could simply say, 'We'll pull out every last cent we have deposited in the United States.'

Not only do we have to worry about the oil, but now we have to worry about the money. And I ask President Sutherland and I ask this nation, could the banks that have all this Arab money sustain withdrawals from the Arab nations? Just the fact that the Arabs could threaten this withdrawal gives them significant leverage over our economy. We have become so dependent on Arab petrodollars that the Arab nations, and OPEC, are the ones with the most deposits in our banks, the most investments in commercial real estate, and even the most investments in United States government securities. From thirty-six weeks of pumping oil, Saudi Arabia earns enough to buy General Motors completely. In forty weeks, they earn enough to buy Exxon, which is still the largest industrial corporation in the United States.

"3M, a large multinational corporation located here in the Twin Cities, could be purchased from the income of a mere twenty-four hours of pumping oil. Senate information reports the Saudis have over 200 billion dollars invested in American banks. Statistics show that two years from now, Arab oil-producing countries might invest more than one trillion dollars in the United States. That would be ten times the total book value of the United States investments overseas and would be one hundred times the value of all gold held by the United States government." Then Starr added sarcastically, "and the question was if we are dependent on Arab oil? Our government doesn't even know about concealed investments that have been made by OPEC, and I believe we need federal legislation right now to correct the problem.

"This doesn't mean that I'm declaring economic war on Arab nations. This also applies to any foreign investment by Israel. I think it's bad policy for the United States to take in all of this money while jeopardizing our position in the world."

Arthur Sutherland was stunned. He thought Starr had gone too far. He not only was opening himself up to the religion issue again, but had gone so far that the average American would realize that he could not separate church from state. He was attacking the Arabs, and since he was a Jew, people would think he would now have a hard time divesting himself of his heritage if a serious dispute arose between the Arabs and the Israelis.

Sutherland realized it was a calculated decision, and he was confident it would backfire.

The last subject to be debated was the country's national defense. Senator Starr knew he had left himself open by attacking the Arabs, but he felt now was the time to fully discuss all of the issues that concerned the country.

When asked about the country's national defense spending and military power, Arthur Sutherland gave a very encouraging report.

In rebuttal, Starr claimed the Sutherland administration had ordered that military budgets could grow only with the rate of inflation. The practical effect of this was to pour billions of dollars into costly strategic weapons, but not allow enough money for the real military forces. The country could have all the fancy missiles and aircraft, or the most expensive computers money could buy, but they needed the soldier to man the weapons. Starr attacked the Republican Congress: "They like to solve problems by just throwing money at them, but they haven't been able to solve this problem. Even if the defense budget was increased by twenty percent over the next few years, the money must be spent in the proper areas."

Starr wiped his brow and turned directly at Sutherland. The president returned his icy stare. Starr began speaking slowly, but his voice projected the words loud and clear. "This universe faces the threat of nuclear war every day. I admit the Middle East is in turmoil . . . the peace of a decade is threatened. But this president, in a last-ditch effort to win reelection and appease Arab oil money, has proposed an executive agreement peace plan, not a treaty, so he can bypass congressional approval. He has made only portions of the plan public."

Starr once again stared at Sutherland. He could feel the adrenaline building. He surveyed the audience before him and saw the anticipation in their eyes.

"The peace plan can't work. Israel can't survive with nuclear power plants in Egypt and Saudi Arabia, no more than we could if reactors were in Cuba. There is no way to safeguard them. Would Syrian President Assad and Colonel Qaddafi stand by? Of course not. Would the plants be safe from terrorist takeover. Of course not.

"These very plants could manufacture nuclear weapons if they fell into the wrong hands.

"This country can't dictate a peace plan. Let the participants decide their own fate. If we want a treaty, then involve the Congress and not use secret negotiations behind the back of the American public. And if this president really trusts the public and wants to be fair to Israel, then make the entire plan public. No more piecemeal disclosures. Let us see it all.

"I haven't even discussed the most important issue facing civilized society. We must enact a nuclear freeze . . . *now*," Starr shouted, banging his right hand solidly on the podium. "For the past ten years, national politicians have used every forum imaginable to promise a freeze . . . both Democrats and Republicans. I'm tired of the rhetoric . . . sick and tired. I pledge to this nation, if I'm president, within six months of my swearing-in, I will personally fly to Moscow and commence negotiations that will lead to a nuclear freeze. Once and for all. This is my solemn pledge."

The moderator was shouting at Senator Starr. He had twice been warned he had gone over the time period, and the debate was drawing to an end. Starr finally smiled, apologized in going too long, and quietly concluded.

"Sorry, I just think this had to be said." For a moment thirteen thousand people sat in stunned silence. Then slowly, and then as if an eruption, the tumultuous crowd broke loose. People cheering, standing on their feet . . . hollering. The applause was deafening. The three panelists were helplessly looking at each other. The moderator used the public address system urging people to quiet down immediately. The outburst was spontaneous and unstoppable. The president was dumbfounded.

In unison, the crowd was hollering "Starr . . . Starr," clapping their hands in staccato rhythm. Over the noise the moderator suggested that, if the president had anything to say in rebuttal, he best say it now, because time was running short. However, the auditorium would not quiet down, and the president's last words were inaudible to the viewing public.

As the two candidates walked over to shake hands with the panelists, Starr thought everything was moving in slow motion. It was almost like a stop-action replay of two players after a tennis match, slowly walking to the judges. When the two men approached the panel, the president of the United States stared coldly at Jonathan Starr. Then the president, feeling the blood rush to his head, unexpectedly moved quickly between Secret Service agents—shouting at the senator, the fury of his anger apparent in his eyes, in his voice. "You don't have to be irresponsible to win an election." The outburst from the president shocked the people around him. The crowd was still cheering, and it was difficult to hear what was being said; though the people in the arena, earlier oblivious to shouting, now could observe the commotion near the panelists' table. Starr screamed back to the president, the veins in his neck stretched to their fullest.

"Somebody had to tell them!" Before he could continue, Paulson Orear grabbed his arm and started pulling him away. The Secret Service agents for both the president and Starr began to push both candidates toward the arena exit. It was a mob scene. Mass hysteria as the people continued to shout "Starr . . . Starr."

Jonathan had no control over his movements. Reynolds had a firm grip over his right shoulder and Orear clamped his left arm. The Secret Service desperately tried to control the crowd, to move them away from Starr, and to move Starr away from Sutherland. The last thing anyone wanted was a brawl between the two candidates for the highest office in the land.

Starr's path to freedom was like a dream. He followed the force of Reynolds . . . as if the inertia of human flesh rubbing against each other was a wave he was riding on. People in the crowd were reaching out, trying to touch or grab Starr, to have something to tell their grandchildren about this historic night.

The Civic Center remained complete pandemonium until the two candidates had left. The unflustered moderator, adjusting his glasses, tried to explain to a shocked viewing audience what had occurred. The wily veteran spoke extemporaneously as all cameras focused on him.

"We have seen an incredible event in American politics. It was a brutal assault on a sitting president. What effect it will have on November 2 is up to you, the American public, the American voter." Then shaking his head and smiling into the camera, the dean of political broadcasters concluded, "Have a good night."

It was forty-five minutes before Starr and Orear were able to get to the St. Paul Radisson, which was only three blocks from the Civic Center. By the time they got to their room, they were both totally exhausted.

Andrew Reynolds, Jo Decker, and Roger Jefferson, along with the other Secret Service agents, had their hands full trying to keep the crowd away from Starr. There had been another mob waiting for him at the Radisson lobby, and had it not been for the hotel management, and their employees on duty, Starr might not have ever made it to the elevator.

"Je . . . sus Christ, I have never seen people react to a speech like that," Orear said excitedly as they shut the door to their suite of rooms. The two stood there looking at each other, both completely drained by the debate and the crowds.

"You know, Paulie, I think the president was shocked. He was pissed off, but he was dazed. I didn't even get into the guts of my speech, the damn moderator rudely interrupted me," Starr joked with a grin, pouring himself a drink and pulling off his tie.

"Jonathan," Orear broke in, grabbing the drink Starr had fixed him, "the damn debate is over. Relax. I want to catch the news."

"You just saw tonight's news."

"I know my reaction, but I want to know theirs," Orear replied, pointing to the three television sets near the center of the large suite. Starr had taken off his drenched shirt, but he was unable to relax. The debate had worked him into a frenzy.

Jonathan rushed into the bathroom and splashed his face with cold water. Orear quickly changed channels so all sets would carry the local news. Starr walked out of the bathroom carrying a small hand towel as he briskly dried his face. He continued talking excitedly, even though Orear's back was to him.

"Shit, I didn't tell them anything that they didn't already know. Hell, I might have told the president something he didn't know."

Orear walked over to Starr, placing a hand on his shoulder.

"Jonathan, the debate is over. Wind down. But I'll tell you

one thing," Orear beamed brightly, "Arthur Sutherland is in a whole lot of trouble."

"I hope so," Starr replied, collapsing on the bed to watch the news, "I hope so."

J.W. McBee sat in a trancelike state before his television, holding a warm can of Texas beer in his trembling right hand. He rubbed his eyes with his left hand, glancing at his watch as he lumbered to his desk.

The light in his den was the only sign of life in the huge deserted Texas home. His wife had been out of town visiting relatives in Dallas. J.W. had spent the entire week in Houston, publicly campaigning for the president's reelection, but privately meeting with Arab leaders in a small hotel, near Hobbe Airport.

He pulled the phone from the receiver and slowly dialed eleven digits. The phone rang twice.

"Long here," the man replied calmly.

"Mr. Secretary," he drawled, "Ah assume you saw TV?"

"Yes, J.W.," the secretary of state replied, recognizing the Texas senator's voice. "What should I do?"

"Git your butt down here tomorrow. Ah'm goin' to need help with the A-rabs."

CHAPTER 32

CAIRO

THE GENERAL'S PRIVATE LIMOUSINE ROLLED TO A STOP TWO blocks from the hotel. The muscular passenger in the backseat methodically rubbed his perfectly trimmed mustache, waiting patiently for his driver to open the door.

"Pick me up in three hours . . . right here," the officer ordered.

The Egyptian general stood ramrod stiff after climbing out of the vehicle, giving the impression he was a man of stern stuff. Peering out from a sun-bronzed face were steel eyes, hard and uncompromising, betraying considerable energy and icelike fanaticism.

"Yes sir," the military attaché replied, saluting his commanding officer.

The general walked quickly toward the hotel, adjusting the many medals he proudly displayed over his left chest. When in public, he always dressed in full uniform.

The general moved briskly through the garden, up the winding staircase, and crossed an almost deserted veranda filled with wicker chairs and low tables. He passed a turban-topped waiter, and ignored his inquiry whether the general was thirsty. The full-dressed officer entered the dark lobby, walking under several slowly rotating fans, and took the stairs to the third floor.

"Have you been waiting long?" the general asked the two individuals in the room.

"No," the short, nervous man replied with a lingering trace of a British accent.

The general approached the woman who was sitting in a small chair in the corner of the room. She gracefully held out her right hand and the general leaned over to kiss it gently.

"Madame, thank you for traveling such a distance on short notice."

She smiled and withdrew her hand. She was just slightly above average height, but because she was slim and carried herself well, she gave the impression of being tall.

The general went to the balcony, smiling when he saw the elaborate tomb of the Aga Khan filling a nearby hilltop. He observed the splendor of the upper Nile—Egypt's great river, dark and slow-moving on such a peaceful day. Layers of clouds now had spread across the far horizon as the general returned to the room, sitting in a chair across from the madame.

"The recent presidential debate in America is the purpose of this meeting," the general began. "Our goals will never be achieved if there is a peace plan. If our people get nuclear reactors, stability, and peace, there will be no political unrest. The civilian government will be popular, and the people won't support any military takeover."

"What is our next step?" asked the short European man sitting on the bed next to the general.

"We support Jonathan Starr for president," the general responded.

The elegantly dressed woman watched the general closely as she uncrossed her thin legs. Her white silk stockings, expensive jewelry, and modern tweed suit gave evidence of her wealth.

"My general," she began, "I see the genius in your plan. We pump money into the Jew's campaign so that there will be no peace plan. We help him win to prevent your government from achieving popularity through this peace plan. Then our real plan continues without Sutherland's stupid interference."

The general smiled, nodding toward the woman.

"My general," she continued, "we have now invested in 13.5 million acres of American land . . . worth eleven billion dollars. Through the assistance of our senator friend, we have sidestepped the Agriculture Foreign Investment Disclosure Act. We should continue to do this?"

"It is true," the general conceded, "that things have worked out well. We have billions invested in American banks, have taken over several legitimate U.S. businesses and purchased vast amounts of government securities. Starr has publicly disclosed some of our activity. We can deal with this. The Jews invest much money as well. Our senator will see to it the Americans hear both sides of the story. Starr's position on this won't stop our buying up bits and pieces of America. But Sutherland must be defeated. A peace plan now, at this time in our movement, could destroy what we've been working for."

The little Englishman, with mouse gray eyes and a thin, almost cruel mouth, nodded his assent. "We must do anything to insure ourselves that our military takeover of the Egyptian government occurs. Both parts of our plan revolve around this."

The general hesitated thoughtfully before answering, slowly rubbing his mustache as he observed the little man to his right.

"As the executive committee of the syndicate, we have the power to commence this new idea. I think we must act now to give Starr the money and political power we have at our disposal. I have seen enough of Sutherland's plan to know my government will support it, and so will our people. We need political unrest . . . not peace.''

The madame rose from her chair, walking slowly around the inexpensive piece of furniture, standing behind the headrest where she placed her dainty hands. She grinned mischievously as she addressed her European counterpart.

"I think our general, once again, has the situation under control."

"We can continue to use our senator friend. He can funnel the money and political support, at the same time, increasing his power. He serves our purpose . . . since we gain more financial and political clout at the same time," the general mused aloud.

"What about the others?" the European snapped. The fidgety little man was constantly pushing his heavy-rimmed glasses up the bridge of his angular nose.

"I've checked with them," the general responded firmly. "Canada, West Germany, and Hong Kong will leave the decision to this executive committee."

The little man adjusted his glasses and smiled. "I agree with this plan of attack. We will defeat Sutherland and his peace plan, even if it means a Starr presidency. He won't be able to stop us once we get close to our final goal. Though it's ironic, the three of us, suggesting ways to help a Jew win the American presidency."

"We're going to do it," the madame snapped with finality. "We're going to destroy Israel, and eventually take control of what is the greatest nation on earth."

The general smiled. He was extraordinarily confident, even ebullient. "The Greek poet Sophocles once said: 'One must wait until the evening to see how splendid the day has been.' Now," he continued, "let's discuss the real purpose of this meeting. Let's review our plans for the annihilation of Israel."

CHAPTER 33

THE VOTERS ARE HEARD

ON TUESDAY MORNING, NOVEMBER 2, JONATHAN STARR, HIS wife and parents voted in San Francisco. The plan called for Starr to make an appearance sometime late afternoon or early evening at the Hyatt Regency, and then quietly watch the election returns in the "secret hideout" that had been secured for him. The hours passed quickly for Starr, bringing the emotional candidate before a throng of supporters.

"And the final point I would like to make," Starr told a cheering crowd at his campaign headquarters, "is that tonight is a new beginning. Politicians say this every four years. Only this time it's true. God bless you all."

The well-wishers flocked toward the handsome California senator. He grabbed many extended hands while Reynolds and the other Secret Service agents tried to move him out of the Hyatt Regency Ballroom. It was 6:15. The polls would close in forty-five minutes. Though network coverage began at 7:00 P.M. on the Coast, Harris and Gallup had "privately" informed Orear their exit polls demonstrated that Starr was doing quite well; that most major electoral college states were leaning toward the Senator. Jonathan wanted to be in his room no later than 6:45 to watch network coverage, a wish he had made clear to Reynolds . . . on several occasions.

"Out of the way," Reynolds pleaded with the crowd surrounding Starr, "make way, please."

Jonathan wanted to spend time with the many dedicated people who had worked so hard for him, but he realized they were running behind schedule. He extended his hand as far as he could reach, grabbing outstretched arms and fingers of the gathering throng.

"Jesus!" Reynolds exclaimed as the group escaped the ballroom crowd, "look at this." Reynolds pointed to the thousands of people packed into the enormous hotel lobby, like sardines, waiting to touch, to hear, to see their candidate.

"Andy."

Reynolds turned around and saw Paulson Orear pulling the sleeve of a well-dressed man who appeared overcome by the crowd.

"This is the manager. He says there's a service elevator around the corner."

"I thought it was out of order," Reynolds said, irritated that they were falling behind schedule. No one had anticipated this many people showing before the polls closed.

"It was fixed an hour ago," the manager replied meekly, feeling guilty he didn't inform the Secret Service about the development. Reynolds took Starr by the hand and pointed to the other agents.

"Now!" he shouted, as the group of men ran to the elevator, Starr like a halfback carefully following his blockers. Once in the elevator, Reynolds took charge.

"Get the limo at the underground entrance . . . Now!" he commanded, using the walkie-talkie to contact other agents. Starr stood by, helplessly. The plans, the security, were beyond his control. He looked at his watch. 6:25. Reynolds felt Starr's anxiety, and his hot breath down his back. He turned to Jonathan.

"We'll make it."

"You always do," Jonathan responded, but there was still apprehension in his voice.

The doors opened and Starr was led directly to his waiting limousine. Reynolds radioed ahead. He handed Orear a box from the glove compartment.

"Put these disguises on."

Orear handed Jonathan his hat and mustache; then he carefully secured his personally chosen disguise.

"Really, Paulie," Reynolds said, shaking his head in disapproval, "I thought you'd do better. A Nixon mask, really."

The two other Secret Service agents in the car remained silent. Their suit coats had been removed and they were now dressed casually, one of them wearing a Giants cap.

"There it is . . . pull over," Reynolds shouted hurriedly, as the limousine pulled ahead of another identical limousine waiting at a taxi stand at the intersection of California Street and Battery.

"Get out and move quickly; to that limousine. Everyone take the same seat," Reynolds said calmly, directing them with confidence.

For the first time Starr noticed they weren't heading directly to the Fairmont. "Andy, why this route? The Fairmont isn't that far from the Hyatt."

"Be patient," he replied tensely. Orear began wondering about the plan himself. "This is Chinatown!" he exclaimed.

"Pull into that alley."

Reynolds directed the driver to a small garage off Grant Avenue, and Starr recognized Roger Jefferson sitting alone in a yellow cab in the empty, seemingly abandoned garage. The curly-brown-haired agent smiled confidently when he saw the vehicle enter the garage.

"All set, Andy?" Roger asked, as the men approached the cab.

"Let's get moving," Reynolds responded, motioning everyone into the cab. As they turned onto Mason Street, within a few blocks of the Fairmont, he explained the scheme.

"We were fearful the press would try to follow us. If they knew we weren't really at campaign headquarters, but at the Fairmont, it would hamper our security plans for tonight. That's why Jo is still at the Hyatt. She'll stay there for a few more hours."

The cab drove near the back entrance of the hotel. The six men quickly exited and moved directly to the back stairs. Reynolds received clearance over the walkie-talkie to proceed. At 6:45 the men entered the end suite on the third floor, directly adjacent to the hotel's back stairway. There were two other men in the hallway watching them. One stood near the elevator, wearing a bellboy's uniform. The second was dressed in coveralls, a plumber to be working on nearby pipes that would start leaking immediately, and leak all through the night. He had a walkie-talkie and a .38 magnum in his tool kit. The coast was clear. Starr was safe.

Jonathan was joined by his wife and close aides, all of whom had used various disguises to get into the Fairmont undetected by the press and public. For three hours they sat watching returns. Jonathan and Orear used the many phones in the suite continuously throughout the night.

Judy Starr, who had been glued to the set most of the night, hollered for everyone to gather around the three sets situated in the spacious living room. And to be quiet.

"We have established a trend and we think we are very close to predicting that Jonathan Starr will be the next president of the United States," NBC reported.

"We would like to make this election night a little more exciting, but it is apparent from the returns coming in that Senator Starr is going to be a winner," CBS speculated.

The ABC news reporter offered his personal thoughts. "Perhaps all of us have learned something by this election. Perhaps the end of anti-Semitism has finally arrived in the United States. The First Amendment tonight really means something, and that doesn't have to be a political statement, but a moral one."

By 2:00 A.M., at the White House, Arthur Sutherland realized what he had suspected all along; Jonathan Starr had won the election. He knew it was time to make a decision about issuing a statement. The president assembled his top advisers for a discussion in the Oval Office. Arthur Sutherland looked around the room in great appreciation to these men and women who had been so supportive of him during his four-year administration.

The president's advisers argued forcefully that, since he was an incumbent president, he should wait until the morning to make his concession speech, especially since Starr had previously indicated he would not make a statement until morning. They persuasively pointed out that the president could concede prior to 9:00 A.M., before Starr made any statement. The president thought to himself, why not? He would wait until tomorrow. What the hell could happen that hadn't already happened to him?

* * *

The FBI director had been gone for one hour. During the past sixty minutes the president had alerted the necessary government officials—summoning them to the White House. He would be meeting them within the hour.

He fingered the FBI papers silently, squeezing each one as he methodically flipped them to one side. His audible reactions were blunt, a combination of farts and grunts.

He reached for the phone and dialed a familiar number.

"Hello."

"J.W. . . . it's Arthur."

"Ah'm sorry, Mr. President. It's a cryin' shame. But Ah think we can still convince the A-rabs . . . we need . . ."

"J.W.," the president interjected, "you, of all people, know how important this deal is with the Arabs. How important it is to me, and this country." The president hesitated momentarily, "But you're *never* going to guess what problem I've inherited this morning." The president sighed, shutting his eyes tightly, fighting the swelling of tears in his eyes.

"What could . . ."

"J.W.," the president interrupted, regaining his composure, "get your Texas ass here . . . now!"

CHAPTER 34

THE SPEAKER

Midnight, November 24

CHARLES DURKIN TURNED OVER THE LAST PAGE OF THE LEGAL memorandum. He placed the document in a basket to the right of his desk. He leaned back slowly in his chair, propped his feet on his desk and smiled at his attorney, who sat apprehensively in the chair before the Speaker's large oak desk.

"Well," Attorney Paul Douglas prodded, "what do you think?"

"I think this country is in the middle of one helluva constitutional crisis. Maybe Starr, maybe Edwards, myself, Sutherland. Will he make the swearing-in? I've never seen so many unanswered legal questions."

"There are," the tall, lanky attorney conceded, "and many go against you."

"But I've got a chance," the Speaker replied calmly. "That's all I want."

"Your campaign with the electoral college must not only defeat Starr, but the vice president elect as well."

"I know."

"One thing is clear," the attorney replied. "If neither Starr nor Edwards gets qualified, Section 19 makes you acting president."

"I know," the Speaker replied, "but it will be tough to convince the college to keep Edwards out. I realize how important this is."

"Keep in mind, Mr. Speaker," the attorney continued, "even if Starr is qualified, he may not be around on January 20. If he's not around by then, the Twentieth Amendment may not apply since there is no *failure to qualify*. If that happens, we argue that Section 19 governs, and you are acting president and not the vice president elect."

The Speaker smiled. "If Sutherland keeps screwing up these rescue efforts, he may convince the college I'm right . . . Starr won't be back, so why qualify him."

"But if the college qualifies Edwards, he could be acting president. Starr's failure to qualify would trigger the Twentieth Amendment."

The Speaker aimlessly tapped his desk and contemplated the situation. He stared at his attorney. "During the primary campaign four years ago it came down to Sutherland or myself in the last few primaries. We met privately after the last debate. He claimed I was a cheap-shot artist who would do anything to win the nomination. He called me a power-hungry demagogue.

I called him a pussy . . . a goody-two-shoes who didn't have the guts to do what was necessary to win the nomination or lead the country. He vowed to destroy me. To do anything he could to make me look bad. He thinks I'm bad for the country. Though we have been on the same side of many issues due to partisan politics, neither of us trusts the other.''

Durkin leaned back in his chair and looked intently at the man before him, searching for the unreachable truth, the solution that would resolve this conflict. He stared at the legal memo to his right. "Give me a quick layman's summary of your brief.''

Without referring to the papers in front of him, the attorney responded confidently.

"Assume Starr is qualified by the electoral college on December 13, despite your great efforts. On the sixth of January, this qualification becomes legally binding when the vote is announced in a joint session of Congress. We've already assumed Starr won't be around for the swearing-in. During the next two weeks, backdoor politics will be played for keeps. And we both know,'' the attorney said winking, ''that you're the best. If Starr doesn't appear on the twentieth, some will scream Edwards is acting president, but that is subject to argument.''

"And subject to his being qualified as vice president elect in the first place,'' countered the Speaker.

"Exactly, but let's assume he is. The Twentieth Amendment says Edwards would be president if Starr is dead. Let's assume there's no proof of that. Since a president, Starr, has been chosen and qualified, then there is nothing explicit in the Twentieth Amendment providing for Edwards to be acting president. Yet on January 20, Starr's not around. Some will argue we have a qualified president, who is not able to discharge his duties, so under Section 19, and the Twenty-Fifth Amendment, the vice president could become full-time or acting president.''

"What law governs?''

"That, Mr. Speaker, is the $64,000 question. We must argue Section 19 applies. The Speaker of the House is acting president, not Edwards. In addition, Section (c)(2), of Section 19, which we talked about earlier, could come into play. The inability would be Starr's failure to be present at the swearing-in. A disability, in a sense. Under this interpretation, as I point out in my brief, *inability* would apply to a *president-elect*, and under *either* part of Section 19, the Speaker *acts* as president."

"Until my Republican House qualifies me as president," the Speaker concluded triumphantly.

"Right. You can have it both ways. First, if Starr is qualified, but not present on the twentieth of January, Edwards is vice president, and the Speaker acting president, until someone is qualified by Congress."

"And second?"

"Second, if Starr is not qualified, Edwards may act as president, assuming he was qualified himself as vice president, but only until a president is chosen by Congress. In either scenario, Edwards never becomes full-time president, and in both scenarios, Congress chooses the president."

"Either way, I'm president. And at worst I have a democratic vice president."

"Right."

"I can live with that. He'll be no problem. Paul, this is amazing. I'm very impressed. However, in all honesty, this plan has a much better chance if Starr isn't rescued by the thirteenth."

The attorney set his glasses on the desk and rubbed the bridge of his nose, showing the fatigue and strain he felt.

"I agree. If he's rescued before the thirteenth, there is no reason for the college not to qualify him. It would be as if he wasn't even kidnapped. But if he's not, you can tie things up. Stall for time. Get this election to the House . . ."

"I know," the Speaker interrupted, "into my own backyard." He paused for a moment and smiled. "I can hear the marine band striking up 'Hail to the Chief' already."

CHAPTER 35

THE EVIL MAN OF SAN QUENTIN

Thursday, November 25

ALL MAJOR NEWSPAPERS CARRIED SIMILAR HEADLINES THANKS-giving Day. Tommy Duncan had granted an interview in San Quentin the preceding day, admitting that he masterminded the Jonathan Starr kidnapping. He wired the president, requesting a hostage exchange. Duncan promised, if he were released from prison and allowed to leave the United States, that Starr would be returned to Washington, unharmed.

By noon, President Sutherland was meeting with Andrew Reynolds, Paulson Orear, and Vice President elect Martin Edwards. The emergency gathering placed Edwards in a delicate position.

There had been an inordinate amount of pressure placed on him to make a public statement concerning his interpretation of the Constitution, and whom he felt should be the next president. So far, Edwards had made no public statements, except to support the actions taken by President Sutherland. However, Edwards had retained his own legal counsel to research the issue. They had advised him that, if he were qualified as vice president, and Starr wasn't returned safely, in all probability he would become president.

"Thank you for coming on such short notice," the president began, as he poured coffee for his guests. The president looked tired. Haggard. The strain of the last month had taken its toll. This gentle man in his mid-sixties was finally looking his age.

219

Large bags had formed under his eyes—a telltale sign of sleepless nights.

"Thank you for inviting us, sir," Edwards replied simply.

The president sat opposite the three men and took a sip of coffee. He played with the rim of the cup, wanting to choose his words carefully.

"In three hours I'm going on national television to inform the country that I'm sending Thomas Whyte to San Quentin to talk with Duncan."

"Will Duncan be released?" asked Orear.

"Not until Starr is released, and even then, I doubt it."

Reynolds looked at the president unbelievingly. "With all due respect, Mr. President, Duncan won't deal unless he gets out, too."

"No way," the president replied angrily. "That sonuvabitch isn't in the driver's seat. He's a convicted murderer. We can't set precedent like this. It would subject politicians, members of their families, hell, even celebrities, to kidnappings."

"Duncan won't do it," Reynolds said flatly. "He has everything to lose and nothing to gain that way."

"Don't underestimate Whyte," the president cautioned.

"Don't underestimate Duncan," Reynolds said, challenging the president's authority.

"Andy," the president said softly, "I know how you feel. I know what you personally have gone through this past month, both physically and emotionally . . . but I can't let this country be blackmailed. It would be a colossal mistake."

The president sipped his coffee. He continued talking with an air of apparent disappointment.

"The Speaker called this morning. He suggested I delay negotiating with Duncan until *after* the electoral college votes on December 13. Obviously, his chances to steal Starr electoral votes would be better served if Starr isn't returned by the thirteenth. Duncan is smart. His timing is almost perfect. He's been reading the papers like everyone else. If Starr doesn't qualify, the election could go to the House. The odds aren't good a Democrat will prevail under that scenario. This way, Duncan is confident the electoral college will qualify Starr because they, like all of us, will assume he's alive and ready to serve. There is no reason for him to fail to qualify. Duncan has his bargaining chip: the real president-elect, instead of someone who won the popular vote, but who became a loser. Starr is priceless as president-elect, but not so if he fails to qualify. Thanks to the Speaker's power play, Duncan had to play his cards.''

The president shook his head in disgust as he turned to Edwards. "You know my position on this issue. Senator Johl is doing everything possible to keep the electors in line, so there's no mutiny. You and Starr won the election—you should have a chance to serve.''

The president paused a moment, then addressed all three men. "I told the Speaker to go to hell. As to my decision with Duncan, I'm afraid," he hesitated slightly, "that decision is final.''

The four men were silent. It was a profoundly moving silence.

"Thank you, Mr. President," Edwards said sympathetically, as he went to shake Sutherland's hand. The meeting was over. Somehow, Reynolds and Orear didn't feel any closer to getting Starr back.

Sutherland wasn't pleased with the meeting. He looked out the window staring at the quiet beauty—the peaceful elegance of the Rose Garden. He couldn't expect Starr's friends to understand his decision. They would do anything to win his release. But Arthur Sutherland had the country to think of. Because Starr had defeated the president, some would claim Sutherland was seeking revenge, not doing everything he could to rescue his opponent. But he knew better.

He sat down and took his favorite pipe from a desk drawer. "Joni," he said over the intercom, "don't let anyone in for half an hour. I want to go over tonight's speech.''

"Damn it," he mumbled in frustration as he tried to light his pipe. After all these years he still ended up smoking matches. He put his pipe away and grabbed a box of cigars. He didn't have any time to waste.

The two men sat opposite each other in Duncan's cell. Whyte was seated on an unstable wooden chair, while Duncan was comfortably sitting in bed, propped up by two large pillows.

"Took ya long enough to get here, Mr. Whyte." Duncan

smiled wryly at the president's counsel. Whyte visibly grimaced as he opened his small briefcase, trying to ignore the surroundings of the rather cold jail cell.

The small cell was oppressive, 10′ × 15′, but for Duncan, featured the special privilege of not sharing the upper bunk bed with another inmate. There was a sink, a toilet, and one electrical outlet. It was malignant and threatening, as if taken right off the set of a Jimmy Cagney movie. In the background, Whyte heard the never-ending noise of radios, shouts, and obscenities. He took a deep breath and eyed Duncan intently.

"Where is President-elect Starr?"

"He's alive, for now," Duncan replied, carefully scrutinizing his adversary.

"We want him returned immediately."

Duncan nodded in mock agreement. "Sure thing, counsel. Then I'm sure the president will negotiate with me in good faith." Duncan stared at Whyte, the sly grin on his face turning to anger, as he spewed profane invective.

"Who the fuck do you think you're dealing with? He's a *dead man* unless I get out . . . now. That's my term, my condition— my deal. Hell, Carter commuted Patty Hearst, Sutherland can do the same."

Whyte sat motionless. His tight jaw slackened, his lips parted, and his face lost all poise of confidence. He had to remain calm, his mission must succeed.

"Mr. Duncan," insisted Whyte, "the president of the United States will not let you walk out of San Quentin, under any circumstances, and you might as well get that out of your head. We want Jonathan Starr back, but we will not be blackmailed. You must understand the position you have put the president in."

"I do understand, Mr. Whyte, and I also understand that if I'm not released from prison, Jonathan Starr will die."

"You're not going to kill Starr because he is the only bargaining power you have. However, it's obvious the president would like him back before December 13."

Tommy Duncan started to pull himself out of bed, a devious smile on his face.

"Mr. Whyte, this meeting is over. Unless I receive the president's permission to be released from prison I will retain Jonathan Starr. I will no longer negotiate. It appears to me that I have the upper hand. I have the Jew." Duncan was irritatingly relaxed, as his voice turned cold and deathly serious.

Whyte was flabbergasted. He couldn't believe Duncan would publicly announce he had Jonathan Starr, write a private letter to the president, and then end negotiations with the president's counsel like this. As Whyte observed Duncan in his blue prison uniform, smiling at the guard outside the cell, he knew the convict wouldn't continue the conversation. It would not be a very pleasant trip back to Washington. Thomas Whyte had been put in tough positions before by President Sutherland, but this problem apparently had no solution. It was the first time Whyte had failed his commander in chief.

CHAPTER 36
THE ATTACK

Tuesday, November 30

THE TALL, ANGULAR MAN SILENTLY WALKED THE LENGTH OF the marina. He opened the folding door to the phone booth and dialed a familiar private number in San Francisco.

"Morgan, here."

"I'm calling from the marina," Len Allen said, his eyes focusing upon a new houseboat docked on the north side.

"How was your Thanksgiving?"

"Fine. The turkey is still with me."

"My client has made a decision."

Allen hesitated momentarily. "What are my orders?"

"Implement Plan A. Leave for Washington today: the task force will meet you."

"How long do I have?"

"The task force suggested four days. But you are to be finished in two days, understood?"

"Understood," Allen responded quickly, hanging up the phone.

Jonathan Starr's oldest daughter, Andrea, walked six blocks to school, Monday through Friday. Normally, she left home at 7:45 A.M. each day, accompanied by two Secret Service agents. However, due to a student council meeting, Andrea was anxious to get to school, and had dragged the agents out of her home fifteen minutes earlier than normal.

Tommy Duncan's task force had determined, through three weeks of constant surveillance, that on Tuesday and Thursday the agents didn't use an advance car or any backup men.

On this particular Tuesday morning Lee Allen rented a car using a fictitious name, wearing a wig and moustache that would have made him unrecognizable to his mother. The group obtained a second car, stolen the night before, from the other side of Washington. A quick paint job and license switch were all that was necessary. One vehicle would be used in the actual murder; the other would be their "getaway car."

"Everything set with the other car?" Allen asked, as he slowly drove his rented car toward the school.

"Check," the tall man in the backseat replied. "It's parked seven blocks from the school, just as you requested."

"Tommy appreciates this," Allen muttered, as he pulled within a half block of the school.

"Anything for Tommy. Tell him for us," requested the short, fat man in the front seat, as he rubbed his smooth-skinned face. He had clear brown eyes, topped by a mass of disheveled brown hair that had managed to stay the same color as during his early New York labor days with Duncan.

The men gazed at the carefree teenagers; the tall man commenting on how the girls' breasts were much larger now than when he was looking for action. Allen's eyes were glued to the rearview mirror. He finally saw what he was waiting for.

"Everyone down!" he commanded, as he grabbed a newspaper, placing it on the steering wheel, pretending to read.

Andrea was cheerfully making her way on the sidewalk toward the school, laughing at the comment one of her unsuspecting protectors had made. They now had passed Allen and his anxious comrades.

Allen slowly turned over the motor. The engine quietly purred.

"Ready," he whispered, never taking his eyes off the target.

"Ready," the men replied in unison, each grabbing two hand grenades as the brown car screeched toward Andrea.

Agent Tommy Connor was still smiling from his last joke as he turned toward the oncoming car. He froze, as his eyes caught the cold stare of the mustached driver.

"Cover Andrea!" he screamed, as the grenades exploded near their prey. The blast picked one agent up, spun him in midair, and plunked his riddled body to the ground. Within seconds, the whole block was a scene of screaming kids, mass confusion, a sickening smoky haze, and seven dead bodies in the vicinity where the hand grenades had landed.

Two members of the basketball team, who were approaching Andrea, were killed instantly, their intestines grotesquely splattered on the ground beneath them. Blood was everywhere.

With no Secret Service backup cars around, the assassins calmly drove to the stolen car, safely parked seven blocks away.

"I'm going to drive about two miles. I'll drop Mark off first. Then Jeff will drop me off where I can take a cab."

Allen continued watching the rearview mirror intently. No cars.

"I'll ditch this car in Virginia," the fat man said, wiping the sweat from his brow.

"Good job," Allen said proudly, smiling for the first time, as he removed the mustache.

Len Allen took a cab to the airport and casually read the morning newspaper. He tipped the cabdriver generously, in plenty of time to catch his 10:55 flight to Los Angeles. He acted as if this were just another day. Seven human beings were dead, but Allen was reading the sports section. Several observant students noticed the license plate of the fleeing car, but the police

would end up with no leads. As usual, Allen had covered his
tracks. He adjusted his wig and felt his thick eyebrows. Simple
disguises. He had used them before.

Planning, organization, and execution. A complicated target,
an easy hit, because Allen knew his job. Tommy would be proud.
They had gotten away with murder. Again.

What Len Allen didn't know, and couldn't know, was the
body count of seven didn't include the intended target. Andrea
Starr had miraculously escaped death. She sustained cuts and
bruises, and a serious concussion, but thanks to a brave Secret
Service agent, she would suffer no permanent injuries.

Tommy Duncan wasn't disappointed when he received word
of the mission's result.

His point had been made.

Arthur Sutherland sat behind his desk, stunned by the day's
development. He violently threw *The Washington Post* to the
floor. It's headline read: "STARR'S OLDEST DAUGHTER AT-
TACKED."

Without being called, Special Counsel Whyte and Attorney
General Paul Gilbertson arrived at the White House. The president had summoned Andrew Reynolds, along with FBI Director Hagstrom.

The room was silent for quite some time. Andrew Reynolds
was physically and emotionally drained. The brutal attack of
Starr's daughter had shocked everyone.

"Mr. President," the attorney general began, getting up to
address the group, breaking the silence. "It's obvious that
Tommy Duncan must be released. I am certain that the political
polls, and the mail you will be receiving, will indicate the country would rather have a live president, with Duncan in Europe,
than a dead president, with Tommy Duncan in San Quentin.
The point is, he's got us by the balls. He's the one that has
Jonathan Starr. I don't like this any more than you, but if we
want Starr back, we've got to let Duncan go . . . it's as simple
as that."

"Can you believe the audacity Duncan has to immediately
take credit for this, like it was something to be proud of," the

president said softly, still trying to accept the senseless act. Sutherland glanced toward Andrew Reynolds, who said nothing.

"Mr. President, we are being blackmailed," interjected Thomas Whyte. "I've negotiated with Duncan, and I'm convinced he'll never let Starr go unless he's released. That by no means assures Starr's safe return, but it's the only chance we have. We've seen the videotape with Starr holding up the *L.A. Times* headline of Friday, November 26. He's alive. The FBI has confirmed it's Starr. So has Judy Starr. Duncan proposes to fly Starr to the airfield north of the prison. When Starr gets off, Duncan gets on, and flies right out of the country. He says that's his guarantee, his only guarantee of getting out. He'll pick the plane and the pilot. He doesn't think you'll shoot him out of the sky."

"In a way, Mr. President, this decision is directly related to what advice you will give the electoral college," added Gilbertson, nervously straightening his bow tie.

"Paul's right," Whyte said quickly. "If you're telling the electoral college to qualify Starr, you need to assure them everything is being done to guarantee his safe return."

"If you don't," the attorney general cautioned, "the Speaker will scream and holler Starr won't be returned . . . and we know we can't give him more ammunition to get this election thrown into Congress."

"You know," the president replied, gently rubbing his right ear, "some woman on a local talk show insinuated I was anti-Semitic and that's why I don't want Starr back. . . . Can you believe anyone would. . ."

"Excuse me, sir," Whyte interrupted, "but time is of the essence. We must act immediately. Both Director Hagstrom and Andy claim we can cover San Quentin from a security point and follow Duncan to the airfield. Duncan wants to be driven by his own men. He doesn't trust us. He fears a double cross. The airfield has been checked out and it can work. But the plane won't land unless Duncan gives his word. He'll probably have a phone in the car that picks him up. He can't get away from us in the short ride from the prison to the airfield. We'll cover him by land and air."

The president got up and paced back and forth. Occasionally, he would take a practice golf swing . . . how he missed the fairways today. His unusual actions worried Whyte. The president appeared to be losing his grip on the situation. He seemed disoriented. The grim-faced president went to his desk and lit a cigar. He turned to his advisers.

"What's the consensus?"

"Well," Gilbertson responded, carefully enunciating every word, "we're not dealing with someone with a room-temperature IQ. Duncan is smart and devious. I think we must give him what he wants."

"As for setting precedent," Whyte chimed in, hoping the others agreed with Gilbertson, as he did, "this has never happened before, and I hope to God never again. None of the events this past month have any precedent. But we can't be concerned about worrying what may happen in the future. The problem is with us now."

"That's not rational coming from a lawyer, Thomas," the president said harshly. At times he could be quite cantankerous.

Reynolds spoke for the first time. His voice rang with sincerity. He forgot his nervousness of speaking at this meeting due to the passion of his conviction.

"Mr. President, I am not a politician. I suggest we do what we have to do to get Jonathan back. Period."

The president sighed. Then he slowly formed his familiar grin. Reynolds took a deep, grateful breath.

"I can't play devil's advocate with you guys," the president said admiringly. "I agree. Thomas, go to San Quentin and do what is necessary. Let's get Jonathan back where he belongs." Sutherland walked over to Reynolds, gently placing his hand on Andy's shoulder.

"Starr has two other daughters, doesn't he?"

"Yes."

"I want top protection . . . for all members of his family. We must be ready for anything. This won't happen again."

CHAPTER 37

A TIME FOR PRAYER

Wednesday, December 1

THE PRESIDENT WAS READY TO ADDRESS THE NATION FOR THE second time this week. Following his first speech, his hard line with Tommy Duncan, police had arrested over six hundred demonstrators who protested the president's decision. It had been the largest mass arrest for a political demonstration in years. Many protestors had been carried away on stretchers to over forty waiting police buses chanting "Free Starr Now."

The arrested demonstrators were photographed, loaded onto buses, issued their summons en route to a booking area, and then released. The demonstrations had angered the president, as any attack on his integrity would.

But tonight's speech would be different. The White House had received letters in record numbers, over ninety-five percent in favor of releasing Duncan to win Starr's safe return.

The French doors to the Rose Garden were open because the intense TV lights generated so much heat. Three silver reflectors stood on tripods behind the camera. The Oval Office had been turned into a makeshift studio.

The president made his way past the wires and white canvas that had covered the green carpet, etched with the great seal of the president of the United States. The president's makeup man placed the finishing touches on Sutherland's face, gently applying a special chemical to stop perspiration, and another to cover the big black bags under his eyes.

The president quickly sat down in his chair behind the massive desk as the sound man clipped the microphone to his tie.

"From the White House," an unidentified voice said, "the president of the United States."

The president paused, took a deep breath, looked straight at the camera and cleared his throat. There would be no script or TelePrompTer—only an outline from index cards.

The president told the country there could be no turning back on past decisions. He assured them his original hard-line stance with Duncan was best for the national interest, but due to Duncan's ruthless and unforeseeable act, the president would immediately begin negotiations to release Duncan, as long as Jonathan Starr was released, unharmed.

The president appeared tired as he outlined the country's dilemma. His two hands rested on the highly polished desktop. The president, who normally faced TV cameras with such confidence and enthusiasm, appeared drawn and somber.

Arthur Sutherland concluded his speech in a most unusual manner. He requested the last thirty seconds be dedicated for silent prayer: for Andrea Starr, Jonathan Starr, and the entire Starr family. After the allotted time, the president raised his face, looked solemnly into the cameras, and firmly said in a loud, convincing voice: "And God Bless America. Good night."

Within minutes after the president's speech, phone calls, cables, wire-service bulletins, and teleprinter messages began to pour into the White House—supporting the president's decision and ignoring any contrary arguments made by the president's opponents, who argued Sutherland had caved in to a blackmailer.

Messages from prime ministers and world leaders expressed sympathy and support for the president's predicament. Everyone was praying for Jonathan Starr.

Including Jonathan Starr.

Starr knew events were moving quickly. He noticed that only Paul Michael Riley and Jim Olsen had been around for the last week. Why hadn't he heard from Allen? The uncertainty was destroying him. He knew that, if he was ever going to come out of this situation alive, he would have to keep control. Stay alert. However, Len Allen had just returned. Soon—too soon—Starr would know where Allen had been.

Jonathan rose from his bed and stretched, extending his arms high, until they touched the low ceiling over him. He rubbed his head gently, feeling for the bump that had knocked him unconscious on the helicopter.

It was gone . . . finally.

He walked over to the only window in his small room, a porthole that was boarded up from the outside. He squinted his eyes trying to see through the small openings of the wood, barely able to detect sunshine.

The small yacht docked on the L.A. waterfront gently swayed back and forth, the waters being quiet this early morning. Other than his bed, the only item of furniture in this prison was a large piece of finished wood hanging from the wall, which in the past obviously had served well as a desk or kitchen table. Jonathan had used it often, quietly eating his meals in silence. In the corner of the room was a toilet and sink. The conditions of his captivity had improved since the warehouse dungeon.

Len Allen and Vicky Roe walked down the steps into the small room, throwing the newspaper and sandwich on Starr's bed. Roe stood motionless, near the center of the room, as Jonathan slowly walked toward his bed. He was hungry and started eating the roast beef sandwich as Allen left the room grinning.

As he turned around, motioning for Vicky to come over and have part of the sandwich, he noticed there were tears streaming from her eyes.

As he devoured his sandwich, his eyes glanced to the paper next to him. "Oh my God," he uttered in shocked disbelief as he got up and staggered to the wall—putting his hands out to brace his body weight. The sound inside his head grew louder, as if an African drum was echoing in his temples. A loud percussion band beating nonstop thunderous music. Everything was going out of focus, he was spinning, then he could feel the darkness.

His mind was incapable of functioning rationally. His shock

was total. He couldn't speak. He still didn't, couldn't, understand the horrible reality of the headlines in front of him.

Vicky started to approach him, but stopped. He was in such agony. It was as if he were falling in space—plunging down the depths of the earth, impossible to catch his breath. Pain was shooting through him—it reached his stomach. Fear, hatred, sorrow, all his emotions were being experienced at the same time.

Tears were flowing down his cheeks. He felt sweaty, then faint. Then sick. He ran quickly for the toilet and vomited his guts out.

For the next twenty-four hours Jonathan's mind filled with memories of Andrea. Vicky Roe was with him. She saw the drawn face, the genuine sadness and sorrow in his eyes.

"I use to tuck her into bed every night when she was little. She never slept in her bed. She could be found on the floor, in the basement, almost anywhere but her bed. On her third birthday my mother-in-law bought her a sleeping bag."

Vicky rubbed his arms gently. He needed to talk, get this out of his system.

"She would crawl into bed with us . . . I liked. . ." Jonathan could talk no more. The hurt almost choked him. Finally he slept.

"Wake up," he barely heard her whisper. "I've got some breakfast."

Jonathan pulled himself out of bed and stretched. He had slept all night in his clothes. He looked at his companion and started to speak, but she moved her hand to her lips. She wanted to talk first.

"I had nothing to do with your daughter's attack. But you should know the paper says she's going to be all right. She will completely recover."

"I know," he said softly, still thinking of Andrea. He ate his breakfast and promised himself he would snap out of his mental hell for the time being. He had to remain strong and alert to survive. He looked at Roe intently, but she seemed preoccupied.

"What's the matter?" he asked.

"I was originally asked to seduce you."

"I gathered that," he said smiling, having fond memories of her success.

"That's all changed. My only job was to find out what you knew about the other crimes Duncan may have committed that weren't made public in those hearings. I've told them you know nothing."

"So what?"

"I'm expendable. I am of no use to them. I didn't deliver what they wanted." She hesitated slightly and then continued. "They will kill me. Listen . . ." she touched Jonathan's arm and looked into his eyes. "I'm not acting this time. Trust me . . . please." She was pleading with him.

"What do you want me to do?"

"We can get out of here. Olson will stand guard tonight. He sits outside your room. I can unlock your door . . . and distract him. While I'm . . . uh . . . *distracting* him, you can jump him."

"What's in this plan for you?"

"My life."

Starr wanted to believe her, but it could be a trap. He desperately needed to trust someone. Anyway, why would they need to trap him this way? They needed no excuse to kill him. They had their opportunities. It was obvious their orders were to keep him alive, for the time being. She did present him with a viable option. What did he have to lose?

"What time?" his voice showing the apprehension he felt.

"3:00 A.M. Listen for the lock to unlatch."

"By the way, where are we?"

"In a small, fancy yacht."

"No, what city?"

"L.A. Listen," she said hurriedly, "should I call someone to meet us?"

"No. No. That might get you caught. Let's get the hell out of here first."

She walked to Jonathan, leaning toward him, kissing his cheek. "See ya soon." She was gone.

He washed up and thought about her proposal. It just might work. Then suddenly he heard the noise. At first it startled him. His heart started beating a mile a minute. He walked quietly to the door. He heard the noise again. It was a cricket. He had heard that cricket for years. Reynolds was *here*. He was saved. All the thoughts rushing through his head, however, came to an abrupt halt. Under the door he saw it. That little odd-shaped black bug. A goddamn cricket. A real cricket. "Shit," he cussed to himself, as he slowly crawled into bed for what he hoped would only be a few hours of rest.

Jonathan could not sleep. He was lying flat in bed, his arms cocked under his head on the pillow, staring at the dark ceiling. He had been in captivity for over a month, and his body ached to get out. He knew it was risky, it might cost him his life, but what could be worse than what he was already going through?

The papers reported the country was in turmoil, and he couldn't believe Duncan would ever let him walk out of this alive. Being a true politician, he looked at the assets and liabilities, weighing each side, and chose to take the daring course. He had no other choice. The minutes seemed like hours, the hours seemed like days as he lay quietly in his bed. He noticed his breathing was very slow, but his heart was beating fast.

Finally, three o'clock came and he heard the door open slowly. A light from the outside hallway shone in as he started to rise. The force of the bright lights stunned him. The room was now well illuminated as Len Allen, Riley, and Olson sauntered down the steps. Something had gone wrong. Allen walked toward Starr. The prisoner could sense the hatred this morning—the bad vibrations he normally felt with Allen were worse than ever.

"I would have thought a smart man like you would know this room was bugged," Allen said, shaking his head.

It was all over. The great escape plan would never work. They had been monitoring Starr's conversations with Vicky. All of those crazy things Starr had talked to her about, thinking it would be kept in confidence, certainly never suspecting there was a perverted third party listening on the other end, now horrified him. What he was most concerned with now, however, was Roe's safety. That question was left unresolved for only a few seconds.

"We killed her," Allen said coldly.

"That's it!" Starr screamed, "*You killed her?* You can calmly stand in front of me and admit you killed another human be-ing?''

"Fuck off, Senator!" Allen thundered, as he motioned for the others to leave the room. "Your time will come. You'll *never* make it to Washington," Allen said icily, as he walked away from Starr in disgust, slamming the door behind him.

Starr collapsed on the bed. Some poor girl, who somehow got mixed up with these ruthless men, had attempted to help him. That effort had cost Vicky Roe her life. These people were monsters and would stop at nothing. He prayed that night like he had never prayed before. He prayed for his own safety, but he also prayed for the safety of his family and the country.

Starr's thoughts went to President Sutherland. He knew the president was making difficult decisions. He had been able to piece together the chronology of his captivity through recent newspaper articles. So on this night Starr prayed for the one man in the world who could help him. Besides Tommy Duncan, the one man who had some control over his future well-being. Jonathan Starr prayed for Arthur Sutherland.

CHAPTER 38

THE PRESIDENT DECIDES

Friday, December 3

NBC BROKE THE STORY FIRST. WITHIN A HALF HOUR, EVERY wire service and national network reported the tragic news— President Sutherland had suffered a heart attack and had been rushed to Walter Reed Hospital.

The president had been scheduled to address the nation this

evening, outlining his decision on the pending constitutional crisis.

"Mr. Vice President, this is Charles Durkin."

"Yes, Mr. Speaker."

"How is the president?" asked Durkin.

"I don't know. I'm going to the hospital now. His chief of staff swears it wasn't a heart attack."

"If the president becomes incapacitated, regardless of whether or not you take over as acting president under the Twenty-fifth Amendment, I think you will have the influence to convince the electoral college that Martin Edwards can't be president."

My God, the vice president thought to himself, this is what he wants. The president's in the hospital and he's talking politics.

"Mr. Speaker, if the president thinks the Constitution provides for Senator Edwards, and the attorney general concurs, far be it for me to differ." The vice president was getting restless. Enough of this.

"My point, Mr. Vice President, is to let Congress have more time. The Twentieth Amendment talks about our role as well. The electoral college shouldn't have the power they do under these . . . most unusual circumstances," the Speaker persisted.

"There's nothing I can do. It's a constitutional decision, not politics."

"Bullshit, Jerry," Durkin shouted back unexpectedly, his tone belligerent. "I'm best for the country. The electoral college should be told to qualify no one. Then Congress, as it should, can decide the issue."

"You're wasting your time," the vice president replied icily.

"Look, the country doesn't want the administration to make a hasty decision. We need time to reflect. I'm the perfect compromise candidate. Hell, Edwards isn't that popular, and without Sutherland pushing him, I doubt the college would qualify him for vice president elect. He just rode in on Starr's coattails."

The vice president heard a knock on the door. A perfect excuse for the Southern gentleman.

"Mr. Speaker, I thank you for your . . . frankness," Stevens said sarcastically, then quickly added, "I must go. Good-bye."

"Mr. Vice President?" Stevens recognized the voice immediately. A welcome voice.

"Come in, Thomas."

"I've been meeting with the attorney general and our lawyers. I just heard. Any news?"

"Nothing," Stevens replied. "Let's go to the hospital."

After talking with the president's doctors for fifteen minutes, Whyte and the vice president heaved a collective sigh of relief.

"That's all it was, Mr. Vice President, a pleurisy attack," explained Walter Reed's heart specialist, Dr. Larry Boss. "The president's doctor wanted to be safe rather than sorry." Then Boss quickly added, "And he was right to do so. Unfortunately, the media got wind of this, and the rumors started flying."

"How long will he be incapacitated?" asked Whyte.

"Thirty-six hours at most. But we should keep him here overnight. Just to be sure."

Whyte noticed Mary Sutherland standing outside the president's room. She looked relieved. Dr. Boss had already told her the good news. Her face lit up when she saw Whyte. The two of them went in to see the president, as the vice president continued talking with the doctor.

It didn't look much like a hospital room. Four telephones surrounded the president, and a full medical team was on standby in the adjacent room. Conference-size tables had been placed in the large room and at least a dozen chairs were scattered about. The Secret Service had secured one wing of the hospital for the president, and a small suite was being arranged for his secretary.

The president waved his two visitors in. Mary sat down on a chair near the head of the bed.

"You look swell," volunteered Whyte.

The president reached for his wife and squeezed her hand softly. "It's going to take much more than this to get rid of me. Sit down," he commanded, as he sat up in the elevated bed, propping two pillows behind him.

"Just got off the phone with Andy Reynolds. I've put him in charge of coordinating surveillance on Duncan from the prison to the airfield."

"Did you read *The Washington Post* today?" asked Whyte, not satisfied with his boss's decision.

"Poppycock!" shouted the president. "The original kidnapping wasn't his fault. Besides, the security setup was perfect, considering the circumstances. And the attempt on the daughter . . . no way Reynolds is responsible for that. If anyone is, I am." The president sighed, remembering the tragic incident.

"Very well, Mr. President," replied Whyte, not wanting to challenge Sutherland.

"You know, Thomas," the president continued, "I like the idea of having one man responsible for the exchange at the airstrip. Otherwise, I'll spend all day reading reports. Honey," he said turning to his wife, "could you give us five minutes?"

Mary flashed an understanding smile and gave her husband another kiss before leaving the room.

"Sit over here, Thomas."

Whyte pulled up a chair. The president was acting strangely.

"I want you to know Reynolds has been given complete authority to act on my behalf. This is national security. And Thomas. . ." the president motioned Whyte closer, "I put it in writing." Before Whyte could protest, the president gently grabbed his arm. "I know you lawyers don't like that kind of thing in writing, but Thomas . . . I'm desperate. If I don't get Starr back alive, my administration . . . hell, my life, will be a failure. I will admit, Reynolds has made some mistakes, but I've gone this far with him—I'm not pulling the plug . . . yet. I *do* still have confidence in him, and my instincts tell me more harm than good would occur by bringing in someone else. Can you understand that?

"Yes," Whyte conceded.

For the next thirty-six hours Thomas Whyte worked nonstop. He finished the final proposal concerning recommendations to the electoral college. He also prepared for the final round of negotiations with Tommy Duncan.

Whyte had become the most important part of the crisis team. He handled power well and wasn't worried about monopolizing it. He was the quintessential staff man, in a position to influence the destiny of the country.

A master synthesizer, Whyte collected divergent viewpoints from his legal staff, carefully shaping their views into a workable plan with real solutions. He was indeed the perfect adviser: characteristically friendly, yet sharp and perceptive. And always the gentleman, rarely raising his voice, almost never swearing. His apple cheeks, light brown eyes, and premature white hair gave him the appearance of a middle-aged, all-American boy.

"It's great to be back," Sutherland beamed brightly as he greeted the marine sergeant, with his neat crew cut and pressed blue uniform, sitting proud and erect behind his desk, adjacent to the tall doors leading to the Oval Office.

The attorneys started to rise when the president entered, but he quickly waved them to their places. He was in no mood for formalities.

Christenson and Griswold were visibly nervous. They knew this was the last meeting—judgment day. Their work ended tonight. The president's would just start. Both lawyers were dressed appropriately, one black pinstripe—one gray. The other men dressed for the occasion in similar fashion, a fact that didn't go unnoticed by the president.

"Why is it lawyers always dress alike? You guys always dress up. So formal," the president chided as he sat down on the couch with a cup of coffee, proudly wearing a casual sweater, white shirt, and soft brown corduroy slacks. No tie, no coat for him. Not today. Too much work to do.

"Paul," he said turning to his attorney general, "any conclusion on the Emergency Powers Act?" Gilbertson cleared his throat and addressed the group in his confident and efficient manner.

"Carter used the act in 1980 for the grain embargo with Russia. FDR banned scrap iron shipments to Japan prior to World War II and used the act again to regulate the railroads during the war. We have precedent."

The president held up his right hand, shaking his head sideways. "I won't pardon Duncan. No way. But I'll let him out under this act. Does that settle the issue?"

The men nodded in agreement as the president hastened to add, "Of course, that assumes Starr comes back alive. The airfield exchange seems foolproof. We'll watch Duncan from San

Quentin to the strip. He gets on the plane *only* when Reynolds confirms Starr is okay. Now to the other issue."

The president walked to his desk and opened the upper right drawer. Would it be a cigar or pipe night? The cigar won, much to the chagrin of Paul Gilbertson, who couldn't stand the smell.

"I've had a chance to review these memos," the president said seriously. His eyes again carefully scanned the papers prepared by Griswold and Christenson.

Sutherland moved to his chair, lighting the cigar as he sat down. Gilbertson, sitting to the president's right, quickly gulped his last breath of fresh air. All eyes were on the president as the room became uncomfortably silent. Taking a long, slow puff from his oversized cigar, the president looked at Griswold and nodded.

The attorney took his notes from a stylish briefcase, leaning over to pull up his socks at the same time. He was both apprehensive and excited.

"Mr. President," he began, his deep and aristocratic voice vibrating through the room. "We must assume under the Twentieth Amendment that the president-elect has not died. Martin Edwards wouldn't become president under that provision." The short, stocky, compactly built attorney observed his jury. Whyte was frowning.

"What is it, Thomas?"

"It's a minor point, but it hasn't been raised before. The definition of president-elect in this Amendment seems to vary within the context of several sentences."

"Such as?" Griswold asked.

"President-elect seems to mean the person who was qualified prior to the swearing-in, but doesn't make it that far—he dies. However, late in the amendment, there is an implication that it refers to the person who won the general election. In this case, Starr. I think the distinction must be kept in mind."

"Very well," Griswold said, "I'll continue. With all the publicity about Duncan's involvement, I feel confident the electoral college will qualify Starr. All we need to do is make sure Edwards is qualified as vice president."

Attorney Griswold paused and looked at the president. "Sir,

should we focus the discussion on the assumption that Starr is qualified?"

The president squirmed on the couch, reaching toward the ashtray to put out his cigar. "Yes, I think so. Senator Johl has been extremely successful in fighting off Durkin's campaign to sway members of the electoral college. I think the college realizes that it's not up to them to alter the course of history. People are still sensitive to power politics, especially since it looks like Starr will be returned."

The president strolled to his desk, opening the top right drawer. "These smell better than cigars, don't they, Paul?" the president joked, smiling at the attorney general. Sutherland sat down and twisted a pipe cleaner in the stem of his Carey pipe.

Thomas Whyte moved his chair closer to the president. The others followed.

"Speaker Durkin called yesterday," the president began. "He suggested that all negotiations with Duncan should cease immediately until after the thirteenth of December."

Whyte was aghast. "That's sick."

"Think about it, for a minute," the president suggested. "If we negotiate his release and we don't get Starr back before Monday the thirteenth, how will that effect the electoral college?"

"They may *not* qualify Starr," the attorney general conceded.

"Exactly," the president sighed. "The Speaker wants to box me in. They may not qualify Edwards, either."

"Sure," Whyte agreed, "if you wait until after the thirteenth, the Speaker has a chance. If Starr is back before the thirteenth, he loses."

"But," the president interjected, "if something goes wrong *before* the thirteenth, we may lose."

Sutherland reached for his pipe, filled it, and lit up with a nearby lighter. As he drew on it slowly, smoke billowing with each puff, his countenance was typical of the academic pensiveness he was experiencing. Maybe it was due to his scholarly audience, who waited patiently for him to continue.

The president smiled. "We got off the track." Turning to Griswold he added, "Assume Starr is qualified."

"Okay. If we. . ."

"Excuse me, Don," the president interrupted. His gaze under the puckered, bushy eyebrows was piercing. "Further assume Starr won't be back by the swearing-in."

Griswold paused a moment, glancing at the legal pad before him. "If Starr is chosen and qualified, but not present for the swearing-in, two arguments can be made. First, that the Twentieth Amendment doesn't apply, because there is no failure to qualify."

"I follow that option," quipped the president, sucking on his pipe.

"Second," Griswold continued, "there is a creative definition of 'failure to qualify.' "

"Where is this definition found? I looked everywhere," Whyte asked earnestly. The white-haired attorney smiled.

"It's my interpretation of the law, Thomas. You won't find it anywhere."

"And it is?" the president asked impatiently.

"We know the Constitution requires a president to take the oath of office. The Founding Fathers used the word '*shall*,' which means mandatory, not discretionary. Starr's absence may be a failure to qualify, because his very presence is mandatory. He doesn't qualify, or he's not qualified, to be president, if he can't be sworn in."

The president nodded his head. "Very clever. We can have it both ways. If Starr fails to qualify, Edwards *acts* as president under the Twentieth Amendment. Or, if Starr is chosen or qualified by the electoral college, but isn't around to be sworn in, we argue his absence is a de facto failure to qualify, once again, triggering the Twentieth Amendment provision in favor of Edwards."

"De facto?" whistled Whyte. "Very impressive, Mr. President," he said smiling.

The president took a long drag from his pipe. "I'm getting into this legal crap," he joked.

"After one month of research, we're finally getting answers to support our position. Starr and Edwards should serve," the attorney general said proudly.

"This is a key point Don has argued. Does anyone disagree with him?" the president asked.

"Arguments can be made against it," Whyte responded, "but I like the reasoning. It makes as much sense as anything else we've talked about. There's no precedent to draw on. I'd say you have better than a fifty-fifty chance to prevail in a court of law."

"I agree," said the attorney general, "but Thomas just raised an issue we should discuss."

"I don't like that frown, Paul," the president said seriously.

"Thomas mentioned a court of law. Let's spend a moment to think out who would make the decision as to whether Starr's unavailability constituted a failure to qualify under the Twentieth Amendment. We know the Speaker will be screaming that the amendment doesn't apply—so Edwards can't act as president."

Sutherland doodled frantically on a legal pad, praying for some mystical idea that would strike his imagination or inner being he had thus far been unable to find. He stared at the attorney general, shaking his head in exasperation, now clasping his hands together in total frustration.

"Wouldn't the Supreme Court grant an emergency hearing and expedite a decision? It seems to me they would have jurisdiction."

"Yes," agreed Gilbertson, "but there's more to it. Who has the authority or power to decide how anyone will be qualified— where is it truly defined? We keep going back and forth. To Article 2 of the Constitution and the Twelfth and Twentieth Amendments."

"I think I know where Paul's coming from," Griswold interjected. "Whatever happens, under almost any scenario, legal issues requiring instant decisions may be necessary."

"Such as?" the president asked.

"First," Griswold replied, "if Starr isn't sworn in, if he's considered to have failed to qualify, by not being available on the twentieth, does that mean Congress must choose another candidate after January 20? That's what it means under the Twelfth Amendment . . . and it must be done by March 4."

Griswold paused for a moment and eyed the president intently. "Additionally, if Starr can't be qualified, it only leaves you and the Speaker to be chosen under the Twelfth Amendment. You two remain from the top three."

Sutherland paled and sank slowly back against his chair. "I'll be damned." His words came in a soft groan.

"Wait a minute," Whyte said, rising from his chair. "Let's get practical. If Starr isn't back by January 20, or March 4, for God's sake, it will mean one thing."

"That he's dead," the president said quietly.

"Exactly," Whyte said, walking behind the president's desk. "And under the Twentieth Amendment, if Starr is dead, Martin Edwards becomes full-time president. Congress won't have to choose anyone."

"I agree," Sutherland said sadly, "but I'm not too thrilled about that backdoor victory. After one month, aren't we any closer to resolving this?" The president mumbled, foiled again by the legal uncertainties. The president's control over his impatience was slipping fast, his frustration at being trapped in a hopeless dilemma was growing.

The tall lawyer, with the long, brown sideburns, stood up. He had silently watched his colleagues debate the constitutional issue for over an hour.

"Well, Mr. Christenson," the president said, feigning surprise, "I wondered when you would put in your two cents worth."

Christenson grinned, pouring himself a cup of coffee from a nearby tray. "I've given you a discount in fees, Mr. President, but it's still more than two cents."

The president politely smiled and motioned for him to continue.

"Today, almost every comment has focused on the ambiguities and uncertainties of the Twelfth and Twentieth Amendments. We can go through all kinds of scenarios, and reach different conclusions, all based on sound legal principles."

The attorney paused and sipped his coffee. "Let's direct our attention to the most recent law covering this topic, Title 3, Section 19. This was the congressional response to the provisions of the Twentieth Amendment. There's no question that, if neither Starr nor Edwards qualifies, the Speaker acts as president until someone is chosen . . . undoubtedly himself. I'm suggesting the president recommend both Starr and Edwards to be qualified according to the popular vote. No problem so far, is there, sir?"

"No," the president replied. "I follow you. Please continue."

"Assuming both are qualified, if Starr is not available on January 20, for the swearing-in, he would be unable to discharge the powers and duties of the president. Under *this* law, the vice president can discharge these powers and duties and can be president."

The president laughed. "Ken, it just can't be that simple. What the hell have we been killing ourselves for this past month?"

The attorney hesitated before responding, carefully placing his coffee cup on the tray. Whyte watched him closely, fascinated by the proposal. The attorney general grabbed his briefcase, looking for a copy of the law under discussion.

"We ignore the Twelfth and Twentieth Amendments. They are not relevant for the legal determination of any issue, because they don't cover the precise problem, or they're ambigious. However, if Starr is qualified, and not sworn in, Section 19 can be implemented as long as there is a qualified vice president."

The attorney stopped himself. He had actually lectured to this esteemed gathering, prancing around the Oval Office as if he were in court. The president was impressed. So was Whyte.

"What we could do," Whyte began, with no-nonsense spontaneity, "is drop our argument that Starr's unavailability means failure to qualify. Why get into the Twentieth Amendment? Take the position Ken has proposed and downplay the others. This is the surest way to get Edwards as president. If we later feel this position isn't going to work, we can always fall back to the other legal arguments we discussed today."

The president was elated. He placed his pipe on his desk.

"I could tell the electoral college to qualify them both. That we feel confident Starr will be returned, but if he's not, their decision will most likely lead to Edwards ultimately becoming president. I don't want to confuse them by getting into the conflicting laws."

"I agree with that," Christenson said, "but I doubt even *you* have legal authority to compel the electoral college to vote for Starr and Edwards."

"Agreed," Sutherland replied quickly. "But I can suggest—based on the law and common sense. And," the president said firmly, "based on what is morally and ethically right."

"Look," Whyte said, "constitutional lawyers and law professors will talk about our decision for years. Some will agree, some will criticize. The point is, the Democrats won. They should have the White House. Some polls show Edwards isn't popular . . . so what? He won the office, it's his. If the president tells the electoral college to vote Starr and Edwards in, they will."

"And that's exactly what I plan on doing," the president said triumphantly.

Paul Gilbertson reached out and shook the president's hand vigorously. "I've never been more proud to have served you than tonight," he said sincerely. "There would have been no problem in getting the Speaker to be acting president. You could have stonewalled the electoral college and kept Edwards out. With a Republican Congress, you could call the shots. They would qualify who *you* chose, with the number one candidate being yourself for another term. By the time it got to the courts, the new government would be in power."

"Here . . . here," Whyte chimed in, saluting his boss. The president was embarrassed. None of these men knew the mental gymnastics Sutherland had performed over the past month. Analyzing different scenarios to keep his power. To keep the peace plan a reality. He knew, if it ever came down to the Speaker or him, he would fight to the end to retain his office. But now, finally, he was at peace with himself. If the issue was between Starr and the president, or the Democrats versus the Republicans, Arthur Sutherland would do the right thing. The office of the presidency required nothing less.

"Experience, when it can't be communicated to another, is the greatest loss of man's resources. We have made decisions today that may help those that follow us. Now, if the electoral college agrees, we're in business. The next item is to get Starr back in one piece." The president was feeling good.

"Mr. President," Christenson said, slightly hesitating, as he slumped his shoulders, his voice serious. "We've been reading in the papers Durkin's claims that Starr may be brainwashed. That he's probably been tortured, so he's not mentally sound. I think we need to talk about this."

"Go on," the president said, feeling his mood roller-coaster once again.

"The issue would be the same even without the kidnapping, if we substituted a car accident, brain damage, or a heart attack. Assume further the electoral college votes for him. I know of no law that says he wouldn't qualify as president. Furthermore, *who* would determine if he was unable or disabled to be president, especially if medical opinions differed?"

The president looked toward his special counsel, but the look on Whyte's face indicated that this possibility was a new thought to him as well.

"Don't you lawyers have anything better to do than come up with these fucking possibilities?" the president shrugged.

The attorney general found the idea intriguing. "If Starr had not been kidnapped but was seriously incapacitated, let's say some doctors said there was brain damage and others disagreed, as doctors will do, I'm not aware of any law prohibiting him from being sworn in. Especially if this takes place after the electoral college has voted him in—qualified him. Nobody ever took the time to define *qualify*, and if the president-elect insisted he was okay, who's going to stop him from being sworn in? Who could prove he's disabled?"

Reluctantly, the president agreed there was a problem. Another one. "I suppose you have a copy of the law with you?" the president asked the tall attorney sarcastically.

"Take a look at the first paragraph of Section 4." Christenson crossed the room and handed the president a portion of the Twenty-fifth Amendment. He circulated copies for the others.

Whenever the Vice President and a majority of either the principal officers of the executive departments or of such other body as Congress may by law provide, transmit to the President pro tempore of the Senate and the Speaker of the House of Representatives their written declaration that the President is unable to discharge the powers and duties of his office, the Vice President shall immediately assume the powers and duties of the office as Acting President.

The president carefully reviewed the document. Something didn't make sense. "How can the vice president and the cabinet act when they don't exist until Starr is sworn in? My cabinet leaves at noon on the twentieth."

"That's it!" Whyte exclaimed, pointing to the document as he continued. "The Twenty-fifth Amendment presupposes the man is already sworn in. It only applies to *presidents*, not *presidents-elect*."

"I agree," the attorney general said. "The amendment doesn't apply *until* Starr takes office. If something is wrong with him, this amendment wouldn't stop him from being sworn in."

"But once in office, then his cabinet could act." Whyte stated his conclusion, but Griswold thought it was a question.

"They could, but would they? Especially if the president insisted he was okay."

"The point I wanted to make, Mr. President," Christenson continued, "is that Section 19 comes into play, even if the Twenty-fifth Amendment doesn't. If Starr has a disability, preventing him from discharging his duties, we better make sure Edwards is qualified, so he can act as president, until Starr's disabilities are assessed. Otherwise. . ."

"Otherwise," the president snapped, "we're back to fighting the Speaker."

"Especially," Whyte added, "if the Speaker argues Starr's physical or mental disability is permanent, which could support an argument he has *failed to qualify*."

"Back to the Speaker, again," the president snarled. "What's the bottom line?"

"That there is no answer," Whyte replied. "Again, this situation, something happening to the president-elect, isn't covered by the laws or the amendments. Unless something physical stopped him from being sworn in, like a coma, anyone qualified by the college could be president. It revolves around what *qualified* means, and who would ultimately make that decision."

"Good," the president snorted, "another issue with no answer."

Christenson turned to the president. "There's no precedent. The physical or mental condition of a president-elect during this lame-duck period has never come up. It's not like the impeachment procedure, where everything is nicely laid out. Here, there's nothing.''

"Gentlemen," the president said flatly, "I think I've made my decision." The aides listened intently as the president methodically delivered his conclusions, speaking in a deliberate monotone. "I'm going to advise the electoral college to vote for the winning ticket. I'll give them, and the country, reasons consistent with our discussion."

The president paused, and slowly pulled himself out of the chair. He was sweating profusely, though the room temperature was very comfortable. He walked to the couch and dropped his tired frame onto the comfortable cushions.

"I'm not going to comment about the possibility of Starr's health. If that becomes an issue, we'll handle it at the appropriate time."

For the third time in two weeks the president appeared on national television. The speech was delicately delivered, since the president didn't want to give Tommy Duncan the impression that Starr would not be returned. However, the president candidly outlined to the country and the electoral college what his specific proposals were, and the rationale behind them.

Thomas Whyte watched the speech at home with his family. He was very pleased with his good friend's performance. It illustrated true statesmanship. He was letting the nation know he was not going to play politics. He was putting the country's interests before any party . . . any individual.

For Whyte, handling the dilemma of the legal conflicts involved the exercise of legal reasoning, the use of his legal skills. That's what he was trained for. The rational, underlying principles of law prevailed in those difficult decisions.

Not with Tommy Duncan.

One slip of the tongue, one improper nuance, could lead to Starr's death. Unfortunately, Duncan was in the driver's seat. Whyte's job, as the clever negotiator, was not to let Duncan know just how powerful a position he held. No easy job with a man of Duncan's perverted abilities.

Satisfy Duncan. Satisfy Sutherland. Satisfy the country. Satisfy himself. He didn't relish his trip to the Coast, but he understood and accepted the challenge. The challenge. That was all Whyte could think of as he tossed and turned the entire night. His vague and troubling dreams were about one man. The convicted felon and ruthless murderer. The man who was holding America hostage.

CHAPTER 39

THE SAN QUENTIN CONTRACT

Sunday, December 5

THEY CONCLUDED THE FOURTH BREAK OF THE DAY. WHYTE WAS sick of Duncan. He had spent the past two days trying to reason with a madman.

"I can't take much more of the sonuvabitch," a frustrated Whyte whispered to his aide. They were gulping Diet Pepsi outside the warden's office, where they had spent their last three breaks.

"You better call Sutherland," Steven Jay reminded his boss. The young, aggressive, rotund lawyer had been Whyte's top associate for six years.

Jay was going through his sheaf of papers when Whyte returned, obviously not satisfied by his talk with the president.

"I told Sutherland we had convinced Duncan no pardon would be granted, that he could never again live in the United States."

"Good," Jay replied, noticing Whyte looked preoccupied. "What else happened?"

"The president watched a program last night that replayed the Senate hearings with Starr and Duncan. Remember when Starr screamed he hoped no president would ever pardon Duncan?"

Steven nodded his head, remembering the scene well. He thought Starr had been damn impressive throughout the hearings. But he had to change the subject. His boss was getting more depressed each day as the negotiations lingered. Whyte's frown made deep crease lines in his already creased forehead. His intelligent eyes showed the anger he was fighting to control.

"Do you think Duncan's ready to deal?"

"I do," Whyte replied firmly, trying to snap out of his self-imposed depression. "He knows we are running short on time and temper, just like he is. We may have to call his bluff. Let's go. And Steven . . ." Whyte grabbed the young lawyer by the arm as they walked back toward the room with Duncan. Leaning close to his associate's ear, he mumbled, "Don't show any emotion or surprise at what I do . . . no matter what."

"All right," Steven replied, not knowing what his mentor had in mind.

They entered the $20' \times 20'$ glass-enclosed room that had been their home for the past two days. The decor was one six-foot table in the middle of the room with four adjacent folding chairs. Three guards were stationed outside the special room. Though they could look in, they heard nothing. The room was soundproof. Whyte's tape recorder would preserve the historic negotiations.

Duncan was wearing his prison blues, the universal insignia of captivity. He watched the two men sit down. He sipped coffee from his hand-carved mug, a sign of his prison status. Whyte folded his arms neatly in his lap as Steven started the tape recorder.

Whyte could sense the change in Duncan. Maybe his gut feeling had been right. It was time to close the deal.

"I've been thinking, Thomas, it's time we wrapped up these negotiations. You want Starr back—and I want out of this pit."

"Tommy, we're prepared to end the negotiations now. As we discussed yesterday, I have authority from the president to release you from prison under the Federal Emergency Powers Act. There will be no amnesty. No pardon. In addition . . ."

"Hey, wait a minute," interrupted Duncan. "Not so fast. If you're not going to let me come back to the United States, if I have to spend the rest of my life in some other country, I want the pardon." Then, slightly pausing, he added whimsically, "For my pride."

"No dice, Tommy." Whyte was bluffing. The president had just given him authority to grant a pardon. The president had no other choice. Duncan knew where Starr could be found, and Sutherland wanted Starr back. But Whyte sensed a change in Duncan. He seemed more apprehensive, restless, apparently anxious to end negotiations, and get the hell out of San Quentin.

"You're calling the shots, Mr. Whyte, and if you say no dice, that's fine. We might as well terminate discussions now. I'd rather spend the rest of my life in this hellhole, and have Jonathan Starr killed, than follow your proposal. Not letting my own people drive me to the airstrip is crazy. What am I going to do? You'll have agents all over. Do you expect me to sneak through the ground? I don't trust the president. I'm doing what I have to do to make damn sure I get on that plane when Starr gets off. Fuck you . . . and fuck Sutherland." Duncan glared at Whyte and pushed his chair back from the table.

"Steve," Whyte said, gathering his papers, "it's time to go." Without looking at Duncan, Whyte motioned for the attorney to pack their briefcase and leave the little conference room for the last time.

Duncan watched in disbelief as the president's special counsel and his associate hurriedly packed their papers. My God, he thought, can this be true? Tommy Duncan played poker as well as anyone. However, he didn't like to bluff when his own life was the stake. Just as Whyte and Jay approached the door to leave the room, judgment time arrived.

"Wait a minute!" shouted Duncan. "Get your ass back here. I guess I can live without the pardon, so let's wrap up these goddamn negotiations today. But I want my own car and driver."

Whyte nodded and Steven returned to his chair. The young lawyer grabbed his pants so Duncan wouldn't notice his uncontrollable shaking.

Whyte had been acting on instinct. He risked breaking off negotiations, directly contrary to his instructions from the president. As he started to leave the room, his back to Duncan, Whyte prayed all the way—praying the labor leader would change his mind.

During the remainder of the day, release logistics were worked out. Whyte indicated he would check with the president, and get back to Duncan the next morning. If the proposals were acceptable, the prisoner would be released from San Quentin; with his own car and driver, to go immediately to a nearby airfield where Starr would be returned by plane. Duncan would then board the plane and leave the country. Never to return.

"Well, as I see it, Thomas, we've got no choice," sighed the president, relieved this part of the crisis was almost over. "Duncan watched my speech the other night. He saw my promise to the public. He knows I've got to get Starr back, no matter what."

"Mr. President, I think under the circumstances, it's all we're able to do. We've got no choice. Really, from a bargaining standpoint, we did quite well. Hell, he's got all the cards, yet he let us call some of the shots."

"At least we think we were able to call some of the shots," the president responded drily. "I have mixed emotions on the date," Sutherland continued. "If Duncan double-crosses us before the thirteenth, Starr might not get qualified. If Starr is back before the thirteenth, it's a shoo-in. Why is he waiting a week? It troubles me."

"I've had a chance to talk to Press Secretary Brandt. I believe we can work out the release with the cooperation of the press. I'll leave it to you to talk with Andy Reynolds to coordinate FBI and Secret Service surveillance from the prison to the airfield. Per his proposal, we're going to have to be damn careful when we follow him. If he shakes loose, we'll never find Starr. Until we get Starr back, keeping watch on Duncan is our only safety valve. If Starr is not released, we take Duncan back to prison."

"Tommy, the president says you have a deal. Under the Federal Emergency Powers Act, he will make arrangements with prison officials to sign for your release, scheduled for noon, Tuesday, December 14, pursuant to your request. Correct?"

"Yes," grunted Duncan.

"As to your other demand, we have agreed you may be picked up by your own people. You know we will be following you, so don't make any crazy attempts to escape from our control."

"Understood."

"Don't double-cross us. We'll be watching you every step of the way. Go right to the airfield and make your arrangements to have Starr there."

"Understood."

"We'll allow you to board the plane when Starr gets off . . . and Reynolds says he's okay. We won't stop the plane or follow you. Once you've left our soil, as far as we're concerned, you're as good as dead."

"Thanks for the kind words, Thomas," Duncan responded sarcastically.

"This isn't very pleasant for me, Duncan, and I would like to get it over with. As you know, on December 13, the day before your release, the electoral college votes for president and vice president. We believe they will choose Jonathan Starr for president. With this agreement, you have promised to produce Starr unharmed. Do you understand that?"

"Understood," Duncan said again.

"And may God be my witness, Duncan, if you don't follow this bargain to the letter, you'll be back in this prison and we'll throw away the key." Whyte was losing his temper. Through all his government negotiations on behalf of the president, he had never lost his composure. His coolness under fire was the one virtue, the one trademark Thomas Whyte had proudly displayed throughout his life. He wasn't about to give Tommy Duncan the pleasure of witnessing a rare burst of rage.

"It also goes without saying," Whyte continued, "if you ever come back to the United States, you'll be immediately returned to San Quentin."

"Yeah, yeah, I know," Duncan said impatiently.

Whyte squinted at Duncan, rubbing his unshaven chin. "We have an agreement," he said matter-of-factly.

Thomas Whyte stood at the desk, waiting silently for Duncan to leave. The small, glass-enclosed conference room of San Quentin was now under maximum security. Guards were accompanying Duncan at all times, as the government feared someone would try to negotiate directly with the labor leader—with a knife—or gun. Whyte took one more look around the tiny room, shook hands with Jay and packed his legal papers.

* * *

During the next week President Sutherland met with Andy Reynolds to discuss the surveillance plans for Duncan's release.

"Mr. President," began Reynolds, "I believe everything is set."

"All right, Andy," continued the president, casually puffing on his pipe, "fill me in on the final arrangements."

"The press secretary has assured me that at noon on the release day, there will only be one cameraman and reporter outside the gates of San Quentin. The three networks are pooling, and I believe NBC will be there, live. Director Hagstrom has given me five of his best men to use as I see fit. The California Highway Patrol, along with their helicopters, will be constantly watching the area for any unusual activity. We'll follow Duncan to the airstrip. Once there, my men will monitor the air space. We've already thoroughly checked the area. It's clear. It's too flat for a shoot-out. We should be fine."

"Good—good," chimed the president. "What about that problem we discussed before?"

Reynolds noticed the president was doodling on a pad, evidently keeping no record of Andy's plan.

"Well, in the tragic event Duncan somehow, someway, eludes us, we believe extreme measures will have to be taken. I have talked with Director Hagstrom, and have been working with top security personnel at the FBI to assist me in a very high-risk, back-up plan. As I understand it, Mr. President, you don't want to hear the specifics of my alternate plan."

"Andrew, I have given you full written authority in this matter. You are authorized, on behalf of the president of the United States, to take whatever, and I emphasize *whatever* action you deem necessary to get Jonathan Starr back." The president was distinctly nervous. His expression became somber.

"I have done that, Mr. President," Reynolds replied.

President Sutherland rose from behind his desk and walked toward Reynolds, putting his hand gently on the Secret Service agent's shoulder. As the president ushered him out of the Oval Office, the two men grasped hands. All they could do now was hope and pray that everything worked out.

CHAPTER 40

HUNCHES

Monday, December 13

THE FOOD AT THE INTIMATE SEASIDE RESTAURANT WAS EXCELlent. An informal atmosphere and private booth were two prerequisites Reynolds had insisted upon for his secret rendezvous before the big day.

After the delicious meal Andy Reynolds and Kate Wilson broke some shocking news to their dinner companion.

Roger Jefferson was stunned, as he silently ran his fingers up and down the length of his glass. He stared in disbelief at his boss.

"I don't believe it."

"Believe it, Roger. Do you think I would accuse her of this if I didn't have the facts?" Reynolds leaned backward against the booth; the firm plastic felt comfortable against his sore shoulder.

"I loved Jo Decker like my daughter. She *was* . . . she *is* my goddaughter." Reynolds glanced at Wilson who remained mute during this exchange.

"Look," Reynolds continued, "we'll go over it one more time. She knew about the special ring, that's why the farmhouse attempt didn't work."

"But that . . ."

"Roger," Reynolds interrupted, "let me finish. She was in my room so fast on the night of the kidnapping, she couldn't have been at her proper post. She arranged for special personnel to be working on the scaffolding. She's undergone a complete personality change. She knocked over a garbage can at the warehouse—alerting the kidnappers of our presence. And finally, she even refused to call for helicopter assistance when I screamed for it.''

Andy took a sip of vodka and eyed his associate closely.

"Should I go on?"

Jefferson shrugged his shoulder and gulped down half of his drink. "Would it be foolish to argue that is all circumstantial evidence?"

"Yes," Andy responded softly, "it would be."

"Have you told the president?" Jefferson inquired.

Reynolds hesitated momentarily before responding, attempting to choose his next words carefully. He sipped his vodka again.

"I haven't told Sutherland. I don't want anyone to know of my suspicions, except the three of us." He looked toward Kate and continued.

"I trust you and Kate with my life, with Jonathan's life, with the goddamn future of this country, but my hunch stays our secret."

Jefferson nodded, straightening the curly hair behind his left ear. "What should I do?"

Reynolds leaned over the table, closer to his trusted aide.

"Tomorrow, before release time, you are to plant a bug on Jo's car. Just in case something happens."

"We're supposed to follow Duncan. Why do we need this?"

"It's a backup plan. The deal the president had to make with Duncan is a security nightmare. It handcuffs us. I'm a little concerned we'll lose Duncan."

"How?" Jefferson asked incredulously.

"That, Roger, I can't answer. I don't think we'll lose him, but I want alternate plans. Jonathan won the election today. The electoral college came through. But Duncan wanted his release after the vote. As if he wanted Jonathan to get qualified. That troubles me. I'm just trying to be prepared for anything . . . and everything."

"Understood."

"I'll tell you the special frequency you and I will use tomorrow. Both of us will use radio phones. If we lose Duncan, I'll catch up to you, and you better be on Jo's ass."

"I will be," the agent replied confidently.

'I know you will."

The three continued to sip their drinks in silence. Jefferson appeared unusually nervous, tapping his ring finger over and over against his glass. He sighed and stared long into Reynolds's eyes.

"Andy, I've got some shocking news myself."

Reynolds calmly placed his drink on the table. "I'm listening."

"I think I've identified the mystery man who shot you and confronted you in the warehouse."

"How?"

"By using your description, his voice patterns, and his bullet. I personally ran it through the computer."

"And . . ." Reynolds said impatiently.

"He goes by the name of Hassan."

"What's his real name?"

"I don't know . . . for sure."

"What does that mean, Roger?" Reynolds's tone was becoming angry. He didn't like games.

"We think it's Carlos Ramirez or Ilich Ramirez Sanchez."

Kate dropped her drink, spilling it on the table.

Reynolds reacted as if hit by a bolt of lightning. "Jesus Christ," he muttered, "what the fuck does the Jackal have to do with any of this?"

Jefferson shook his head. "I'm not sure, but the word is he's on a project with Fayez Jaber, a known anti-Israel rebel."

"But the Jackal is normally employed by sophisticated revolutionaries. Why is he in this country?" Kate asked, regaining her lost composure.

"To kill Starr," Reynolds responded with finality.

"But he's had the chance. He's beat us to Starr twice, yet he didn't kill him . . . or you, Andy," Jefferson said, trying to make sense from this new mystery.

"Maybe Duncan beat him to Starr . . . and the Jackal is waiting, or has received new orders," Reynolds offered, finishing his vodka. The black agent was concerned—with all his problems he now had evidence of an international plot.

"Will you tell the president?" Kate asked, looking intently at Andy.

Reynolds leaned against the booth again, his eyes fixed on the light above. "Not until tomorrow's over. We all should sleep on this. Roger, who knows of this?"

"The three of us," he said softly, slightly squirming in his seat.

Kate raised her empty glass over the table. "To tomorrow," she toasted.

"To the three of us," Reynolds added, raising his glass to meet theirs, "and to President Jonathan Starr, whom I hope to God I see tomorrow."

CHAPTER 41

BREACH OF CONTRACT

Tuesday, December 14

HUSBANDS AND WIVES STRUGGLED OUT OF BED, JOLTED BY THE obnoxious ringing of alarm clocks, as much of the nation prepared for another day of work and school.

But something was different. There was no laughter . . . just anxiety.

Tommy Duncan release day.

The news media had abided by the president's edict. NBC representatives were outside the small white gate of San Quentin by 8:00 A.M., running their cables to a nearby truck. At the same time, another crew was assembling their equipment at a nearby airfield so all of America could witness the return of their next president.

The famous California prison sprawled over 440 acres of Marin County, on land jutting into the bay north of San Francisco. In addition to Duncan, the prestigious prison guest list read like a Who's Who in American Crime—more than sixty percent of the confined felons were in for life, many of whom awaited death by poison gas.

Andrew Reynolds and his platoon of agents had been walking the grounds for two days. There were no people hidden in the fields, no ships at sea, no surprise attack anticipated. But Reynolds was worried. The president had made several concessions to the convict, which made Andy's job more difficult. Two helicopters from the California Highway Patrol were available, and the weatherman had even cooperated with bright sunshine. FBI agents had been strategically placed along the highway near the airstrip, as a precaution, in the event the three chosen Secret Service agents lost Tommy Duncan's trail. Reynolds had gone over all of the contingencies during the last few days. All systems were go.

"Hey, Andy!" shouted Ray Stewart, "we've got a report from the helicopter that there's a convoy of moving vans approaching San Quentin."

"Let me have that," growled Reynolds, as he grabbed the radio earphones from Stewart, almost ripping the big agent's ears off.

"This is chief at base, come in copter one."

"Yeah chief," the helicopter pilot shouted loudly. "There's four big moving vans headed in your direction, not really toward San Quentin, but on the highway. Hey wait a minute—they're stopping."

Reynolds frowned. He didn't need to hear anymore. He reacted quickly and decisively.

"Ray, get in the car and see what the hell is going on with those moving vans," boomed Reynolds. It was 11:20 A.M.

Jo Decker heard the confusion from her position directly behind Reynolds.

"I'll go, Andy," she volunteered loudly as she approached her boss.

Andy stared at her momentarily before responding. "No way, Jo, I need you here."

"Should I go?" wondered Stewart, watching his two superiors discuss the situation.

"You go . . . now," Reynolds barked impatiently, walking by Decker without saying anything further.

Ten minutes later, Agent Stewart apprehensively approached the first van in the convoy. He noticed that one of the drivers appeared sick. As he moved closer to the cab he smelled the distinct odor of human vomit.

"Hey man," said one of the drivers, "my friend's sick. We're coming over this way because we felt the prison doctor could help us. Two other guys in the back there," motioning to the vans behind him, "are also sick. We're all headed toward Frisco, but we ate at a truck stop a few miles down the road, and evidently the fuckin' chili we had was bad. I don't know if we're getting food poisoning or not, but we've got to see a doctor."

"Well, there's no secret who I am," Stewart said, his eyes squinting to get a better look into the cab. "I'm a Secret Service agent. You can't go to the prison now. Tommy Duncan's getting out in an hour."

"Yeah, we know that, but can't we go in when he leaves?" queried the man in the cab.

"I'll check," Stewart responded suspiciously, flashing an annoyed look toward the two men. He walked alongside the long moving van, trying to determine if everything was in order.

He approached the two men sitting in the second cab. "Hey buddy, we're sick. Can't we get to that doctor?" the man on the passenger side hollered. Stewart gripped the handle and pulled the door wide open—the stench forced him back three steps.

"Shit," he screamed, "what's that?" He answered his own question seconds later when he saw the vomit under the feet of the two men. The smell permeated throughout the area.

Stewart quickly made his way to the third cab—just in time to observe the driver in the act of throwing up, vomit spewing out of his mouth like a fountain. The agent gingerly approached the man sitting in the passenger side—smelling the distasteful odor from the cab.

"I want to look in the van."

"Be my guest," came the quick reply.

Stewart opened the van and noticed office furniture stacked to the ceiling. Desks, filing cabinets, tables and couches, making one solid wall of furniture, with literally no openings—a collage of fancy office decor. Though he couldn't determine how deep into the van the furniture was stacked, he presumed the entire van was full.

He made his way to the fourth van, purposely avoiding the men in the cab—his nose had already suffered enough. Upon raising the truck's back door, he observed furniture similar to the previous van.

He strode quickly to the first van, moving to the driver's side of the cab.

"Everything checks out. When Duncan's gone, you can see the doctor." Stewart glanced at his watch. 11:50 A.M.

The stoic-faced agent slowly strolled to his car and reported to Roger Jefferson.

"Stay there, Ray, but if anything gets suspicious, call me immediately.'

"Roger . . . Roger," Stewart chuckled into the microphone, dropping it on the front seat. He grabbed his walkie-talkie with his left hand and waved to the helicopter pilot hovering above.

"Hey agent, secret agent, look at this cargo." One of the drivers motioned for Stewart to view the back of the first van. As he approached the end of the truck he was grabbed from behind, another driver snatching his walkie-talkie.

The first driver took a knife and jammed it into the unsuspecting agent's gut, pulling it out and simultaneously hitting Stewart with his left fist. The driver gripped the agent by the throat, and lifted him off the ground, his legs flying as he went through the air, striking his head on the side of the truck. Ray Stewart tried to struggle to his feet. His training had taught him survival. He was in misery as he reached for his blood-soaked stomach. He knew he was dying.

Len Allen studied the agony on Stewart's face. Enough was enough, he thought, as he reached down with his knife and slit the agent's throat. The second driver lifted the agent into the back of the truck. They motioned the other drivers to start moving. It was almost time.

They quickly removed the office furniture from the middle of the truck, piling it to one side, making room for Duncan's escape vehicles to exit—two black limousines, one racked on top of the other, each with a sturdy ramp.

"You guys get your masks on! The others will back out the limos. Let's *move*!" Allen shouted, strutting around the area as a military commander would move in his domain.

"Pearson!" Allen screamed, "you get ready to take care of the copters. Everyone else should be in full uniform. Let's hit the cars . . . and go," Allen commanded, getting in the passenger side of the first limousine.

Eight black limousines formed a perfect procession heading to the prison's main gate. Two vehicles had been backed out from each of the four moving vans, where the office furniture had served as perfect cover.

Allen smiled as he glanced over his left shoulder. The three trailing limousines each kept perfect distance from the other, as the first vehicle screeched toward Tommy Duncan.

Andy Reynolds held his binoculars fixed on the main gates of San Quentin. He glanced at his watch. It was time. Duncan was walking from the main prison office, toward the front gate, where the little guardhouse was a hub of activity. The NBC camera was centered on Duncan as he approached the main entrance. So far, no car had arrived to meet Duncan, but there were still a few minutes left before the gate would actually open. Curious, Reynolds thought to himself, that Duncan would be dressed in a black, three-piece, pin-striped suit on the day of his release.

Duncan's agreement with the president required the Secret Service to station themselves no closer than five hundred feet from the front gates. However, Duncan knew he would be followed to the airfield. The front gates had now opened—it was high noon.

Suddenly there was confusion. Reynolds was staring ahead at Duncan but heard screams and shouts from the agents behind him. Agent Jefferson sprinted to receive a frantic call from one of the helicopters circling above.

"This is copter one . . . come in, Chief . . . come in . . .

There are . . ." The frantic helicopter operator would speak no more.

From the moving van, a marksman centered the aim of his M-72 anti-tank gun rocket launcher on the rotors. Centering the gun on his shoulder, adjusting his sight, he squeezed the trigger. The armor-piercing shell found its mark, blowing the helicopter from the sky, the crash echoing throughout the area.

The sound of death.

Within ninety seconds the second helicopter suffered the same fate. The marksman had hit his target with ease, using a second rocket launcher.

Reynolds smelled the smoke from the explosions as he helplessly watched eight black limousines, similar to those used in political motorcades, come tearing down the roadway directly in front of the guardhouse gates of San Quentin.

The Secret Service agents drew their guns, but Reynolds still had the presence of mind to bark orders preventing a discharge of bullets. The last thing they needed was the death of Tommy Duncan.

What Andrew Reynolds saw next completely dumbfounded him. All the preparation—all the plans—all the careful analysis of possible escape routes were shot to hell. Sixteen men darted out of these black limousines, dressed identically to Tommy Duncan, whose facial masks made them undistinguishable from Duncan himself; from a distance of five hundred feet. They intermingled so quickly with Duncan there was no way to discern which of the seventeen running men was actually the labor leader.

The NBC announcer who had been covering the release stood speechless, as the rest of the country witnessed the incredible scene on live television.

Reynolds tried to take charge, sweat coursing off his shocked face. Most of the agents stood by with their guns ready to fire. Reynolds's order still stood. No shooting.

The scene was one of chaos and confusion. Seventeen identical twins ready to go eight separate ways. No one had anticipated following this many cars. The original surveillance plans were worthless.

"Let's get going," Reynolds commanded, joining Decker

and Jefferson as they sprinted to their own cars and began following three of the eight limousines. Reynolds grabbed the microphone in his car, which directly fed to a predetermined police frequency.

"Follow as many limousines as you can," Reynolds barked, noticing his speed was over 80 mph. "Maybe we'll get lucky and follow the right one. Notify the patrol to follow all black limousines. Don't stop them, just follow them. And get me every goddamn available helicopter."

Reynolds followed his limousine for another few minutes. He suddenly saw brake lights. He put down the microphone and tried to control his car, frantically pumping his brakes. By the time he pulled over, he saw the driver, also dressed as Duncan, run out of the limousine into a light blue Chevrolet Impala. Instantly, both vehicles took off in opposite directions.

As he grabbed for the microphone to report the news, he noticed there was no license plate. Then he heard from the other agents. The same switch occurred all over the highway. There were now eight limousines and eight other vehicles to follow. Duncan's rescue squad had strategically placed the second layer of cars at different locations surrounding the area. One of the sixteen vehicles carried Duncan. But which one?

A roadblock outside of San Francisco stopped one red Mustang and a black limousine. The only occupant of each was the driver. Neither was Tommy Duncan. The labor leader was having a relaxing trip in the back of a 1984 VW, having switched cars again fifteen miles earlier. He was dressed casually, lying on two pillows, listening to the radio reports of his escape. His driver had a communications system installed in the front seat. Len Allen was pleased.

"Great job, Lenny," Duncan grinned maniacally from the backseat. "When's the next stop?"

"If the cops set a roadblock outside of L.A., like they've done in Frisco, I've got a place for us to stay a day or two. I doubt they try it, though. They know they lost."

"Lost *again*," Duncan proudly corrected him, placing a delightful emphasis on the last word.

The labor leader was grinning ear to ear. He had once again

committed the perfect crime. He was on his way to commit another perfect crime . . . the murder of one Jonathan Starr.

The scene outside the gates of San Quentin was pathetic. The NBC camera crew silently collected their cables and cameras, the shock of what had just occurred still very visible on their drawn faces.

Reynolds sat stunned, alone in his car ten miles outside the prison. For the past thirty minutes he had listened to reports from the FBI and California Highway Patrol. Almost everyone had already given up. With eight vehicles becoming sixteen in such short time, there was no conceivable chance to locate Duncan. Except by complete luck.

Five more vehicles had been stopped within a thirty-mile radius of the prison, but Duncan wasn't in any of the captured vehicles. The agents previously assigned to designated locations on the highway kept up with a few limousines—until the first switch occurred. No one had been prepared for this exchange, no one had foreseen the unforeseeable.

Reynolds drove his car back to the prison. He had some unfinished business to take care of. When he pulled to the front gates he observed agents and prison officials wallowing in defeat, heads dropped down, unable to face the reality of what occurred.

Andy observed Josephine Decker comforting a sobbing Roger Jefferson, both of them sitting on Decker's car hood.

"What's the problem?" Reynolds asked as he approached the two agents.

"Ray Stewart is dead. They butchered him," Jefferson uttered softly, trying to control himself.

"He thinks it's his fault," Decker offered, her arm still around the agent's shoulder.

"Roger," Andy said gently, "I was the one who sent Ray . . . even after Jo volunteered. There's no need for you to feel guilty."

"What do we do now?" wondered Decker, jumping off her car, moving next to Andy.

"Will you do me a favor?"

"Anything," she replied.

Reynolds gently grabbed her arm, trying to give her the impression of sincerity.

"I think Duncan will get to L.A. I believe Starr is still there. I want you to drive your car straight to L.A. Go to bureau headquarters so I can reach you."

"Why don't I take a plane?"

Andy smiled, and softly squeezed her arm. "You can't . . . because of my second favor."

"Which is?"

"On your way to L.A., I want you to check on the roadblocks. See if anyone can give you leads. We're not out of this yet."

"Okay," she replied, nodding her head.

"I want you to keep me posted every three hours for the next twelve hours. Use this special radio frequency," he said, handing her a piece of paper. "Only the two of us will have official access to this."

"What about after today . . . what should I do?"

"Sit tight, wait for further instructions. I'll reach you through the L.A. bureau."

She placed the paper in her back pocket, pulling up her blue slacks at the same time. They both looked toward Jefferson.

"I'm fine," he said gently.

Decker pulled out her car keys and opened the door.

"I've got to check out with prison officials," Andy said, briskly walking to the front gate. Both Decker and Jefferson waved.

Reynolds flashed his identification to the guard and entered the confines of San Quentin. He was on his way to visit the prison's doctor. No one asked—no one wondered what Reynolds's mission was.

By this time, no one cared.

CHAPTER 42

THE WHITE HOUSE

Tuesday Afternoon
December 14

THE PRESIDENT WENT RIGID WATCHING THE ESCAPE ON TV. HE stared at the screen without batting an eyelash. For some unexplained reason, the president had insisted that FBI Director Hagstrom, Thomas Whyte, and the attorney general be present to witness the release of Tommy Duncan.

A deathlike hush fell over the Oval Office. No one stirred, or even breathed. They were all thunderstruck.

"Ah fuck," snarled the president as he rose from his couch and walked back to his desk. The president's eyes stared around the room. When his protruding eyes finally came back to them, they were cold and unsympathetic.

The three men in the room remained silent. Thomas Whyte knew the president better than anyone present. He had been watching his reactions during the last few minutes, and though the president was angry, he did not have a defeatist attitude. Something was going on.

"Mr. President, it's Andrew Reynolds on the security phone," his secretary said flatly over the intercom.

"Yes, Andy," answered the president. "Wait a minute—let me put you on the box." The president motioned for the three men to come closer so they all could listen to the conversation.

"Mr. President, we never anticipated this situation," Reynolds said apologetically.

"Let's get to the other thing, Andy," the president said impatiently, squirming around in his chair, pulling on his right ear, his eyebrows furrowed in anger. Second thoughts about Reynolds's ability came to mind . . . again, as the president listened to the response.

"Yes sir. I have talked to Dr. Berkin and he has assured me that the TRC was injected properly last night."

"All right, Andy, why don't you explain what that is," suggested the president.

"TRC, and I'm not going to give you what that technically means, because I can't pronounce the word, stands for trace. Director Hagstrom is aware of what the FBI and CIA have been doing with this drug."

For the next fifteen minutes Reynolds methodically explained the background on a top security project, involving an experimental drug, TRC, which had been injected into the bloodstream and digestive systems of small laboratory animals. These experiments demonstrated that much of the liquid passed through the intestines, but the relatively small remaining portion lined both the large and small intestines of the subject animals. At least theoretically the same would happen with humans. However, no human had ever been injected.

Dr. Berkin, who at first hesitated injecting the untested drug into Tommy Duncan, received classified information that Andrew Reynolds was acting under the auspices of the president of the United States. Dr. Berkin also received a call from FBI Director Donald Hagstrom, indicating that the drug was being used by the FBI, and under these particular circumstances could be injected into Duncan for national security considerations.

Berkin had been assured by the FBI staff doctors that the drug could not harm Duncan. The only question was whether the drug would be effective in a human being. TRC was to serve as a "liquid homing device." The drug, after coating the small and large intestines, would stay in the system for approximately one week. Then, it would dissolve or be excreted, as most of the liquid did when first passing through the system. Unfortunately, the drug took twenty-four hours before its substance could be traced, due to the chemical reactions within the body.

Specially designed electronic scanners served as a "sonar" system. By using these instruments, the government had been able to observe the movements of mice and rats on video screen from distances of up to one hundred miles.

"We have set several sonar systems in place . . . between San Quentin and Los Angeles. The Oakland and San Francisco airports were also watched closely, but we figure Duncan won't risk that escape route."

"Any results?" questioned the president.

"Yes," Andy replied quickly. "If preliminary results are correct, the sonar readings indicate he's headed to L.A. He's close to half way between Frisco and Los Angeles. He was injected about thirty hours ago."

Thomas Whyte was curious. He had to ask one question before Reynolds left. "Andy, this is Thomas Whyte."

"Yes, I can hear you."

"How did you get the TRC into Duncan?" It was the same question Attorney General Gilbertson was about to ask.

"Duncan was told a contagious virus had spread in his cell block. It was necessary to inject all the men with antibiotics. So twenty-four men were given shots in their butts yesterday. Duncan was present during all of them . . . but he was the only one getting TRC."

"I'll give that doctor an award." the grateful president added.

"He should get an Academy Award. You should have heard him explain how the shot would work and what the virus could do to them. The doctor even suggested we pull two guys from the cell block and tell the others they already had the virus. It worked beautifully."

"Now we're cooking," the president replied enthusiastically. "It's about time we got some momentum. Andy, do you still have that phone in your car?"

"Yes, and I will keep you advised at all times. I'm on my way to L.A. now." His car had its own TRC sonar kit, and Reynolds also had a field unit available.

The phone went dead. The president leaned back in his chair and interlocked his fingers under his chin, revealing immaculately clean nails. He felt better.

"TRC has been used only on rats and mice; can it work on Duncan?" Gilbertson wondered.

"It should," Whyte replied with a twinkle in his eye. "It's been injected into the biggest rat of all time."

"Thomas," the president said, ignoring the attempt at humor, "I want you to get together with Griswold and Christenson. I need advice on Starr's potential mental or physical disability—and how that relates to his ability to discharge his duties. The more I think about it—the more worried I become."

"I'll get on it immediately," Whyte replied.

"Well," the president said, addressing the group, "I'll let you folks go. We all have a ton of work to do. But remember," the president cautioned, "not a word to anyone on what we've got cooking with Duncan."

"We're going to take heat . . . all of us," FBI Director Hagstrom said sadly.

"Yes," the president agreed, "but no one must know of the TRC. No one. We can take the heat until then." The president leaned over his desk, bringing his hand to his forehead, feeling the beads of perspiration.

"Thanks, men," the president said, as the advisers exited his office. "Wait up a minute, will you, Thomas?" the president requested, rising from his chair to meet Whyte halfway.

"Call Judy Starr. Tell her what's going on. She deserves to know."

"Consider it done," Whyte responded, shaking the president's hand.

The president walked briskly to his desk, grabbing the phone and dialing simultaneously.

"J.W. ?"

"Ah was wonderin' when you'd call. Ah don't believe mah own eyes. Duncan wins again."

"Did you see Kate Wilson's article this morning?"

"No. Ah haven't got 'round to readin' it yet."

"She smells something brewing in the Middle East. She claims her 'sources' think a major diplomatic development is ready to unfold."

"Shit."

"Well," the president said, reflecting for a moment, "she can't know of Hussein's role. No way. Tell your friends, no matter who is president, the part of the deal regarding the West Bank will be honored by this country. Give them my word.''

"Arthur . . . ah don't . . .''

"J.W.,'' the president snapped, "give them my word. We must give the king everything he wants to get this off dead center.''

"He may want to wait to see who will be president,'' McBee responded.

"I know,'' the president reluctantly agreed. "He knows Starr has been qualified. Maybe he should just go on that assumption.''

"Ah'm not sure he will after today. They are draggin' their feet. Ah don't think anyone will sign it. Everyone's waitin' to see what happens to Starr.''

Sutherland grimaced. "Do what is necessary. We can't stop now. Have you told the Israelis what I wanted conveyed to the prime minister?''

"Yes.''

"Their reaction?''

"Not very good.''

"Call me after you talk further with them.''

"Ah will,'' McBee drawled.

"I'll wait for your call,'' the president mumbled as he put the phone in its cradle. He gazed at an unlit pipe next to the phone. "Goddamn it!'' he screamed, as he threw the pipe across the room, shattering it into several pieces. Sutherland stopped, his chest heaving. He could feel the thudding of his heart, racing to the fury just unleashed. He collapsed back into his chair, overwhelmed by the fear, anger, and uncertainty facing him.

Most Americans had witnessed the San Quentin fiasco on live television. Wednesday morning commuters were talking about the "great escape'' with a mixture of bitterness, anger, and some grudging admiration. Overnight polls indicated eighty percent of the public blamed the president for the security breakdown.

Sutherland leaned back, locking his hands behind his neck, staring at the ceiling above. Could Reynolds handle the pressure? How long would, or could, Sutherland support the agent who had been through so much? The president's credibility now rested on the battered shoulders of one man. Even worse, Sutherland's most tender part was caught in a veritable vise. Unfortunately, Duncan's hand was on the vise handle.

CHAPTER 43

FOLLOW THE LEADER

Friday, December 31

REYNOLDS CHEWED A BITE FROM HIS COLD SANDWICH, STARING at the phone next to him. The small table was overcrowded with the most sophisticated electronic equipment ever utilized by the Secret Service, but it was the phone connected directly to the White House that had Reynolds's undivided attention.

Roger Jefferson sat on a footstool, peering through a small hole drilled in the white garage door. His attention was directed to the red brick house across the street at 2040 Broadway, Tommy Duncan's home for the past week.

"It's still hard for me to believe Jo is involved with this," Jefferson said, shaking his head in disbelief, staring through the small opening, "but she led us straight to Duncan."

Reynolds nodded, rising from the folding chair located in the middle of the garage—their makeshift stakeout headquarters. For seventeen tortuous days the two men waited for Duncan to make his move—praying that Jonathan Starr was still alive.

"What are the odds of Duncan hiding out across the street from a retired cop?" Reynolds wondered, stretching his arms above his sore shoulders, slowly rotating them back and forth. "I think our luck is changing," he said, walking to the phone.

"How come you were so sure Starr wasn't across the street?"

Jefferson asked, quickly looking over his shoulder, before returning his stare through the small opening.

"Glendale isn't the best place to keep a president-elect. Too many people in this neighborhood . . . too risky. Besides, this location is too close to the area's police station. They had to land that helicopter close to where they are keeping Jonathan. And as far away from cops as they could."

"They would want us to think that, wouldn't they?" Jefferson countered.

"Not necessarily," Reynolds responded, facing the back of the agent, whose eyes were again focused on the house across the street. "Anyway, Duncan hasn't made his move to get away. If Starr was dead, Duncan wouldn't stay in L.A."

Jefferson sighed, shaking his head slowly. "These have been the longest days of my life, sitting across the street knowing that shithead is over there. I guess it's all moot now anyway. When are you calling the president?"

"Now," Reynolds replied, picking up the phone from the card table next to him.

"Mr. President," the agent began, "we were right all along, Duncan will make his move tonight."

"The bastard," Sutherland whispered in a disgusted tone.

"It makes sense for him to travel New Year's Eve," Reynolds continued, "more people in the crowd with him. Our phone tap indicates he's flying to a private airfield in Connecticut."

"Venelli?" asked the president in a wondering tone.

"Right. He's going to have plastic surgery tomorrow. They're flying in a foreign plastic surgeon . . . from London."

"Were you able to trace his calls to the kidnappers?"

"No, he only talked for a few seconds. He told them he would arrive at 8:00 P.M. We still don't know where he's keeping Jonathan. And Decker's going with him." Reynolds had to force the last few words. The betrayal was a brutal fact.

"Where do you think they're keeping him?" the president asked, both elbows leaning on his desk as he cradled his phone with his left shoulder.

"Probably near L.A. International, so he can leave town immediately. I have alerted Special Agent Roodman. He has twenty of his best men ready to go where I tell him, as soon as I tell him."

"Good, Andy. I know these last few days have been hell. But we both knew Starr wasn't in that house. Duncan had to be certain he wasn't followed. He would never go directly to Starr until he knew it was safe. Starr's always been his ticket to safety."

"He thinks it's safe now."

"That bastard is predictable," the president grunted. "We both knew when the time came *only* Duncan would pull the trigger."

Reynolds nodded, but said nothing. He began to pace in front of the card table.

"Andy, you know the press has been after me about your whereabouts. The official response has been you're undergoing medical treatment. I know you understand—Duncan can't have any suspicions. We even planted a picture of a black agent through a hospital window for AP. The lad looks like you."

"We all look alike," Reynolds cracked. But he still felt the large lump in his throat.

"How will you follow Duncan?" The president's voice was serious, his mood solemn.

"We think he'll go in Decker's car. The tracer's still in place."

"How can you be certain?"

"We flattened his tire," Reynolds replied, hoping his voice wouldn't give away the uncertainty he was feeling.

"I presume this is the last time we'll talk. I'm sending Air Force One to L.A. International to bring you all home. It will land on the strip farthest from the terminal, and the press . . . *after* you get Starr back. Is there anything else we should discuss?"

"No, we're ready on this end." Reynolds stared toward Jefferson, who had been listening intently to the conversation. He wanted to say something else to the president, but the words weren't there. He finally spoke again. "President Sutherland . . . *this time* we'll get him." Andy stopped pacing, realizing for the first time he was trembling.

"You must, for the country's sake, and your own. I've stuck with you throughout this ordeal, never taking you off the investigation—for which I've been blasted in the press. Make it work this time. There will be no next time for you . . . or for Starr. I hate scapegoats, but we're out of time.'' The president's usually strong, resonant voice was subdued and defeated. He placed the phone on the receiver and leaned back in his chair, slowly turning to the right, staring out the window behind him.

The cold rain of night lingered with diminished strength and the sky was now almost pitch black. The president rubbed his forehead, his hands gently running through his gray hair. Within the next few hours he would finally know whether his presidency would end with dignity . . . or disaster.

"Let's go," Duncan snarled as Decker helped him with his overcoat. The labor leader was neatly dressed in a brown suit, wanting to make a good impression on his Connecticut friends.

Duncan and his bodyguard followed Decker out the front door. It was dusk. The sun's receding rays did very little to warm the evening's brisk wind.

"Tommy . . . look," the bodyguard exclaimed, pointing to the rear left tire. It was flat. Duncan stared toward the back of the car, his shoulders hunched forward, the overcoat collar sticking straight in the air, serving as a shield for his hidden face. He glanced at his watch and flashed an annoyed look at Decker.

"No problem," she muttered, pulling keys from her coat pocket. "We'll take my car."

The apelike man next to Duncan opened the back door of Decker's car for his boss. The three drove away in silence.

"Good work, Roger," Reynolds sighed as the vehicle across the street pulled away from the curb.

"We'll wait five minutes . . . then follow them using the alley . . . in case others are still in the house." Reynolds had difficulty controlling his excitement, his voice became uneasy and hurried. Like the pregnant woman suffering through several false alarms, Reynolds knew the final confrontation would occur. The L.A. farmhouse and the warehouse district fiascos had been his labor pains; but it was now time to deliver. Life would continue . . . or there would be death. No middle ground existed any longer between the two.

By using a prearranged secret radio frequency supplied by

Special Agent Roodman, Reynolds made contact with the FBI. Because there was a remote chance Decker's car was equipped with a monitor to intercept police communications, even under special frequencies, Reynolds devised a plan. He would report travel and movement, in opposite directions, disguising his voice with a deep guttural tone.

"Patrol car 18 . . . come in," Reynolds said, the handkerchief partially covering his dry mouth. Jefferson kept his eyes fixed on the road, then the radar screen, not moving within three miles of their target.

"This is 18 . . . go ahead."

"Believe suspected dope dealers are traveling north on Highway 5. They appear to be heading toward Glendale. They came from Highway 10, probably Culver City. We will monitor and report back in ten minutes. Over and out."

"Do you think Decker heard that?" Jefferson asked, feeling the stiffness in his arthritic left hand, which was sweating from his firm grip on the steering wheel.

Reynolds shook his head sideways. "I don't." He leaned forward returning the microphone to its cradle.

"Roodman will move his men just south of L.A. International. Decker's route won't go that far south, I don't think."

"Even if she does, we can go back on line and advise Dick."

"Right," Andy replied, "but I'd rather not communicate again until their car stops."

Jefferson wiped his left cheek using his upper arm; sweat appeared over his eyebrows. "Where are they headed?"

"Possibly the ocean. I don't think it's their escape route, though the idea is fascinating."

"Amazing," Jefferson muttered, a hint of grudging admiration in his voice.

"That they are," Andy conceded, "but wherever they stop, Roodman won't be far."

The two agents rode in silence—their thoughts were private. They both realized the fate of the free world was in their hands.

"How many miles have we been on the Pacific Coast Highway?" Reynolds asked, his eyes fixed on the beep in the screen before him.

"They're turning!" Jefferson exclaimed, feeling his heart pound faster as he glanced at Reynolds.

"Marina del Rey, I'll be damned," Reynolds uttered, reaching in the glove compartment for his silencer. "Stay two blocks away . . . no closer," he ordered, fastening the silencer to his gun.

"They stopped," Jefferson said, trying to catch his breath. Reynolds reached for his walkie-talkie and barked his command.

"Call Roodman, surround the area. Give me a four-block radius. I don't want them too close. Everyone should wait for my signal." Andy exited the car and turned to Jefferson, pointing both thumbs in the air. "By the way," he added, "have Roodman alert the Coast Guard, just in case. If I use the radiophones, you'll know within five minutes."

It was now dark outside, the flaming sun had settled, leaving little light for Reynolds as he ran to the marina. He sprinted down a hill toward a car parked on the north side of the long parking lot adjacent to the docks, shielding himself from his unsuspecting targets. Duncan and Decker were talking to the bodyguard.

"You stay here," Duncan snapped. "Jo will go inside with me. I'll send Allen and the boys out here. I'll be ready in thirty minutes." Duncan was still hunched over, hiding his face behind the stiff collar of his coat.

The cold rays of the moon streaked down from the dark sky and bounced off the rolling surf, which burst into tiny sprays of white off the sides of the small boats docked on their respective slips. The stretch of beach to the south of the marina was lifeless. Broken bottles and other debris were gently nudged by the waves that pushed against the shoreline.

Duncan and Decker made their way to the southernmost slip on the dock, where a small yacht swayed slightly back and forth from the steady force of the Pacific Ocean's current.

Andy scanned the parking lot and was relieved to find no one around. One less complication to worry about.

"How are you, Len?" Duncan inquired as he stepped aboard the yacht. Decker followed him in silence, her eyes surveying the area for nosy neighbors.

"Your man is down below. What should we do?"

Duncan looked around the large room. It could have passed for a comfortable living room for most home owners. The table to his right still had the dinner dishes scattered about. Duncan reached for a dinner roll from a wicker basket, taking a bite as he walked around the wooden floor. The two couches in the middle of the room were empty, but several suitcases were neatly lined up in front of them.

"Good roll . . . still warm," Duncan said, as he shook hands with Olson and Riley. "Why don't the three of you go outside for about thirty minutes. I want to be alone with Starr."

Duncan noticed the concern written all over Allen's face. He smiled and patted the taller man on the back. "Don't worry, Len. Decker will stay, and Alfred's by the car."

"There's a hot-dog stand on the north end of the marina," Allen said, as he motioned for Olson and Riley to leave. "We'll get some coffee and wait for you."

"Fine," Duncan replied. "Then we'll all leave in the same car."

The three men left the yacht together and slowly walked toward the hot dog stand. And toward Reynolds.

Andy quickly placed his gun in the right pocket of his waterproof vinyl jacket, zipping it shut in one motion. He stuffed the walkie-talkie into his left pocket. He had only one option. And seconds to do it.

He dropped to his knees and scampered on all fours across the dock into the icy waters next to a houseboat on the northern tip of the marina. He cursed to himself, fighting the urge to scream. The water cut through his body like a knife. Dog paddling as quietly as he could, he pulled himself around the west side of the boat, out of sight from the three men who were quickly approaching the area. Reynolds peered down the row of boats peacefully docked down the south side of the marina. He couldn't risk going back on the swaying wooden planks—the hot dog stand behind him gave Allen and company a direct view of the entire dock. He also couldn't risk being detected by the man sitting in Decker's car. He gasped for air as another wave pushed him into the boat. He started pulling himself toward the faraway yacht.

Most of the houseboats and yachts he passed were empty. He periodically pushed his powerful legs against the boats—like a mountain climber swinging up hill—to give him momentum and to use the tide. In between the slips he had to swim on his own, forcing himself to use every ounce of energy he possessed. He kept staring to his right, praying the distance between himself and the yacht would miraculously shorten.

He no longer had any feeling in his legs. His arms felt like barbells. But he continued. He had come too far to quit now. He rested for a moment, gripping the side of the boat with both hands, gently resting his head on the fiberglass material. Pushing the cold water from his eyes, he looked to his right again. The moon proudly shined above, casting its powerful light over the shifting, dark blue water.

He was only halfway.

CHAPTER 44

THE CONFRONTATION

THE PRESIDENT-ELECT RECOGNIZED THE LOUD, OBNOXIOUS voice from above. Starr quickly rolled out of bed and began pacing the small room. Though he had anticipated this meeting for weeks, his stomach felt like a bottomless pit, as though all the energy from his weak body had been drained.

Duncan pulled the door open violently, quickly descending into the room below. His devilish grin had the ruthlessness that only the really evil possess. He gripped a large handgun with his powerful right hand. The two men looked at each other. There was a long silence. The air was heavy. Starr was tense. He was conscious of his heart pounding as he waited for Duncan to make the first move.

Duncan walked over toward Starr, pointing a warning finger directly at him, his tone frigid.

"I'm going to blow your brains out tonight," Duncan said coldly. "I've been waiting for this ever since I went to San Quentin over eighteen months ago. I don't need you alive any longer. Tomorrow I'll have a new face and new identity."

Starr's eyes moistened. He was numb . . . too numb to reply. He looked at Duncan in shocked fascination. His square, broad shoulders made him look like a military man from central casting; or maybe it was the gun pointed at Starr's head.

"You think you did a lot to benefit the country, to help labor unions, don't you?" Duncan snapped harshly. "Well, let me tell you something. You had no idea who you were dealing with. Do you really think you're dealing with a common hoodlum?"

Starr stared at Duncan in horror. The man holding the gun could see Jonathan's fearful eyes. Duncan pursed his thick lips.

"The president of the United States thought he could negotiate with me. What a fool that Sutherland is. Did he really think that I would return you alive, with his Secret Service agents, FBI, and God knows what following me wherever I go, to return me to San Quentin? I wasn't about to let that happen." Duncan was in control of his emotions as he kept the gun pointed toward Starr, a ghoulish smile forming around his red lips.

For the first time Starr moved. He walked closer to Duncan. His voice was strained, nervous.

"Let's get this over with, Duncan," Starr said, his heart beating rapidly, face flushed, skin hot.

Duncan's arm suddenly swung as he laughed sadistically, striking Starr in the face with the butt of the gun. The piercing pain shot from Jonathan's ear through his brain. His head was about to explode. His spine stiffened, every nerve and muscle tightened to the limit. Starr clenched his teeth and somehow managed not to scream. Gradually and painfully, his body loosened, slowly growing numb, finally immune to any more pain.

"Oh no," Duncan snarled, "I'm not going to kill you yet. I've got a few things to talk to you about. And if you get any ideas about charging me . . . I won't just hit you in the head, I'll shoot you in the nuts."

Starr moved away feeling haggard, drawn, lifeless. He rubbed his eyes, hoping he would wake up from the nightmare. But he knew it was real. His pain was real.

"You know," Duncan began, "during those hearings I thought, at least for a while, that you knew some of the crimes I'd committed in the past. You only touched the surface during your so-called investigation. I thought I would clue you in on what you missed."

Duncan took out a cigar from his pocket, lit it with a lighter held in his left hand, and nonchalantly began puffing. Duncan's voice was harsh—sounding like rock rubbing rock. His evil eyes glared at Starr.

"Before I get to that, I presume you know how I planned the kidnapping?"

The prisoner failed to respond, returning Duncan's penetrating stare.

"Jo Decker," Duncan continued, "did most of the work from the inside. Once you chose the nigger to head your detail, I knew you were mine. I know all about the government cover-up of her father. I saw to it she found out. Your abduction was really quite simple. I find," he concluded proudly, taking a long puff from his obnoxious-smelling cigar, "whenever you need to beat the government, a little planning and muscle always does the trick."

Duncan took a small stride toward Starr, motioning with the gun. "Sit on the bed, I've got much more," he barked, taking another drag off his cigar. He leaned against the wall, standing over his one-man captive audience, lowering the gun as he spoke.

"Enough about the kidnapping. You've read the papers. You know about the Fairmont, the farmhouse, the warehouse, and San Quentin . . . all government fuck-ups," he said triumphantly, carelessly flipping gray ashes on the floor.

Duncan lowered his voice slightly and leaned closer to Starr. "Before I blow your fucking head off, I want to tell you about another one of my perfect crimes. Do you remember November 22, 1963?" Duncan felt the chill of excitement shake his entire body, as it always did when he remembered the glorious past.

All his life Duncan had been a collector of information, fascinated by facts and details of all types, especially about his crimes. He savored them, remembered them, collected them like kids collected baseball cards.

Starr reacted as if jolted by lightning—instantly dazed by the new revelation. He stared numbly at Duncan. His hands began trembling uncontrollably.

"After two years of Kennedy," Duncan began seriously, "we knew, if he stayed in power, organized crime would be destroyed. Only Don Venelli was willing to plan the hit. Marcello, Trafficante, the others, just wouldn't risk it." Duncan's voice began to rise with the ring of authority as Starr sat silently on the bed next to him, biting his lower lip in utter disbelief.

"Once you mentioned Venelli's name at those hearings, I thought you were withholding information about the JFK killing. We hired the whore," Duncan said sarcastically, a mischievous grin appearing on his cleanly shaven face, "to blow out whatever information you had."

Duncan drew several puffs from his cigar. "It's obvious to me from your reaction, this is new information."

Starr gently wiped the tears from his eyes. He wasn't crying. Duncan's cigar smoke had completely filled the small room. The silent man moved his sleeve over the left side of his nose, the smoke shifting up his nasal passages as he sniffed and snorted, hoping for relief.

"I don't need to tell you the specific details, but my plan was brilliantly *executed*," he said, emphasizing the last word proudly. A smile formed on his round face as his cheek muscles tightened.

"We had Dallas cops on the payroll, the perfect patsy, and we covered our tracks by sending off phony trails to Cuba and Russia."

It had taken several minutes for Duncan's words to sink in. Finally, reluctantly, Starr began to believe the terrifying tale of horror. He stared at Duncan, speechless, examining his face, looking into his eyes. Over the years Starr had developed a working knowledge of body language. Duncan's actions, the stroking of his chin, the occasional covering of his mouth, the nervous scratching of his arm, did not indicate falsehood, but rather a person with misplaced emotion. One filled with great excitement.

"Why are you telling me all of this?" Starr asked harshly.

"Look, when you were running for the presidency, you were the subject of magazine and newspaper articles every week. Everyone had to read or hear about Jonathan Starr. Well, I can't have my glory or be written about. Obviously, I haven't been able to tell too many people about my perfect crime." Duncan's voice was breathless, eager, tinged with elation.

"Yes, but. . ."

"Shut up," Duncan fired back. "We're almost to the good part. You might as well listen, because the longer I tell the story, the longer you live."

Starr recoiled with the thought of being shot. The bizarre, shocking story had left him numb. He could see the glimmer in Duncan's eyes as the assassin proudly continued his sick story.

"I was the one who arranged for the second gunman. It took the government another fifteen years to conclude he was even involved. It was my idea to use Ruby as the safety valve if Oswald got by Tippit. We worked with Ruby for six months, setting him up all the way. With all the false trails I left, nobody could ever link Ruby and Oswald together, or back to organized crime." Duncan dropped his cigar, violently crushing it with his right foot.

It finally ended. The most grotesque story Jonathan Starr had ever heard came to an end. During the morbid story, Starr had almost chewed a hole in his lower lip. His handsome face showed the strain of his captivity.

"Hell, we left everyone so confused that the two of us, sitting in this room, other than Don Venelli, are the only people who know the real story. I haven't had time to tell you everything, but you got the basics," Duncan gleamed, pleased that he could inform his arch nemesis of the crime of the century.

"And you know, Johnny boy," chuckled Duncan, "it didn't end there. Hell, that Hale Boggs started to get smart in 1972, thinking about reopening the Warren Commission. If you recall, in October of 1972 his plane vanished during a flight in Alaska. And to this day," Duncan said, smiling, "they've never found a trace of that twin-engine plane.

"Shit, we had to take care of Jimmy Hoffa when he got out. He was getting so anxious to run the union again, we couldn't take any chances. He wouldn't listen to reason, so he ended up in the same place you're going to be in about . . . oh . . . ,'' then looking at his watch Duncan finished the statement, "two minutes.''

Clammy, wet fear began crawling across Starr's skin. He could feel it spreading over his body. He knew he was going to die. His brains were going to be blown out in some godforsaken boat in Los Angeles.

Insanity.

Starr's face was arrested in shock. His eyes devoid of life, just like a blind man's. His lips began trembling as he started to speak.

"Why?'' he muttered. "How could. . .''

"Why!'' Duncan laughed, his thick jowls shaking like Jell-O, "to protect organized crime.'' Duncan explained his statement. "Many years ago I was at an initiation. I saw the revolver and dagger crossing one another. In Cosa Nostra you come in alive, you go out dead. It comes before family . . . anything. My index finger was pricked, I was in. I was a member. I had *power*.''

Starr tried to speak again, but words wouldn't come out. His garbled voice was filled with phlegm. His eyes were moist and red with fatigue and rage as he awkwardly brushed the tears away. He was exhausted. Hope was gone.

"Yes, Senator, I'm glad we had this talk. I'm the greatest criminal mind of our time,'' he said with exaggerated modesty, "but who can I tell? I'm not like Booth, or Sirhan, Oswald, or Hinckley, everyone knows them. But the mastermind . . . ah, the genius behind the plot . . . that's who history never knows.''

Starr shook his head in disgust and scooted against the back of his bed. He loathed the man standing in front of him.

"Well, it's probably best for you,'' Duncan tartly noted, "that I kill you tonight. The PCP in your system would give you a lifetime of problems.''

Jonathan went pale, an almost grayish pallor seeped over his haggard face. He knew all about PCP, or 'angel dust.' His Drug Commission had studied its effects. Abuse and overuse could cause long-term mental problems and bouts with infectious diseases.

Starr looked up at Duncan, trying to collect his thoughts. He inched his way closer to the labor leader. "This time you're wrong, Duncan," he said icily. "Your henchman only injected me once with PCP."

"Don't you wish," Duncan laughed. "You really don't know, do you?"

"Know what?" Starr mumbled.

Duncan leaned against the wall adjacent to Starr's bed. "Weren't you the least bit suspicious about all the mayonnaise used on your sandwiches?"

"The mayo," Starr uttered in disbelief. "That fucking mayo." He recalled a portion of the California study concluding that angel dust, in some individuals, caused a severe form of schizophrenia. Maybe it was for the best he would die this evening. A president with hallucinations and delusions couldn't govern. Not from an institution.

Starr swallowed hard, feeling the tension constrict his throat. He squeezed his eyes shut, shaking his head, with the sick realization that his body was infested with angel dust.

Tommy Duncan had won.

Duncan slowly rotated his neck from shoulder to shoulder. The gun in his right hand was aimlessly pointing toward Starr's bed. For a split second Jonathan considered lunging for the weapon . . . but a split second was all the indecision time his captor would allow.

"Well, Senator," Duncan sighed, pointing the gun in Starr's face, "I do believe . . . your time has come."

Reynolds struggled beyond the small houseboat and glanced south. Mercifully, the yacht finally came into view. He couldn't see anyone on the main floor, the dim light focusing over a small table in the corner of the room.

He made his way to the back of the yacht. The moon illuminated his wet path as cold waves continued to slap his face. He pulled himself on board, struggling to lift his body weight from the strength of his arms and shoulders. His normally powerful legs were like two dead weights tied to his lower torso. He prayed to himself. Please, please, O Lord, let him be alive. Let me get there in time. The agent's respite lasted only seconds.

He began violently rubbing his legs, willing his circulation to return. He unzipped his jacket. The gun was dry.

He resecured the silencer, stretching his legs in the air, extending the knees, turning the ankles. Some feeling was back. It would have to be enough, there was no time to waste.

"Shit," he muttered to himself, removing the soaked walkie-talkie from his other jacket. "Waterproof, my ass," he whispered as he flipped the only hope of communication with his men into the chilling waters below.

Reynolds had an unreal sense of having been in this dilemma before—the deathly silence. Sometimes the stillness was more frightening than the expected burst of gunfire.

The waterlogged agent pulled himself upright, standing for a moment, listening. No human sound broke the water's staccato rhythm.

He cautiously tried a knee bend, lowering his body slowly, in stages. Success. Other than the barely noticeable cracking sound, his legs and knees were ready to take him further around the boat. The wind sighed briskly in his face as he silently moved to the yacht's entrance. He looked carefully all around—holding himself rigidly, listening for intruders. With a sudden panther-like quickness he crashed into the room.

"Freeze!" he shouted at Decker, aiming his gun toward the surprised woman. Andy's heart plummeted, his face turned grim and purposeful.

"Bravo," she said, smiling wryly at her godfather. Reynolds took two steps, glancing around the room for a clue on Jonathan's whereabouts. He noticed light from a stairway near the back of the yacht.

Decker's smile turned into an expression of hate as she reached for her shoulder harness. Reynolds fired once, his bullet piercing through the palm of her right hand.

"Damn you," she screamed, clutching her wounded hand to her bosom, bending over in pain, rocking back and forth on the couch.

Decker's agonizing scream echoed throughout the yacht. Duncan glanced toward the top of the steps. "What the. . . ."

Jonathan charged Duncan with all the stored energy he possessed—tackling the off-balance Duncan in the midsection, pushing him violently against the wall as he struggled with Duncan's right hand. The mafiosos' strong fingers were still glued to the trigger.

The two men rolled across the floor, Starr banging the wrist of the man below him continuously against the wooden floor. Finally, the gun was bumped from Duncan's fingers. The labor leader forced his left hand into Starr's face, pushing the chin with all of his strength. Jonathan fought back, leaning his entire weight on Duncan's struggling hand as he felt his back muscles tighten. Starr saw the gun out of his left eye, inches from Duncan's stretching fingers. Starr strained to raise the left side of his body. After forcing himself several inches above Duncan, he repositioned and barreled his left knee into Duncan's groin, using every ounce of energy left from his torn body. Duncan moaned, a guttural sound that shook his entire body as he recoiled in pain. Starr lunged for the gun with his left hand, aching fingers extended to their limit.

He pushed himself from the still groaning man, collapsing against the wall, the gun in his right hand. Aimed inches away from Duncan's temple.

"It's all over, Jo," Andy said softly as he approached Decker. "I'm going to get Jonathan. I want you. . ."

Decker lunged at the unsuspecting agent. Her left hand held a knife which she forced into Reynolds's right shoulder. He groaned as the two fell to the ground.

Reynolds's eyes watered as he tried to push Decker off his body with his right hand. Her entire weight leaned against him, preventing him from aiming the gun. The pain in his right shoulder was excruciating. He grabbed her hair with his left hand, pulling her head back with all his strength. For a split second their eyes met, glaring at each other as two wild animals.

She was the enemy.

She suddenly raised the left side of her body, her left arm and hand aimed the knife toward Andy's neck. Simultaneously, and without hesitation, Reynolds twisted his agonizing right shoulder away from her, squeezing the trigger of his gun. Decker's eyes widened, her body shook as she collapsed on the floor, her left hand dropping the knife on impact.

Andy struggled to his knees and crawled over the fatally wounded woman, pushing her over on her back. Tears streamed down her cheeks as she watched Andy in silence.

"Why?" he finally mumbled, noticing the large hole of blood in her stomach.

"Congratulations," she muttered icily, "you have single-handedly killed off the Decker family."

He stared in horror as her entire body shook.

She was dead.

Reynolds swallowed hard, an empty feeling shooting up from his gut. His head was spinning. He felt sick, paralyzed by a new kind of loathing. And a new kind of pity. He stood silent for what seemed like an eternity. Finally, he was able to choke out, "May God forgive me . . . again."

He heard someone cough from downstairs. Was it Starr? Duncan? Or someone else? He quietly inched his way to the stairs, noticing the blood from his shoulder dripping on the floor. His first reaction was to charge down the steps. But what if Duncan held the gun? Jonathan would be killed instantly. Maybe Duncan was waiting for Decker's signal.

He stared down the steps, his heart beating so fast he thought it would burst through his chest cavity.

Then he had an idea.

Starr heard the noise, his gun still pointed at the moaning Duncan, who now watched his captor through piercing eyes. The veins in Duncan's neck surfaced, tight and ugly.

Starr heard the noise again. It sounded like a cricket.

"Andy?" Starr asked with uncertainty, "if that's you . . . get in here . . . now."

Reynolds descended the six steps quickly. He walked over Duncan's supine body, and reached down to help Starr to his feet.

Jonathan extended his left hand.

"Up you go," Reynolds said, pulling the president-elect to his feet, grabbing the gun from Jonathan's hand, placing it securely in his jacket pocket.

The men stared at each other for several seconds, neither quite believing they were actually in each other's presence.

"I never thought I'd see you again," Starr said softly, smiling, reaching out to hug the grateful agent.

Jonathan pulled back quickly after observing blood all over his left hand.

"It's just my shoulder," Reynolds said assuringly, keeping his penetrating eyes focused upon Duncan and his own revolver clasped tightly in his right hand.

"We've got to get out of here. Now," Reynolds snapped, quickly looking around the room.

"Just call for help," Starr responded, staring at Andy's shoulder, thinking of all the pain and sorrow his abduction had caused.

Reynolds shrugged. "Nothing's ever that easy. My walkie-talkie is gone." He pulled Duncan to his feet, pushing the labor leader on the bed. Duncan's face was ash white, his impenetrable plan had been foiled.

"There's no rope to tie him up," Reynolds said, trying to make a tourniquet from his ripped jacket. "Tie this, will you, Jonathan?" Reynolds asked, still glaring at Duncan. Starr made a tight knot from the vinyl material hanging from Andy's shoulder, which had been torn during his struggle with Decker.

Suddenly, without warning, Jonathan lunged for the weapon in Reynolds's hand. He grasped the handle and violently pulled the gun toward him. Reynolds was stunned, trying to comprehend what had just occured.

"What the fuck are you doing, Jonathan?" Reynolds scowled, surprised by Starr's action.

"Don't stop me, Andy!" Starr screamed as he pointed the gun directly at Duncan, his breath exploding from his throat. He was livid. His face turned beet red. Tears were flowing down Jonathan's cheeks and he began shaking, almost uncontrollably. He was on the brink of a nervous breakdown. When he spoke his voice was filled with hatred. With revenge.

"This son of a bitch. This son of a bitch attacked my daughter. I've been sitting here for an hour listening to this asshole tell me how he killed John Kennedy, Hale Boggs, and Jimmy Hoffa. I've been held like an animal for weeks, with drugs being pumped into my body from goddamn mayonnaise." Then looking Duncan square in the eye, with a glazed expression that Reynolds had never seen before from his good friend, and seemingly with no regret, no apprehension, he placed the gun to Duncan's right temple.

"Take it easy, Jonathan," Andy said softly, not wanting to alarm his disturbed friend. "Don't do anything foolish. Duncan will get what's coming to him." Andy could see the cold hatred in Jonathan's eyes.

Starr's shaking stopped. He took a deep breath and a quiet calm appeared to come over him. His eyes raked Duncan like claws. He cocked the trigger of the gun and slowly, deliberately, moved his forefinger. At the same instant Reynolds grabbed Starr's arm as his finger pulled the trigger. Duncan's scream pierced the early-morning air. Reynolds and Starr both recoiled at the spitting-like sound that ricocheted around the room.

And then there was silence.

CHAPTER 45

THE GETAWAY

JONATHAN STOOD STARING AT DUNCAN. HIS LIPS MOVED BUT no sounds were audible. Reynolds gently removed the gun from Starr's stiff fingers.

"You owe me . . . asshole," Reynolds snapped at Duncan, who sat petrified in stony silence on the bed next to Reynolds.

"Jesus," Duncan muttered, his eyes open wide in astonishment at what had almost occurred. The quiet bullet missed his head by inches. Reynolds's catlike reflexes had saved Duncan's life.

Andy moved toward Duncan, the gun gripped firmly in his right hand. Duncan raised his head in time to see Reynolds's hand and arm come crashing down on the back of his neck, knocking him unconscious.

"I liked your solution better, Jonathan. But my way is preferable. We don't want a murder-one charge for our next president."

Jonathan leaned against the wall, staring at Reynolds. "Thanks . . . isn't enough. I completely lost my. . ."

"Forget it," Reynolds said, interrupting Jonathan's apology, "help me with his raincoat."

They pulled the coat off the lifeless labor leader.

"Put it on me," Reynolds commanded, as the two struggled to pull the coat over Andy's injured shoulder.

"This place will be crawling with Duncan's men any minute," Reynolds said, motioning for Jonathan to walk up the stairs. "I'm going to escort you to the car . . . as Duncan."

Jonathan cringed when he heard the plan, stopping on the third stair, looking down at Reynolds, who had pulled the collar as high as it could go.

"You're black," was all Jonathan could say. Reynolds smiled, pushing Starr up the stairs.

"Jesus!" Starr exclaimed as he stepped over Decker's sprawled body in the middle of the room.

"Keep moving," Reynolds cautioned, not even looking at the fallen traitor.

"Wait, Jonathan," Reynolds muttered suddenly, turning back at Decker's body. He leaned over her, reaching into her pocket. "The keys," he said, dangling the small chain in his left hand.

They exited the yacht, briskly walking toward the nearby waiting car. Reynolds tugged the sleeves down with his hands, his fingers cupped the fabric tightly in his palms. He hunched forward, trying to lower his head in between the raised collar. He occasionally pushed Starr in the small of the back with the gun held in his right hand.

The two quickly made their way off the wooden dock, each step they took sounding like horses kicking to get out of a stall.

Duncan's bodyguard scampered from the front seat. "Boss," he inquired, "where's Decker?"

"Inside," Reynolds coughed, hoping the hacking would disguise his voice. The wet vinyl coat he was wearing under Duncan's overcoat gave him the added bulk to temporarily fool the unsuspecting bodyguard.

"In the car," Reynolds barked at Starr. His coughing causing the bodyguard to take a closer look. Andy moved toward the front of the car but a nearby streetlight's illumination exposed the charade. His black face was no longer concealed from the apelike man.

"Christ!" the man screamed, reaching for his gun. Reynolds took one shot, the impact propelling the wounded man solidly against the car as his body shook in agony. Andy kicked the bodyguard's gun away as the man aimlessly crawled around the ground in almost unbearable pain, clutching his midsection with both hands.

"Fuck!" Len Allen bellowed as he watched the man he thought was Duncan kill his boss's bodyguard. "Let's get to the car!" he barked, dropping his second hot dog as he dashed to his nearby vehicle.

Reynolds stared out the windshield in disbelief.

"DEAD END."

The menacing sign penetrated the car's four anxious eyes. Reynolds glanced in the rearview mirror.

"They'll be waiting for us. The only way out of here . . . is the only way in. I didn't have enough time to case the area." Reynolds put the car in reverse, backed up, and peered down the long, almost empty parking lot.

"We've got to get up that hill," Reynolds said, pointing toward the only blacktop road, which served as entrance and exit to the marina.

"Give me your gun, Andy. While you drive, I'll lean out the window and shoot their lights out . . . or the driver," Starr suggested, surprised he wasn't nervous about the prospect of crashing cars. After weeks in hell, being out in the open, with Reynolds, was much more palatable.

"No way. You get in the backseat. Lay down, and buckle yourself up. I don't want you bounced around . . . or hit by a bullet. . ."

"But Andy . . . I. . ."

"Jonathan!" he shouted, "there's no time to argue. I have enough to worry about . . . now do it."

Starr shook his head in frustration as he climbed into the backseat. Reynolds's eyes noticed a car slowly moving away from the area of the hot dog stand. The driver nervously wiped the sweat from his brow.

"When he makes his break," Allen said, "shoot to kill the driver. If you can't, I'll ram them."

Olson and Riley aimed their weapons toward the dark car at the far end of the marina, one perched in the front seat, the other stationed behind Allen in the back.

Reynolds closed his eyes briefly and prayed he wouldn't soon hear the staccato burst of gunfire splitting the night air.

"Give me a Jewish prayer . . . here we go!" Reynolds shouted as he moved the gear to drive and floored the gas pedal. He flashed his brights and estimated he was three blocks from the waiting car. He turned the steering wheel slightly to the right. Maybe he could drive on the adjacent hill, at a deep angle, and avoid the collision.

Just maybe.

The glass to his right shattered suddenly as the dreaded gunfire began. The other car screeched its tires as it headed directly on course toward Reynolds, the bright lights almost blinding the agent. When he was less than two blocks from the oncoming car Reynolds noticed a set of headlights to his right.

Suddenly, this strange car peeled out of its parking stall and headed at an angle toward the collision course chosen by the other two drivers. Reynolds could no longer go to the right, the mystery car cut off his access. To the left were other parked cars . . . and the boats . . . and the ocean.

Starr heard the gunfire all around him; his arms covered his head as he lay on his stomach in the backseat. He could feel the speed of the car taking the parking lot potholes. It was worse than the most terrifying roller coaster.

Reynolds stared at the rushing car from his right. His instincts beckoned to him once again. He kept his hand just above the steering wheel, slumped in the seat, dodging the fury of bullets spewing in his direction.

"Brace yourself!" he screamed as he slammed on the brakes; the tires screeched and the car swayed left and right, almost out of control. Reynolds desperately gripped the steering wheel, using his forearm strength to prevent himself from flying through the windshield. The veins in his arm almost popped through his skin as the vehicle came to a violent stop.

Starr was pulled forward, almost to the floor. The seat belts wrapped around his shoulders and legs strained to hold him, cutting through his clothes with enormous stress, burning the skin underneath.

Suddenly, Andy saw the occupant of the third car jump out of the driver's side and roll over several times on the pavement to his right. The large, driverless Oldsmobile crashed into Allen's car with a terrific surge of power, pushing the vehicle and its three screaming passengers into several cars parked next to the dock. The violent impact caused an enormous explosion, the hot yellowish flames immediately spreading to the surrounding area. Several occupants from nearby houseboats began shouting for their neighbors to evacuate. The peaceful night air was permeated with smoke and fire from the incinerated vehicles . . . and bodies. Debris was scattered all over, metal crashing into the nearby ocean with violent fury.

"I'm getting up," Starr muttered excitedly from the backseat, trying to unfasten the seat belt to his right.

"Stay there," Reynolds snapped, pulling himself out of the car, walking to the area where the mystery driver leaped from his suicide mission. Even with the moon, and the sickening light from the nearby flames, Reynolds saw no one.

Then he heard a click. Someone had cocked a gun. Andy sighed and closed his eyes. He was at the mercy of the unseen driver.

"Turn around," came a command from behind in a strong resonant voice. A voice he had heard before from another dark corner . . . on another dark day.

Andy glared into the penetrating eyes of the man before him. His eyeballs were large, not grotesque, just unusual. He held a gun in his right hand, but it wasn't aimed at Reynolds.

"The Jackal," Andy said, his tone evidencing the admiration he felt for the daring rescue attempt.

"So you know."

"But why. . ."

"Mr. Reynolds," the Jackal interrupted, "don't try to figure it out. You're a good man . . . worthy of your position. But more trouble is on the way. If I were you,'' he pointed to the car, ''I would drive your friend to safety.''

The Jackal began stepping backward, never taking his eyes off Reynolds.

''Hey . . . I know you.''

Reynolds turned around. A small overweight man in his bathrobe had approached him, confusion written all over his concerned and unshaven face.

''I've got to go,'' Reynolds hurriedly replied, turning around toward the Jackal.

He was gone.

''What happened here?'' the curious man inquired, pulling the bathrobe tightly around his rotund midsection.

''Read about it in the newspapers tomorrow,'' Reynolds replied as he drove the car up the hill.

''Can I get up?'' Jonathan asked.

''No. Stay down. You're safer there.''

''Who were you talking to?''

''A confused boat owner.''

''No . . . the other guy.''

''I'll tell you later. More trouble is ahead.''

Andy carefully traveled the next two blocks with his headlights off. Every other streetlight was on, radiating some light over the deserted roadway. Christmas tree lights shone through some living-room picture windows, and a nearby cat scampered for cover as the car invaded her territory.

Then he heard the gunfire. Two men behind a car were shooting. Reynolds couldn't see their target, but he inched closer. He strained his eyes, peering through the broken glass in front of him . . . formerly the windshield.

''Jonathan . . . somehow these guys got through the roadblock. They're Duncan's men. I'm going to back up and turn down another street. The FBI is around here somewhere.''

Starr strained to lift his head up, wanting to look out the window. But the seat belts held. He had become so twisted within the several belts and buckles he had used, he wondered if he ever would get loose. ''This is worse than the trunk,'' he mumbled in disgust.

Reynolds quickly glanced to the backseat as he reversed the car's direction. The gunfire was becoming more intense.

"Hey, look!" one of Duncan's hoodlums shouted from behind the car as he was reloading his gun, "over there."

The other man quickly turned around, lowering his head behind the vehicle. "That's Decker's car. Let's get it . . . it might have Starr."

The two gunmen dashed into their car and turned it around quickly, pulling into a now-awake resident's front yard. Their heads remained low as they avoided the barrage of bullets blasting their car.

"Shit!" Reynolds exclaimed, "they saw us." He hurriedly completed backing up the car, turned up the next street, and floored the accelerator while staring into his rearview mirror.

"Stay down. They're coming from behind."

"Oh great," Jonathan mumbled, "now they can rear-end me." He dropped his face on the seat, feeling the sweaty vinyl, and once again covered his head with weary arms.

Reynolds saw another roadblock several intersections away. If he didn't do something quick . . . his own men would shoot at him. The car behind him was gaining, one of their bullets shattering the side mirror.

Andy started flipping his brights on and off . . . on and off.

"Come on, Roger . . . be there," Reynolds whispered as he headed directly toward the waiting police vehicles that blocked the roadway.

"Don't shoot!" Roger Jefferson screamed. "It's Reynolds . . . don't shoot," he shouted, waving his arms over his head as he ran in front of the roadblock so everyone could see him. Agent Roodman reached for the bullhorn.

"Let the first car through—move those cars out of the way," he commanded, as the agents scrambled to give Reynolds some space to pass through the roadblock.

"When the first car passes," Roodman ordered, "move the cars back into the blocking position."

Over two dozen special agents took their positions. Several aimed their high-powered rifles at the area immediately in front of the roadblock. Others scampered for cover behind nearby vehicles, all prepared for the inevitable confrontation.

"Thank God," Reynolds said softly, witnessing the opening in the roadblock as he crouched low in the front seat, his eyes barely over the dashboard.

Then he heard the sickening noise. "Hold on Jonathan . . . a tire's gone!" he screamed excitedly, fighting to keep his speeding car under control as a bullet blew parts of the rubber off his right rear tire. He struggled, using all his strength to keep the car centered on the roadway. The small opening in front of him seemed even smaller as he approached the waiting cop cars. Everything was moving in slow motion as the right front of his car angled for the small gap in between the roadblock.

"Hold on!" he shouted, closing his eyes and bracing himself as his car collided with one of the police cars in front of him, the impact pushing both cars off the side of the roadway. The crunching sound of metal to metal echoed throughout the area as Reynolds's car stopped, after jumping a curb and bouncing over a fire hydrant, geyserlike water spraying the entire area.

"Shoot to kill . . . don't let them collide!" Roodman shouted excitedly over the bullhorn. Two FBI sharpshooters found their mark at the same time, blowing both sides of the driver's head off simultaneously; brain matter sprayed all over the stunned passenger's body. He lunged for the steering wheel, barely able to touch it as the car steamrolled out of control through the roadblock, violently crashing into a building over three hundred feet away.

"Andy . . . Andy," Jefferson yelled into the car, finding Reynolds slumped over on the passenger side. Water sprayed the frantic agent as he pulled the door open. He reached to grab Reynolds when he observed Andy's right hand go in the air and point toward the back seat with his thumb, as if he were hitchhiking.

Jefferson stepped back and moved to the back door. "Dick," he commanded Roodman, "help me get the door open," cussing silently as he pulled on the door with all his strength.

Roodman pushed the nervous agent aside. He leaned into the car and reached around to unlock the back door. Jefferson didn't have time to be embarrassed. They both stared at Starr. His body lay still . . . lifeless . . . as the agents quickly tried to unravel the seat belts, both silently praying the man wasn't injured . . . or dead.

"Can I get up . . . *now*?" Starr uttered, his words bringing instant relief to the haggard agents around him.

"Thank God," Reynolds whispered in the front seat, finally believing the ordeal was over. "Get me out of here," he grunted, as he felt Jefferson's wet hand reach around his right shoulder.

"Don't touch it, Roger," Andy said, "I was knifed."

Jefferson straightened the agent's legs, and with Roodman's assistance, pulled Reynolds out of the front seat as if unloading a long piece of plywood.

Andy hugged the waiting Jefferson, gently patting him on the back. "Well done, my friend," he said appreciatively, turning around to watch several agents assist Starr from the backseat.

"I'm a firm believer in seat belts," he said, grinning as he approached Andy.

Tears were welling around Reynolds's eyes as he grabbed Jonathan and embraced him tightly. God, he thought to himself, how long had he waited for this moment.

They became embarrassed by the sudden outburst of cheering and applause from the nearby agents and officers who had gathered around to make sure their mission was a success. Many didn't care that the hydrant was drenching them—they wanted a chance to tell their children they were with President Starr.

"Unbelievable job," Roodman said, as he carefully removed the coat over Andy's wounded shoulder. "There's a doctor on Air Force One . . . he'll check you both over."

Reynolds nodded and placed his left arm around Jonathan's shoulder as they were escorted to a waiting police car. Jonathan shook hands with as many agents as he could as he briskly made his way to the curb.

"I'm honored to meet you . . . and to have been of service," Roodman said shyly, as he extended his hand to Starr.

"No, Agent Roodman. *I'm* the one who is honored," Jonathan replied sincerely, gratefully taking the agent's hand between both of his.

Jonathan entered the backseat, sliding next to Reynolds. He patted Andy's left knee softly with his left hand.

"What now?"

"Air Force One is ready at L.A. International."

"This has been one helluva New Year's Eve," Starr cracked.

Reynolds looked to the front seat. "Let's go, Roger, we've got a long trip ahead of us." Andy collapsed against the vinyl behind him. Exhausted. He glanced at Jonathan. And smiled.

Perhaps the ordeal was finally over. Or was it?

CHAPTER 46
THE RETURN TRIP

THE PRESIDENT WATCHED THE FLECKS OF WHITE SNOW FALL from the sky. He had been sitting alone in the Oval Office for hours, waiting to hear from Andrew Reynolds.

The telephone's strident signal produced an abrupt tightness in the president's throat. He felt a slight paralysis overcome him as he grabbed the phone.

He paused for a moment, uncertain whether he really wanted to hear what Reynolds was about to say.

Slowly, Sutherland placed the phone to his right ear and heard breathing on the California line, and pounding in his own chest.

"He's safe," were the first words from the receiver.

Finally.

The president struggled for control as he brushed a tear from his cheekbone. "Andrew, thank you," the president muttered softly.

"Mr. President, we're about ready to board."

"Tell Jonathan, by the time he arrives, his family will be waiting."

"I will," Reynolds replied quickly. "We've dispatched several agents to Connecticut . . . that arrest is being made now."

"Good. To say I'm anxious to see Jonathan would be a gross understatement. I . . ."

"Mr. President," Reynolds respectfully interjected, "I've got to board. Jonathan and I will call you from the plane."

"God bless you, Andy," Sutherland said sincerely as he gently placed the phone in its cradle.

He pulled his weary body from the chair and stretched his arms high above his aching shoulders. Looking around the room—his office—he understood he was enjoying one last graceful moment alone. A joyous, victorious conclusion to four years of meetings, decisions, and crises. Now, if only he could pull out the Middle East peace plan from his bag of tricks, his name would be etched by historians forever.

He stared at the large portrait of George Washington smiling at him from above the fireplace. At least he thought it was a smile—never before noticing Washington's small subtle grin.

Sutherland carefully poured himself a drink, raising his glass toward the picture of George Washington.

"Long live the presidency," he proudly toasted, sipping from his glass as he walked to his desk. He leaned over and pressed the intercom.

"Get me Thomas Whyte."

The president gently placed his drink on the side of his desk and turned slowly to face the first president once again.

"*All right!*" he shouted triumphantly, raising his right fist in the air. He scampered out of the room and hurried toward the master bedroom.

He finally had some *good* news to share with his wife.

Jonathan Starr boarded Air Force One for the first time. The upholstery was expensive, the carpet luxurious. The elaborate passenger cabins were partitioned into several sections, including a communication center, presidential quarters, and passenger and staff compartments. The seats were separated by upholstered armrests, with an inset wood table surface. Candy and cigarettes were neatly arranged in nearby trays.

Jonathan stared stonily, wordlessly out the window. The plane was halfway to Washington. To his left sat the man who had saved his life. Andrew Reynolds was trying to catch forty winks, but there were matters the two of them had to discuss before landing.

"Andy . . . Andy, wake up," Starr said gently. Reynolds immediately opened both eyes, moving forward in his seat.

"Did you really think I'd pull the trigger?"

Reynolds shook his head slowly and turned to face Starr.

"Not at first. But I saw a look in your eyes I never saw before. I thought about all you must have been through during the past two months, and for a second . . . just a second, I was ready to let you do anything."

"What changed your mind?"

"I couldn't let our new president be a murderer. Though in this case, it would have been justified."

"You cut it close."

"Yeah," Reynolds grinned, "too close. That bullet didn't miss him by much."

"Duncan about shit on the spot, didn't he?" Starr quipped, finally cracking a smile.

"Yeah," Reynolds agreed. "He's on his way back to D.C. . . . top security."

Starr said nothing, but nodded his head in approval.

"Listen, Jonathan," Reynolds said quietly, "I wanted to wait until we were alone, and until you were emotionally ready."

Starr flinched and grabbed the armrest for support. He searched Reynolds's eyes and saw tears.

"I can't tell you how sorry I am for Andrea. With all you've been through. I feel responsible."

Starr gently placed his left hand on Reynolds's knee. "You're not to blame," Jonathan said firmly. "You weren't even in charge of her protection. No one was to blame. Besides," Jonathan added, tapping Andy's knee, "Andrea is going to be fine. The doctor told me when I boarded she would make a complete recovery."

Reynolds wiped a tear from his eye and nodded appreciatively. "Thanks, Jonathan."

"How's Judy?"

"Remarkable woman. She has been strong . . . really strong."

Jonathan nodded his head and glanced through the window again, peering down at the squared fields from the farm below.

"Arthur Sutherland's a pretty good man, isn't he." Starr said, speaking softly, still peering out the window. It wasn't a question, but a statement.

"He's a great man, Jonathan. He took heat from everyone—but was determined to get you back and keep the presidency above politics."

Starr's eyes accepted the statement. "I owe him my life."

"Yes," Reynolds agreed, "both literally and politically."

"I understand," Starr responded, his hands slightly trembling, "from reading the papers that the Speaker tried to steal the election from me."

"Yes," Reynolds sighed, "but Sutherland convinced his own party to rally around you and campaign against the Speaker."

"That son of a bitch was trying to steal *my* presidency." Jonathan's voice rose with anger; his body started to shake.

"Take it easy," Andy said, trying to comfort the man on his right.

"If he had prevailed," Starr continued, still shaking, his voice strange, taut, and cold, "someone else could have been qualified, even though I'm back. I would have lost the fucking election—even though I won." Jonathan's mouth twisted in anger, his left hand tightened into a fist.

Then suddenly he became calm. A contorted smile appeared on his face, as he tapped Reynolds on the knee.

"Fuck 'em."

"What?" Reynolds asked, noticing Jonathan looked mean, almost frightening.

"Screw them all," Starr snapped. "I don't want the fucking job. Who needs it? I'll be a senator and spend time with my family . . . before they try to kill all of us."

Reynolds eyed Jonathan carefully. His moods changed by the minute. Perhaps he was just tired. After all, he had been through hell.

"Shit," Jonathan continued, "who needs politics? I'm a goddamn good lawyer. I'm . . ."

"Jonathan," Andy said firmly, "calm down. You need rest.

You'll see Judy and the girls pretty soon. Then you're going to see some doctors at Walter Reed. They'll help you.''

''Help me!'' Starr shouted, turning to face Reynolds. ''What kind of help do I need, Andy? Am I wacko just because I'm pissed off?''

''No, no,'' Andy said reassuringly, waving his hand, ''that's not what I meant. Everything will be fine. You'll see.''

Starr returned his gaze to the window. Andy wanted to bring up the drug issue. What had Jonathan meant by his statement in front of Duncan? What drugs had he been given, if any? Maybe once Reynolds knew this, Jonathan's bizarre behavior could be explained. The drug topic could wait.

Another topic could not.

''We've got something else to talk about.''

''Let it wait until this afternoon,'' Starr replied softly.

''It can't,'' came the tense reply.

Jonathan eyed Andy with curiosity. ''What's it about?''

Reynolds gritted his teeth, his mood became solemn. ''The Jackal,'' he responded coldly.

CHAPTER 47

NATION'S CAPITAL

Saturday, January 1

JONATHAN HELD HIS WIFE TIGHTLY IN HIS ARMS. AFTER A TEAR-ful reunion with his daughters, the president-elect found privacy in a bedroom-like compartment on Air Force One. He desperately needed these quiet moments with Judy, prior to the hastily called press conference just minutes away.

He whispered, ''I never thought I'd see you again.''

She squeezed him. "It's all over. I just want to be with you."

They heard the knock on the door. "Sorry, Jonathan," Reynolds said loudly, "but they're ready to start."

"Two minutes," Jonathan responded. "Just two more minutes."

"Okay. I can stall them."

Jonathan bent over and kissed his wife. His fingers brushed away her tears.

"I'll make this short," he said assuringly. "Then we'll go home. I want to be with you and the girls for a while—no one else."

She nodded, grabbing his arm while he opened the door.

As Jonathan and Judy walked down the steps of Air Force One, they were greeted with thunderous applause from the assembled news and print media.

"Ladies and gentlemen," he began, speaking directly into several microphones, placed together on the podium in front of him, "it's great to be back home."

The throng cheered, sincere and grateful smiles were everywhere. Photographers pushed forward, and the clicking of cameras could be heard over the afternoon's gentle breeze.

"I don't have a prepared text. I haven't had a chance to meet with my staff," he quipped, inching nearer the microphones.

Camera close-ups, beamed throughout the world, showed large black and blue bags puffed under each eye. His face was drawn. The blue suit he wore showed his twenty-five-pound weight loss of the past two months.

"Mr. President-elect, how are you feeling?" shouted a reporter from a distance.

"President-elect," Starr replied with curiosity. "Even though I won the election, others had to campaign in a second election so the electoral college wouldn't succumb to power-hungry politicians acting like vultures hovering over dead bodies."

There was a sadness in his voice. Judy moved closer to her husband.

"Sir, have you spoken to the president?" asked a nearby correspondent.

"I have," Starr replied. "We talked twice on Air Force One. I'm going to the White House from here."

"Do you expect to become president?" asked a reporter standing to Starr's left.

"Of course I do," snapped Starr indignantly. "I haven't done anything to disgrace myself or my future office. Why shouldn't I be president? What other legal or political obstacles will my opponents throw before me?" His voice rose in anger. "Why should I lose the office I worked hard to get?" He shook his head, adding, "Damn it, that's how I feel."

Judy reached for Jonathan's right hand, squeezing it tightly. Her husband was getting agitated and angry.

Andrew Reynolds was concerned. He had known Jonathan for twenty years. Yet today, he had heard and observed more mood changes than all the previous years combined. He hoped the press conference would end soon.

"How do you feel, now, sir?" a reporter asked with some hesitation. Starr turned to him, contemplating his answer. Before he responded, another question was shouted from the crowd.

"Do you feel capable of discharging your duties as president?"

"Who asked me that question?" Starr said harshly, turning his fiery gaze to the left of the crowd.

"I did, sir," a small woman reporter responded meekly. All eyes focused on her, then back to Starr.

Reynolds took a deep breath, catching Judy's worried glance, hoping Jonathan would calm down. Judy squeezed her husband's hand again. This time, he pulled away from her and pointed a menacing finger at the shaking reporter.

"Why, in God's name, would you ask such a question?"

"Speaker Durkin is claiming, after two months of captivity, you would have mental problems that could make you unfit for the job. He says he bases the claim on what a leading psychiatrist has told him."

Starr gritted his teeth, trying to control his rage. He glanced at Judy. He saw the confusion in her eyes. His hand pushed hair off his forehead as he eyed the reporter. The crowd was silent. He didn't feel right. He was losing control and he didn't care.

"One advantage I had during the past two months, not shared

with my countrymen, was being able to avoid Charles Durkin's nonsense.''

There was forced laughter from several reporters. Reynolds wondered if they had reached the eye of the storm.

"Of course, I'm fit to be president," he continued, "I just need rest. I'm fine. The president's personal physician examined me on the trip here. Pretty soon I . . ."

"Then why are you scheduled to see several doctors at Walter Reed tomorrow?" a reporter rudely interrupted.

"That's just routine," Starr replied, completely annoyed by the line of questioning. He appeared to have taken control of himself again. Reynolds started toward the microphone. This was the perfect time to end the press conference.

"What happened to you, mentally and physically, during these past two months? The public has a right to know." The NBC correspondent moved closer to Starr, wanting to hear his response.

Jonathan nervously bit his lower lip. This time he reached for Judy's hand. He stared at the reporter, uncertainty and anger showing on his face.

"I haven't had a chance to talk with my family, or the president," Starr responded coldly. "Before the public knows, I owe it to others to keep silent. For a while. Besides," he continued, "the public's right to know doesn't interest you, Mr. Litzman, or your network. The public may not care. It's you!" he shouted, pointing his finger, "and the piranhas in the press who care."

Reynolds lunged for the microphones, gently pushing Jonathan to the side. "This session is over," he said with finality.

Speaker Charles Durkin rose from the chair and walked to the television, switching off the set. He turned to his boyhood friend, Dr. Jim Stunyo, chairman of the department of psychiatry, Walter Reed Hospital.

"Well, Diamond Jim," he began, "that's your patient."

The broad-shouldered doctor frowned, leaning back in his chair, staring at his medical degree from the University of Illinois. He faced the Speaker.

"Charlie, I just can't do it," he said, his gaze returning to the wall.

"Oh, you'll do it," the Speaker snapped. "There's a girl in Jacksonville who says you'll do it."

"You've blackmailed me enough. All my life for that. I took an oath. I can't phony up a medical report on the next president."

"I'm going to be the next president, if you follow instructions."

"Besides," the doctor pleaded, "my top assistant will be with me. I can't fool her."

"Did you ever think for a moment, that maybe, just maybe, Starr is sick? Maybe he has that hostage syndrome you've written about. Somewhere in these goddamn books," the Speaker grunted, pointing to the several bookcases that surrounded the doctor's private office.

"Look," Stunyo reasoned, feeling pangs of guilt. "If he's sick, if he can't serve—I'll say so. But I . . ."

"What about that hostage syndrome?" the Speaker interrupted.

The doctor sighed. "Years ago, a colleague, Dr. Janis Ruth, and I did a research study. This hostage syndrome is an understandable phenomenon in which some kidnap victims, rather than being irate at their predicament, emerge from their tortuous experience bubbling warm praise for their captors—who, in a sense, turned out to be fine people because they didn't kill their hostage. Like Patty Hearst."

"So, why not Starr?"

The doctor shook his head. "From what I saw on TV, he doesn't think much of his experience. In fact, he's pissed off at what happened to him. A very normal reaction. I suspect he's got problems . . . but not what you're talking about."

The Speaker moved next to Stunyo, standing over his desk. "You've worked long and hard, Diamond Jim. You have a fine reputation. I'll ruin you," Durkin said coldly, "if you don't come through for me. I want a report I can hold up to Congress that will *prove* Jonathan Starr can't serve as president, by having a permanent, irreversible condition. Then I'll fight Edwards in the courts . . . everywhere . . . to obtain the presidency."

Stunyo stared at the Speaker. The power-hungry congressman had lost his sense of reality. His obsession with the presidency, Stunyo thought, had made the Speaker unfit for official duty.

"I can't do it," the doctor muttered softly.

"Forty years ago!" the Speaker screamed. "You could do it forty years ago!" His eyes bulged with anger as he pounded the doctor's desk.

"My sister has been in a state sanitarium for forty years because of you." The Speaker was shaking uncontrollably, tears streamed down his red puffy cheeks. "When she got pregnant," he continued icily, "*you,*" he shouted, pointing his finger in the slumped-over doctor's face, "you performed an abortion . . . on your own child."

The Speaker leaned against a nearby filing cabinet and stared in disgust at the helpless doctor.

"Sure, you finished medical school, to atone for your sins. But what about my sister? What about her? She went crazy," the Speaker bellowed. "What about her, Diamond Jim?"

The Speaker turned toward the door, taking several steps before he stopped. He glared at the defeated, beaten physician. "This is the last favor you owe me. We'll be even after this. But if you don't come through," the Speaker warned, "I swear to you, I'll expose you for what you are."

Arthur Sutherland had aged considerably during the past two months. The energetic glow of strength and purpose he brought to the White House several years ago was fading under the enormous pressures of power.

Sutherland looked at Whyte, consternation and astonishment on his face. "Well," he began, "that was a most interesting press conference earlier today."

Whyte nodded. "I don't know what it means. But I have completed the research on the disability issue."

"Does much of it depend on medical proof?"

"Some of it. But as usual, there's no solid answer . . . and no precedent."

The president rapped the desk with his knuckles. "Before I leave office, I want to find an issue where there is a clear, concise answer."

"Since Starr is back alive, in one piece," Whyte said, "I

expect there's no way to prevent him from being sworn in. If he has some type of disability, where he can't govern, the new vice president and a majority of the Cabinet can force him to step down under the Twenty-Fifth Amendment, until his disability is removed.''

''That sounds reasonable to me,'' Sutherland said. ''Thomas,'' he continued, ''have you determined what the Speaker's up to?''

''No, not yet. But Johl and McBee are giving it top priority. They're checking every possibility—every angle. If the Speaker tries to pull anything on the disability issue . . . we'll be ready.''

There was a light knock on the door. ''Come in,'' Sutherland said, nervously glancing at Whyte.

Jonathan Starr made his way slowly into the Oval Office. He held his lips tightly together, overwhelmed he had made it this far—after two months. He was in the Oval Office.

''Mr. President, I owe you my life.'' Starr extended his right arm.

Suddenly, the president embraced the man who had defeated him. Whyte fought back tears as the two men patted each other softly on their shoulders.

''Welcome back,'' Whyte said sincerely, shaking hands with Starr.

''Sit down,'' the president said softly, motioning to the couch. ''I think what we've been through makes first names in order.''

''Yes, Arthur,'' Starr replied awkwardly, ''I agree.''

''See,'' Sutherland said, ''in only thirty seconds we agree more today than we ever did before,'' he said smiling.

Jonathan nodded and looked around him. This would be his office in less than three weeks.

''I've waited a long time . . . to . . .'' The president fought to control his emotions.

''I know,'' Jonathan responded quickly, ''there's a man outside who told me all you did.''

''Andy?'' the president asked.

Jonathan nodded his head, smiling.

Sutherland journeyed to the door. ''Mr. Reynolds, I presume?'' he quipped.

Andy grinned and vigorously shook hands with his commander in chief. The president's eyes glittered with appreciation.

"You came through. This nation owes you a great debt."

Andy smiled gratefully. "Thank you for sticking with me." Then he added quickly, "Though a two-week vacation would be nice."

Sutherland laughed. "Ask your new boss," he suggested, pointing to Jonathan.

"Listen, fellas," the president said, addressing Reynolds and Whyte, "why not give Jonathan and me some time alone?"

Sutherland sat down opposite Jonathan as the two other men left the room.

"Hectic day?"

"Yes," Starr said. "I did have a chance to call Orear. He's putting some things together."

"Like a cabinet?"

"Yes," Jonathan smiled, "little things like that."

"There's so much to discuss," the president said, "I'm not sure where to start. I suppose," he hesitated slightly, "we start with the legal problems."

Starr squirmed and scooted in the couch. The president sensed his uneasiness.

"I get the feeling you sense my . . . difficulty."

"Maybe," Jonathan replied awkwardly, "but I'm not sure."

"I'm just going to get it off my chest," the president sighed. "I feel terrible about the attack on your daughter. I've felt guilty and responsible since the day it happened. I just . . . ."

"Arthur," Jonathan said quickly, "please . . . I understand." Jonathan's eyes watered as he brushed a tear away. "It's hard on all of us. Thank God she's making a super recovery. But," he said firmly, looking toward the president, "I don't blame you. I would have done the same thing."

"Thank you for your compassion."

Jonathan took a deep breath. "Let's move to another topic."

"Back to the present situation."

"I've been brought up-to-date," Starr replied. "I sincerely thank you for your efforts. Without you, I wouldn't have had a prayer to be qualified."

"Even with me," Sutherland said, "it was nip and tuck."

"I suppose I should spend time choosing a cabinet?"

"Of course," the president replied. "We need to put together a transition team. Maybe Whyte and Orear should head it?"

"Fine with me," agreed Jonathan.

"Too bad," the president reflected, "that neither of us had time to recover after the election."

"It's a grueling experience. I suppose," Starr added, "that's an understatement."

"Someday soon," the president said, "you and I will talk about the debate, the hotels . . ."

"I would like to know," Starr interjected, "more about the rescue efforts, and what was happening here."

"We'll do that," Sutherland replied quickly. "But we must talk about something else first."

The president walked to the fireplace and picked up a trinket from the mantel, aimlessly rolling it through his fingers. He motioned to the picture above.

"George and I went through a lot together, these past few months," he said, turning to Starr. "But what you and I have to discuss would curl old George's ponytail."

The president walked to Starr, sitting next to him on the couch. "I know you've been through hell. I also sense you're not feeling well," then added quickly, "and I understand, and appreciate that. But we need to discuss something urgent."

"Okay.'

"I know you want dinner with your family, but can you stay for another hour?"

"Sure."

"We can spend five minutes, before you go, posing for those damn photographers outside."

"Fine."

"But for now," Sutherland said, clearing his throat, "I want you to sit . . . and listen."

Starr nodded, looking at the president with curious uncertainty.

Sutherland told him about the executive agreement. He told Starr everything, not leaving out one minute detail. The Middle East was on the brink of a violent confrontation. The Sutherland peace plan might be the only way to avert a war.

Starr sat mesmerized. He didn't say a word.
He couldn't.

CHAPTER 48
BACK HOME

"PASS THE POTATOES, WILL YOU, AMY?" JONATHAN ASKED, EX-tending his arms toward his twelve-year-old daughter.

"Daddy," Abby said cautiously, looking at her mother, "will all these men be living with us?"

Jonathan smiled. "Yes, dear, but it won't seem that bad when we move to the White House."

"When will that be?" Amy wondered.

"Next month," he said, winking at his wife.

Judy smiled, chewing a piece of pot roast, pleased that her husband seemed to be in complete control again.

"It's nice to have you home, Daddy," Abby said sincerely, watching her father closely.

"It's great to be home. I missed you all."

Andrea took a bite of her potato. Most of her facial injuries had healed, with the exception of a large cut above her right eye. She smiled warmly at her father.

"I'm feeling great."

"That's wonderful, honey." Jonathan said, squeezing her hand softly. "We all came out of this in one piece."

"Daddy," Abby said, "my classmates say those kidnappers did bad things to you and hurt your feelings . . . or your brain."

Jonathan stared at Abby, but said nothing. He bit his lower lip as he sipped his iced tea. He wasn't ready for this discussion—not yet.

Amy started crying uncontrollably. She darted out of her chair and ran to Jonathan.

"I'm so glad you're home."

"There, there," he whispered softly, patting his daughter tenderly. "I'm home to stay."

Amy brushed away her tears. "Abby and I don't understand what happened to you, or why. Mom hasn't really explained it."

Jonathan hugged her. "We'll talk about it, maybe tomorrow," he said. "Tonight isn't a good time."

"Okay, Dad," she said, dejectedly returning to her chair.

"Johnny," Judy said, "I told the girls they could spend the night at a friend's house. I . . ."

"No, Jonathan snapped. "Tonight we stay together."

"But Daddy," Abby responded, "Mom said . . ."

"Damn it," he shouted, angrily pushing his plate away, "I said no." He peered at Abby. His forceful look was unfamiliar and frightening to his youngest daughter.

Jonathan had a sick feeling in his stomach. He felt no control over his emotions. The dinner table became a scene from television or the movies; he wasn't really there. He was just watching. His hands began to tremble slightly, his forehead was covered with huge beads of sweat.

"Abby," he said, taking a deep breath, "Mom shouldn't have told you that."

"Johnny," Judy said calmly, eyeing her husband intently, "maybe we should be alone tonight. I didn't think you'd care. You never did in the past."

"In the past," he repeated, shaking his head, staring at his wife, "we had a normal family life."

The room was silent. The three young girls were watching a metamorphosis. My God, Judy thought to herself, could all the talk about his captivity be true?

Jonathan nervously folded his napkin, then threw it on the table in disgust, striding out of the room.

"Girls," Judy said softly, "Dad's been under enormous pressure. The campaign was hard and he never had a chance to celebrate. He just needs time to rest."

"Can we sleep in the living room?" Amy asked.

"Sure," Judy responded. "You unfold the couch and make

sure Abby brushes her teeth. Andrea can sleep in her own room.''

Judy walked down the stairs into the finished basement. Andy Reynolds was watching television. The other Secret Service agents were outside. The house and neighborhood were surrounded by agents. Crawling with agents. Reynolds wasn't about to let anything else happen to this family.

He looked at Judy. She was crying.

"I heard," Andy sighed. "I couldn't help it."

Judy nodded. "I know. What's wrong with him, Andy? You know him better than almost anyone."

"Except you."

"He's different. He goes off—unexpectedly. No warning." She shook her head in frustration.

"The doctors will take care of him tomorrow. It will pass. He's been through hell."

"I wonder if he wants to be alone?" she said, rolling her eyes toward the upstairs.

"I doubt it," he replied. "He's been alone for two months."

Andy rose from the couch and walked to Judy, kissing her gently on the cheek. "I'll talk to Paulie tomorrow. If we keep him out of the public's eye for a few days, things may be better."

"Thanks, Andy." She tried to smile, unpersuaded by his reassurance. For a woman who eschewed publicity and confrontation, Judy Starr found herself in the middle of a brewing controversy.

Was the man in the upstairs bedroom fit to be president?

She kissed the girls good night and made her way to the master bedroom.

"Johnny, what are you doing?"

Starr was sitting on the bed, thumbing through a stack of letters. "I found these in the closet. I thought you threw them away years ago."

"I hid them in the attic for years. I just couldn't throw them away."

"Why were they in the closet?" he asked suspiciously.

"While you were gone," she replied awkwardly, "I felt a need to reminisce."

"By reading old love letters from old boyfriends?" he asked incredulously. "Some of these must be thirty years old."

"Most of them are from you."

He stacked them neatly, tapping the letters on the old shoe box before putting on the lid.

"Sometimes I wish we could go back in time—relive some of the good days."

"The good days are now. Starting tonight," she said, sitting next to him, stretching her arm around his shoulder. Their eyes met. She leaned over and kissed him tenderly on the lips. "I missed you."

"I missed you, too," he said quietly. "I was just thinking," he continued. "Remember the night I was elected to the Senate?"

She nodded, squeezing his shoulder more firmly.

"We went to the Washington Square Bar and Grill in North Beach. Everyone who was anyone in San Francisco politics was there that night."

"And you were king."

"King for the day," he said, remembering.

"After you're sworn in, we'll go there again. Let's go back home soon."

"After the swearing-in," he murmured.

"I'm going to take a whirlpool, care to join me?"

"I will in a minute, you go ahead."

Jonathan hung his pants in the big walk-in closet. It looked the same. Everything looked the same. The large bedroom was immaculate. The navy blue curtains were drawn and the dresser was dust-free. Even the mirror was clean. He rubbed his bare feet on the white carpet. It felt good.

"Amy, stop that."

"No, you, Abby, you started it."

Jonathan turned around, but Judy was already in the bathroom. He journeyed downstairs in his underwear.

"Will you two stop it," he snarled, entering the living room. "It's late . . . just go to sleep. You don't know how lucky you are to sleep in a nice house with your sister, Amy."

"Oh Dad, she . . ."

"I don't care who started it," he interjected, "just stop it."

"But Dad, Abby . . ."

"Damn it, Amy, don't talk back," he shouted unexpectedly.

"Gawd," she mumbled.

"What did you say?" he snapped. She didn't respond, but she turned her back to him.

His eyes widened as he reached to grab her. He started shaking her. He couldn't control himself. Abby watched in stunned silence. "Don't you ever turn your back on me," he said harshly. He raised his right hand, positioning himself to slap her. He caught Abby's terrified gaze. But it didn't stop him. He slapped Amy hard, his right hand leaving an imprint on her cheek. The stunned girl fell into her pillow.

"Dad . . . dy . . . wha . . . wha," Abby stuttered. She had a slight speech disability that had improved over the past few years. Now she only stuttered when she was tired . . . or frightened.

He took both girls in his arms. "It's okay . . . Daddy was bad. I just lost my temper. Will you both forgive me, especially you, Amy?"

Sobbing, they both nodded suspiciously as he kissed them each on the cheek. He closed his eyes tightly, slowly shaking his head, disgusted with himself. He had never slapped any of his kids before. "You're not old enough to understand. I'm not sure I am, either," he said, teary eyed, pulling the covers over their bare legs. "Good night, girls . . . I love you."

"What was the screaming, Johnny?" Judy asked as he entered the bathroom.

"I slapped Amy, for no good reason at all. I just lost control. Poor Abby, she was so terrified. She began that stuttering again."

He stripped off his underwear and looked at her. She was beautiful. Her nipples were erect—her breasts sensual.

"Add ten more minutes."

He pushed a button next to the tub and the powerful whirlpool jets circulated the warm bath water.

"Boy, does this feel good," he said, stretching his legs next to her shoulders. They sat opposite each other—taking in nude bodies that for the past two months had been only fond memories.

He rubbed her ankle tenderly. She leaned forward. Her eyes squinted. "What's that on your arm? It looks like a bruise."

"It's nothing."

"Do you want to talk about it?"

"It's from a needle," he said matter-of-factly.

"Oh, Johnny," she gasped, "what have they done to you?"

"It's okay. They only did it once." He wasn't ready to talk about it, even to his wife.

Not tonight.

She started massaging his leg. It felt good.

"I had trouble sleeping for weeks. I even took pills."

"I know," he replied thoughtfully. "I've had trouble sleeping too."

"Any nightmares?"

"All the time," he responded.

She moved her hand forward, caressing his inner thigh tenderly. "We've got a lot to talk about, but it can wait until tomorrow."

She crawled over to him on her knees, repositioning herself next to him. He put his arm around her.

"You must be horny, if I am," she whispered seductively, flipping his ear with her tongue. He stared at the mirror next to them, but didn't reply.

He touched her hair gently as he kissed her. She opened her mouth, their tongues intertwined. He felt like he was far away. The same distant feeling he had experienced several times earlier in the day. Suddenly, he couldn't discern in his daydream world whether he was with Judy or Vicky Roe. His back stiffened as his body shook uncontrollably.

"What's wrong, Johnny?"

"I'm okay. It's like being a virgin. It's been a long time, like you said," he lied. His wife was right. Tonight wasn't the time to talk about the past.

She scooted down his body, taking his penis in her hands. She rubbed and pulled him, finally lowering her head to his groin. She touched the tip of his penis with her tongue.

He pushed her head away. "What are you doing?" he asked angrily.

"Johnny, I don't understand," she said, confusion written all over her face.

"Why are you going to do that?" he grunted.

"Because I thought you'd enjoy it."

"Don't pamper me," he said, his voice rising.

"Sshh," she responded, "you'll wake up the kids."

Judy got out of the tub and reached for a towel. He looked at her, shaking his head. "I'm sorry," he uttered.

"You've said a lot of things tonight." She started crying, turning away from him. She leaned over to the sink and splashed cold water in her face.

He got out of the tub and moved behind her, rubbing her naked back. "Remember before," he said, "when we used to fight. You said when we walked out of a room, into another, we would forget the argument, and start again."

She finished drying off, dropped the towel, and embraced her husband. She moved her body into his, feeling his erection.

"I love you," she whispered.

They went to bed. Still, he was haunted by recurring images of Vicky Roe. When he finally climaxed, he screamed, perhaps unloading both the unbearable pleasure and the tormenting guilt.

What was it? Perhaps Vicky Roe? Maybe his ambivalence toward becoming president? Or maybe it was the PCP.

Whatever it was, Starr pledged that night to exercise the same mental determination that weathered almost two months of captivity.

As he tossed and turned, however, it wasn't guilt that kept him awake. His cold sweat wasn't related to the past. He now understood.

It was Arthur Sutherland's Middle East plan.

CHAPTER 49
THE DOCTORS

JONATHAN STARED OUT THE WINDOW AS HIS LIMOUSINE approached the main entrance of Walter Reed Hospital. And old iron-bar fence surrounded the huge multi-building complex.

The military police at the main gate saluted Starr as his vehicle made its way to the main hospital via the circular drive.

"There they are again," Starr said, pointing to the swarm of reporters in front of the building.

"I told you there was a back way," Reynolds said.

"No, Andy," Jonathan replied, "I wanted to see them—to set the record straight."

Jonathan exited the limousine and waved at the journalists as they approached him.

"It's okay, guys and gals," he quipped, "I won't bite."

"Mr. Starr," a reporter chimed, "any comment on this morning's *Washington Post* survey, disclosing off-the-record interviews about your present condition?"

Jonathan pushed the hair off his forehead, walking from the driveway to a spot near the front door.

"First," he said sincerely, "let me apologize for my comments yesterday. I was out of line."

"No apology is necessary," muttered a *New York Times* reporter. "We lacked restraint."

"Here, here," several added, pushing their way closer to Starr.

"Well," he continued, "I just wanted you to know that for eight weeks I was out of practice. I wasn't doing much talking—and I sure wasn't responding to questions."

"Does your statement about the Speaker still stand?" wondered a nearby print journalist.

"Yes," Starr grinned, "I meant that. As to this other development . . ." He paused, looking for the questioner.

"Yes, you," he said, pointing a finger to the middle of the crowd, nodding his head. "I think I'm in good physical shape. There's no truth to personality changes and brutal beatings during my captivity. I'm just tired . . . and I *am* qualified to be president."

He turned to Andy. "Where did Judy go?"

"I'm over here," she waved, still standing near the limousine.

"Folks," he said, "I better get inside. "I've got a heck of a day."

Jonathan walked toward Judy, holding out his hand, as they met on the curb. Reynolds conferred with two of his agents as the Starrs approached the hospital's entrance.

"Good luck, Mr. President-elect," a reporter offered as Jonathan walked by.

Starr turned to the throng of reporters, searching for the familiar voice.

"For God's sake," he said warmly, leaning over to kiss the reporter on the cheek. "How the hell are you, Kate?"

"I'm fine," she beamed, embarrassed by the reaction and sudden attention from her jealous colleagues. "I was standing in the back, but thought I'd get a closer view. You look terrific."

"Well," he smiled, "I don't know about that."

"Hi, Judy," Kate said, extending her hand.

"Why don't you come over to the house. We both would love to see you." Judy offered, squeezing her husband's hand.

"I'll do that—real soon." Her eyes weren't focused on Jonathan or Judy. She stretched her neck, searching for Andy.

The Starrs entered the hospital, escorted to the fourth floor by a Secret Service entourage. One agent stayed outside.

"How are you?" Andy asked, pulling Kate toward the still parked limousine, rubbing her hand gently.

"I missed you."

"Me, too."

"Listen," she said, lowering her voice as she moved closer,

"I've heard the Speaker is still trying to get Jonathan disqualified. That he's planning a big battle on the sixth. I wanted you to relay this to Paulson. Durkin and his lawyers have been burning the midnight oil."

Andy's eyebrows furrowed, a look of irritation, then confusion flickered over his dour features.

"That's what I'm hearing, too."

"What can it mean?"

"I don't know—but I'm going to talk with Jonathan. He and Paulie are working with the president, and I know they have a strategy. I don't know the specifics. It's out of my area."

She smiled and, standing on her toes, kissed Andy on the cheek. "I know your *area* of expertise," she quipped. "I'll call you later, I've got to run."

"Mr. and Mrs. Starr, my name in Jim Stunyo, and this is my associate, Suzanne Gee."

Jonathan shook hands with both doctors. He already felt uncomfortable, engulfed by the sterile surroundings of the large examination room.

Judy was seated near the corner of the room. She was there for moral support.

"As you undoubtedly know," Stunyo began, "our report and our conversation is privileged. Only you and President Sutherland will get copies. What you choose to do with those reports is your business."

"Understood."

"Mr. Starr," Gee said politely, "if you would sit down, I'm going to take a history from you. We need to know what happened—everything, or else our diagnosis could be affected."

The tall, dark-haired doctor was direct and efficient. Jonathan liked her, but his feelings for her boss were mixed.

"May I come in?" Reynolds asked, slightly hesitating before he entered.

"Yes, Mr. Reynolds," the doctor responded, recognizing the black agent from his recent media exposure. "What is it?"

"I would like to be present."

"Well, that would be . . . ."

"Why not, Doctor?" Starr interrupted. "I'll waive my privilege for Mr. Reynolds."

"See," Andy offered, "it's my job to protect him. To do that job, I should know what problems he may have now—or in the future. I must know what makes him tick."

"Very well," the doctor conceded, "please sit next to Mrs. Starr."

For the next two hours Starr related the bizarre events of his captivity. The kidnapping, the rescue attempts, the solitary confinement, and the torture. He described his meals and lack of exercise. He recounted all the bumps, bruises, and slaps on the head.

"What happened to this Vicky Roe?" Gee asked.

"They killed her."

Judy recoiled, grabbing Andy's arm. The agent sat silently, showing no emotion. A trained military professional would have had a difficult time during this imprisonment. But he was amazed that Jonathan had come through so well.

Or had he?

"Do you feel guilty or responsible for Roe's death?"

Jonathan peered at the doctor. Then he glanced toward Judy. She wiped her eyes with a handkerchief. She was starting to understand Jonathan's erratic behavior—and for that, she willed herself to remain in the room.

Jonathan smiled at his wife and responded to the doctor's last question. "No. I don't feel guilt—just regret about her death."

"Anything else you have to say about Vicky Roe?"

"No," Starr lied.

His wife shot him a glance, but quickly looked aside, feigning lack of interest.

"But I do," Starr pointed out to the doctor, "have guilt feelings about Andrea. I told you before they wanted me to choose which daughter should die first. I couldn't—no father could. I think about the attack. I think about how she could have been killed. Could have been . . . "

"Go on," the doctor urged, her voice snapping the dazed man back to reality.

"Okay," he cleared his throat, the pain of remembrance still registering on his face. "That's how I feel on the subject. I know realistically, there is nothing I could do. But I can't help how I feel. The pain is in my stomach."

Dr. Gee placed her notepad on the desk next to her. She glanced at her mentor, who was jotting notes in his file.

"Mr. Starr," Gee said curiously, "I notice the president's doctor's report says there were no major bruises on you, except the arm. Everything else, I presume, had gone away before your rescue?"

"I suppose."

"What happened to the arm?"

"They kicked it and stepped on it."

Judy squirmed in her chair, staring at the tile floor. She couldn't look at her husband—but she wanted him. to tell the truth.

The stocky, square-shouldered senior physician approached Jonathan. "May I look?"

"Sure," Jonathan replied, extending his arm.

Dr. Stunyo ran his fingers over the area of the bruise. If he found anything significant, his poker face didn't show it. "Thank you," he said, returning to his seat. He reviewed his copious notes.

"Mr. Starr," he finally said, rising from his chair, "Dr. Gee and I need to confer." He glanced at his watch. "Why don't you eat lunch. We've arranged for a private room. After lunch we can discuss matters further."

"I need to freshen up," Judy said, standing outside the door to the private dining room. "I'll be back soon."

"Judy," Andy said, "could you give us about ten minutes?"

"Sure."

"Roger!" Reynolds called for his assistant. "It'll be a few more hours. Let everyone know."

Roger Jefferson motioned for a nearby agent to position himself outside the dining room. "I'll get right on it, Andy," he said, nodding his head toward Jonathan.

They entered the small, cozy dining room. There was one table and four chairs. Nothing else.

"Hi, I'm Ann Heggemeyer. I'm your waitress. Can I take your order, or do you need a menu?" she asked cheerfully.

Jonathan grinned at the short, young, friendly girl. "Hi, Ann. I can order for Judy, are you ready, Andy?"

"Sure," he responded.

"Okay, Ann. I'll have a club sandwich. But Ann," Jonathan's tone became serious, "I want it plain and dry, nothing on it."

"I understand," she said patiently. "What about your wife?"

"Do you have chicken salad?"

"Yes."

"She'll have that."

"Make that two," Reynolds added. "And Ann," Andy continued, "can you give us ten minutes with no interruptions?"

"Sure."

"Thanks."

"Okay, Andy," Jonathan said, "shoot."

"I'm not going to beat around the bush," Andy began. He looked at Jonathan and sighed. "Are you leaving anything out?"

"What do you mean?" Jonathan asked, his face puzzled.

"You made some comments about Duncan before you almost shot him."

"You mean about Vicky Roe?"

"No. I mean about drugs."

"Andy," Starr began hesitating thoughtfully, "there are some things I'm not ready to deal with or disclose."

"Maybe the doctors can help you."

"Do you think I need help?" Starr snapped.

"I don't know." He stared at Jonathan. "Look," he said softly, "you've been through hell. You're under strain. You're going to be president. Let it all out, for your own good and the good of the country."

Jonathan nodded his head slowly. "I know you mean well, but I'm not ready to disclose everything today. My mind is cluttered with Sutherland's peace plan."

"What we talked about yesterday?"

"Yes."

"Aren't you opposed to it?"

"Of course," he replied firmly and convincingly. "But Andy, I've changed a bit." Jonathan smiled. "I'm not wacko, but I understand you can't always negotiate. You can't always avoid violence or confrontation. I'm becoming more conservative. Maybe it's more realistic—even my views on nuclear weapons.''

Andy started to respond, but Jonathan cut him off. ''Don't get me wrong. I'm against them. What I said in the debate still holds true. But I understand the other side a little better.'' Jonathan watched his friend closely. ''Do you understand what I'm saying?''

''I'm not sure.''

''Look. I'm against the Sutherland agreement. I think it's bad and dangerous. But I also believe the president when he tells me war is around the corner without this executive agreement. Israel can't exist forever with hostile neighbors plotting its destruction every day. Because of that, I'm in limbo. I'm looking for a way to avoid it, while at the same time I concede there is some method to his madness.''

''So, what do you do?''

''I'm not sure, but I think a compromise may work. Maybe serious discussions with Egypt, Saudi Arabia, and Israel can take place so they have input with any agreement before it is signed. So it's not crammed down their throats.''

''When would this take place?'' Andy wondered.

''Not *until* I'm president. There won't be any agreement before the swearing-in that I'll honor.''

''Nine minutes, fifty-eight, nine minutes, fifty-nine.''

''Come in, Judy,'' Jonathan said, ''even though your watch is fast.''

''I timed that perfectly,'' she quipped, sitting next to Jonathan.

''Listen,'' Starr said, ''since you're both here, I wanted to say something. I've been acting strange, I know, but I'm feeling better. I woke up this morning, and for the first time, in a long time, I really wanted to be president.''

''Good for you,'' Andy said approvingly. I . . . ''

''Soup's on,'' the waitress said, carrying in their food. ''I waited eleven minutes.''

Jonathan eyed his sandwich and flashed an annoyed look at the young waitress. ''Goddamn mayo!'' he snarled, throwing the sandwich to the floor as his rage erupted. He glared at the waitress, shouting, "I told you I wanted it plain." Jonathan stalked out of the room.

The waitress was stunned, shaken to her toes by the outburst. She had straightened up as if Jonathan had slapped her on the face.

"Sorry, for this," Reynolds said sympathetically to the waitress. She pulled away from him and stormed out.

"My God," Judy uttered, "he's not any better. I've never, in all the year's I've known him, seen him display such . . . such inconsistent behavior." She approached the agent cautiously. "I'm really frightened for him."

"Mayonnaise," Andy whispered under his breath, as he escorted Judy back to the examination room. He rubbed his chin, deep in thought.

"Well, Mr. Starr, back so soon?" Stunyo asked. He glared at Jonathan. "Anything wrong?"

"No. I just lost my temper."

"Has it happened before?"

"Yes, it has," Judy said firmly, entering the room with Reynolds.

Jonathan's tired back stiffened in defense of the impending trouble.

"Would everyone sit down," Stunyo gestured toward the chairs.

"Mr. Starr, my colleague and I disagree about your condition. I'll start by discussing our consistent findings, since we did agree in some areas. Suzanne will make her points when I'm finished."

Judy put her hand on Jonathan's thigh. He reached down and grabbed her hand, holding it firmly.

"We think you suffer from post-traumatic stress reaction. I'll explain many of the symptoms. You may recognize some, some may not apply."

"Is it disabling or permanent?" Starr asked nervously.

"I'll get to that," Stunyo replied. "First, our area of medicine isn't perfect. It's not like reading an X ray, or performing surgery. Many times there is no right or wrong. We just try to diagnose situations." The doctor paused for a moment, taking a deep breath. He appeared nervous and uncomfortable.

"You've been through a great deal. You were humiliated, tortured, both physically and mentally. Your daughter's attack is a complicating factor. Your lack of nourishment, lack of sleep, and growing guilt feelings contribute to this condition."

"How will it manifest itself in my daily life?" Starr asked.

"You will become overprotective of your daughters."

Jonathan glanced at Judy. She squeezed his hand.

"Your relationship with your wife can change—physically, emotionally, and sexually. You may become jealous, due to increased insecurity and depression. And," the doctor added awkwardly, "if you haven't been completely candid with us about your relationship with Ms. Roe, you could have guilt feelings about that."

A nervous roll of Jonathan's Adam's apple, the quick dart of his tongue on his lips, betrayed the composure he so desperately wanted to display. He prayed no one noticed.

"We've ruled out drugs. There's no evidence of it. But as you know, we do need to run some tests. These simple neurological tests will be reviewed before we issue a final report. We also will run standard tests to confirm you have no foreign substances in your body."

Reynolds was watching Suzanne Gee intently. It was readily apparent she was straining to stay emotionless—detached. Especially when Stunyo mentioned drugs. Reynolds could read body language. He would talk to the good doctor.

He had to.

"So, Mr. Starr," Stunyo continued, "you will have some pain. Though most bruises are gone, you have complained of aches and pains. If it's chronic, it can lead to anxiety, depression, loss of appetite, profound fatigue, and sleeplessness. Dr. Gee and I disagree on this diagnosis. I think . . . or project you may have chronic pain for an indefinite time."

"Permanently?" Starr asked.

"Close to that. Dr. Gee says it's too early in your evaluation to make longterm predictions. There is merit to that position. However, we as doctors, under your unusual situation, have an obligation to predict the next four years."

The doctor was coldly courteous and, at times, almost condescending.

"Are you telling me, that I'm not fit to be president?" Starr asked in disbelief.

"Yes," he replied, "I am, but with an explanation. Pain is difficult to understand. Sometimes it's more mental than physical. The spinal cord and the brain . . . "

"Wait a minute," Starr snapped, "what pain? I told you of minor aches . . . you've made me out an ambulance candidate." Jonathan turned to Dr. Gee. "Are you going to write your own report?"

"I am."

"Am I fit to be president?"

"Yes," she hesitated slightly, "with a few conditions."

"Such as?" he asked suspiciously.

"Ongoing therapy. Continuing contact with a nonpolitical neutral third party and verification of certain test results."

"Is that all?"

"Basically."

Starr rose from his chair. "Dr. Gee, you've got a new patient, if you want me?"

She smiled nervously. "I'd be delighted."

Dr. Stunyo cleared his throat. "Mr. Starr, I am truly sorry, but after I review your lab results, my opinion will go to the president."

Starr nodded silently, baffled by the contradiction in the tone of his voice and the smile in his eyes.

The phone rang. Dr. Stunyo hurried to pick up the receiver. "I'm with a patient . . . no, I can't talk. Yes, that's right, I've taken care of your problem. Good-bye."

The doctor turned to apologize, but no one was there. He walked to the window and gazed below.

He and Charles Durkin were even.

"Dr. Gee, I appreciate your seeing me."

"Mr. Reynolds," she responded, "quite frankly I'm pleased. I know of your relationship to Starr. We should discuss a few items. It's off the record and it won't be part of my report."

"I'm going to have to trust you."

"You can. I have no ax to grind. I think he should be president."

"Fair enough."

"Was he given drugs?"

"Why do you ask?"

"His arm. I'd say one or two shots. Otherwise, there would be much more discoloration."

"Why didn't Stunyo notice it?"

"Oh, he did," she replied, stretching her long legs under her desk. "But if Starr had drugs, once or twice, there probably wouldn't be a long-term problem. No permanent disability. His actions would then be attributed to the drug, nothing else."

"So why didn't Stunyo say something?"

"That's my problem. Something's fishy. He's too good a doctor to miss that."

"What drug do you suspect?"

"I've ruled out morphine and heroin. Those could cause severe nightmares, nausea, constipation, and hallucinations. He hasn't had those, has he?"

"Not to my knowledge, except nightmares."

"Nightmares are okay," she smiled. "You know what I meant?"

"Right."

"He's feeling guilty. That's *normal*. He certainly hasn't been brainwashed—nor does he identify with his aggressors."

"No Patty Hearst syndrome?"

"Right." She snapped her finger. "I may have it. Let's go back to the drug angle. He knows a lot about drugs, right?"

"Yes, he headed a commission."

"He may be overreacting to the fear of the drug's effect, more than the effect itself."

"Like a form of . . . hysteria?"

"Exactly," she replied.

"Look," Andy said, "I'm a medical neophyte. Where does this take us?"

"If he's had drugs . . . maybe I can get him to tell me. Then, if he's only been injected a few times, I can convince him the drug isn't causing his trouble—it's the fear of the drug's effect."

Reynolds stared at the doctor, a smile crossed his face. "I've been in the habit of trusting women lately. Let me tell you one of my hunches."

"Go on."

"Can a drug be given to someone through mayonnaise?"

She shrugged her shoulder. "I'm not sure. I suppose it depends on the drug. Maybe angel dust."

"PCP?"

"Yes."

"How would he know he was getting it . . . really receiving it. In contrast to someone lying to him, trying to trick him into believing he received it?"

"We could run tests. Look, if he thinks he got angel dust from the mayo, and he did, we can do things for him. If he didn't, then he's overreacting. Either way, we can help him."

"What can PCP do?"

"Enough of it can screw up the immunity system and leave him vulnerable to infections. There are many other bad effects, as well."

"We have to get him to level . . . with both of us."

She smiled. "That's your job. I'm confident we can help him under either predicament."

"One last item," Andy said, "I read somewhere that World War II generals and Vietnam commanders who were POWs oftentimes after their release had no desire to accept leadership roles."

"Does he still want to be president?"

"He does, but he's had some doubts."

"I think he'd be crazy if he *didn't* have doubts. But the fact he mentioned it is another reason I should see him. He's got problems . . . but we can help him."

Easier said than done, Reynolds thought to himself, as he left to join Starr.

CHAPTER 50
THE SYSTEM WORKS

THURSDAY MORNING, JANUARY 6, FINALLY ARRIVED FOR AN ANX-
ious Jonathan Starr and an apprehensive nation. President Sutherland's brain trust gathered for their 7:00 A.M. meeting.

"Good morning," the president said cheerfully, striding with
confidence to his desk. "Sit down," he waved, as the men rose
automatically.

"You see, Jonathan," Sutherland quipped, "when you become president, all these guys will treat you like a lady."

The president grabbed several file folders from his desk.

"Let's see," he mumbled, "I had that stuff last night."

The president pulled two medical reports from a small manila
folder. He put them on top of the desk and addressed the group.

"Jonathan Starr, Martin Edwards, welcome to the secret society of the Grand Old Party," he cracked.

"Thank you," Starr replied. "As you all know," he said
turning his head to the others, "it's a great pleasure to be here.
I sincerely appreciate everything each of you did for me."

"Here, here," several chimed.

"I wanted senators Johl and McBee here to discuss what
we've got planned for the Speaker today," Sutherland said.
"Paul Gilbertson," he continued, winking at the attorney general, "is to keep us all in line, and Thomas Whyte," he concluded, nodding toward his special counsel, "has coordinated
this entire project. Thank you all," Sutherland said gratefully.

"Everyone in this room," the president continued seriously,
pausing to clear his throat, "is acutely aware of what the kidnapping has cost this nation. The stock market has been erratic

332

for the past two months. Investments and foreign trade have been affected. Various industries, such as housing and banking, didn't know how to prepare because they didn't know who would be president. Well," he concluded proudly, "this meeting is to insure that *we* know who will be president."

The president raised his eyebrows and peered at Jonathan, looking deeply into his eyes. "This next topic may be uncomfortable for you," Sutherland said, grabbing the medical report from his desk.

"I understand. We've got to discuss it. Especially if Durkin goes public," Starr replied.

The president caressed his chin thoughtfully with one hand, tapping absentmindedly on the desk with the other. He clasped both hands together, staring at Dr. Stunyo's report.

"I think" the president said, "Dr. Stunyo's report is full of shit. Gee's report makes sense to me."

"Mr. President," McBee said, hesitating thoughtfully, "the medical report is the basis on which the Speaker will claim that the disability Jonathan has should prevent him from being sworn in."

"J.W. and I," Johl chimed in, "have been working on this potential problem. I think we've got it solved."

"How?" Jonathan asked, surprised there could be a simple solution.

"Well," Johl said confidently, "we couldn't understand why someone like Stunyo, with his reputation, would take a dive. The report just doesn't wash. We found out."

Jonathan looked at Sutherland, then to Johl. "Well, go on, Jay."

"The Speaker's been blackmailing him. We tapped his phone. He called Stunyo while you were there."

"I'll be damned," Starr murmured. "I'm beginning to feel better already."

"Even if the report had merit, our lawyers have concluded that the Speaker has no power to use that report," Johl indicated. "There's no procedure, no judge, no jury, no set of laws. Jonathan would be sworn in on the twentieth of January, and if he was disabled, Marty Edwards as vice president, with the new Cabinet, would handle this under the Twenty-Fifth Amendment.

"So, if Durkin makes his play," Johl concluded proudly, "J.W. and I will head him off."

"Super." The president looked at his watch. "We don't have enough time to get into another topic, but after the vote, we should all return here. We'll have a luncheon for the winning ticket, and then get back to work. Okay, Jonathan?"

Jonathan rose from his chair, moving to a bookcase near the president's desk. Sutherland's eyebrows twitched into peaks of incomprehension.

"No matter what happens on the Hill in a few moments, I want you all to know how grateful I am for what you've done." Jonathan paused just an instant to catch his breath, then he was off again. "Arthur," he continued, "you're really quite remarkable. You did everything in your power to rescue me. You know how much that means to me. I'm convinced, without your support, I wouldn't have had a prayer today.

"Now the medical issue. You could have sat back and let me fight my own battle. But you didn't. You tried to keep me president-elect. You did this knowing my feelings on your Middle East agreement. By keeping me out of this office, you could have enhanced chances of this agreement's success."

"Thank you, very, very, much, Jonathan," Sutherland said, deeply moved by the passionate remarks.

Starr walked to the president's desk and extended his hand. "We'll talk this afternoon. Now I want to win my election. Again."

As the senators were announced, one by one, they walked onto the House floor to their preassigned places.

When the junior senator from California was announced, the House and gallery spontaneously erupted. The demonstration lasted several minutes, much to the chagrin of Speaker Charles Durkin, who, with Vice President Stevens, the president of the Senate, presided over this joint session of Congress.

Jonathan waved to his family seated in the Family Gallery overlooking the floor of the House. The Press Gallery, along one entire side of the Chamber, was so crowded that reporters were sitting in the aisles and between chairs.

The Vice President began reading the electoral college results. As each state was announced, Starr began to breath easier, caught up in the excitement of the moment, as colleagues started congratulating him on the House floor.

Speaker Durkin exhibited little emotion, standing silently next to the vice president, almost oblivious to the celebration on the floor.

When the roll call of states ended, Jonathan Starr had been qualified to be the next president. Only eighteen members had defected. They all had cast their vote for Charles Durkin—a small consolation for a man who wanted the presidency.

After the vote, senators Jay Johl and J.W. McBee approached the next president. They shook hands, and in a strange gesture for such controlled individuals, slapped palms in a high-five manner like basketball players celebrating a slam dunk.

"This is the way to start a bipartisan administration," Starr joked, surrounded by fellow legislators.

"If I may have order!" the Speaker's baritone was heard throughout the chamber. Out of the corner of his eye, Jonathan saw J.W. McBee approach the podium.

"Order. Quiet." Durkin angrily pounded the gavel.

"Jonathan Starr is not fit to be president!" he shouted into the microphone, his accusation ringing through the chambers. Several senators near Starr were aghast.

"I have proof that he cannot discharge . . ."

"Mr. Speaker," Jay Johl shouted from the floor, "point of order!"

"The majority leader is out of order!" Durkin bellowed, pulling the medical report from his coat pocket.

"Mah friend!" McBee yelled, approaching the podium, "Ah need a moment."

"Not now, J.W.," Durkin snapped, once again trying to restore order with his gavel.

"You better listen to him, Charlie," Vice President Stevens said, amused by the trap set for the Speaker.

"What is it, J.W. ?" Durkin snarled with disdain.

"We know of the blackmailin' with Stunyo."

The Speaker recoiled. A tense silence followed as he grappled with his thoughts.

McBee put his hand on Durkin's shoulder. "It's over, Charlie. Ya won't be president," he said without malice.

"Starr is not fit. A leading doctor says so."

"Are you blind, deaf, or just dumb?" McBee asked incredulously. "The doctor's credibility is gone. He did the report for *you*."

"But the report speaks the truth . . . it . . ."

"Even if it *is* the truth," McBee said, his eyebrows rising as he made his point, "no one would believe it now. Stunyo owes you—the report is the payoff."

"Prove it," Durkin replied icily.

"Would the phone conversation between you and Stunyo be enough proof?" he responded sarcastically.

The Speaker stared at the podium, uncertainty registered on his face.

"Don't do it, Charles. Don't ruin your career," he pleaded.

Durkin nodded and opened his mouth, but then said nothing.

"All is not lost, Charles," he said softly, "you're still the Speaker. Give up this silly charade that kin cause only pain to everyone involved. You won't win. But many young congressmen will look up to you . . . if you stop . . . now." McBee concluded, placing his hand on the Speaker's shoulder again.

Durkin nodded his assent.

"Mr. Vice President," McBee said loudly, "Ah believe the Speaker has had a change of heart."

"Very well," Stevens replied, banging the gavel.

"Ladies and gentlemen, fellow legislators, the Speaker has graciously reconsidered his past remarks and has no plans to make any challenge to the certification of this election."

Durkin tried to regain his composure, digging deep within him for a reservoir of will to see him through this setback. But it was a temporary defeat. He had received eighteen votes—the largest deviation ever—by the electoral college, from the popular vote.

"Come on, Charlie," he whispered to himself. He was still the Speaker. And this was *his* House. Arthur Sutherland and Jonathan Starr had only won round one. They still had to deal with him.

The Speaker strode to the microphone, nudging the vice president to the side.

"I want to apologize," the Speaker began earnestly, "to

President-elect Starr. I have been told the information supplied to me is not accurate. I support, and will support this new administration, and urge," the Speaker's voice rose with passion, his right hand pointed upward, "a renewed spirit of cooperation between the White House and Congress."

Durkin acknowledged the enthusiastic applause, waving his arms, as he stepped down from the podium.

"He thinks he's won," Starr said bitterly to Johl.

"Don't worry about it," he replied calmly. "This is your day."

"May I have your attention?" Vice President Stevens shouted, pounding the gavel. The Chamber became still.

"On behalf of Arthur Sutherland, the outgoing administration pledges full cooperation to the new Starr-Edwards regime.

"It was a tough campaign," Stevens continued, "and since that time there has been much turmoil. But this nation survived. We survive because we have great men to lead us."

There was a spattering of applause. Stevens motioned for quiet. "I must add a personal note," Stevens said seriously, looking at the crowded House Chamber, now quiet and attentive.

"I congratulate Jonathan Starr on his bravery and courage. I wish you Godspeed. But today, I also congratulate another patriot. A man who has put his oath of office, to defend our Constitution, above anything else. A man who pulled our nation through the past two painful months with dignity and wisdom. I salute you, Arthur Sutherland. God bless you."

The teary-eyed vice president choked up as he concluded his remarks.

"Here, here!" Jonathan Starr bellowed, rising to his feet to lead the Chamber in thunderous applause.

CHAPTER 51

CAIRO

Friday, January 14

"I WOULD LIKE TO THANK YOU BOTH FOR COMING," THE GENeral said warmly, opening the door for his two guests.

The frail, elfin, sixty-two-year-old man nodded, moving to the bed. The madame, wearing the same white silk stockings and tweed suit from last month, sat on a chair near the desk. These two travelers handled the syndicate's money. They made the investments and controlled the banks. Their job had been accomplished. They anxiously awaited the general's final report.

"Starr will double-cross us. Now of this we have no doubt."

"The bastard," the Englishman mumbled with uncharacteristic venom.

"I share your sentiments," the general responded, surprisingly calm considering recent developments. "But we have another plan. One thing is for certain. There will be *no* peace plan."

"What about the troop deployment?" inquired the man on the bed.

"Delayed," the general snapped. "There will be no movement until we've resolved this *temporary* setback."

"And how, my general," the madame inquired, "do you accomplish this?"

The general smiled. "With the syndicate's permission, I will order the Jackal to kill Jonathan Starr."

The madame slowly twisted her neck and eyed the English-

338

man. He nervously adjusted his glasses and squirmed on the bed.

"There are no other options," the madame said, after several seconds of silence.

"I agree," said the man from the bed.

"Good," the general responded. "Confirm to me within twelve hours. I have plans to make. With Starr dead, the peace plan will die . . . at least for a while. The indecision in America and the world will be felt. After all the political turmoil in America will seemingly have been solved, we will create worldwide chaos. A peace plan won't be high on the agenda for the new president. Our people will once again become frustrated and impatient and will welcome any change in government. We will take swift action, taking advantage of the international confusion. Our civilian government won't be able to stop us, or rally the people. That is why I say the Jew's double cross is only temporary. We thought he'd stop the peace plan, which fit our purpose. That's why we sent the Jackal to America. To allow Starr to be rescued so he could prevent Sutherland's plan. Now he will express gratitude for his rescue by selling out our aims. He has betrayed us. Now we will kill him because *this* fits our purpose. There must *never* be a peace plan before we take action. And there won't be. And with the Jackal," he concluded triumphantly, "no one will ever trace the murder back to us."

"Before we go further, my general," the madame said, "the syndicate wants to know about the weapons."

The general nodded, twisting his mustache as he addressed the group. "As you know, we have secured plutonium and uranium through syndicate fronts. We have utilized the information from Libya, which they received from France years ago. We are using the new reactor at Libya. We have assembled several nuclear engineers, paying them large sums of your money to develop our weapons and technology."

The general eyed his attentive audience. "The key to our plan is surprise. Our nuclear attack will destroy Israel. They won't be ready. They don't know we have this capability. If they did, they would go after us like they did with Iraq in 1981."

"Doesn't Israel have a nuclear plant?" the madame asked.

"Yes," the general responded, adjusting a small medal on

his chest. "That's the key to our victory. We have a very important man on our payroll. We are paying him many a shekel."

"What's his role?" The Englishman wondered.

"It's twofold. First, he's been giving us Israeli nuclear technology. Without it, we couldn't build our bombs. We're using the plutonium and uranium. With their technology, and our scientists, we are building bombs that will destroy the Jews.

"This man will also be told when we are to attack. He will see to it we can overtake the power plant without destroying it. We will destroy Israel, but the power plant at Dimona is ours," the general said enthusiastically.

"This man must be very important?" the madame suggested.

"He is in charge of security. For the past ten years he has worked in this underground uranium processing plant at the Dimona reactor in the remote Negev desert. They have a nuclear capacity far greater than most understood."

"And it will be ours," the madame snarled, sounding like a wild animal.

"Our man works in a section known as Machon 2, a factory with six underground levels." The general's voice rose as he felt a sudden exhilaration. "He's involved in processing uranium to extract plutonium, which is used in nuclear weapons. Israel has exploited this experimental reactor, secretly built by the French in the early sixties to produce eighty-eight pounds of plutonium a year, enough to build ten bombs."

"Those Jew bastards have been violating international law themselves," the madame whispered savagely.

"Could he be a double agent—setting us up?" the man asked sheepishly.

"No," the general grunted. "We are solid with him."

"What will you do with the power plant?" the madame asked.

"The power plant," the general chuckled. "Excuse my levity, but the Jews have a sign near the plant, outside of Dimona, that suggests it's a textile plant. Anyway," he continued, "we will then have the capability to convert an already existing nuclear power plant to nuclear weapons."

"Atomic bombs," the man whistled.

"More than that, my friend," said the general. "A thermonuclear bomb or four-megaton hydrogen bomb is much better. We have assembled the team that can do that.''

"How so?'' the man asked quizzically.

"Three competing processes must be put in perfect balance under extreme conditions of temperature and pressure. It gets complicated, I know. But eventually, there is an explosion that compresses the fuel, driving it up to the incredible temperatures needed for ignition. This perfect quantitative and qualitative interrelationship between these three competing elements I told you about does the trick.''

The general strode to the balcony. Although his face was lined, he looked years younger than his age. Much of his youthfulness was expressed in the animation of his features, the almost constant gesturing with his hands when he spoke. He looked over the panoramic view of Cairo from the hotel room. Parts of the city had a population density more than four times the density of Manhattan. The prevailing winds blow north or south. One brings toxic fumes from the lead and zinc smelters in Shubra El Kheima, north of the city. Tonight, the shifting wind brought fumes from the steel and cement factories from Helwan.

"Have you received the total cooperation from your other generals?'' the madame asked, breaking the general's momentary reverie.

"Yes. At least most of them. We will take over our civilian government, immediately taking control over all oil fields, as well as the Dimona plant.''

"My general,'' the man on the bed spoke. "The Americans, won't they attack?''

"We've given considerable thought to that eventuality. We will have the oil fields. And we will have destroyed Israel. What good will America's retaliation do? There's no more Israel. We will control it. Will they risk a world war over that?''

The general stared at his coconspirators. "We think not,'' he said icily. "If we're wrong, then we'll perish.''

"The syndicate has been working on this, too,'' the madame offered. "We will inform the United States that if they take action against this new Arab nation, we will withdraw our funds from their banks. It will cripple their economy.''

"Very good," the little man nodded admiringly. "But what about a freeze of assets, like their Iranian crisis?"

"We're ironing out the details now," the madame replied calmly. "Since no aggression will be taken against the United States or its citizens, we don't think international banking law will allow a freeze. Besides, we don't have debts like the Iranians did. There is no legal justification for them to escrow funds."

"You may kill U.S. citizens in Israel?" the man argued.

"True," the madame replied thoughtfully. "If we think a freeze is possible, we'll pull our money out during Israel's demise. There will be no time for a freeze. Then, if the Americans don't attack, we can return the money."

"We'll need to work out more details on this part," the man suggested. The little man with slate gray hair adjusted his heavy-rimmed glasses, walking to the balcony, shoulders slightly stooped. His dour, dark-eyed face had been etched over the years with down-turning lines, but was still capable of all the familiar flashes of emotion: the rare, stray wisp of a smile, the characteristic sag of one side of his thin mouth to denote disapproval, or sudden animated contortions of carefully thought-out anger. He faced the general.

"A remarkable plan. I endorse it wholeheartedly. We kill Starr, destroy Israel, and soon, within years, in our lifetime," he cried triumphantly, "we can take over America. We keep buying land and businesses. With Starr out of the way, we won't have to worry about a president limiting foreign investments. During the next four years we can buy more land and control businesses and banks. They will be ours."

"Yes, my friend," the general smiled warmly. "I, too, dream of that day. Israel has bombed Palestinian refugee camps with U.S. planes for too many years. American guns kill Arab women and children and seize our brothers' land with illegal settlements."

"Americans are such hypocrites," the madame hissed venomously. "They created nuclear weapons and were first to use them. They stockpile them, sell them, and threaten with them. No more."

"Let me ask you, my general," the man said, "how you plan

to win the approval of your people when this military coup occurs?''

"I have spent considerable time on that matter," the general responded, pleased the question had been asked.

"When the army toppled the monarchy in '52, there was general support, but not throughout the twenty-six provinces. We need total support, and I think we'll have it. People have suffered under our president, as they did under Mubarak and his predecessors. I'm counting on the Dimona reactor to assist in improving the quality of life."

"I suppose," the madame interjected, "you could tell your people that you did in one day, getting Dimona, what it would have taken their former government ten years, plus, you will have eliminated Israel."

"Yes," the general concurred. "We will communicate those points in our eight newspapers. Only ten million our of our 150 million Arabs read a daily, but those are the ones we must convince. Society's leaders. We can shape the news they read as well."

"How so?" she asked.

"Newspapers now are under quasi-public ownership. Senior editors are government insiders. We'll place our people at *Akhbar al yom, Al Ahram*, and others. We will also take over the government radio and television stations."

The madame rose and approached the general. "A tremendous plan. The syndicate is with you." She extended her hand and the general graciously bowed to kiss it.

The short man offered his congratulations as well. "The day will come," he said sincerely, "when you, more than others, will enjoy the fruits of labor."

CHAPTER 52

THE PEACE PLAN

Friday, January 14

THE PRESIDENT WALKED ACROSS THE ROOM AND TURNED OFF the machine. Eight pair of eyes watched him in silence, each one in suspended animation, locked in time, forced to be part of a tragic, ghoulish nightmare. The Situation Room in the basement of the White House West Executive Wing had served as the administration's communication center after the kidnapping. Twelve weeks later it was, once again, in full use.

The president nervously tapped the machine next to him, staring at the group before him. Sutherland thought it incredible how much could go through a person's mind in just a few short seconds when one has to make such crucial decisions. "Gentlemen," he began, determination flaring from him like a flame from a struck match. "We must take immediate action. But I want it understood that any decision I make must be approved by Jonathan."

Sutherland glanced at his watch. "It's 1:30. I want written recommendations on my desk in three hours. Everyone is to stay at the White House. J.W. and Thomas will join Jonathan and me in the Oval Office. I want the two vice presidents to coordinate assignments from here—work with the CIA and Secretary Long." The four men quickly made their way upstairs. No one spoke, each frightened and unsure.

The president sat behind his desk, as he grabbed a yellow pad from a drawer. "Move the chairs closer," he requested, reaching for a pipe.

344

"J.W.," he began, "you've had direct negotiations with the Arabs. Did you have any idea things were this bad?"

McBee was aghast. "Ah've bin duped." His speech was laced with invective.

"The CIA tells me," the president continued, "that this tape is valid. Their operative overheard these Egyptian soldiers discussing a military move against Israel. Why the Egyptian president would stand for this is beyond me. We've still been negotiating with them."

"Does their president know?" Starr asked. "It could be a military coup."

"Good point," Sutherland conceded. "The Israel invasion of Lebanon has everyone frightened. How can we talk peace to the Israelis when their allegedly peaceful neighbors place tanks on their border?"

The men watched the president, with measured, habitual movements, empty his pipe into the ashtray on his desk. Sutherland instinctively reached for his tobacco pouch. Realizing his pipe's bowl was still warm, he changed his mind and didn't refill it. He crossed his fingers, resting both hands on his desktop as his penetrating gaze traveled through the room, making brief eye contact with each of his attentive listeners.

"Could this move be tied in with the Jackal's recent involvement?" Whyte wondered.

"I doubt it," Sutherland answered, "but we've had to make changes because of it. The swearing-in ceremony will be held in the Rotunda, not outside. Jonathan will make his speech and it will be televised. We have precedent for this. President Taft took his oath inside and, in 1833, Andrew Jackson held all inaugural events indoors because of the weather. And most importantly," he added with emphasis, "it's safe. After all Jonathan's been through, we don't want him shot after his swearing-in."

"Originally, I was against this," Starr added. "I thought it was poor precedent because of a *suspected* threat. But I've been convinced by Reynolds and others to go this route."

The president sighed. "Poor Jonathan. He campaigns his ass off, wins, then gets kidnapped, tortured, beaten, and humiliated. When he's finally rescued he has to fight Durkin, and when the dust settles, he's sworn in inside.''

"The tape doesn't disclose when the A-rabs plan this move,'' McBee pointed out.

"No,'' Sutherland retorted, "but the CIA feels within the next several weeks. It doesn't give us much time to get this peace plan worked out.''

Jonathan looked at the president, hesitating slightly before proceeding. "The agreement can't work,'' he said simply.

Sutherland twisted a pen in his fingers, subconsciously playing for a few seconds to examine the alternatives.

The president slowly shook his head in frustration. "I thought that agreement was the only way to peace. I'm really out of ideas,'' the president gloomily conceded.

"I have one,'' Starr replied gently.

"Go on,'' Sutherland urged.

"As you know, I haven't chosen an attorney general or secretary of state.'' Jonathan rose, stretching his arms and neck. He stood behind the chair and carefully eyed the president. He wiped moisture from his lip. He tensed and swallowed with difficulty; biting his lip, Starr exhaled. "I want you to be my secretary of state,'' he said matter-of-factly.

Sutherland shook his head. "Jonathan, you . . .''

"Hear me out, Arthur,'' Starr firmly interrupted, "you need to know the whole story.''

"All right.''

Jonathan remained standing. "President Starr and Secretary Sutherland go to Israel.''

"To be killed by the Jackal,'' McBee drawled.

"Listen,'' Jonathan pleaded, "to the whole plan. Then, if you don't like it, fine. It won't make sense until you hear it all.''

"If then,'' McBee muttered to himself.

"We go to Israel. We meet with the Arabs and the Israelis on a modified peace plan. My administration's peace plan. Before the tape, I was thinking about going over there anyway. I even talked to Andy about the security problems . . . and the Jackal. Because of the controversy of the plan and my election, we both need,'' he gestured toward Sutherland, "to meet them face-to-face. If the people of the Middle East know that a plan can still be worked out, they should rally around their civilian governments and be less likely to support some military action or takeover. We know their *people* want peace. We need to do something dramatic in a hurry. When Israel hears of this potential military action, they will take action. Soon, both sides gear up for a war neither wants . . . and which *we* can avoid.''

"But the Jackal," Whyte pointed out. "What's your solution?"

"Simple. We plan a four-day trip. On the last day we'll organize a massive outdoor activity. A speech . . . a peace rally, something like that. An event with many people. We would be sitting ducks. The Jackal would plan the hit that day."

"And how do you avoid the hit?" Whyte asked curiously.

Jonathan smiled. "We leave on the third day."

"Interestin'," McBee mused.

"As to the Jackal," Jonathan continued, standing up and pacing before the others, "we still don't know what his role is. If he wanted to kill me, he had ample opportunity before. Anyway, we don't need all the details now, but we must take some public action to calm the Arab government and the Israelis."

"Mr. President," Whyte said reflectively, "I'm thinking about what Jonathan said before. I think it is likely a military coup is planned. The Egyptians, and Saudis, for that matter, want a peace treaty. It makes no sense for them to start a war."

"During the first two days," Jonathan said excitedly, "Arthur and I would meet only with the civilian leaders of the peace-plan parties. We would disclose what we know, which could save their governments. We will also hammer out the agreement."

Starr sat down, taking a peek at his legal pad. "As president, I need to build a personal relationship with these leaders. I need to do the same thing with the Russians. By communicating and expressing a common desire to avoid mutual annihilation, we can relieve world tensions."

"Jonathan, how will the Arabs react to a *Jewish* president?" Sutherland inquired.

"Much better if you're next to me as my secretary of state, showing the stability and continuity of our commitments. Plus, Arthur," he said seriously, "you need to tell them you were wrong on your agreement. That area of the world isn't ready for everything you proposed.''

"Arthur," Whyte said, "Jonathan is making a strong case against your early retirement from government.''

"The Arabs will trust me," Starr suggested, "because I'm giving them back their own country. Otherwise, that region becomes a military dictatorship. You and I, Arthur, will work with them to save their nation. If we stop this military coup, think of the goodwill that could come out of this. Especially since Israel benefits, too.''

"We're saving them from destruction. It will also tell the Israelis that the Arabs want peace," Whyte said.

"Yes," Starr replied. "But Arthur's agreement can't work. Maybe someday we can convince Egypt and the Saudis to go along with Hussein's coup. Without giving them reactors. The other parts of the peace plan have great merit. But for now, Hussein's role must be stopped. We need time to evaluate the entire plan, after Egypt and Israel are safe. Getting them to work together, for their mutual survival, can also go a long way toward rebuilding their trust in each other. With this uncertainty and turmoil, there's no way Hussein could pull off the coup. It's apparent some faction of the military not only wants to take control of Egypt, but by placing troops on Israel's border, they want Israel, too. If this group could place their hands on Egypt's nuclear reactors, as the original peace plan called for . . . well . . . we all know the consequences. Fanatics and nuclear weapons can't coexist.''

Jonathan stopped, turning to the president. "Sound familiar?''

"Yes," he responded warmly. "Only it sounds better, now. Maybe it takes something like this to change my thinking.''

"I hope we're lucky, this time," Jonathan replied, "and we only have to deal with the *threat* of nuclear war. We've hit the cold day of realism for the Middle East. Mutual possession of these god-awful weapons of mass destruction promises them no brighter future than these weapons gave us or the Russians. We all have the potential for mutual suicide.''

"You know," Sutherland said, "you'll have to watch Israel closely.''

"That's true," Starr admitted. "That's why every detail of our strategy must be ironed out."

"Givin' em thirty billion dollars over the years may have bought us some influence," McBee quipped.

Jonathan studied the president. "We've answered several questions so far; many remain unresolved. But I'm still waiting for my secretary of state."

"Jonathan," the president said firmly, "I'd be proud to serve under you."

Jonathan leaned across the president's desk, extending his hand. "Thank you."

"I will voice my own opinion, as you well know, but you'll have my loyalty. The final decision will be yours. But I will support it."

Jonathan smiled with appreciation and sighed. "I think I should address the nation in several days to explain that you and I will go to the Middle East within the next several weeks on a new peace plan. That you and I will develop a plan with the assistance of Egypt and Israel, with the direct participation of their leaders. We can move behind the scenes to calm Egypt and Israel before we get there so *no* troops will be on any borders. Let's keep the status quo. The secretary of state can hold their hands for a while."

"And the military coup?" Sutherland asked.

"We'll come up with a way to get word to the Egyptian government to stall that action."

"Life is strange," the president mused. "Several months ago we were at each other's throats. Then I end up campaigning for your *second* election. Now, the cycle is complete. I'm serving under you." Sutherland shook his head sideways. "Damn," he muttered, forcing a grin.

CHAPTER 53

THE INAUGURATION

Thursday, January 20

THE TWO MEN SAT OPPOSITE EACH OTHER, WAITING FOR THE
president. The Oval Office was otherwise unoccupied.

"Have you moved in yet?" Reynolds asked, motioning toward Sutherland's desk.

"Not yet," Jonathan Starr replied, smiling at Reynolds. "I
can hardly believe the two of us are alone. After all these months,
we're just hours away."

Reynolds looked at Starr seriously and glanced at his watch.
He walked to Jonathan's couch and sat down next to the man he
had rescued.

Starr watched in silence. He could sense Reynolds was troubled. "Are you going to tell me what's bothering you?" Jonathan prodded.

Reynolds looked at his watch again. "The president will be
here in five minutes. I don't think I can cover it in five minutes."

Jonathan frowned. "Let's have it, Andy."

"I know about the mayo," he spewed.

Jonathan noticed the bags under the tired agent's eyes. He
looked terrible. But he was telling the truth.

"How?"

"You mentioned drugs . . . right before the gun incident with
Duncan. Then, at the hospital, after you and I discussed the
possibility of drugs, you almost assaulted a waitress who
brought . . ."

"Mayo on my sandwich," he said, ending the sentence.

"What drug?"

"PCP. But I haven't told anyone. I wanted to see if I got better. I did. If I had told others, I risked that disability argument again. People overreact, you know that. Can you imagine, after today, what would happen if Edwards and my cabinet thought drugs had disabled me?"

"Scary."

"Will you keep the secret?"

"I will. But there's no guarantee Duncan will."

"That's right," Jonathan said, his tone telling Andy he hadn't thought the issue through.

"If Duncan goes public, it could embarrass you—make it appear you were hiding something. You've already lied to the doctors, so this could be another overreaction—only in reverse."

"Suggestions?"

"See Dr. Gee. The counseling won't hurt you. Then you can go on record telling her about the mayo and PCP. Let her do tests. If Duncan goes public, you can down play it—you would have told your doctor."

Jonathan contemplated the proposal. "There's a drawback."

"What?"

"If Gee finds a serious problem. Then we go back to the disability issue."

"Wouldn't you want to know if there's a problem? Can you really serve this country, if you lose your temper over a sandwich?"

What Andy suggested struck home. Jonathan desperately wanted to be president. His passion to serve had returned. But he also had a responsibility to the nation. Now, more than ever, leadership was necessary. Leadership uninhibited by nightmares, temper tantrums, or irrational behavior.

"Do you think I can handle it?"

"After what I saw this week, sure," Reynolds answered. "But what about tomorrow? Say you're alone in the Oval Office and forced to make an instant judgment. What if you snap? Who watches over you?"

"This job would be grueling for anyone under any circumstances," Jonathan sighed. He stared at Andy. "Tell you what,

I'll think about it. If I don't let you know by Monday, bug me
again. Then I'm pretty sure I'll agree to do it. Deal?''

"Deal," Andy replied, patting Jonathan on the shoulder.

It was better than nothing.

The aura of history and tradition permeated Washington. The
familiar event had never happened quite this way before, en-
closed within the classical, white geometry of the Capitol Rotunda. This ad hoc theater-in-the-round hosted virtually the
entire American government. Two hundred officials connected
with the White House, five hundred members of Congress, the
Supreme Court, other assorted power brokers, and the nation,
through live television, would all witness Jonathan Starr's biggest day.

The soothing tones of the network announcer described the
scene for the viewing public:

". . . This rotunda, packed with all the powerful personali-
ties of government, has erupted as Jonathan Starr makes his
second triumphant return to the Capitol. The next president is
striding down the aisle, grabbing extended hands offered by
smiling congressmen. The noise, as you can hear, is almost
deafening. Starr looks exceptionally fit . . . neatly dressed in a
navy blue three-piece suit . . .''

Jonathan felt exuberant. Fatigue and exhaustion had left his
body. This was his moment.

Finally.

Jonathan scanned the crowd before him. He could see the
look of gratitude and pride on their smiling faces as they remained standing, cheering and applauding their new leader.

He winked at Kate Wilson, standing to Judy Starr's left. Behind them stood the beaming Paulson Orear, making no effort
to conceal the tears streaming from his eyes. Jonathan blew a
kiss to his daughters and gave a nod to his parents as he tried to
silence the enthusiastic welcoming.

He briefly thought about the inaugural address. For the first
time real butterflies hit his stomach. Until now the waving and
smiling had sufficed. Soon, he would address the nation . . .
and the world. The chief justice tried to get Jonathan's attention.
It was noon. He had become so mesmerized by the crowd, the

chief had to tug on his suit sleeve to get his attention. Jonathan placed his hand on the Bible. He could feel the lump in his throat, his dry throat. He noticed something unusual about the Bible. He looked again. It was his. His parents' Bar Mitzvah gift to him. He sneaked a wink to them, acknowledging that he had noticed.

I do solemnly swear that I will faithfully execute the Office of the President of the United States and will to the best of my ability, preserve, protect and defend the Constitution of the United States. So help me God.

After the oath of office had been administered, Jonathan smiled and waved to the crowd, motioning for them to sit down. He walked to the other side of the lectern and embraced Arthur Sutherland, a gesture that brought the crowd to its feet again.

Jonathan nodded toward Andrew Reynolds, who stood to the right of the lectern, out of sight from the panning network camera. Reynolds smiled and saluted his commander in chief.

As Jonathan approached the podium, he looked out into the mass of people before him. He was confident he could save Egypt and Israel. Confident he would convince the Arabs and Jews to work together and to trust him. The surprising tandem of Starr and Sutherland, together, just might achieve their mutual goals for an everlasting Middle East peace.

It was 12:05 P.M. Jonathan Starr was the president. He took a deep breath and delivered his inaugural address without notes. His speech was interrupted by prolonged applause when he reaffirmed his pledge to visit Moscow.

Israel, then Moscow. Starr's ambitious course was publicly charted. He would be a one-man crusade to diffuse current tensions that threatened world peace.

"Great speech," Reynolds shouted, as he grabbed Jonathan's left arm. Starr waved to the audience as he was escorted from the Rotunda. The new president and his Secret Service entourage exited the Capitol from the south side.

Reynolds and his men formed a protective pocket around Starr as he walked down the steps to his waiting limousine. A crowd had gathered at the foot of the steps to catch a glimpse of the president. Uniformed policemen had barricaded the area and had no problems controlling the orderly crowd.

Reynolds scanned the gathering of well-wishers, but noticed a man standing next to a car on Independence Avenue, about one block from the steps the president was descending. He held something in his hand.

"Roger!" Reynolds hollered, "give me your binoculars."

Andy focused the glasses on the distant man. His body became tense, his shoulders stiff, his hands tightened into a fist.

The Jackal was observing the president with his own binoculars. He knew Reynolds was watching him. He lowered the binoculars, smiled, and saluted the agent.

Reynolds pushed Jonathan in the small of his back. The President turned around, frowning at the agent.

"What the . . . "

"Run to the car . . . now," Reynolds ordered, as the agents surrounded the president, pushing him toward the limousine.

Andy nervously focused his binoculars on the Jackal. He was sitting behind the wheel of his brown sports car. Reynolds's outward signs of strength and purpose were losing to inward anxiety and fear.

"Don't drive yet," Reynolds barked, as he pushed Jonathan toward the middle of the limousine's backseat.

"Lay on the floor, Jonathan," Reynolds ordered, his voice thin and weary. Jonathan eyed him intently, but did as he was told.

The Jackal made a U-turn and left the Capitol area via Independence Avenue. "See you in Israel," he whispered as he watched the limousine through the rearview mirror.

Reynolds was dumbfounded, confusion written on his face.

"Make a U-turn and exit from the Senate side . . . head toward Union Station. We'll take a circuitous route to the White House."

As they traveled through a barricade, Reynolds helped Jonathan up.

"What the hell is going on, Andy?" he snapped.

"This is leader one. I want pursuit of brown sports car, BAK 113. Subject dangerous. Shoot to kill—the Jackal."

"He's here?" Jonathan gasped. "It doesn't make sense . . ."

"I don't understand either. He wasn't here to kill you."

Jonathan stared out the window, waving at several school-children standing on a corner near the White House. He turned to Andy, his eyes wide with excitement.

"Just think of it. Soon, Air Force One is going to the land of Israel. Ben Gurion Airport. I . . ."

"Jonathan," Andy asked harshly, "how can you be so elated when the Jackal's here?"

Jonathan laughed. "Don't be so uptight. You'll get an ulcer before we arrive in Israel. Aren't you looking forward to the trip?"

The president rubbed his hands together in anticipation of his mission.

Reynolds observed his boss, closely. Was it another mood change—or simply enthusiasm for achieving a lifetime goal?

"I can hardly wait," Reynolds replied half-heartedly, turning to look where the Jackal had been. "I can hardly wait."

ABOUT THE AUTHOR

STEVEN KIRSCH was born in 1951 in St. Louis, Missouri. He grew up in Quincy, Illinois. He received a Bachelor of Arts degree from the University of Missouri, Columbia Campus, in 1973. He graduated third in his class from the Hamline University School of Law, St. Paul, Minnesota, in 1976.

He has been a partner since 1983 with the St. Paul law firm of Murnane, Conlin, White, Brandt & Hoffman. He practices extensively in state and federal court, and his speciality is civil litigation, focusing on insurance defense matters, products liability, and toxic torts.

Mr. Kirsch is the author of a well-known three-volume practice manual published by West Publishing Company, entitled *Minnesota Practice—Methods of Practice*, 3rd Edition, which is approximately 2,000 pages dealing with almost every subject of law, with the exception of criminal law. It is the most widely used and accepted practice manual in the state of Minnesota.

Oath of Office is his first novel. He is currently working on his second novel.

Mr. Kirsch resides in White Bear Lake, Minnesota, just north of the Minneapolis/St. Paul area, with his three children, Amy, Abby, and Brian.